CAVE

ALI COOPER

Standing Stone Press

Published by Standing Stone Press

Copyright © Ali Cooper 2011

Ali Cooper asserts the moral right to be identified as the author of this work.

ISBN 978-0-9564811-2-2

Printed by Lightning Source.

Acknowledgments

Many thanks are due to people who have contributed to this book, both directly and indirectly, especially to Moira Dahlberg for edit suggestions and to Robin Lewington for proof reading. And of course to all the people with whom I've explored caves, especially to members of the Brighton Explorers' Club and the Bristol Exploration Club. Everything to excess!

Caves

Quarry Cave, as described in this novel, is completely fictional. All the other caves mentioned by name are real and can be visited. Wookey Hole and Dan-yr-Ogof are open as show caves and, for the more sporting, Gaping Ghyll can be descended by members of the public at winch meets. Other named caves should only be visited with a reputable caving club. Please note: caving is a strenuous and potentially dangerous activity.

Characters and Events

This book is a work of fiction. However, some of the events are based on my own experience of underground exploration and others are based on anecdotes told by friends and fellow cavers.

All characters are fictional with the exception of Simon Prat (Sprat). Mr Prat is based loosely on the late Tony Jarratt (Jrat) of Priddy and of Bat Products, Wells and was included at his request. The book is dedicated to his memory.

In memory of Tony Jarratt (Jrat), 1949 – 2008.

Chapter 1

Cave - a hollow place in a rock, sometimes extending into a large system of underground passages and chambers.

'Die happy!' Those were the last words I heard.

It was three or four hours ago and I was climbing the wire ladder that stretched above me to the cave entrance and the welcome glow of afternoon light. It had been a strange trip underground and I was glad to be returning to normality.

The way out was via a vertical pitch, measuring seventy feet from the floor of the entrance shaft up to the opening in the hillside above. As always I tackled it slowly and methodically. I moved steadily upwards, wedging each foot, one after the other, onto the boot-wide rungs; right toe in front, left heel behind, like a dance; simultaneously weaving my arms through the mud-streaked framework, hauling myself upright, heading for that everyday world on the outside.

Today I felt an urgency that made me want to clamber faster, but I knew that if I hurried I'd be exhausted after forty feet. So I breathed deeply, gasping in the energy that propelled me upwards, and held tightly onto the ladder. Normally I'd have had a rope clipped onto my belt, a lifeline; but this wasn't a normal day.

I'd gained twenty feet, thirty at most, when I paused and looked up. High above me beckoned the ever-widening circle of light, the door to the outside world. But it seemed I wasn't welcome in that world. Far away, in the sunlight, voices argued in harsh rasping discord. Then the ladder began to swing, twisting and lashing like an angry snake, throwing me against the knife-edged boulders that surrounded me. My head crashed against stone and, despite my helmet, my brain buzzed with the shock. My shoulder hurt, my cap lamp went out, I lost my footing as my knee slammed into a rock, and I let go – only for a second, but enough for the ladder to slip out of my grasp. I

1

plummeted to the bottom and landed in a painful heap.

And the words clattered down around me.

'Die happy!'

Fucking hell, man! I had no intention of dying, happy or otherwise. Not for a very long time. And preferably of old age.

Chapter 2

Pitch - a steep climb (or sheer drop) often requiring a rope or ladder.

It all started because I split up with Carole, or more precisely because she split up with me. I suppose I should have seen it coming. Perhaps if I were a more touchy, feely kind of person, I'd have read the signs and noticed that something was wrong. As it was, I didn't even know we had a problem. OK, our marriage wasn't exactly exciting. It wasn't like the passionate flings you have in your teens, when women get butterflies at the mere thought of their loved one and men get – well they get constant proof that everything's in working order. Fair enough, our relationship wasn't like that. But it was comfortable. Isn't that what we all settle for once we get past thirty?

Then Carole went on this personal development course. It was a work thing, arranged by her employers. What does a legal secretary need with something like that, for goodness' sake? I swear she was fine before. But she came back full of all this nonsense about identifying goals and transforming her life. She never really settled after that. Instead, she fretted and questioned everything she did. I thought she'd snap out of it once we were on holiday; but when we returned home, after an unusually chaste fortnight on Knossos, she enrolled on a college course. What with her lectures and my shifts, I hardly saw her. I suspected, too, that she might have a bit of 'women's trouble', a mid-life crisis or an early menopause or something. I didn't say anything though. One thing I've learned is that women tend to be sensitive about these things. I decided that, all in all, it was best to leave her to figure it out for herself.

So, when she said she was going to sort her life out, I expected her to say she was taking HRT, but instead she suggested that we should have counselling; and I felt I didn't have much choice but to go along with it.

It was really embarrassing. Each week we sat in a faceless

3

room. It reminded me of the rooms they have at the hospital, with comfy chairs and strategically placed boxes of tissues, where they break bad news to grieving relatives. Anyway, in this room we were interrogated by a total stranger and answered all sorts of personal and irrelevant questions about our marriage. When the counsellor suggested we do some exercises, I thought she meant those sex therapy things they talk about on television, where you have baths together and massage each other before jumping into bed for a bout of rampant rumpy-pumpy. So I thought, fair enough, especially if it means I get a shag at the end of it, I'll go along with that. However, it turned out to be some deep and meaningful self-analysis, where you write down your targets for the next five years and question the meaning of life. Well frankly I just couldn't be arsed. Carole got really into it though, and filled sheets of paper with all this scribble of unfulfilled dreams.

The counsellor said it might be best if, during this time of self-exploration – I didn't want to explore myself for God's sake, I'd spent enough years as a bachelor doing that, I wanted to explore a woman – anyway, she said it might be best if we slept in separate rooms. Now, I'm hardly a qualified psychologist but even I realised that this would only make things worse. Carole thought it was a great idea, however, and it all went so well – or badly, depending on your point of view – that after three months she suggested I move out for a trial separation.

Move out? Where the hell was I supposed to go then? Carole had already thought this out. She reminded me of a conversation we'd had a couple of weeks previously with one of my work colleagues. Personally I'd completely forgotten the details (how do women remember all these things?) although I could hardly forget the occasion because it was so rare for Carole to come out for a drink with any of my mates.

'Mike was saying he could do with someone to share.' She said this casually but definitively as she carefully folded my T-shirts, socks and underpants into a suitcase. 'So it would solve two problems at the same time.' She closed the empty drawers

4

and began removing my shirts from the wardrobe.

I was pretty taken aback of course, but I was confident that, once the novelty of starting the car on cold mornings, or having to mow the lawn every week, had worn off, and once her doctor had prescribed HRT, Carole would get back to normal. Don't get me wrong; I'm not a bad person. I wanted my wife to be happy, of course I did, but I didn't think anything was seriously wrong. I simply thought this was a hiccup in our relationship that would resolve itself if left alone. The moving out was a nuisance but ultimately it was just a temporary thing while Carole resolved her 'issues'.

Over the next few weeks it became apparent, during our fortnightly counselling sessions, that this arrangement really suited Carole. She spent her evenings (the ones when she didn't have college) reading books on transactional analysis, discovering her 'inner child' and embracing her new-found freedom. I, on the other hand, rediscovered my inner slob and got very grumpy because I wasn't 'embracing' my wife. I was, quite reasonably, feeling sorry for myself. Mike wasn't exactly sympathetic either. After a couple of months he said he was getting fed up with me hanging around the place like a lost puppy, waiting for Carole to call.

'Get off your bloody arse and get yourself a life,' he said, one evening. Well I thought he could have been a bit more understanding given the circumstances. And considering he was divorced himself, acrimoniously, he was hardly qualified to give advice on happy relationships. I told him to sod off and pointed out that I'd relinquished most of my life to Carole, along with the house.

'Well rediscover the life you had before, then.' He was undaunted. 'Haven't you heard of Friends Reunited?'

Do what? For God's sake! I wasn't going to turn into some sad loser, wallowing in the past, trying to recapture my lost youth. We grow up. We move on. We move back in with our wives – once they've come to their senses. I couldn't be bothered to argue about it though. Luckily I managed to stay out of Mike's way for the next few days; it wasn't difficult, I had a lot on at work.

But I suppose the seeds were sown and I got to thinking about them; Rick, Joe, Fish and Taff. I hadn't seen them for years. Then there was Beth. I tried not to think too much about Beth; that was too unsettling. I thought about the lads more and more, though; about our time at university and how we used to spend our weekends exploring caves deep beneath the mountains. And when I made the decision to get in touch with them again, I had no idea of the chain of events that I was about to set in motion, or the ghosts I would unleash from the past.

Chapter 3

Prusik - to climb up a rope with the aid of rope loops and/or metal ascending devices.

So here I am, Martin Wight, a man in one hell of a hole, up shit creek without a paddle, or to be more accurate, down shit pot without a ladder. Whatever you want to call it, I'm in one hell of a mess.

In the past couple of hours I've gone through every emotion I possess. I've been shit-scared and shaking, and I've cried wet, blubbing tears. But deep down I know that my best chance of getting out of here alive is to stay calm and think rationally, to try and imagine what Rick would do, or Joe.

The last thing I remember was climbing the ladder. Needless to say, it's gone now. It must have been hauled to the surface while I was out for the count. When I came to, I realised that it wasn't there and that I wouldn't be going anywhere soon. So I closed my eyes again and rested my foggy head, hoping that I would wake up later in my bed at home and discover it had all been a dream. No such luck.

Despite the fall, I don't seem to be seriously injured. Not surprisingly, my head aches. I don't think I was unconscious for long, but doctors always seem to worry when you get knocked out. I'm trying not to think about that though, because even if I've got some life-threatening clot or haemorrhage, there's bugger all I can do about it. Cautiously, I flex my arms and legs. My shoulder still hurts, my knee too, but I can move them OK. Further than that, I haven't inspected myself too closely. I'm telling myself it's because I don't want to get cold getting undressed, but basically I'm not too good with blood and gore and all that stuff, so if there is any I don't want to see it. Funny, considering I work in a hospital lab; but somehow it doesn't seem so bad when it's in a test tube and it belongs to someone else.

It's partly my own fault. I wouldn't be the first person to get into difficulties underground. Caves are dangerous places and accidents happen all the time. But my fall didn't happen by chance. I bite my lip as I allow myself to consider the events of the last twenty-four hours. Even now, up in the outside world, under the harsh sterile lights of the City Hospital's intensive care unit, one of my dearest friends is lying in a coma – may already be dead for all I know. To cause one fatality might be considered an accident. Killing two people is murder. There's no getting away from it. The knowledge that I have been left down here because someone wants me to die sends a shiver down my spine that is so sinister it chills me even more than the draught from the entrance shaft above.

I take a deep breath, and, forcing myself to focus on the here and now, I switch on my cap lamp and look about me.

I'm sitting on a clammy boulder in the middle of a small and dreary chamber. The space around me is ruggedly bell-shaped, the sides taper away towards the ground, disappearing into jagged, shadowy crevices. All around, the rock is dank and forbidding, it swallows the torchlight and gives nothing in return. At head height it funnels upwards into a vertical shaft, a chimney. It's a natural feature, carved out of limestone, first by ice freezing the earth apart, then by the action of water cascading down. But that happened eons ago, only a fine spray comes down these days.

High above at the top of this chimney is the cave entrance, the same one I was heading for earlier. At the surface the opening is protected by an iron grille, so small boys with fatal curiosity, and dogs chasing rabbits won't plunge to their doom. In the daytime it beckons, like a halo, offering salvation. Sunlight trickles down teasingly. It dangles swathes of silk and threads of sparkling jewels, always just out of reach. Right now there is nothing. Night comes early in a Welsh winter and even my torch beam doesn't stretch that far. Only water slips past the metal bars, dancing on rocks as it tumbles down, ringing optimistically in delicate tunes, until, at the bottom, subdued by constant night, it drops dismally to the ground, squelching into muddy puddles amongst the rubble. In short, this is not a place of hope.

I switch off the lamp and listen to the dull thud of water droplets hitting the ground. They're more frequent than before. It must be raining heavily in the outside world.

On the positive side, I try to persuade myself that things could be worse. I could have been abducted and dumped in some unknown basement or knocked unconscious and left to freeze in a ditch. Although unwelcome, at least my surroundings are familiar.

I've been here before. Many times. With Rick and Joe and the others. Laughing as icy water splashed down our necks, revelling in the mud and the teeth-chattering cold, shivering and shouting as we clattered through golden torch-lit tunnels, grasping ropes and ladders with rubber-gloved hands. But it was never like this. However tired we were, however cold and wet, we always knew that in a couple of hours we'd be warm and cosy, eating dinner beside the inglenook of The Quarryman's Rest, reflecting on our adventure. This time is different. Because this time I'm alone and there's no way out.

The water falls faster now and a chill down-draught sharpens the air. I shiver and hunch my shoulders and clasp my arms across my chest, protecting my precious body heat. One thing's for sure, I can't stay here on this boulder much longer. I'm going to have to decide what to do. I take another deep breath and consider my predicament.

Part of it's my own bloody fault. I broke the two golden rules of caving.

1. Never go underground on your own.
2. Always tell someone where you're going and when you expect to be out.

But who sticks to the rules? Especially when you're experienced and confident, that's when you get complacent, that's when things go wrong. The fact is that if I'd told someone about this trip then, even as I sit here now, they'd be looking anxiously at the clock, making hurried phone calls and setting out to rescue me. If I'd told the right person, that is. But there's no point in brooding over what might have been. I've got to make the best of things, got to keep my head, got to be ruthlessly single-minded. My survival may depend on it. I grit my teeth. I'm not going to panic; I'm going to think this out logically. There will be a solution; I have to believe that. Anyway, fear and panic use up energy like nothing else on earth, I'm going to need every ounce of strength if I'm going to get out of here alive.

I count to ten as I breathe in and try to think rationally.

Basically, I have two choices: either to attempt to get out of here right now, under my own steam, or to accept that I'm going to stay underground for the night and wait (I force myself to think the word 'wait' rather than the word 'hope') to be rescued tomorrow.

I think about the first option. It would mean free climbing up the entrance shaft; there'd be no rope, no ladder. I consider the possibility carefully. Part of the route is narrow; I remember studying the rocky walls on the numerous times I have travelled past, stepping sedately on a ladder, whistling down on an abseil or prusiking, froglike, upwards. It would be straightforward to chimney the lowest section, bridge across with my feet pressed on the rock in front and my back braced against the surface behind me. That would account for about thirty feet, but what of the rest? Some of it bells out – you couldn't reach the sides from the rope, let alone without one – and although there are holds and ledges jutting out in places, in others the rock wall is smooth and sheer. Not only that, but higher up, where sunlight reaches in the daytime, the surfaces are treacherous, slippery with algae or brittle with frost damage. Even if I did manage to reach the top, the iron grille would almost certainly be in place and padlocked shut. And what if I fell? Not just a short drop like earlier but from near the top? I'd be lucky to escape injury. Most likely, even if I survived the fall, I'd lie crumpled and broken at the bottom of the shaft and be dead from hypothermia before morning.

10

I know that if I am going to attempt the climb, I should do it immediately, before I become too cold and tired. I turn my lamp onto full beam and look up for exactly one second, contemplating the ascent, before deciding immediately against it. Then I switch off the torch, returning to total blackness, and think again.

People get rescued from caves. It happens all the time. Hell, I used to be a member of the local rescue team myself, I went to practices and hauled pretend casualties on stretchers up waterfalls. I even helped on a couple of real life call-outs. Sooner or later, I'll be missed. People will come looking. I'll be found.

I begin to feel quite optimistic.

There's the downside though. So much has been happening, everyone has a crisis to deal with. Today is Saturday. The weekend. Only when I fail to turn up for work on Monday morning will the alarm bells ring. My heart sinks. I breathe in slowly, conscious of the cold air filling my lungs. I have to stay positive. My best hope is that there'll be some walkers on the top tomorrow. There may even be a caving group come down on a trip. Sooner or later I'll be rescued. It's inevitable. And, in the meantime, all I have to do is stay alive.

Chapter 4

SRT - single rope technique. As an alternative to using ladders, cavers abseil down a static rope and prusik back up. Sometimes referred to as 'on string'.

In the week following Mike's outburst, I spent a lot of time thinking about my old mates, my caving buddies. I remember, twenty years ago, meeting them for the first time.

It was my first year at university, first week in fact, and to tell the truth I was feeling a bit homesick. There was this quiet chap in the room next to mine in the hall of residence. He owned an acoustic guitar on which he strummed stuff by Dylan and Deep Purple and belted out a mean version of *Free Bird*. Apparently he had a couple of electrics too, a Fender Stratocaster and a Gibson Les Paul copy, the one with the sunburst finish; but he'd decided to leave them back home with his Mum the first term. I had comical visions of her doing a quick burst of Eric Clapton between the washing up and the ironing. Joe was the typical innocent, fresh faced, first-time-away-from-home student. He was slightly built and his hair was embarrassingly short at that time because he'd stayed on at school to do his 'A' levels and had only had the summer holidays to grow it. At least it was just long enough to signify that he wasn't into punk.

It was a Friday night and I knocked on his door.

'Yeah? It's not locked.' The voice was soft and smooth with a somewhat unexpected Geordie accent.

I pushed the door open a few inches and stuck my head round. The room was unnaturally neat – by my standards anyway. On the wall were pinned a poster of Gandalf from *The Lord of the Rings* and a surrealistically airbrushed print by Roger Dean: the one he'd designed for the album sleeve of Yes's *Tales from Topographic Oceans*. Joe was sitting at his desk, a textbook and a ring binder open in front of him; he was wearing unfashionably new jeans and a Genesis tour T-shirt, slightly faded but carefully washed and ironed. He looked up and smiled.

I opened the door fully and stepped inside. 'Hey. Wondered if you fancied coming down the union bar?' I don't think I was particularly sociable in those days but I wasn't overly confident either and I didn't feel like going out on my own. I figured that Joe, being obviously less outgoing than I was, would be glad of the company and tag along. I looked at the work in front of him. 'Unless you're busy, it isn't...you know...important.'

He pushed his books aside. 'It isn't anything really, I was just filling in half an hour before I go out.'

'Well if you've got something planned...'

'Look, I picked this up at the Freshers' Fair.' He reached over his shoulder to a pin-board and passed me a paper flier.

It was typed in capital letters, no frills:

UNIVERSITY CAVING CLUB OPEN EVENING
NEW MEMBERS WELCOME

This was followed by small print describing the details.

'I've seen a couple of TV programmes on potholing, I wouldn't mind seeing what it's all about.' Joe sounded enthusiastic.

I shrugged.

'Why don't you come along too? They've got a slide show and stuff. It might be interesting.'

I shook my head. The words slide show conjured up pictures of relentless holiday snaps and as for the idea of going down cold, wet caves for fun...well frankly even Aunt Molly's photographic record of Majorca beat that one. Then I read the bit at the bottom of the paper that announced there would be a free barrel of beer. 'On second thoughts it might be fun. OK, why not? Grab your coat.'

Suitably, for a bunch of speleologists, the get together was held in a basement room in one of the older buildings. We descended a gloomy staircase into a surprisingly bright and lively dungeon. Apart from a few token women wearing scruffy jeans, the room was full of blokes. There was no music but it was certainly noisy, with bursts of eager conversation penetrating through the cigarette smog. It was like one of those parties where most people already know one another (the second and third years, presumably) and you have to find someone who looks as lost as yourself to talk to. I was glad I was with Joe because I didn't recognise anyone there. He did though. He waved across the room and a tall graceful chap made his way over to us.

'This is Fish,' Joe said. 'He's in my tutorial group.'

'P-p-pleased to meet you.' The willowy and somewhat mysterious stranger bowed and shook my hand, his dark hair swinging across his face, sweeping a veil of secrecy over his eyes as he bent down to my level. I'd never met anyone quite like Fish before. Nor since, come to that. I wouldn't normally say this about a bloke but the fact is he was just gob-smackingly beautiful. Not in a girly way exactly, but there was something about his bone structure and the proportions of his face that reminded me of an art history class at school, about sculptors striving for aesthetic perfection. His most striking feature was his hair. It was long and sumptuous, gleaming like ravens' wings draped over his shoulders. Anyone else would have blown this image with stooping posture or clumsy movements, but Fish was balletic, as if every step, every gesture had been carefully choreographed. He was so perfect that, after the first sentence, I didn't even notice his stammer.

I don't know to this day whether he was called Fish because of the way he swam or the way he drank. Either would have been applicable at the time as I was soon to find out. Still holding on to me, he paused to take a long gulp from the glass in his other hand; then he turned to Joe. 'You d-didn't say you were a caver.'

'I'm not – yet. But I'd like to give it a try. And Marty here will come along too, I'm sure. Have you had a go already then?'

'Yeah, started with the scouts then joined a real club. I've just done a d-d-diving course. That's w-where it's really at.' He finished his pint and stared down mournfully at the empty glass, his dark lashes creating wispy shadows across his cheekbones. Then, quick as a flash, his mood brightened. 'This way,' he beckoned. 'We've got a barrel.'

Oh magic words. Drinking beer was like a new game to me; now for the real business of the evening.

We pushed through a huddle of people, catching snatches of conversation as we went.

'That was when I dived my first sump...'

'How are you on ladders or do you prefer SRT?'

'I swear there was only an inch of air space...'

'I'd rather do it on string any day.'

I didn't take much notice of what was being said, it was all a foreign language to me.

Although the room was quite small, Fish soon gave us the slip. Despite the fact that he was taller than Joe or me, he seemed to have this knack of slithering through the crowd. He was like a vanishing act, dissolving into the ether to slide through infinitesimally small spaces. Perhaps it was the result of his caving experience. When Joe and I finally reached the famous barrel, Fish was already leaning against the wall, beaming quietly having downed the first few inches of his next pint.

A tall thickset guy with a wide mouth and dark curly hair seemed to be in charge of the beer. 'Let me fill you up, lads!' he bellowed, reaching for a couple of glasses. He had the sort of confident manner and somewhat posh accent that must have been cultivated by a public school education. I'd noticed him across the room as I came in; you could hardly miss him, he'd been engaged in loud conversation and I'd assumed he was at least a second year, maybe even a finalist. He peered at Joe and Fish. 'Think I've seen you two in a maths lecture,' he said. 'Do you know how we sign up for our first trip? My name's Rick by the way.'

I figured Rick was my best chance of tracking them down. Joe and Fish had always been more elusive. I had no idea where

15

they were working these days. But Rick was on the physics faculty at the university, I'd seen his name in a prospectus less than a year ago, when I'd been vaguely contemplating a study sabbatical.

At first I'd been nervous about contacting him. I mean, what if he and Joe had split up or something? Like we had – Carole and me. What would I say? In the end I'd rung the department at the university. I was secretly relieved when the secretary said he was giving a lecture. She suggested that I email him and gave me the address.

So that's what I did, nice and impersonal, a cop out really. I summarised what had happened with Carole (it would save having to say it out loud) and said I'd be down the Red Dragon on Saturday night.

When the time came, I didn't know if they'd be there. Rick hadn't replied. Not before I left work on Friday afternoon, anyway, and I didn't have a computer at home back then. So I had a drink before I set out, just a couple of cans to get me in the mood, then I took a deep breath and dived back into the past.

The Red Dragon had always been the cavers' pub. Every Saturday evening we used to meet there, anyone who wasn't away on a trip. It wasn't just the university crowd but people from other clubs too. Each week this unofficial convention happened. It was an opportunity to exchange information, relate anecdotes of trips underground, to tell tales of where you'd been and ask questions about the places you wanted to go. In short, if you were into cave exploration, it was the place to be.

I hadn't been in there since I got married to Carole and I admit I was apprehensive as I pushed open the door. It was only eight-thirty but the public bar was already heaving. It contained an amorphous lump of life, a collection of bodies seeming to move as one within their restricted space, wriggling to and from the bar to replenish their sustenance, like maggots on a piece of rotting meat. All around me, broad shoulders

16

jostled for space, bulging biceps were adorned with colourful designs, affirmations of their owners' manhood etched forever into the skin: snakes, dragons, 'Black Sabbath', 'Motorhead'. Above the hum of conversation, with its occasional crescendos of shouted exclamation and raucous laughter, the till pinged, coins clattered and the drawer crashed shut – to be immediately re-opened. Beer-filled glasses changed hands, the frothy head of ale overflowing, slopping into slippery puddles on the floor and clinging to moustaches and beards like freshly fallen snow. The air hung thick and heavy with cigarette smoke and testosterone while sweaty condensation formed spidery rivulets on the steam-obscured windows. It was like a time warp. Nothing had changed. It was exactly as it had been when I was a student.

'Weed!' Rick's booming voice hit my eardrums at exactly the same moment his heavy ape-like hand clapped on my shoulder. Then I was engulfed, squeezed to within an inch of my life in an almighty bear hug. I could smell the aftershave on his chin and feel the furry pelt of his arms where they pressed against my neck. At last he released me and stepped back. 'It's good to see you, Marty,' he said.

He was just the same – big, muscular, gorilla-like; the dark tangle of hair was receding slightly, perhaps, but hey, the tide goes out on all of us.

'It's good to be back.' I found myself saying those words, even though they sounded corny, like a prodigal son returning to the fold.

'We're over here,' Rick put an arm round my shoulders and steered me through the crowd, 'over by the window. Joe's kept a seat for you.'

Joe. Thank God. They were still together then. I felt my breath whistle past my lips with relief. As we eased our way across the room, I looked between the shoulders and the beer glasses towards the far end of the bar. Sure enough, there he was, skinny as ever, blond hair spilling fine and wispy over his face, he wore skin-tight leather trousers and a bike club T-shirt, his right forearm rested on a fringed and weathered black leather jacket draped over the arm of the bench. He stood up as I approached and reached across the table to embrace me.

'Marty!' His touch was lighter than Rick's and his voice quieter, even the soft Geordie lilt had been mellowed by twenty years of living in Wales. 'It's good to have you back.' He reinforced his words by patting me on the shoulder.

I put my beer glass down and sat on the wooden stool that Joe pushed from under the table. Thankful that the difficult bit was over, I began to relax and settle myself down for the evening.

Rick, on the other hand, was just warming up. 'We've got so much to tell you!' He waved his hands, like he was an actor giving a soliloquy, taking charge of the stage. He always had been theatrical. 'The strangest thing,' he continued, 'is that we were about to contact you. Synchronicity or what?'

A couple of pints later, I was feeling more at home. I'd worried about what it would be like, meeting up with old friends after so long. I'd feared there'd be this chasm between us, a void that couldn't be crossed. Instead, it felt like I'd only been gone a couple of weeks and within minutes we were laughing and joking just like old times. The Red Dragon was a free house. It sold guest beers from all over the country along with ciders that tasted of silage and an ale from a local brewery that went through you like a dodgy Vindaloo. That night we played it safe with Marston's Pedigree.

Rick took a long gulp of his drink. 'Do you know we moved house, back into Benson Street?'

'Back to the old stomping ground,' said Joe.

'Just like old times.'

'Only the posh end of the street this time.' Joe grinned and pushed the tip of his nose upwards with his thumb.

'I remember Benson Street,' I mused fondly, 'number forty-two.' That was where we lived when we were at university, Joe, Rick, Fish and me. We spent the first year in Hall of course – most people did back then – but after that we got this place together. It was scruffy, a slum almost, but it was our home.

'One hundred and one, this time.' Rick jolted me out of my daydream.

'Huh?'

'Number one oh one. It's easy to remember, like Room 101, in 'Nineteen Eighty-four', you know, everyone's worst nightmare!'

'I hope it's not that.'

'Actually it's highly desirable and sought after,' Joe laughed. 'That's what the estate agent said!'

'But what about you?' Rick fixed his gaze on me. 'This split with Carole, are you coping OK?'

'Of course.' I shrugged. 'I'm better off single. I haven't thought about her all evening.' That wasn't strictly true. I'd tried to call her before I left the flat and again from my mobile just before I came in the pub, but the number diverted to the answering machine both times.

Rick went to the bar to buy another round. Meanwhile. Joe took out his tobacco tin and rolled a cigarette. I'd forgotten what a soothing activity that was, what a good diversion, like cats washing. I'd started smoking again myself since I moved into Mike's but I'd gone for the packet sort, instant gratification. Joe was just licking the paper and sealing the tobacco inside as Rick arrived back with the drinks. Both Rick and Joe were drinking out of pewter tankards. I guessed the landlord kept them hanging above the bar, just like he had when we were students. As I sipped my beer out of a straight glass I wondered what had become of my own tankard. It was in the loft, probably, or the garage, worst-case scenario it had ended up in a charity shop or a jumble sale.

'Have you done much caving recently?' I asked this tentatively.

'Not as much as I'd like.' Rick looked slightly wistful. 'We occasionally do a day trip, just the two us. And now and then we go out with the university club – I'm a full member of course, being faculty – but mostly that involves taking novices down Bridge Cave. Fish and Taff haven't been out with us recently because of family commitments. But that's another

19

story. You?'

I shook my head. 'I gave all that up a long time ago.' I paused to take a gulp of beer. 'What about work? I know Rick's a physics lecturer, obviously.' I turned to Joe. 'Are you still in the same job?'

He nodded. 'Still a computer programmer but I work as a contractor – a consultant – these days. What about you?'

'Still in the lab,' I confirmed.

'Never could quite come to terms with you doing that.' Rick shook his head. 'Ironic really.'

'Someone has to do it and I'm well qualified.'

Joe put the cigarette to his lips and flicked the lighter. 'And more experienced than anyone could guess.' He accentuated the word 'experienced' and chuckled to himself. He was referring to the fact that not all of my training in chemistry had been strictly academic. Some was – shall we say – extracurricular. But that was a long time ago. I'd moved on.

'So tell me about Fish and Taff.'

Rick did most of the talking, just like he always had, Joe nodded agreement now and again. Fish was married, Rick told me; he'd got hitched a couple of years back and had two stepdaughters. Taff was divorced; his ex-wife, Megan, had custody of their boys. Rick paused for breath. 'Give us a drag of that ciggy, Spider.'

Spider. Rick using his pet name for Joe brought back a pang of nostalgia for university days. By the summer of our first year, Joe's hair had grown long enough to fall in fine fair wisps about his shoulders. With his pointed chin and long finely chiselled nose and especially when he wore tight jeans and played his guitar, he looked exactly like Mick Ronson – the guy who played guitar in David Bowie's band. You're a Spider, Rick used to say, a Spider from Mars.

'And of course you'll want to know about Beth,' Rick continued.

I was taken aback. 'I didn't realise you were still in touch with her.'

'We certainly are. Now let's see, where shall I begin?'

20

I was caught unawares. Beth and I had been an item when I was at university. However, that was over years ago. History. It shouldn't bother me talking about her after all this time, but for some reason it did. On the one hand I didn't want to know anything. I wanted her to stay in the past where she belonged. On the other there were dozens of questions I wanted to ask – but only if I heard the right answers. I wanted to know that she was successful and that she had a good job. But if she was happily settled with a rich husband and children then I didn't want to hear about it. I know it sounds mean, especially seeing as I'd been married myself for ten years, but suddenly it mattered. Maybe it was because of splitting up with Carole. Like life had suddenly turned into a competition to see who was happiest.

Rick looked at me. 'Don't worry,' he said, misunderstanding my expression. 'She's OK. She's done very well, actually. Got into PR. She landed a big job in the States a few years back.'

I breathed a sigh of relief. Like I say, I wished Beth well. But I was very glad she was pursuing her wellness a long way away.

I went to pay the beer tax and got another round in on the way back. There was a bit of a disagreement going on at the other end of the room but that was nothing new for this place.

'Joe and I have had an idea,' Rick announced as I set the tray of drinks down. 'We've been talking,' he continued, as the two of them exchanged conspiratorial looks, 'and we both think it would be a great idea if you moved in with us.'

I was taken aback. I wondered what it would be like, sharing with them again. 'Well I'm not sure,' I hedged.

'At least think about it,' Rick urged. 'We've got plenty of space.'

I was so tempted. I had no doubts that their place was far more luxurious than my present abode. Plus it would solve the problem of Mike getting pissed off with me. Then again, maybe he had a point; maybe I really had become an unbearable misery. If that was the case then I didn't want to risk annoying Rick and Joe as well, not when we were just getting to be friends again. I took a gulp of beer to give me courage.

'Thanks,' I said, 'but I'm kind of settled for the time being – and anyway it shouldn't be for long.'

'Of course,' Rick nodded, 'you'll be looking for a place to buy yourself once the divorce is settled.'

I was thinking more in terms of moving back in with Carole but I didn't say anything. Instead I moved on quickly. 'So what was it you mentioned earlier? This thing you wanted to talk to me about.'

'Ah yes.' Rick paused for dramatic effect, and also because there was quite a bit of shouting going on somewhere in the crowd. 'Joe and I have been worried, really worried, about something.'

Joe nodded in agreement.

Further down the bar there was a yell and the clatter of a chair hitting the floor.

Rick continued. 'And we've decided we have to try and do something to help.'

It was my turn to nod. 'But what is it and where do I fit in?'

I was fired up with curiosity now, eager to find out what they were talking about so mysteriously. Then I saw the landlord pushing his way through to our table.

'Would you mind?' he shouted across to Rick. 'Only it's one of yours.'

The request was nothing new. Rick had practised martial arts as long as I could remember and that, combined with his physique, meant he'd often been called upon to break up squabbles.

He nodded to the landlord. Then he leant across to me and, in a hushed voice, answered my question. I was just taking in what he'd said when he leapt to his feet. 'Come on,' he said, flexing his arms as he stood up. 'No prizes for guessing who's playing fisticuffs.'

As he led the way through the crowd, I kept a few paces back. I didn't want to get involved in any trouble, I don't like pain and I didn't want to get hurt.

The throng had backed away from the scene of the fight. Clearly I wasn't the only one with cowardly sentiments. As it turned out, by the time we got there the action seemed to be over. A man I didn't know was picking himself up from the floor, rubbing his chin. On the ground another man lay on his back. He had dark gipsy looks and an unshaven growth that wasn't quite designer stubble. I recognised him immediately.

'Taff!' I leaned over him in amazement.

'Weed!' he gasped in reply. Then he passed out.

But it wasn't the sight of Taff, spread-eagled in a drunken stupor, that haunted me over the next few hours; his brawl was proof that he was the same as ever. What bothered me were Rick's words before we were interrupted. 'We need your help,' he'd said. 'One of our friends is in trouble. It's a matter of life and death.'

Chapter 5

Cows' tails - a piece of climbing rope divided into two different lengths and attached to the caver's belt or harness in the middle. A safety aid and an essential part of the SRT kit.

All I have to do is stay alive. It sounds easy enough. In the outside world, in the warmth of summer, survival would be straightforward. But in March, down a cave in the Welsh mountains, that's a different matter.

There are basically three things you need down a cave: light, food and warmth.

My worst enemy is the cold. The temperature outside will doubtless drop below zero. Underground it will be warmer, perhaps six or seven degrees, more in the dry and sheltered chambers. I shiver slightly. I'm wearing a one-piece fleece suit, like an overgrown baby suit. It's designed to drain quickly when it gets wet and to wick moisture away from your body. This is just as well seeing as I got soaked through a few hours ago. If I'd been wearing ordinary clothes I'd be well on the way to hypothermia by now. On top of the fleece I'm wearing an oversuit. This protects me from spray, from wind chill and from ripping my fleece on every rock I brush against. It also gives an extra layer of insulation. On my hands I wear industrial rubber gloves and on my feet neoprene socks inside steel-toe-capped lace-up boots. Round my waist is secured a webbing belt with a battery pack for my lamp and a set of cows' tails threaded onto it. On my head I wear a protective helmet. Normally, in this weather, I'd wear a balaclava underneath, but hey, there didn't seem any point for just a couple of hours. If I were constantly on the move, all of this would keep me quite cosy. But it isn't designed for sitting around in, much less sleeping the night.

The combination of rain and a rapidly dropping temperature above ground are creating one hell of an icy blast from the entrance. One thing's for sure, I can't hang around here much longer. If I'm going to get out of here alive I need to stop feeling sorry for myself; I need to take stock of the situation and decide what I'm going to do.

I take a deep breath. Stop the fucking self-pity, Marty, and get your act together.

Strictly speaking, the entrance above me isn't the only way out of the cave. Somewhere there's another way. We know the water goes through; we've tested it. We did it last year. High up on the hillside, where the stream goes in, we tipped a bottle of bright, glowing dye. Sure enough, further down the valley, up bubbled an orange spring. And we think there are others. However, that's not to say I could get out the same way. There could be boulders blocking my path or a passage totally submerged in water – a sump – too long to dive on a single breath of air. Let's face it, we've spent the last few months searching for and failing to locate a way through, so what are my chances of finding one now? Not something you'd want to bet your life on, that's for sure.

I can feel a dark despondency creeping over me again. One thing is clear; I'm not going to get out of here tonight. I have to make plans now, for how I'm going to get through the next twelve hours.

Food and drink: I'm going to need something to keep me going. Water is no problem, there's plenty of it flowing through the cave. More gallons than I could ever drink gushes and rushes along streamways, bounces over boulders and spills down cascades. It's as pure as you'll get too. The original mountain spring, unpolluted by chemicals.

Finding enough to eat could prove more tricky. All I've got with me are the two Mars bars and the packet of nuts and raisins I squashed into the cradle of my helmet before I left the car. On second thoughts, make that one Mars bar; delete the one I ate earlier. It's hardly a gourmet feast but it'll keep me going till morning. At least, it would under normal circumstances, but I'm going to burn up a fair bit of energy keeping warm; not to mention moving about; because I can't stay where I am for much longer.

Light. I'm going to need light while I'm underground. There's no natural light down a cave, none at all. It isn't like walking down the road on a dark night. All you have is what you take with you. I switch my lamp on again, playing the beam over the dank, jagged terrain. There are perhaps six hours of light left in the battery, more if I use the dim pilot bulb. Then there's the micro torch I carry for emergencies. I take a deep breath and breathe out whistling the air over my teeth. I had never foreseen an emergency such as this. I do a quick calculation. If I only use it when I'm travelling it should see me through. I rummage between the rubber glove and the sleeve of my oversuit and reveal my left wrist. My watch indicates that it is just after four p.m. The same time it showed when I looked earlier – presumably the time when I fell and when some part of it got broken. I tap it and shake my wrist but the display remains the same. Not good. I'll have to guess timings and, more importantly, lamp time. Feeling even more insecure, I turn the lamp off and return to total darkness.

I'm starting to feel uncomfortably lonely. I've been caving on my own before and it's never bothered me, but this time is different. A bed for the night, that's what I could really do with. Now I really must be cracking up, thinking I'm going to find a bed down here in this cold, dark, God-forsaken place. Hell no! There is though! A bed, that is. I've slept down here before, when we were exploring. It was a while ago, admittedly, and I wasn't on my own; but it was OK, snug even. We'd set up a proper camp with sleeping bags and a gas stove and kettle and everything. The rest of us took our sleeping bags out in February because we needed them for a trip to Yorkshire. But Fish had bought a new one. I remember him saying he might as well leave the old one down here at the camp ready for next time, no point in taking it all the way out just to carry it back in again a few weeks later. I rack my brain trying to remember if I saw it last time I went past the camp. Certainly we left a stove there and what was left of the night-lights and candles, maybe even some food.

I mull it over for a bit but really there's only one option. I'll go to the camp. It'll be cosy enough – even better if Fish's sleeping bag is still there. Then in the morning I'll make my way back here, climb as far as I can up the entrance shaft and shout for help. I stand up, switch the lamp onto pilot and make my way purposefully along the passage.

Chapter 6

Streamway - general term for an underground watercourse.

I remember one night when we were students. The pubs had just reached kicking out time and we'd swayed and swaggered our way back from the Red Dragon. Somewhat the worse for alcohol, we turned the key in the lock of number forty-two, Benson Street. The door creaked open and we stumbled in, Rick and Joe, Fish and myself, all laughing helplessly.

'Why do you always run away from policemen?' I spluttered, gasping for breath.

Rick grinned. 'Must be my guilty conscience.'

'You haven't done anything illegal.'

'No, but I'm about to. Get the goods out, Spider.'

The sitting room was a collage of decaying upholstery; creative, Joe called it. There was a weary carpet, patterned with intertwining leaves, threadbare at the roots. The curtains were bold and glaring, the sort described in the early seventies as trendy and thereafter as tasteless. Two winged armchairs and a sofa competed with their varying colours and designs. In one corner stood the television, a bulky ex-rental, in another a motorbike engine lay in pieces, leaking oil onto a newspaper.

Joe collapsed face down on the sofa, reached underneath, and, after much scrabbling, pulled out a small foil-wrapped package. He threw it across the room to Rick who was now seated in one of the chairs, with his Dr Marten-clad feet resting on the coffee table.

I went through to the kitchen and took four cans of Ruddles out of the fridge.

Back in the front room Rick sprinkled brown crumbly resin onto the tobacco. Someone had put a tape on: it was playing 'Court of the Crimson King.'

Rick looked up at me. 'Hey, we've only got one joint's worth left! Can you do anything about it, Weed?'

I ran upstairs two at a time, to my room, which was in the attic. I switched on the light. There was a bed (unmade) with an Indian throw draped untidily over it. A similar throw was pinned onto the far wall, covering up a damp patch. A chest of drawers stood open with T-shirts hanging out and over in the far corner an ancient wardrobe clung onto the wall. In the roof was a skylight and directly under this, surrounded by screens of mirrors, grew a veritable garden. Five full-grown cannabis plants spread their finger-like serrated leaves, reaching greedily for any glimmer of light.

Downstairs, Rick was getting impatient. 'What're you doing up there?'

'Coming!' I picked a handful of leaves, left the light on to help the plants regain their energy and ran back down to the living room.

'They're a bit fresh, I'm afraid.' As I spoke I arranged the leaves on the rack in the grill-pan and lit the gas.

'Hey!' called Joe. 'Isn't that all greasy?'

'Yeah,' I replied. 'They'll taste of bacon.'

'Well turn the heat down, man, or you'll incinerate them,' suggested Fish.

I didn't think they were quite up to rolling so we tore the charred aromatic leaves into small pieces and put them in the teapot together with two spoons of Earl Grey. The resultant brew wasn't bad, though as far as taste goes I'd have preferred another can of Ruddles. Rick, Joe and I spread ourselves over the furniture, while Fish sat on the floor and played an imaginary guitar until eventually his fingers started to shake.

'Hey!' he shouted above the music. 'I'm all weirded out!'

I remember, that night I fell asleep in the chair and dreamed I was being chased by the Fire Witch.

Weed: green-fingered cultivator of cannabis plants. That was how I acquired my nick-name, though if they'd waited another year I'd probably have been christened Speed which sounds much more respectable. But all that was twenty years ago. This time it was number one hundred and one (the posh end of

Benson Street, like Joe said) and instead of Fish, it was Taff who made up the foursome. Joe unlocked the door and we stumbled in, Rick and I struggling to keep our footing as Taff slumped and swayed between us.

'We'll put him in the lounge,' Rick instructed.

'Fancy seeing you again, boyo!' Taff had always called members of our crowd boyo. I never heard any other Welshman use the word and figured it was a piss-take in return for us calling him Taff. I ducked as he took a swing at my head. He wasn't trying to hurt me. On the contrary, I think it was meant to be an affectionate gesture, ruffling my hair or something; but, whatever the intention, there was only ever one outcome when Taff was pissed, and it was best to stay out of range. We sat him down and while I kept an eye on him in case he puked or started smashing the place up, Rick and Joe went through to the kitchen to organise drinks.

I'd never felt entirely comfortable with Taff. I know I sound like a snob, but when the rest of us were at university his lack of education grated on me. While we studied and went to lectures, his status alternated between labourer and layabout. He was an old mate of Fish's though and as such he became an honorary member of our crowd.

But Fish wasn't around on this occasion, so, ten minutes later, Rick, Joe and I sipped coffee and discussed what we should do about the inebriated Welshman.

Joe thought we should take him to casualty just to be on the safe side, but he was outvoted on the grounds that Taff had done this sort of thing plenty of times before and never suffered more than a bruise or a cut lip. Besides, none of us wanted to spend the night in a waiting room with a horde of rowdy drunks. So Rick decided that I should check him over, seeing as I worked in a hospital. I wasn't too keen – I mean, it's not as if I'm a doctor or a nurse – but I'd seen them sort out head injuries often enough. I checked his pupils, shining a Maglite into each one in turn. This didn't go down too well seeing as he was snoring on the sofa by then.

'How many fingers am I holding up?' I enquired

30

professionally.

This prompted a rude reply such that I was satisfied his brain was OK. So, figuring it would be safer and easier to leave him downstairs, we made up a bed for him on a mattress on the lounge floor, arranging him in the recovery position with old blankets spread around nearby in case he puked up during the night.

It was only after Rick and Joe had bade me goodnight that I realised they hadn't told me what it was, that life and death thing they'd mentioned earlier, or what part I had to play in it.

Chapter 7

Rift - cave passage, often narrow, and with high, vertical walls.

The cave system in which I'm trapped is the largest explored in Britain. It drops to a depth of four hundred feet and its known passages total more than thirty miles. Deep into the mountain they go. Some follow rivers, to plunge into pools and disappear beneath the rock then re-emerge, sweet and clear, on the hillside. Others dwindle, dry and unused and trail, forgotten, into nothingness; they branch and honeycomb, burrowing through the rock. The mountain is like a termite mound. And I am the termite.

I'm feeling a bit better now. Don't get me wrong, I'm not exactly happy about the situation. Given the choice between being tucked up on the sofa with the central heating on full blast and a can of beer and a plate of fish and chips in front of me or being trapped down a cave facing starvation and hypothermia – given any other option in fact – well, there's just no contest. But now I've got a plan, a purpose, something to focus on. Now I can keep going.

From the end of the passage that leads out from the entrance chamber, there are two ways on. The first leads to the upper series, where low and dusty scraped-out tunnels spread dendritic arms towards the surface. We spent many an afternoon up there, scratching at the coarse dry rock, imagining we could feel the steady draught that promised a way out onto the hillside. But we never found one. All the paths were blind. The other way leads down, deep into the earth, into a labyrinth of caverns, rifts and streamways. It's this route that I take now.

I dreamt about Beth, that night at Rick and Joe's, after Taff's tussle in the pub. When I say dreamt, I don't mean some bizarre thing conjured by my unconscious during a period of rapid eye movement, I mean that state when you're halfway between waking and sleeping, when your mind slips into neutral and memories surface spontaneously, memories that you'd normally keep buried firmly in the past where they belong. Anyway, that night I'd been assigned the double bed in the spare room but I decided to doze on the chair for the first half hour or so, just to be sure Taff was all right. Having to help look after him had both sobered me and woken me up and at first I sat there, wide awake, thinking.

I'd trained myself, over the years, to detach myself from anything painful or disturbing. Initially it was a defence mechanism, a way of dealing with difficult memories. Gradually it became more like a filter. If anything in my life was likely to shake up my emotions I simply didn't let it in. Perhaps that sounds like a cop out, but I'd never have been able to do my job without cracking up if I wasn't able to distance myself sometimes. Consequently, all my memories of Beth had been temporarily erased. No particular reason, we had a good time together, we had a carefree time. If you want to be romantic about it, I suppose you'd say she was my first love. But you can't be thinking about ex-girlfriends when you're married to someone else, can you? Fish told me once that in Tibet there is no word for regret because, unlike most of us, the Tibetans put the past behind them and move on; they don't spend their lives beating themselves up over past mistakes. I'm well aware that, if I allowed myself to wallow in the past, there'd be plenty of guilt and plenty of regret. So, until such time as the Dalai Lama gives me a good talking to and tells me how to deal with it, I prefer to live firmly in the present.

But that night, what with Rick talking about Beth and everything, it had got me wondering; it raked up stuff I hadn't thought about for a very long time. And as I relaxed in the chair, and dipped my toes, cautiously, into the shallows of sleep, I got to thinking about her. About the first time we met.

I'd gone to the concert on my own. It was a Saturday night in the summer term and Rick, Joe and Fish had gone on a caving club trip to the Mendips. Normally I'd have been right there with them but this time things clashed. Peter Gabriel was climbing up on Solsbury Hill and there was no way I was going to miss it.

The gig was in the main university hall, nominally standing but in reality most people were sitting on the grubby floor, which was already sticky with spilt beer and gritty with cigarette ash. When I say I was on my own, I mean there were plenty of familiar faces in the crowd, but I was more intent on finding a good pitch – somewhere with a decent sound balance and a good view – than being sociable. Even before the support act came on, people were strewn across the floor, like litter on a beach the night after a bank holiday; so I picked my way carefully, stepping over outstretched limbs and plastic cups of beer, and settled myself down.

She was only a couple of feet away, sitting on an outspread Afghan coat, snuggled into the soft hair of the goatskin. She wore an Indian wrap-around skirt and a black cheesecloth top. The heavy lace that bordered the neckline partly obscured her cleavage and the whiteness of her skin gleamed in contrast with the darkness of the fabric. I could happily have stared at her tits all evening, but perversely I was even more fascinated by the stud that sparkled just above her left nostril. At that time, body-piercings weren't the everyday fashion item they've become today and I'd only seen Asian women wearing nose studs. So I sat gazing at her, transfixed. Her legs were crossed and she sat, poised, over an open tobacco tin, as she rolled a cigarette. I watched as she put it to her lips and took a lighter from her handbag. She flicked the flint a couple of times. Nothing happened.

I was half watching her and half aware of the support band strumming through their first number.

'Do you have a light?'

At first I didn't realise she was speaking to me.

'If you're going to stare at me, the least you can do is offer me a light.'

'Sorry.' I took a box of matches out of my pocket and threw it into her lap – immediately cursing myself for not lighting it for her like they do in the movies.

'Thanks.' She took a long drag of her cigarette, held her lungs full for a few seconds then blew the smoke out stylishly through pursed lips. She had big baby eyes and big baby pouting lips; her face was partially hidden by a mass of curly blonde hair. In short, she was like a doll. She looked at me for a moment, like she was weighing me up. 'Look, would you do me another favour? If I give you the money, would you get me a glass of wine from the bar?'

I raised my eyebrows.

'Only they won't serve me, you see, because I don't look eighteen,' she explained.

'Yeah. OK.' I stood up. 'Perhaps you should carry some ID with you.'

She shook her head. 'It would only prove that I'm not – eighteen, that is.'

'Oh.' I'd assumed she was a university student like me. 'Perhaps you shouldn't be doing that either then.' I nodded at the cigarette, which smouldered with the unmistakable smell of dope.

She gave me a withering look. 'I've been smoking joints since I was fifteen. What's your problem?'

'Wouldn't your parents be shocked if they knew?'

She laughed. 'They both smoke it themselves, they got me into it, actually.'

I stared in disbelief, picturing the unlikely scene of my parents ever offering me a spliff. I didn't know whether I was impressed or horrified.

'Well, are you going to get me that drink or shall I ask someone who's less of a fuddy-duddy?'

I scrabbled quickly to my feet, aware that I was on the verge of blowing a serious opportunity. 'Don't worry,' I assured her, as I shook my head at the money she held out to me. 'This is my treat.'

It occurred to me, as I queued up at the bar, that I'd never actually had a proper girlfriend. Not that this precocious child-like creature was likely to fill that role, obviously, but the interaction with her got me thinking. I'd been at university almost a year now and my experience with girls was virtually nil. I mean, I wasn't some shy, innocent virgin, I'd had a couple of flings, one night stands, call them what you will, with girls I'd met in the union bar. But that was it. All my spare time seemed to be spent with Rick, Joe and Fish, grubbing around down caves. I hadn't got round to a regular relationship. None of us had.

I made my way back with the drinks and got into listening to the support act, which was surprisingly good for a local combo. Then, in the interval, I got talking to the girl as she kicked off her clogs and stretched her legs out, displaying socks that had a separate partition for each toe – another fascination for me. She told me that her name was Beth; that her father was a professor of philosophy and her mother taught yoga. She'd travelled to India with her mother earlier that year and while her mum had retreated to an ashram to fold herself into lotus position and chant 'Om', Beth had wandered round the streets of Bombay, acquiring a pierced nose, an assortment of silk sari fabric and joss sticks, and an unpleasant dose of amoebic dysentery. The latter was entirely her own fault she assured me. 'My mother had warned me not to eat salads, but after a week I was just so desperate for something fresh that I had a side salad with a curry. I should have stuck to lychees.'

Later that evening, when we were leaving, she asked me if I'd maybe like to meet up sometime to listen to music and share a couple of joints. I asked her if she fancied coming down a cave. Either way, she gave me her phone number. And as I lay in bed that night, the fact that Peter Gabriel had been shit-hot cosmically good was not the foremost thing on my mind.

I smiled to myself and looked over to where Taff was lying motionless on the mattress. The lights were dimmed and I was beginning to feel drowsy, half sleeping, half listening to his breathing. Although I'd suppressed them for years, the images, which drifted into my consciousness, were not entirely unpleasant. I let myself doze, hoping for some more.

'I'm the king of the castle,' sang Beth. She was perched high on a rocky pinnacle, stark against the skyline. 'And we all fall down!' And she jumped, out into nothingness.

'No!' I leapt up and caught her in mid air.

The two of us tumbled onto the sheep-cropped grass, laughing helplessly. I kissed her on the chin and on the tip of her nose and on the silver scarab that pierced her nostril. She rolled on top of me, spilling blonde corkscrew curls onto my cheeks. She was not large but retained a hint of puppy fat that gave her a voluptuous perfection, a smooth fullness that exists only in the teenage body's ability to defy gravity. I squeezed her tightly against me.

'I'm going to hold you forever.'

'You'll have to catch me first!'

She wriggled free and slithered down the steep slope towards the river. I followed along the treacherous path, dislodging small pebbles beneath my feet and sending them bouncing onto the rocks and the water below. Neither of us paid any heed to the signposts announcing 'danger'; only tourists would be stupid enough to fall.

The path came to an end. There was nowhere else to go. She missed her footing and slipped on the loose gravel.

'Beth! Hang on!'

She clung to tree roots, suspended only by her arms. I climbed upwards and anchored myself to a branch, holding out my hand to her. But she was too independent for that; she pulled herself up, arm over arm, like a monkey. Straight past me she climbed, then turned around grinning.

When, later, we scampered back down the hillside, she took my hand and we skipped along in step.

'What have you got me for my birthday?'

'I'm not saying.'

'Go on.' She teased pulling the hair that grew, unchecked, about my shoulders. She laughed and ran past me down the path. The breeze caught her skirt, like a purple sail, and played with the fringes at the hem.

37

I caught up with her as we reached the first houses.

'Tea shop?'

'Is there time before the bus?'

I looked at my watch. 'Half an hour.'

'Come on then.'

We squeezed into a space by the window. They were the only seats free and the table was still cluttered with cups and saucers and crumb-covered plates.

She reached into her jacket and presented a handful of coins. 'Empty your pockets,' she commanded.

We had just enough money between us to share a scone and a mug of tea.

I opened my eyes briefly. The room was hazy. Taff was spark out. My mind returned to Beth.

I remembered the first time, just the two of us, sitting in the darkness.

'Ssh! Don't wake Joe and Rick.'

Beth smothered a giggle. 'I can't help it, I've got hiccups.'

'I'll get you a glass of water.'

I fetched her the drink, it was in a chipped mug. 'This is all that was clean, sorry.'

She sipped it slowly, perched on the edge of the bed. I stroked her cheek and kissed her earlobe. 'You've got mud in your hair.'

'You've got mud in your ears.'

'I'm not surprised.'

We'd been out that afternoon. Down dark and gloomy tunnels which the rest of the caving club shunned. Deep in the bowels of the earth, squelching through the surface layer of sodden clay, finding some perverse, gothic enjoyment in the disagreeableness of the surroundings. Then we'd had a mud fight, laughing hysterically as we hurled handfuls of sticky ammunition at one another. Later, we'd walked back to the hut, delighting in the looks of horror on the faces of passers by, as they stared at our darkly grotesque forms. We'd staggered with suppressed laughter like a pair of zombies freshly escaped from their graves.

I took the mug from her hand and set it on the bedside table. There was a glittery thread woven into the fabric of her dress; it caught the lamplight, sparkling like a hundred fireflies. She turned towards me and took my hand. Her eyes were clear with health and youth, it made her look innocent, trusting, vulnerable.

'Sure?' I asked.

'Sure.'

I kissed her on the lips, then again more intensely. We fell back onto the bed. There was a loud creak of rusty springs. We froze.

'Ssh, quiet a minute.'

The sound of Deep Purple seeped subdued but decisive through the wall. We both laughed. I reached out to the cassette player and we spent the next half hour listening to *Silver Machine* and *Running with the Pack* with bed springs for extra percussion.

Jesus! I didn't remember Beth snoring like that! I pulled myself awake and heard the full force of Taff, now lying on his back, roaring and snorting in the middle of the room. I took my cue and after rolling Taff onto his side (ignoring his mumbled, senseless protests) I turned out the light and went upstairs to bed.

Chapter 8

Stalactite - cave formation that hangs from the ceiling, formed as water drips down. Sometimes shortened in speech to 'stal'.

Now that I've left the entrance behind, the cave is taking on its own character. I remember, soon after we met, trying to describe to Carole – who'd never even been in a show cave – what the underground world is like. Even then, I didn't really know where to begin. How can you convey something that's a whole new experience? It's a world within a world, a totally different place with its own set of rules that seem to defy the laws of nature. You could be just yards beneath the surface of the ground, yet many hours journey, through a sometimes hostile environment, from the outside.

Caving is a sensory experience and an emotional one. You can show someone photos of brilliant glistening stalactites, yet there are no words to describe the way you felt when you discovered them, when you touched them, the first human being to see them, ever. Then there's the sound. If you're near a streamway or a waterfall, the noise is deafening. Amplified an infinite number of times as the sound bounces and echoes from rock to rock, it engulfs you, a totally sensurround experience. It flows like waves, first dipping into comparative quiet then rising in unexpected crescendo to a booming climax. And strangest of all is the smell. I don't know quite what it is, a composite I suppose, earth, dampness, minerals, stale air. The components mix together to produce a scent that can only be called cave.

'No,' I said, definitively. 'Absolutely not. No way.'

We were sitting round the kitchen table in Benson Street, Rick, Joe and myself. Taff was sleeping off his hangover in the front room. It was the first opportunity we'd had to continue the conversation that was cut short by Taff's untimely brawl the night before.

I took a bite out of my bacon sandwich. 'You don't rescue someone from a marriage,' I insisted.

Rick shook his head and reached across the table to push the plunger that forced the ground coffee to the base of the cafetière. Joe said nothing but looked serious.

The subject of the conversation was Fish. He was the one they were so worried about, the friend in trouble, the person who, in Rick's opinion, was in a life or death situation. My job, apparently, was to save him: from his demons, from depression and, specifically, from a disastrous marriage. I knew what Carole's view would be. Marriages have to be worked at, not interfered with. If a friend was unhappy, then, unless there was violence involved, the most you should do was encourage them to see a counsellor. And on this occasion I was inclined to agree with her. If I'm honest, I don't think I particularly shared her high morals; I was more concerned with not wanting to get the blame if things went pear-shaped. Don't get me wrong, I'd always been fond of Fish, and if I thought he was in any sort of danger I'd be straight in there. But I hadn't even seen the guy for more than ten years. I only had Rick's version to go on – Fish worked at the university, apparently, in the computer services unit, so they saw a fair bit of one another – and the fact was, Rick had always tended to over-dramatise things.

I sat there chewing my breakfast, feeling uncomfortable as Rick stared at me expectantly. 'What about Taff?' I suggested, trying to pass the buck. 'The two of them have been mates since they were kids after all, surely he'd be the best person to help out.'

Rick nodded. 'You're quite right of course. They go back a long way.' He gestured towards the lounge. 'But unfortunately he's hardly reliable. Plus he's got family problems of his own. And Fish's wife thoroughly disapproves of him of course. We need someone she respects if this is going to work.'

'Well what's wrong with you two then?' I was clutching at straws.

Joe grunted. 'She's homophobic. Won't have us in the house

41

for fear we might contaminate her children.' I remembered they'd told me the night before, that Fish's wife had two daughters from a previous marriage.

'The thing is,' Rick continued, 'normally we'd agree with you, none of our business and all that. But we've seen Fish changing over the last six months, and some of the signs...well...the truth is we're worried he might be heading the same way as before.'

I went hot and cold. Rick was referring to an episode in the past when Fish had had what was then termed a breakdown. But it had all happened years ago. It was part of a time that I thought I'd successfully erased from my memory. Suddenly my head was like a pot being stirred. Images resurfaced in my mind. The flashing lights and siren of an ambulance, Fish lying limp and useless in a hospital bed after the remains of the beer and barbs had been siphoned out of his stomach, me sitting in the corner, overwhelmed by helplessness and guilt.

Joe went on. 'Of course, we don't know exactly why he took the overdose back then. Drinking too much probably didn't help; and then there was...' he lowered his voice to a barely audible whisper, '...the other thing.'

Some kind of safety valve clicked in my brain and my mind went blank. I stared straight ahead. We all sat in silence for a few moments. At last Rick spoke, cutting through the chill atmosphere.

'Did you know, they reckon more cavers die as a result of suicide than in accidents underground? Maybe it's the nature of the sport, attracting personalities who are already close to the edge. Who knows? The point is, given Fish's history, we just can't take the risk, we feel we have to at least try to do something.'

I took a gulp of coffee out of a fashionable stoneware mug. The whole place was like that, fashionable, expensive, luxurious, the complete opposite of where I was currently living. I began to wonder if I should reconsider their offer to move in. My mind firmly focused on the present day and, my composure regained, I turned my attention to the problem in hand and what to do about Fish. 'OK, I've not seen him for years but I'm happy to trust your judgment. If you think he needs rescuing from his wife then perhaps you're right. But I don't see how I can do anything useful; it's not like I know the woman.'

'Oh, but you do!' Rick clapped his hands with glee.

I looked up, confused.

'It's the Valkyrie!' He announced it triumphantly.

'The what?' Bloody hell, I couldn't believe it! I was so gobsmacked I dropped my sandwich. In that instant everything changed. An icy chill crept over my skin and an invisible fist reached into my body and grabbed my stomach. Valerie, or the Valkyrie as we secretly called her, was truly the most fearsome woman I had ever met. I remember our first encounter as clearly as if it were yesterday, or, more to the point, I remember the terror.

It was during our first term at university, before we moved into Benson Street, before I met Beth. We used to go out, a crowd of us from the caving club. We'd borrow the university minibus at weekends and drive out to the club hut up in the mountains, near the caves. I say hut, it was an old miner's cottage that the club had bought for peanuts, in a village, the name of which I still can't pronounce. What used to be the lounge had been converted into a common room and there was a lean-to kitchen out the back and a shower and toilet that drained into a septic tank. A flight of twisting stairs, steep as a ladder, led to the upper floor, where iron-framed bunk beds nestled under the eaves. But just like those fairy stories, where the monster lurks in the enchanted wood, taking occasional children to feast on, there was a price to be paid for staying at the cottage. The Valkyrie, elected hut warden that year, imposed a reign of terror in the idyllic mountain retreat.

It was my first stay at the hut; in fact I'd just been down my first ever cave. The university minibus pulled up outside and we tumbled out, fresh (well actually not so fresh) from our initiation in the underground world of Ogof Fechan. It had been a big deal for me, my first cave. I'd been nervous about it of course. My insides had been tense with excitement. Would it be dangerous? Would it be scary? It was neither of those as it turned out. The cave, in retrospect, was not so much difficult as uncomfortable, consisting mainly of flat out crawls through unwelcome water. Nonetheless, back at the hut I was exhausted, overcome with the tiredness that sets in when you come down from a big adrenalin rush. I just wanted to eat and sleep and unwind. I wanted to switch my brain onto automatic and simply chill. The last thing I wanted was another challenge.

'Go and tick our party off the board.' The leader of the group, a second year called Jeff, had instructed me as I lumbered out onto the street. So, while Rick, Joe and the others trooped down the side passage to get changed in the shed that passed as a kit room, I dutifully stepped through the front door of the cottage into the common room.

On an old school blackboard, nailed to the wall, details of each trip were scraped in chalk by the leaders. There was a column for the date, another for the name of the cave plus another for the area if it was a big system, the number of people in the group was recorded and the main purpose of the visit, such as exploration, survey or digging. Lastly, and very importantly, was the ETO or expected time out. If this was exceeded by more than a couple of hours, then someone thought about coming to look for you or even calling out cave rescue. That was the idea anyway. I took the grubby piece of rag that resided on the shelf beneath the board and wiped off the details of our adventure, taking care not to erase any of the information about the group visiting the Abyss in Dan-yr-Ogof that was written underneath, or those going to Gnome Passage in Ogof Ffynnon Ddu, described directly above.

'Just what do you think you're doing?'

The sharp female voice cut straight through me, causing me to drop the cloth. Slowly I turned round. The first impression I got was that she was huge. I suppose she was only a couple of inches taller than me but, Jeez, she was so much heftier. I guess I was a pretty scrawny build in those days, having never done much exercise to build up muscle. Valerie, by contrast, was endowed with a beefy bulk covering her arms, shoulders and thighs. It was fearsome. Plus she had this short blond hair gelled up into spikes that made her look even taller. I felt like she could obliterate me as easily as swatting a fly.

'I said, what are you doing? In here? Dressed like that?'

I shivered and looked down at my inadequate form. I didn't have a proper caving kit at that stage; instead I was dressed in a strange muddle of clothes that could have been the leftovers from a jumble sale. Over an old tracksuit I was wearing an ancient ripped boiler suit, provided by Fish, tucked into Wellington boots. The frayed sleeves of an item that had once been a jumper protruded from beneath the outer layers and hung raggedly over my wrists. I felt like a dog that had been let off its lead in the countryside, a mutt that had swum across a polluted river then rolled in a load of badger shit. Slimy brown water dripped from my clothes onto the floor and behind me a trail of mud led to the door.

'I'm Valerie,' she went on, 'I'm in charge here and there are rules. Rules which you are breaking.'

'I'm sorry,' I muttered, 'but I was told…'

'Never mind what anyone else says. I'm telling you now; that's what counts. I don't suppose you've read that,' she indicated a poster headed Hut Rules on the wall, 'or you'd know that caving gear isn't allowed inside.'

I shook my head.

'Some people treat the place like a pigsty and I won't have it. Do you know what happened to the last person who broke the rules?'

I shook my head again.

'I shaved him!' she declared, triumphantly.

I fingered my chin gingerly, glad that I didn't have a beard she could defile.

She laughed. 'Not his face, you idiot!' And she nodded at my flies. 'God, you are green aren't you? He'd really messed up the place and he'd sworn at me so he needed teaching a lesson. A couple of the girls held him down while I did the honours.' She looked pityingly at me. 'You'd better clean up that mess you've made and we'll say no more about it.'

I stared at her in dread and disbelief. Rick, the only one of us who'd attended public school, had already told us tales of some of the unpleasant initiation rites they practised there, but this really took the biscuit. She must have read my thoughts.

'Don't look so horrified,' she reassured me as she retreated to the kitchen. 'I wore rubber gloves!'

Well that made it fine didn't it? I shuffled hastily towards the door, my hand cupped protectively over my crotch.

'Bloody hell! The Valkyrie? I just can't imagine it.' I retrieved my sandwich from my lap but I'd quite lost my appetite for it.

'Scary memories huh?' Rick laughed. 'But you better believe it.'

I shook my head. 'How could someone as gentle as Fish be married to a…'

'…an overbearing bitch like that?' Rick completed my sentence.

Joe began rolling a cigarette. 'I think he felt sorry for her after Tom walked out.'

'Pity he didn't stop to think why he moved out.' Rick shook his head.

My increased age and experience did nothing to boost my confidence. The mere thought of the Valkyrie reduced me to terror. This new piece of information changed everything. I realised now, why they were so worried about Fish, and morally right or not, I knew I'd have to help. 'OK,' I said. 'What do you want me to do?'

Chapter 9

*Electron ladder - a typical caving ladder has narrow (approx 6 inch)
rigid cylindrical rungs and flexible wire sides so it can be rolled up. It
is anchored at the top of a pitch.*

A few days later, on the Wednesday, Mike and I were in his
lounge eating a Chinese takeaway.

Mike finished the last scrapings of his meal and set the foil
cartons on the floor beside his chair. I did the same in the
interests of male bonding.

If I'd still been with Carole, we'd have eaten the food off
plates and they would have been collected and put straight in
the dishwasher. But this was Mike's flat. Tomorrow, or the day
after, one of us would go round with a black plastic bin liner
and collect the debris of the week: cans, wrappers, dead
cigarette packets. We'd empty the ashtrays, maybe, but not
wash them. I reminded myself that it was Carole's idea that I
move in with Mike. If she'd ever seen the inside of his flat then
I'm sure she'd never have suggested it – except maybe as a
punishment, or out of spite. I wasn't surprised that Mike was
divorced, only amazed that he'd managed to get married in the
first place. His home and his habits were far worse than
anything I'd encountered as a student. And yet, in some
perverse way, living like this was comforting to me. It was a
personal rebellion against the split with Carole. It was as far
removed from her neat and orderly life as I could possibly get.

I knew Mike through work. We weren't colleagues or
partners or anything, we weren't even employed by the same
people. Mike worked for the police whereas, technically
speaking, I was a civil servant. We just came across one another
sometimes during the course of our working day and went for a
beer occasionally.

I looked across at him as he slouched back into his chair and
flicked his lighter at a factory-rolled cigarette. There were

similarities between him and Taff, I supposed: the unshaven chin, the straggly hair, the tendency towards too much alcohol and tobacco. But there was an underlying difference; not something you'd notice if you saw the two of them in a pub, but glaringly obvious when you got to know them. Taff was simply himself; no frills, no graces, no pretensions, what you saw was what you got. He was the product of a depressed working class background, or, for his generation, a class that had lost its work. Yet, apart from his drunken binges, he had some kind of dignity, something instilled in him by his parents, an inheritance passed down through the generations. Mike, on the other hand, was pretty well educated and pretty well paid. Yet somewhere along the line he had rejected his upbringing, chosen to be a slob. Of course I hadn't really thought about this until I moved in with him. Before that we were mates. We shared a few beers, although conversation had never gone beyond the safe subjects that men discuss at the bar: commiserations over the football results, appreciation of the new barmaid's tits, that kind of thing. Now that we were in closer proximity I'd expected to see a softer side. But so far, if there was a gentler more domesticated aspect to his personality then he kept it well hidden. I knew his job involved his mixing with the less savoury elements of society, that he had to fit in, be unobtrusive, play a role. Yet I found it disconcerting that I couldn't see the line where the work persona ended and the real Mike began.

He put his shoe-clad feet on the coffee table and reached for the television remote control. 'Let's see if there's a match on,' he muttered.

I nodded out of politeness seeing as it was Mike's flat, though I'd never really been into watching football. I took my mobile out of my pocket. No messages. Really I knew there wouldn't be, I'd have heard it beep if anything had come through in the half hour since I checked it last. But I'd sent a text to Carole earlier and I was sure she'd reply eventually.

I first met Carole at work, one lunch hour. I remember the first

48

words I said to her. 'May I sit here?'

The canteen was really busy that day. I didn't like it. The rows of tables were regimental and institutionalised. It reminded me of school dinners, that momentary sense of order when everyone stood to say grace, like a military drill, then the word 'amen' and suddenly chaos was unleashed and we dived like vultures onto the food. I didn't like eating in at the best of times but on this occasion I didn't have time to go out to a cafe or even take a sandwich back to the office because I was due in court at two. It was my first time giving evidence as an expert witness and I was feeling nervous. So I just made a beeline for the nearest empty chair.

The woman sitting opposite me wasn't particularly pretty or striking, I mean, I hadn't sat there with the intention of chatting her up or anything. I sprinkled salt on my egg and chips and glanced across at her. I didn't recognise her, but that was hardly surprising; hundreds, maybe thousands of people worked at the hospital and I only knew a handful of them. She could have been a consultant or a cleaner. I saw her looking back. I'd have to say hello or something just to be polite.

'Hi, I'm Marty.'

'Carole.'

'I don't think we've met before, what department are you in?' I figured she was something in admin. She had that office look, neat short styled hair, carefully manicured nails and freshly ironed blouse.

Carole smiled. 'Oh, I don't work here, I'm on a course.' She flicked her fingers through a wad of typed sheets beside her plate. They were full of technical looking diagrams and I guessed she'd been studying them before I sat down.

I raised my eyebrows.

'I'm learning how to use a defibrillator. There's a group of ten of us, we're here for a couple of days catching up on new technology. The others have gone off to make phone calls and things – actually I think most of them have gone outside for a smoke.'

'You'll be practising on them later then,' I joked.

49

'You can't talk.' She smiled and indicated my plate of concentrated cholesterol.

'So where do you work then? A nursing home or something?'

'Goodness no! I wouldn't have the patience to be a nurse. No, I'm a legal secretary, but I do a bit of voluntary work for St John's.'

What a lady, I thought. While I spent my spare time down the pub she was out saving lives. I had so much respect for her. We chatted for a bit and, although she wasn't the sort of woman I was usually attracted to, I just found she kept going up and up in my estimation.

'You'll get indigestion,' she warned, as I gulped down my food.

'I'm afraid I have to rush to an appointment,' I explained. I hesitated. I didn't have any smart chat up lines except the sort you might use in nightclubs when propositioning a prospective one-night stand. 'But perhaps I'll see you in here tomorrow,' I suggested. I would find out what time her course finished for lunch and I'd make damn sure I bumped into her again. And I didn't even know if she was married or anything.

Mike fished the remote from under a cushion and turned up the volume on the television. Then he lit a cigarette, coughed, farted and settled back in his chair.

I did the same without the cigarette or the gaseous expulsion. Ten years of marriage had trained me, somewhat.

The landline phone rang. I reached for it on the first ring.

'Carole?'

'Sorry, no.' It was Rick's very cultured but definitely masculine voice.

'Oh.'

'Well, sorry to disappoint you. Were you expecting to hear from her then?'

'What? No, of course not, just habit.'

'Well I was hoping you could come round, that's if there's nothing you need to stay in for – like a phone call for instance.'

'Of course there isn't. Shall I come to the house or do you want to meet in the pub?'

'The house. Soon as possible.'

'OK. See you in a bit then.'

'Oh – and Marty?'

'Yeah?'

'Have a shower and get changed first – we don't want you smelling like a biochemistry lab.'

'Why? Is something going on?'

Rick laughed. 'Just get over here!'

'OK.'

I was puzzled but I knew I wouldn't get anything more out of him. Probably they were planning for me to go and call for Fish, make a good impression on Valerie and all that. We'd agreed that, initially, my contribution to Fish's rescue would be to collect him from his house sometimes, make it difficult for Valerie to stop him spending time with us. That was very likely my job tonight. So I got up and set out to follow Rick's instructions, tripping over the chow mein carton on the way.

It was just before nine when I parked the car in Benson Street. The house was an Edwardian terrace with bay windows and the occasional course of decorative brickwork. It didn't look anything special from the outside but I'd noticed at the weekend that it was like the TARDIS; once you went through the front door it seemed to spread out in all directions into a series of spacious rooms. A privet hedge separated the property from the footpath and a small area of crazy paving and flowerbeds lay between this and the front door. Their cars, Rick's Golf and Joe's Cavalier, were parked on the road adjacent to the neat front garden. But the 'real business', as Joe called it, was kept in a shed round the back, accessed by a tarmac pathway between the houses a couple of doors down. There, at the end of their garden were kept the Triumph Bonneville they'd had at university and the more recently acquired Kawasaki. Their other shared passion, beside caves, had always been bikes. I'd admired the mean machines when

51

they'd showed me round last Sunday morning. 'What we'd really like,' Rick had said, 'is a Harley. If we had one of those I could get into bikes almost as much as caves.'

'In your dreams!' Joe had replied very definitively.

Cloud cover obscured the moon and the road was illuminated by streetlights. I crossed the crazy paving and rang the bell. Moments later the door opened. But it wasn't Rick or Joe standing in the hallway. I stood and stared. For far longer than is considered polite. At last I spoke.

'Beth?'

I once learned, on a forensic biology course, that if you meet someone five years on, everything about them has changed. Their skin, their eyes, their hair, every part of them has been replaced. Old cells have died and new ones have been produced, instructed by the secret code of their DNA. All that you can see, touch or smell, is completely new, you have never experienced it before. It was more than fifteen years since I'd last seen Beth, time for everything about her to have changed three times over. I stared, open-mouthed, at the replica before me.

'Hello Marty, good to see you!'

For what felt like ages I stood, awkward as a teenager, feeling that I would stumble over my words so saying nothing. I know it sounds stupid but I'd never been reunited with an ex before. Not anyone who mattered, whom I'd really had feelings for. I didn't know what I was supposed to do or how I was supposed to feel.

At last, Beth broke the silence. 'You could say, "Hello, good to see you too."'

She stretched out her arms towards me. And I let go – of my reserve, my emotions, everything. I stepped forward and hugged her, burying my face in her neck.

'Beth, of course it's wonderful to see you!'

'I was beginning to think you didn't recognise me.'

'Don't be silly, but you have changed rather.' I broke away from her, somewhat reluctantly, and stood back, still holding both of her hands. 'And I wasn't expecting to see you.'

The woman before me was a vision of beauty and elegance. Like a china doll, expertly crafted and painted, too perfect to be real. She wore a dark blue suit, almost black – midnight blue, Carole would call it – and underneath, a white blouse of shimmering silk, even the buttons shone. A short skirt covered the tops of her legs, legs clad in an identical colour, extending almost forever, until finally they disappeared into slim, pointed shoes. I was utterly transfixed.

'Come in.' She stood back and ushered me through the door.

Beth seemed taller than I remembered. Partly because the tapered heels lifted her a further couple of inches and also, I think, because she'd lost weight. Her hair still curled its blondeness down her back but was secured in a dark blue tie.

Corny, clichéd thoughts went through my mind; like how, if I had gone to seed, Beth, by contrast, was in full bloom. I reeled, like some soppy romantic film was playing in my head. I still didn't dare open my mouth for fear of the embarrassing drivel I might speak.

But Beth seemed totally unperturbed by the situation. 'Sorry about the formality,' she said. 'This is to impress the clients, I've come straight from a meeting.' She pulled her hair out of the ribbon and shook wild springy ringlets about her shoulders. 'That's better.'

Still I stared. I felt dizzy, breathing in her perfume; it wafted around me and tickled the inside of my nose. Even I knew it was something more cultured, more expensive than the patchouli she used to wear as a teenager. I stood back.

'I'm just so surprised to see you,' I spluttered. 'I thought you'd gone to the States. That's what Rick and Joe said.'

She giggled. 'But they forgot to tell you I'd come back.'

I was surprised how much it shook me up, seeing Beth after all that time. Later I would marvel at how brilliant it was but right then I felt slightly vulnerable and uncomfortable. I followed her through to the lounge. Rick and Joe's home was luxurious, full of sumptuous carpets and cosy sofas with lots of cushions, a far cry from our student days. Almost a woman's touch, I thought to myself. There were lots of blokey things too:

gadgets, hi-fis and computers with all the latest attachments. It hadn't looked quite the same last weekend with Taff in a drunken heap on the floor. There was a Steely Dan CD playing. 'Katy Lied'. Shit! I hoped that wasn't the one with 'Haitian Divorce' on. There's only so much emotion a man can cope with after all.

'I'm cooking pizza. Have you eaten?' Joe's voice drifted through from the kitchen along with an appetising aroma of roasting vegetables.

'Yeah, but I can eat again,' I reassured him.

Many a time in the past, Joe's culinary skills had saved us from the standard student diet of beans on toast. I sniffed appreciatively and wondered, yet again, if I should reconsider the possibility of moving in here.

Rick appeared with a bottle and some glasses. 'We're on red wine. Or there's beer or whisky if you prefer.'

I accepted the wine and turned to Beth. 'Have you really been in the States or were Rick and Joe just winding me up?' I asked.

'They weren't teasing you, honestly,' she assured me. 'I've only been back in the country a few months and I've been working in London the past fortnight.'

'And we weren't expecting her back until the weekend at the earliest,' confirmed Rick. 'First we knew was when she turned up on the doorstep just over an hour ago, asking if she was in time for dinner.'

'It's on the way to my place.' Beth sipped her wine and licked her lips delicately with the tip of her tongue, like the provocative way they do on adverts, trying to make you think of sex so you'll buy the product. I tried very hard not to think about it. 'I haven't even been home yet,' she continued.

'But you're here now and that's all that matters.' Rick put an ape-like arm around her shoulders and pulled her close. 'I could never understand why Marty let you go. I certainly wouldn't have done – if I'd been that way inclined!'

I gulped the rest of my wine down in one, suddenly embarrassed. I wondered if this was a set up, an attempt on the part of Rick and Joe to get Beth and me back together after all these years. I doubted Joe would contemplate interfering but I could imagine Rick deciding it was just what I needed to take my mind off Carole. I mean – don't get me wrong – a set up might be quite nice. But I was still in shock at seeing her; I couldn't think straight. Luckily a bell pinged at that moment, indicating that the first pizza was ready. I went into the kitchen to help Joe serve up.

'Come on lads! Tuck in!' Joe carried the tray of pizza, ready sliced into manageable portions. I held a plate of garlic bread in one hand and a bowl of salad in the other. We set it all down on the low coffee table and loaded our plates, before settling ourselves back onto inviting upholstery. It was altogether more civilised and enjoyable than my earlier meal.

'This is all just so good!' Rick beamed. 'Now we're all back together again. We're going to have some great times. We'll get Fish and Taff to come along and we'll all go exploring, just like we used to.' He turned to me. 'It's just what you need, Marty. We'll get you underground on some seriously exciting trips. Believe me, all your domestic problems will pale into insignificance!'

He couldn't have guessed how prophetic his words would turn out to be.

Chapter 10

Neoprene - rubbery material used to make wetsuits. Also used by cavers for knee and elbow pads.

As I make my way, tired and chilled, back into the darkness, I think briefly of the first few times I went caving. I was permanently high from the buzz of this new experience. I'd wake up on a Monday morning, bruised and aching from the weekend's exploits, vowing never to do it again. But by the middle of the week, as my body healed, I'd be craving my fix once again.

Ten minutes into the cave, cold, hurting and not feeling entirely positive, my thoughts turn to how I felt some years later, when the novelty wore off once and for all.

It was just one of those things. Once I'd finished my doctorate and started work I didn't go caving as much. Sure, my job, which involved shift work, got in the way; but mostly the magic had gone and I didn't get the same buzz any more.

The crunch came when we got arrested.

It happened like this.

Rick, Joe, Fish, Taff and myself (Beth had long since moved on to pastures new) were out one Saturday afternoon. We were exploring a mine – more an underground quarry really – in Wiltshire, where, a couple of hundred years ago, they dug out the stone that forms the elegant buildings of the nearby city of Bath; and all without leaving a blot on the landscape. Anyway, it's a really interesting place. In one area there're all these graffiti the miners inscribed during their breaks: cute poems in curly embellished writing and pictures of dashing Gatsby-like figures smoking clay pipes. Then there's another section where all the tools have been left, just as though the miners were coming back tomorrow, everything from little chisels to huge cranes, like an underground museum, or the Marie Celeste.

A couple of other interesting facts about this mine: one, it's huge, over twenty miles of passage; two, the roof tends to fall in.

We'd been down there a couple of hours and had stopped for lunch. It had been mostly straightforward walking. The main tunnels were designed to get machinery and probably horses and carts down, not like a sporty cave with waterfalls and swinging ladders; the most we'd had to do was scramble over heaps of boulders, the debris left from roof falls. It was also much warmer than a natural cave, you could amble at a relaxed pace and not worry about chilling down if you stopped for more than five minutes. This being the case, we'd brought small backpacks with bottles of water and a decent picnic instead of just the customary Mars bar apiece.

Taff looked at his watch. 'Time to turn back I guess.' He stuffed the plastic wrapping from his pre-packed cheese, lettuce and mayonnaise sandwich into his pack.

'Yeah, in a minute.' Joe handed round a pack of chocolate digestive biscuits.

It was meant to be a quick 'in and out' trip. Make our way in, exploring a bit along the way, stop for a snack and a breather, then retrace our footsteps back out. No serious route finding, just go out the same way we came in. Which was just as well because none of us was very familiar with the place and the map that passed for a survey was hardly comprehensive.

I nodded in agreement. 'Yeah, time we were off,' I mumbled through a mouthful of crumbs.

Fish just sat there quietly. He was often quiet in those days, even more so than when he was at university.

'Right-oh then!' commanded Rick. 'Let's get the hell out of here and into the pub.'

We switched our cap lamps back onto main beam and set off back the way we'd come. What happened next we shrugged off as a nuisance although, looking back, I guess we had a pretty narrow escape from something far worse.

The rock down there is called freestone; basically that means it naturally occurs as huge individual blocks rather than continuous strata. The miners used this to their advantage, when planning safety procedures, by driving wooden wedges between blocks in the roof. If the wedges started to creak or, worse still, fell out, it was an early warning sign that the stone blocks were moving and a roof fall was imminent. This gave the miners time to get out of the way and casualties were kept to a surprisingly low minimum.

We were in a wide passage with a flat slightly muddy floor. Fish, unusually for him, was in the lead. Suddenly he stopped.

'What is it, boyo?' Taff drew level with him.

Fish pointed at the ground. 'I'm s-s-sure that wasn't there when we came in.'

Rick glanced briefly at the wooden wedge. 'Course it was! Come on, it's perfectly safe!' He walked on down the passage.

Fish shook his head. 'P-please Rick. I'm not kidding.'

I stooped to examine the piece of wood. It was blackened and weathered at the wider end but crisp and new where it had been squeezed against stone.

'Stop!' I caught hold of Joe's arm as he walked past to catch up with Rick. 'Fish is right. This has fallen out recently.'

I don't know whether Rick and Joe would have taken me seriously but at that moment there was a low rumbling sound and the passage began to fill with dust. Rick, caught in the middle of it, looked briefly in front and behind then ran back to where Joe was waiting for him and from where the rest of us had already backed out of the way. It probably wasn't sensible to run because that was likely to stir more shock waves and increase the extent of the fall. But we did anyway.

Then suddenly there was this ear-splitting crash. It paralysed us, like time was standing still. It was several minutes before any of us dared speak, let alone move.

'Shit!' I rubbed the dust out of my eyes.

We stared open-mouthed at the heap of rubble where we'd been standing a few moments earlier.

'Freaky!' agreed Joe.

'Well done, boyo!' Taff patted Fish on the back. 'That was a bit of a close one.'

We stood there a while longer, kind of coming to terms with

the situation and privately thanking whatever gods, Buddhas or hands of fate that might have smiled kindly on us.

At last Joe broke the silence. 'The only problem now is how we're going to get out of here. We could see if there's a way to climb over it I suppose, but personally I don't want to push my luck in case any more comes down.'

We all agreed with this. At least, no-one volunteered to go first. We'd have been idiots to try.

'No problem,' declared Rick. 'We've got the survey. We'll just have to find another way out.'

He pulled the said document out of his boiler suit. It was printed on five separate sheets, two of which were falling apart along the folds and all were streaked with mud.

'See here.' He pointed to an area on the second sheet. 'Here's where we had lunch; here's the roof fall. Now, if we go back to the lunch stop and on a bit, carry on down here, then turn left and left again that should bring us back onto the main drag. Everyone agreed?'

I shrugged. I was probably the only one close enough to read the map over his shoulder and I wasn't entirely convinced. For one thing, one of the passages he'd indicated was outlined in dotted lines and I wondered whether this meant it was impassable. With hindsight I wonder whether he'd got the 'we are here' bit right, or even if he was looking at the right sheet. But hindsight, as they say, is a definite science and in the case of underground route finding it rarely becomes clear until you read the survey in the pub later. Anyway, we didn't have a choice; we couldn't go back the way we came so we had to go on.

'Let's just get on with it.' I pulled my pack onto my shoulder and set off down the passage. Rick overtook me and assumed his preferred position in the lead.

We did as he'd suggested, left and left again.

'Are you sure we're going the right way?' I asked, certain that we had passed a pyramid-shaped boulder on the left at least once if not twice already.

He turned his head. 'Oh ye of little faith! But if you don't trust me, look for yourself. I could do with a break to cool down anyway.' He stopped and leant against a wall and undid the top button of his suit, wiping drips of sweat off his brow with his other hand. Instead of our usual thick fleecy suits we just had on jeans and T-shirts under cotton boiler suits, but even so, this deep in the system it was stuffy.

'I don't need the survey to know we're going round in circles,' I said. 'Just up here, where we're about to turn left for the third time, we need to go straight on and look for a passage on the right, see if we can double back that way.'

No-one argued with this and we all trooped down a nice wide entrance to the right just a few yards on. But there were no obvious side turnings to left or right and eventually the passage closed down. It wasn't a roof fall, we'd just come as far as the stone had been quarried.

'Any more bright ideas?' asked Rick.

We were all getting disheartened now.

'Back to the turning and carry on until we reach a recognisable landmark on the survey,' I offered. 'In any case, there're other ways out of this system. Perhaps we'll find another entrance close by.'

So we did, as it turned out, though it wasn't quite what I'd intended.

We carried on, taking any turning that looked more well-used than the route ahead. Eventually we dropped down into a long wide passage. It felt somehow neater than anything we'd encountered so far in the mine. The ground underfoot was smooth and level and there were no boulders or loose bits of rubble to trip over. It was as though someone had come along and tidied it. I started singing 'My Brother Jake'. There was a wonderful echo. Joe joined in as well. Then Fish.

'Halt!'

We stopped in our tracks.

'Put your hands above your heads!'

The voice came from behind us. It wasn't the sort of voice you argued with, so we all did as commanded, no-one daring to turn round and see who was speaking.

Then Taff began to chuckle. 'It's another caving group playing a practical joke...'

'Silence!'

Shit! Suddenly I realised what this was. And it was certainly no joke. We were in the only part of the mine that was out of bounds. We'd inadvertently wandered into a Ministry of Defence establishment. We all knew about it of course. There had been some trouble a few years back when a bunch of cavers had deliberately forced an iron gate and broken into the restricted area. Whereas all we'd done was to lose our way; we must have entered the MOD tunnel via a previously unknown passage.

By now another figure had stepped out in front of us. He was wearing some sort of uniform. Was it military police? I wasn't sure. But more sinister than this was the leather pocket on his belt that looked suspiciously like it contained a gun.

We all knew this wasn't a time to argue so we did as we were told. We were led down a passage lit by a string of overhead electric lights and into a dreary, featureless system of corridors that formed the military base which occupied the heart of this underground maze. Up a series of flights of stairs, we climbed into the nucleus of the place we weren't supposed to be. In a grey depressing room we blinked at the glaring fluorescent light that stung our eyes painfully after the hours of near darkness and served to make our 'interrogation' more convincing.

'We're very sorry. We didn't mean to come here,' I began, feeling like a spy in a Cold War film.

'You surely know that this area is out of bounds!' snapped the commander or whatever he was.

Rick explained about the rock fall and how it had blocked our way out. The officer walked over to a map on the wall. It was a survey, I noticed, far more detailed and professional than the one we had. He pointed at a point on the map with something that looked like a drumstick and muttered something to Rick. Rick nodded and the officer hmmed and hahed for a few moments, seemingly satisfied.

'It seems this violation was not strictly your fault,' he agreed at last. 'Nonetheless, there are procedures that will need to be adhered to.'

I don't know how long it took, an hour, maybe two. We were questioned, first separately then again together. We were frisked for cameras, tapes and weapons. We had to fill in forms and sign them. The questions went on and on. What were our full names, ages and addresses? Who were our employers? What were our parents' occupations? Were we members of any political parties, pressure groups etc? Did we have criminal records? It was just as well Beth wasn't with us. With her father's political involvement we'd probably have all been thrown straight into prison.

At last we were led back into the commander's office. He glanced through all the paperwork and nodded. 'Don't let this happen again.' His voice was gruff, though not threatening. 'And please inform your potholing friends that turning up here is not treated as a joke.' To the officer at the door, 'Escort them out.'

So we were led up flights of stairs, past more faceless grey corridors until we finally emerged into daylight and a grey, concreted yard where a truck was waiting, the driver idling the engine. I don't think this was out of concern for our wellbeing, this lift back to our car, so much as an opportunity for the guard to note our registration number.

It had been a long day and we didn't talk much as Rick drove us home. We felt like idiots and were just glad it was all over.

Except it wasn't.

When I got into work on Monday there was a message summoning me to report to Personnel. They had been contacted to cross check my details and weren't impressed. What was worse, by then I was already wearing two hats. I'd been helping out with forensics enough to be registered with the Home Office and had signed the Official Secrets and everything. On several occasions I'd had to work closely with the police. The dressing down I got from both of those institutions was just more than it was all worth.

A couple of months after the mine incident, something else happened that made me turn my back on the underground world for good. It was a Tuesday morning and I was making my second cup of coffee – I generally needed two before I could face work – when I heard the post arrive. It fell onto the mat with a loud resounding splat and, hopeful of something interesting and not too expensive, I wandered into the hall to pick it up, mug in hand. There was a bank statement, a circular offering me a loan and the latest edition of the caving magazine to which I subscribed.

I returned to the kitchen and tore the cellophane wrapper off the magazine, intending to browse through it while I finished my toast and marmalade then read the articles more fully that evening after work. But a paragraph in the 'recent news' section caught my eye. It described how the body of a cave diver had been discovered; the person concerned having gone missing, presumed drowned, three years earlier. The individual had been identified from an engraved ring found with the remains, the 'body' having long since been reduced to soup inside the wetsuit, jelly in a neoprene mould.

I felt suddenly nauseous. I threw the magazine and the remains of my breakfast into the bin, then called work and told them I was sick (which was pretty much true). Then I tipped the rest of the coffee down the sink and refilled the mug from a bottle of whisky. And I never went caving again.

Soon after that I met Carole and found better things to do with my spare time.

Chapter 11

Boulder choke - a passage jammed with rocks, often partially cleared to allow a way through.

'Come on, Marty. You know you want to do it really. When's it to be then?' Rick was staring at me, straight-faced. That was part of his dry sense of humour. Inside, I knew he was laughing.

We were back in the Red Dragon, Saturday night, exactly a week after our reunion. Fish was there too, leaning his elbow on the table, his thumb under his chin, tilting his face slightly upwards, his long slender index finger framing his cheek. A snapshot would have produced a prizewinning photograph; a sculptor could have moulded a classical bronze. He'd always had that easy casual elegance, his movements effortlessly graceful, as though he had just stepped from a stage. Of all of us he was the least changed – outwardly at any rate – his hair was a bit shorter, skimming his shoulders in thick dark waves, but his aesthetic presence smoothed out any wrinkles. It was the first time I'd seen Fish since the old days and I was watching him closely, trying to ascertain whether Rick and Joe's fears were justified.

Taff was sitting at the table this time, which had to be an improvement on being sprawled across the floor. I guess it was pretty incongruous really, Taff being part of our crowd. Apart from caving we had nothing in common. But Fish had grown up with him. They'd started out at the same primary school, then, when, against all odds, Taff had passed his eleven plus, they'd both gone to the grammar and consequently attended the same schools for ten years. It would have been twelve but Taff had left at sixteen to work down the pit like his father and grandfather before him, then, when the mine closed less than two years later, he'd taken a labouring job on a local building site, the first of many in his chequered career of semi-skilled job hopping.

And then there was Beth. She had me feeling confused, happy and uneasy all at once. On the one hand it was slightly disturbing being with someone I used to know so intimately, a haunting yet not entirely unpleasant experience as I spontaneously recalled the joys of adolescent (well that's how it seemed now) sex. Yet, in another way, I wasn't sure if I knew her any more, or if indeed I'd really known her at all. It was like 'then' was something different from 'now'. Neither could I separate Beth-one-of-the-crowd from Beth-my-ex-girlfriend. I don't think I've ever understood my feelings, and really I've never seen the sense in trying, best leave the deep and meaningful stuff to the girls.

I looked at her as she took a sip from her pint of beer. She was an enigma, comfortably boyish yet strikingly sexy at the same time. At least she was easier to cope with now she'd swapped the executive gear for jeans and T-shirt like the rest of us. Even so, I couldn't decide if she was one of the lads like she used to be or some misplaced alien presence: the token woman.

We sat round the table, the six of us, with our half drunk pints of Wadworth's 6X in front of us. Except for Fish. I noticed that his tankard contained lemonade. Had he been teetotal all this time? Surely, if he was as messed up as Rick and Joe seemed to think, he'd have started drinking again. Like I say, I'd been watching him since we arrived, looking carefully for signs of depression or mental illness. If I was going to take an active part in Rick and Joe's scam then I wanted to be as sure as I could be that it was the right thing to do. You never could tell with Fish. His emotions – what you could see of them – were as carefully controlled as his physical movements. But years of working alongside doctors forced me to take a more distanced, more medical view of the situation.

The fact was Fish had always been prone to highs and lows. These days he'd probably be diagnosed with manic depression. Bi-polar disorder, the doctors call it, though that always makes me want to laugh, like someone's got problems with their magnetic field or their ice caps. Whatever you want to label it, if

Fish went to a doctor today he'd probably be prescribed anti-depressants or mood stabilisers. But what was I supposed to do about it? I was hardly going to say, 'Excuse me but I think you're mentally ill. Had you thought of seeing a shrink?' Yeah, he looked fantastic, the best preserved of any of us blokes, yet I couldn't help feeling that, in his case, inner pain only added to his beauty, giving him an irresistible faraway look. At that point I closed my mind to further speculation and concentrated on the here and now.

'So,' Rick continued. 'When are we going to get you down a cave again?'

'I'm not sure…' My protest was half-hearted.

'What do you say, boys? Shall we take him on a trip tomorrow?'

There was a chorus of agreement.

I had mixed feelings. It had never been my intention, when I decided to contact Rick and Joe, to get into caving again. But providing it was just a couple of easy trips, nothing dangerous or taxing, where was the harm? And it might help get Fish back on track.

'What about you?' I turned to Beth. Her answer would be the deciding factor.

She nodded. 'They've been wearing me down too,' she explained. 'I haven't been down a cave since I went to the States but Rick's been pestering me and a few weeks ago I even went out and bought some new kit. I've been in London since, though, so I haven't had chance to try it out.'

'Tomorrow then?' Rick was persuasive.

'I'm afraid I'm seriously out of practice,' I warned, 'and I don't have my gear with me.' It was factual rather than an excuse, my caving kit was packed away somewhere in the loft or the garage at Carole's house – our house – where it had resided, unused, all the years of our marriage. I'd have to go over and get it. That mightn't be a bad thing though: it would be a good excuse for us to spend some time together. 'I mean, I don't think I could get hold of it in time for a trip tomorrow. In fact I definitely couldn't because the lamp would need charging.'

'You can borrow some of mine.' Joe licked the paper of his roll-up and pressed it gently between his fingers. 'We're about the same height.'

Rick nodded emphatically. 'And I've always got a spare battery charged in case of rescue call-outs.'

'And don't forget I haven't been caving for years either,' added Beth. 'We can be novices together.'

That prospect cheered me up. I was almost getting into the idea. 'OK, so where are we going to go then?'

'Actually I've g-g-got a request.' Fish had been so quiet I'd almost forgotten he was there, sitting in the corner silently sipping his lemonade. He brushed his hair back from his face, running his fingers through the long dark tresses. He stared at the table though, didn't look us in the eyes. I should have guessed I wouldn't like what was coming. 'I'd really like us to have another look at Quarry Cave.'

There was silence. I swear it was a full minute. That's how long it took for the disbelief to sink in.

'You've got to be kidding!' Rick was the first to speak, and I think I can honestly say he spoke for all of us.

'Ugh! That shite hole?' Beth's language took me by surprise after the gentle vocabulary Carole used. But as far as the cave was concerned, I knew how she felt.

Fish continued to look downwards. 'You remember it then?'

Remember it? How could we forget?

It works like this. Every reputable caving club gets one or two caves assigned to it for kind of maintenance purposes. You keep an eye on your club caves, make sure access agreements with the local farmers are OK, check there's no damage, that sort of thing. And once or twice a year you do a housekeeping trip where you collect any rubbish – tin cans, Mars bars wrappers, scatters of spent carbide and the like – that inevitably get left behind in the course of cavers' eagerness to get out alive, or more likely their eagerness to get to the pub before closing time. In this grand scheme our club had the misfortune to be allotted Quarry Cave. It had another name too, a Welsh one, something long and unpronounceable but more often we just used to refer to it as The Quarry or Quarry Cave. We always used to dread drawing the short straw and being sent to check it out because basically it had absolutely nothing going for it. Firstly, the entrance was high up in the mountains, more than a mile's hike, across rough terrain, from the nearest road; secondly, when you eventually got there you were greeted by a seventy foot entrance shaft that had to be laddered or abseiled and, on reaching the bottom, there was little else to do besides turn round and come back up again. OK there was a series of dusty airless passages but none of them went far before petering out; except for one, and that was soon blocked by a boulder choke.

'I don't mean to be rude,' began Rick, 'but I want to get Marty and Beth out with us again on a regular basis. I don't want to put them off for life!'

Fish was quietly unperturbed. 'N-no, really. I was down on a clean-up a few weeks ago, with a couple of students, you know? And w-when we stopped at the boulder choke, Damian took his battery off while we were having a snack and he dropped a krab; it slid under that big slab – you know – the one we used to try and climb over, and he had to get d-down on his stomach and wriggle underneath to get it back. And he said, "Hey, you know it's chilly down here." So I got down there to see w-what he was talking about and it was d-draughting. Honest to God!'

We sat in silence for a few moments, digesting the information. It was draughting. At home, cosied up in your sitting room, a draught is a bad thing, but down a cave it's a reason to celebrate, it's the first sign that there's a way through, either to the outside world or to an area of previously undiscovered cave passage. Even I couldn't deny a small tingle of excitement.

Rick was the first to speak. 'What do you think, Taff?'

It was a political move on Rick's part to single out Taff; on the one hand knowing he'd be loyal to Fish but at the same time knowing he'd never been one to mince words.

But Fish didn't give him time to answer. 'Look. Sarah and Damian are over at the bar. They were both there. I'll get them to tell you about it.' And with that he leapt up with unusual speed and hurried across the room.

'Unlike him to be so forceful,' remarked Joe. 'He clearly believes there's something in it. What do the rest of you think?'

'I think we should go,' said Beth. 'Even if the cave's a bit tedious, we'll still have fun, we'll all be together again. And after what you said about Fish, well maybe we should do this if it's going to cheer him up. Anyway, we can go to the Quarryman's Rest afterwards. If it's still open?' She looked at Rick who nodded.

How much had they told her about Fish, I wondered, and how much about everything else? She'd been long gone when it all happened. There was no need to rake it up again. I decided there and then to mention only the fact that Fish seemed a bit down at the moment and hoped that Rick and Joe would do the same.

Fish came back with two fresh-faced young students. Damian was tall and skinny with red hair and freckles. He looked wiry and was clearly keen. Sarah, his girlfriend had also been on the trip. Anyway we quizzed the two of them about what they'd found but really the outcome was already decided. Fish asked if they'd like to come along tomorrow but they both said no thank you they had exams to revise for. I think we were all secretly pleased that it was just going to be the six of us again.

Chapter 12

*Bad air - air which is less than adequate or even dangerous to inhale,
either polluted with toxic gases or too high in carbon dioxide.*

I know the first section of the cave – the area between the
entrance chamber and the boulder choke – almost as well as I
know the route from Benson Street to the Red Dragon. I've been
this way so many times before in the past year that I could
practically walk it in my sleep.

In caving terms it's straightforward. There are no side
passages, none that go more than a few yards anyway, no
precipitous drops, no pools of water waiting to suck me down
into hidden depths. I don't really need to concentrate. But I give
it my full attention all the same. Because while I'm focusing on
what's around me, thinking about the rock on either side, above
my head and beneath my feet, I'm not worrying about the
really frightening stuff. So I listen to the clumping of my boots
on the ground and count the corners around which I steer.

We named it Snake Passage because of the way it twists and
turns, first waving as a river in gentle meanders then looping
back on itself like a shepherd's crook. It is dry and airless. It has
a crumbly orange floor, crumbly orange walls and generally
possesses the ambience of a dusty old cellar. The porous
surroundings eagerly absorb the subdued beam of light, adding
to the dismal atmosphere. I've never suffered from
claustrophobia before but I'm distinctly worried I might start
now. I'm getting hot so I unzip my oversuit and peel it down to
my waist. The heat I give off in this arid, stuffy atmosphere
should dry out at least the upper half of my fleece.

The next part of this passage had been dug out back in our
student days, mostly by Rick's broad spade-like hands. He was
always very popular when there was digging to be done and in
this case removed the clutter of broken rock and silt which had
clogged the way. The result is a series of turnings with sharp,

angular corners; plenty of opportunity to collect bruises on your body and tears in your clothes. Without the movement of water there is nothing to freshen the air with moisture and oxygen, or to soften the harsh, abrasive edges of the limestone. It's not exactly bad air, but not good either. Today I'm making heavy weather of it, my breaths panting and rasping and my body lumbering clumsily and painfully as I clatter along.

Eventually I arrive at the Big Slab. I'm only intending to catch my breath and to get back into my suit ready for the more physical stuff ahead, but my shoulder is hurting and my ankle too. I decide to have a short break and also to eat the other chocolate bar. My rational voice tells me I should be rationing my supplies but my stomach and my state of mind say stuff it. So I do, straight into my mouth in two bites. Chocolate is supposed to be an antidepressant after all. Come to think, Beth once told me that your brain thinks chocolate is the same as sex. Now that's pushing it a bit far. I know exactly what I'm getting right now and sure as hell I'm not getting my leg over. I laugh out loud. The sound echoes around and laughs back at me. I shudder and stuff the empty wrapper into my pocket.

It was less than a year ago that we found the way through. On that first trip with the six of us back together.

At first it felt really strange, being underground again after all that time. It was like I had to relearn all the skills, all the rules. I had to stop and think about all the things I'd done automatically in the past. Like switching my lamp onto the pilot bulb to conserve vital electricity whenever we stopped. Like not dazzling someone with my torch beam when I turned to talk to them. Like the technique of climbing up or down a wire ladder – I'd always done this by wrapping myself around it, keeping my right leg in front of the ladder, placing my toe directly onto every other rung, and hooking my left leg round the back, gripping alternate rungs with my heel – otherwise a free-hanging ladder will swing away from you, leaving you dangling helplessly by your arms. These and other concerns took up my concentration and I followed Joe robotically,

71

encased in my own micro-world.

'Hey, Marty! Are you deaf?' It was Beth. She was a few yards in front of me, following Rick.

'Sorry,' I replied.

'I said, I don't remember it being this far.'

She was doing better than me; I hardly remembered the cave at all. 'You're beginning to whine like a girly!' I joked.

'Fuck off!'

One of the things about caving, one of the 'rules' I was remembering, it tends to induce expletives from even the most mild-mannered persons. Not surprising I suppose. If you're hanging over a precipice or stuck on a waterfall with icy water pouring down your neck then you're going to say something a bit stronger than 'oh dear'. And somehow, the words that would shock your grandmother seem to diffuse the fear and the danger of the situation. Not that we were anywhere dangerous just then. We were in what is commonly described in underground guidebooks as 'easy walking passage'. That is to say, for much of it, if you are taller than a pixie you will have to stoop and if you are an adult with no problems of retarded growth you will need to bend double. It's like describing a studio flat as a spacious family home. I've often suspected that caving guides are written by estate agents.

'My back's aching...ouch! Bugger it!' There was a clatter as Beth's helmet hit a low spur of rock projecting from the roof. Although we weren't in any danger, Beth and I were out of practice. When you first start caving, or when you come back to it after a long break, as I was finding out, it's a painful business. You seem to be constantly collecting bumps and scrapes as you stumble through underground passages like a clumsy oaf. And what's worse, it's like the cave's out to get you, setting huge boulders in front of your feet to trip you up, and squeezing you with knife-sharp rocks as you slither through tunnels. After just a couple of hours underground you spend the following week watching your bruises change colour, as though your skin is stained with the minerals that permeate the cave, like tribal tattoos showing where you've been. But over the weeks you grow accustomed to the underground world. You learn to read it in advance, to judge time and distance, bending just enough to give your helmet a half inch clearance, to understand your body, discover which parts you can press against rock without any damage. Your movements become graceful, flowing and efficient, automatically taking the way of least energy and pain. Plus of course you buy lots of protective gear: knee pads, elbow pads and super reinforced suits to cushion your precious limbs.

'Damn!' Beth had caught her battery pack on a rock.

'Just be thankful you haven't got to carry a tackle sack,' Taff called from behind me. He and Rick were carrying the gear between them. There wasn't too much. We'd decided not to take any serious digging equipment on that first trip, just a couple of hand trowels and a small shovel and bucket, plus a short length of rope and some slings to haul things about. The whole lot was packed into two tackle sacks: long, thin, shiny, cylindrical bags with straps to go over your shoulder.

'We're coming up to the boulder choke!' Even Rick's voice was muffled by the engulfing dusty interior. 'Here's the infamous slab, we're approaching the moment of truth, folks!'

At that point the passage belled out; not a huge chamber but enough that we could occupy a common space and stretch our arms and legs. It was luxury after walking in single file for so long. I made my way over to Beth and hugged her, nothing sexual, just a reassuring squeeze around the waist. 'Well done,' I said.

She positively glowed, despite the mud already smudged across her nose and cheek. 'Isn't it great? It's been so long, I'd forgotten what it was like.'

I'm not sure that I thought it was great right then. I was tired and aching and more than a little uncomfortable in Joe's kit which was somewhat on the small side. But Beth looked so beautiful it more than made up for the discomfort. It could have been twenty years ago. Fragments of a thousand memories came back to me and I wallowed in them for a while until Rick's voice brought me rudely back to reality.

'Work to be done, Weed!' he boomed.

73

I remembered, then, that this wasn't just a tourist trip. We'd come down here to do a job. Once the bags were unpacked we wasted no time getting on with it. Having each prostrated ourselves on the cold, hard ground and agreed with Fish about the draught, we organised ourselves into a working party. Then we got down to the real business. We took it in turns to wriggle on our stomachs under the slab, scratching and scraping somewhat unproductively with our trowels, blind as moles – or might as well have been – and not half as efficient at tunnelling. It was hot work, partly because of the awkwardness of trying to dig in an uncomfortable and confined space and partly because the air was low on oxygen, or, more precisely, high on carbon dioxide. Not dangerous, death to the canary, kind of high; but enough to make you get out of breath more quickly than usual. We each worked for about five minutes then took it easy while the next person took over. As we each sat back panting after our shift we were all seriously wishing we'd brought more drinking water.

The main problem, as far as the digging was concerned, was that only one person could fit under the slab at a time. OK, another could be on hand to dispose of the spoil, but that was hardly a full time job. That left four of us sitting or standing around at any one time. It was hardly exciting, but the promise of breaking through and our desire to support Fish kept us from complaining.

We'd been down there about an hour and a half and it was Fish's turn. By now we were getting bored and Rick and Joe had started talking speleology, filling in the missing years of cave exploration for my benefit and for Beth's. We kind of forgot about Fish and instead of yanking him out after his five minutes we just left him to it. Twenty minutes must have passed before we realised he hadn't had a break, he'd been under there working away while the rest of us told jokes and remembered anecdotes from the past. At last his feet kicked wildly in the air showering us all with dust and he squirmed his way out. His face was flushed red with effort and the bright iron-stained earth was streaked across his brow and cheeks. He looked like a Red Indian.

He shook his head. 'The t-t-time isn't right,' he professed sadly as he sat upright, 'the cave will decide when it's ready to be discovered, when to give up its secrets.'

We sat there for a few moments in a kind of silent despondency. Then Taff jumped up.

'Bollocks!' he said. 'Don't give me that New Age crap, boyo. Pass me the shovel!' And with that he slid beneath the slab and set to work with determined vigour. 'This tunnel's going to go!' he shouted. 'And soon!'

It wasn't going anywhere fast though, certainly not on that first trip. But even so, even though we'd spent so long tired, fed up and thirsty, once we got to the pub it all seemed worthwhile. That was another aspect of the sport that I'd forgotten. You can spend the best part of the day cold, wet and aching; sometimes you can hate every minute of it. Yet, once you're warm and dry and you've got a beer in front of you, hindsight converts the pain and the fear into the most spectacular day you've ever lived. I had to admit to feeling like that later as we sat round the fire in the Quarryman's Rest. That's when I realised I'd got the caving bug again.

Chapter 13

Karabiner - (krab) metal loop held closed by a spring clip. Used for joining various items of kit or as a safety aid on a rope.

When I turned up at Rick and Joe's the following Wednesday, I was hoping Beth would be there. I'd been thinking about her a lot during the past week but more so since we went underground. It made me realise how well she fitted in with the crowd – and indeed with my whole lifestyle – in a way that Carole never could. There was still that easy familiarity and youthful innocence despite the fact we'd both grown up into responsible adults. It made me question whether I'd made a mistake when I'd let her go. What possessed me to finish such an idyllic relationship? I don't know. I never actually told her to go away, but neither did I make any effort to keep her. Blame it on youth and immaturity and not appreciating when you're onto a good thing.

As soon as I finished my degree I was off. Like a wild animal trapped in a cage, that shoots out when the door is opened. Not with purpose or direction but haphazardly, running this way and that, happy simply to have found freedom. It wasn't that I didn't want Beth, more that I was totally absorbed in myself. Listen to 'Free Bird' by Lynnrd Skynnrd and you'll know what I mean.

So I put my music collection and hi-fi, together with my caving kit, in the loft in my parents' house and set off to see the world, taking only what I could carry in a backpack. It never occurred to me to stay in touch more than writing the occasional postcard.

'India: sound. Wish I could send you a curry. Yours, Marty.'

'G'day Poms. Ayres Rock high and hot. Lots of desert. Saw kangaroos and crocodiles. See you, Marty.'

Things are different today of course. When kids leave home, go away to university or go abroad, even, they stay in touch. A few words on an email or a few letters on a text message are all it takes. No effort at all. Like Joe says, you're never further than a digital electronic signal away. You can even be in the middle of the Sahara or at the North Pole and call your mum on a satellite phone. But I left university in the days when you still had to put pen to paper and, let's face it, for the average bloke that's a pretty tall order.

I might as well have been on another planet that year away. When, suntanned, broke and not admitting to be as homesick as I felt, I returned to the UK, Beth had gone. Without a word she'd disappeared, gone away to university to study economics.

So all these confusing thoughts ran through my mind as Rick handed me a glass of single malt and we settled ourselves in the comfortable and comforting front room of number one hundred and one, Benson Street. Don't get me wrong; it wasn't like I'd suddenly given up on Carole. I still texted her every day, I still hoped more than anything that the two of us would get back together; I was sure that we would, eventually. I suppose Carole was a constant and Beth was an extra factor in the equation. It wasn't like I was in love with Beth. We'd only just met up again. We might discover, with time, that we disagreed on all sorts of fundamental issues. Maybe it was just a bloke thing; I was sexually attracted to her back at university and I found that, twenty years on, my brain and body were responding in exactly the same way. But however they came about, these feelings were a welcome distraction from the problems with Carole.

'So how was she? How did the two of you get on?' Rick's question caught me unawares.

'Great,' I said, picturing Beth in my mind. 'I was a bit worried about it at first but it's really good to spend time with her again.'

They both stared at me like I was mental.

'Are we missing something here?' Rick leaned forward, screwing up his eyes like he was trying to figure out a scientific anomaly. 'First you're terrified of her and suddenly you're

77

telling us she's wonderful?'

Shit. I realised that he was talking about Valerie, about me calling for Fish at the weekend.

'Sorry,' I said. 'I was miles away.' I swigged my whisky; half of it gone in one go. It helped a bit.

Joe laughed, 'I think Weed's preoccupied with someone else!'

Rick reached over and topped up my glass. 'Let's start again,' he coaxed. 'Valerie – that's the big scary one – how was she?'

I took a smaller sip this time; already I could feel the warmth spreading through me, soothing me. I wasn't a serious drinker, of course, not like Taff. I just appreciated a decent bevy. I pondered for a moment before answering Rick's question. It was a debriefing on the Fish situation, about my part in Rick's plan to rescue him from doom, drudgery and imminent mental breakdown. And the fact was, it had gone surprisingly well.

I told them how I'd arrived at Fish's house on Sunday morning. It wasn't without trepidation that I'd walked up the path to the front door and rung the bell. Hell, quit the macho routine, I'd been shit-scared. Sophie, his elder daughter – or rather, Valerie's daughter – had let me in. Fish was upstairs, she informed me, getting his things together. She showed me through to the kitchen where I sat at the pine table to wait. There were scrawly, childlike hand-painted pictures stuck on the cupboards, and bright plastic alphabet magnets on the fridge. Just what you'd expect in a house with kids, nothing sinister at all. I began to relax. I thought I'd got away with it, so to speak, that perhaps Valerie wasn't at home, but my feeling of relief didn't last long. It was obvious in retrospect, I mean, Fish wouldn't go out and leave the kids on their own.

'Marty!'

I jumped.

She still had that knack of taking me by surprise, just like in the old days. That had always been her secret weapon, she caught you off guard and immediately you were at a disadvantage. Meanwhile, she took control of the situation. From that first moment you didn't stand a chance.

I'd foreseen this meeting, played it out in my mind,

rehearsing what I'd say. But all that was lost now. I opened my mouth but no words came out.

'Still as talkative as ever, I see.' She laughed, 'it's been a long time, Marty.'

Yes, it had, I thought, gratefully. 'It's good to see you too, Valerie,' I managed to splutter. 'How are you?'

'I'm well thank you Marty, and I must say you're looking fitter than I'd have expected. You must have been trained by a good woman.'

Was it a dig or had Fish not mentioned the fact that Carole and I had split up?

Valerie went on. 'Perhaps I'll get to meet her sometime.'

Clearly he hadn't said anything, no point in me disillusioning her then. In any case, Carole and I would almost certainly be back together again soon, so it was irrelevant.

'Perhaps,' I agreed.

'So, I gather you've come to take my husband out to play.'

'No point in taking two cars to the cave.' I shrugged. I was gaining confidence now.

She looked surprised. 'Oh! You mean it's just the two of you? You're not meeting up with those queers then? No, on second thoughts don't answer that; I don't want to know. I expect you think I'm prejudiced, but it's all very well turning a blind eye when you're young and have no responsibilities, it's quite another thing when you have children, you just can't risk mixing with these perverts. Perhaps you'll find out for yourself one day. Anyway, what brings you back – or rather what kept you away all this time?'

I hesitated. 'Well…you know…I have other commitments, what with being married and everything.'

She beamed. 'Putting your wife first, you mean? Well I'm impressed with you, Marty. I admit that I was more than a little concerned when Fish told me you were going caving with him, but if that's your attitude these days then you're welcome round here any time. Perhaps you could teach him a thing or two.'

I was getting in dangerously deep. I willed Fish to come

downstairs right then so I could quit while I was ahead. As it was, I was spared further conversation with its implicit risk of putting my foot in it.

Valerie smiled at me. 'Well I'd love to stop and chat but I'm taking the girls to see their grandparents; I'll tell Fish to get a move on.'

'Well done.' Rick patted me on the back as I finished recounting the event.

Joe clapped his hands. 'I knew you were the man for the job!'

I shuffled in my chair. I knew Valerie only approved of me because of several misunderstandings. 'What happens when she finds out the truth?' I asked. I couldn't help feeling there would come some terrible day of judgment when she found me out; because she would, it was only a question of time; and then all the subterfuge would be held against me.

Rick chuckled. 'You'll just have to keep up the innocent, sensitive, new man act,' he said, 'at least until we've retrieved Fish from under her thumb.' The phone rang and he stood up and walked out to the hall to answer it. 'Put some music on, Spider,' he called over his shoulder.

'What does Beth know about all this?' I found it easier to be direct and honest with Joe than with Rick. Maybe it was all those late night chats at university or maybe it was just his personality.

Joe shrugged. 'About Fish, you mean?'

I nodded.

'Only that we think he needs cheering up.'

I hedged around a forbidden subject. 'She doesn't know anything about...you know...the past?'

He shook his head. 'Why should she? It would only upset her. I certainly don't intend to say anything and neither does Rick. Whatever Taff chooses to impart in a drunken stupor is, I'm afraid, out of our control. As regards the rescue mission, that's strictly on a need to know basis, in other words, you, Rick and myself. Safer that way considering we're dealing with the Valkyrie. I think we all remember how she and Beth used to get on.'

I certainly did. To say they disagreed was an understatement; they'd come close to a catfight on more than one occasion. These days they were best kept well apart.

Joe stood up. 'I'm going to make a start on dinner,' he declared, 'to which you are staying, no excuses, you've certainly earned it. Pick a CD, you know where they are.' He went into the kitchen and hopeful sounds of cupboard doors opening and closing and the chink of a knife on a board as food was chopped filled the evening.

I did as I was bid. After choosing something by REM and pressing the appropriate 'power' and 'start' buttons on the remote, I browsed round the room. A bookcase stood next to the CD rack. I recognised some of the contents immediately, from university days. There were paperbacks by Asimov, James Herbert and Ray Bradbury; these all belonged to Joe. Rick never read novels; by contrast, his books were mainly technical; an encyclopedia of engineering, various works on the geology of Britain and Richard Feynman's lectures in physics – the complete set – adorned the shelves. And of course there were books on caving; dozens of them, specialist volumes on underground photography and cave formation as well as guides to underground exploration in various parts of the world.

Rick finished his phone call and he and I went through to the kitchen where we made a feeble attempt at helping to prepare vegetables.

'So what do you think about the cave?' I asked. 'You know, the Quarry.'

'I'm trying not to get my hopes up,' Rick said, carefully. But you could tell by the sparkle in his eye that he already had.

'It might come to nothing.' Joe was philosophical. He took the carrot chunks I had cut and skilfully converted them into wafer-thin slices. 'We might dig for weeks and find another few yards of cave passage then it might just close down.'

He was only being realistic. After all, that's what had happened every time we'd been there in our student days.

'At any rate,' Rick continued, 'for the moment it's keeping Fish happy so I'm game to go on with it.'

We chatted on through the rest of the preparation and eating of the meal, making provisional plans for future trips down the Quarry and other caves, discussing what equipment we would need to take and the fact that we would need to make earlier starts in future if we were to get anything constructive done at all.

Later, as I settled myself into the spare bedroom for the night, I got to thinking about the current situation. Rick and Joe were lovely people. They'd already tried to persuade me to move in with them and if I wasn't back with Carole soon I might well take them up on it. No doubt if Fish left Valerie he'd be welcomed into the fold too. Then the four of us would be together again, just like student days. We could go caving, take drugs and pretend we'd never grown up. On the one hand it felt like some kind of group mid-life crisis. But on the other it was quite an appealing idea.

Chapter 14

Stalagmite - (stal) formation growing upwards from the cave floor, formed by water dripping from the ceiling or from a stalactite above.

After the entrance pitch, the boulder choke offers the first taste of technical caving on the journey to the camp.

A boulder choke starts life just like any other stretch of cave passage. Then, somewhere along the way it gets crammed with rocks, either from a roof fall or carried by the violent current of a fast-flowing river.

When you discover a boulder choke, the first thing you have to do is dig your way through. Just like we did when we discovered this one beyond the Big Slab. Often there are natural gaps, between large rocks that have jammed together, leaving just enough room to wriggle through. But more often smaller debris has clogged up the spaces and you have to scoop out all the rubbish that's found its way in. You have to be careful though, because often that unwelcome muddy gunk is all that's holding the rocks together. It's like one of those games where you have to take it in turns to remove pieces of a puzzle. Only with a boulder choke, if you take away the wrong piece, it isn't just a handful of marbles that will come crashing down on top of you.

Even when you've painstakingly scraped out a route by hand (bang is rarely a good idea) and travelled it a hundred times, you still have to take care. These things are often unpredictable. Sometimes the boulders are moving – microscopically slowly of course, but continually travelling nonetheless. You can hear them grinding and groaning, like the snoring of a sleeping giant. So you pick your way, silently, cautiously, for fear of waking it up.

This particular one is pretty stable and I push and kick, urging my body through the tight openings. It's tedious more than anything, and energy-consuming; climbing narrow

83

chimneys with no sizable holds in which to lodge my feet, only to slide across a slab at the top and drop back down the other side. As I make my way under, over and around the obstacles, I feel thankful that I am the simple male of the species, whose brain, according to the women I know, lacks the ability to concentrate on more than one thing at a time. At least, for this short while, I'm spared the fear and the worry of brooding over what has happened, what might have happened and what is yet to come.

By the time I emerge into open passage I'm starting to think about food again. All I have left are the nuts and raisins. I was sure that last time I'd been at the camp there were some supplies there, but that was several weeks ago and other people have been down since. We had a policy of always taking a bit more than we expected to need, a sort of stockpile for emergencies. But now here I am in a real life emergency and relying on it seems a hell of a gamble.

I compromise by eating a couple of handfuls of peanuts then I move on.

Soon I'm aware of a noise in the distance, the streamway. It's very faint at this stage and the sound is no more than a background hum, perceptible only because I know it's there. The nature of the cave is changing too. The crumbling aridity of before has given way to a glistening freshness. Moisture coats the firm, dark rocks that form the walls, and droplets of water hang in the air, I can smell it, cool and sweet.

But first I have to cross the Snowy Mountains, a wide area full of huge mountainous stalagmites, many of them more than six feet in diameter. They are pure white, sprinkled with tin and zinc but untainted by the salts of iron, copper and manganese that colour so much of the underground world. All around me, the walls are covered in flowstone, it has poured, dripped and solidified, forming a shiny coating over the underlying rock. In places it has rippled and surged, finally setting in the shape of a giant cauliflower, glazed with milk and honey; in others it hangs from the ceiling in translucent curtains. Whenever I've come down here before, I've paused a moment and looked

84

around me, just awestruck by the wonder of it all. Not today though. For the first time, I'm oblivious to the beauty around me. The millennia that passed as it formed are meaningless to me now. I leave the whiteness behind me and continue down a dark tunnel, following the now unmistakable sound of moving water.

Suddenly, the passage emerges into a black echoing chasm. Far below the water is rushing, crashing and swirling about the sharp, jagged rocks that lift their heads above the torrent. To my right, the river enters the cave as a waterfall, squeezing through some invisible inlet in the roof to thunder downwards in a mist of spray, generating a sharp, cold rush of air as it falls. There is no sound like it anywhere else on Earth, the magnificent thunderous roar of water crashing against rock. Outside in the open, the noise would drift away and mix with an ambience of wind, rustling trees and birdsong. But underground there's nowhere for it to go, and it bounces back and forth like a thousand drums and cymbals.

I remember when we first discovered the streamway, last May it must have been. It was just Rick, Joe, Beth and myself on that occasion, who climbed the electron ladder down the entrance shaft and wriggled our way through the boulder choke.

The depleted numbers meant we'd made good time. That's how it works down a cave; the more there are of you in the group, the longer you take. However experienced you are, there are so many bits you have to do one person at a time, and all the minutes of waiting around soon add up. So we reached the Snowy Mountains ahead of schedule, but from that point on we began to slow up. Joe had brought his camera to get some shots of the magnificent formations we'd discovered on our previous visit. All this meant that for once I was out in front. Rick had stopped to hold a flash unit for Joe while the latter took a photo of one of the Snowy Mountain stals, and I'd taken the opportunity to get ahead. It made a welcome change to be leading. It wasn't so much a competitive thing – OK, Rick liked to feel he was in charge and generally the rest of us didn't feel the need to challenge him – it was just that I was sick of walking or crawling down narrow passages, constantly staring at someone's backside. In my new position I relished the luxury of having a panoramic view of the way ahead.

As it turned out the passage widened and Beth was able to walk alongside me. We passed the point where we'd turned back the previous week. It had really galled us to turn round when we could see at least another thirty feet of previously unexplored cave passage ahead but we'd set off late that day (a Sunday) and a couple of us had early starts at work the following morning. Today, though, we had all the time in the world.

I reached across and took Beth's hand. 'We're the trail blazers now,' I said.

'You bet!' She squeezed my fingers briefly before letting go her grip and pointing ahead. 'Look,' she said, 'water.'

She was right too. We walked up to the point where drips fell steadily from a crack above. She stood directly underneath and tilted her head back, open-mouthed, catching the droplets on her tongue. 'Delicious,' she proclaimed. I tried it too. It was sweet and icy cold. 'I'll bring a tankard in next time,' I said. 'We can leave it on the ground here and there'll always be a drink waiting for weary travellers.' We laughed at the idea but I fully intended to do it. I remembered how they'd done the same thing in St Cuthbert's down on Mendip. Somehow, when you were hours from civilisation, it tasted almost as good as a pint of beer. We dawdled there a few moments longer, inspecting where the water came from (no sign of a stal forming) and where it went (basically it formed a shallow puddle before draining away).

Water is the lifeblood of a cave. The chemistry of it goes something like this. Carbon dioxide dissolves in water to form a dilute solution of carbonic acid. This in turn dissolves limestone, the rock in which most caves are formed. Further into the cave, this liquid rock then gets deposited in its crystalline form of calcite. It forms glistening stals and coats the floor with the sugar icing we call flowstone. Or to put it more simply, water sculpts and polishes, transporting energy and oxygen, and creating beauty in the darkness.

Apart from the moisture on the Snowy Mountains, this was the first water we'd encountered in the cave and a sign of greater things to come.

'Should we wait for Rick and Joe?' Beth asked.

I shook my head. 'I can already hear their voices; they're only a few moments behind. Let's crack on. After all, there's no point in letting them get ahead.'

Beth laughed and we set off deeper into the cave. I think we both felt a competitive instinct kicking in. After a few yards, the walls of the tunnel began to glisten, the roof stretched high above our heads and we could hear the rush of moving water. Excitement arced between us like electricity. Over the next few minutes the noise level increased and our torches seemed brighter as their light was reflected by the water that dripped down the walls and gleamed like a polished floor beneath our feet.

We knew it was coming yet still it took us by surprise.

'Look out!' I shouted, at the same time flinging my left arm out to the side, preventing Beth from stepping forward. We'd rounded a corner when suddenly the ground dropped away in front of us. The near wall of the rift plummeted a good forty feet just inches away from where we stood. On the other side of the gap the far wall was sheer and stark. To our right the water cascaded in, falling in vertical rods to the riverbed below. Immediately beneath us it rushed ever faster into the cave.

'Whew!' Beth took a step back. She looked somewhat shaken and to be honest so was I. Apart from the initial rope or ladder at the entrance, there had been nothing in the cave so far which you could describe as dangerous. OK, the boulder choke was hard work but it wasn't life threatening. But, essentially, caves are dangerous places and this one was just beginning to show its teeth.

I peered over the edge. 'I reckon I could climb down,' I suggested.

Beth grabbed my arm. 'Please don't! I always used to hate it when you took risks. And you haven't done this kind of thing for ages, don't forget.' We were both shouting, struggling to make our voices heard above the noise of the water.

'OK.' I stepped back beside her, secretly quite glad not to be trying any heroics. 'Tell you what, we'll wait for Rick and Joe. Rick's got a rope, he can belay me down.'

Beth was more comfortable with this arrangement and we crouched on our haunches, backs against the rock, to wait for the others.

When they arrived, Rick and Joe were suitably impressed with the river. It was lucky that Rick had brought a short length of climbing rope with him. We hadn't brought any safety equipment before but he and Joe had thought it might come in handy to get into tricky places for the photography. Rick readily agreed with my idea of belaying the climb down to the streamway. 'The route itself looks straightforward,' he nodded, 'but we don't know how deep or fast flowing the river is.' So he used a sling to anchor himself to a spur of rock and threaded the rope through a karabiner on his belt. I tied the end onto my belay belt with a figure of eight knot.

It was an easy climb down, just a scramble really, but I was glad of the rope because the route was exposed and the holds where I placed my hands and feet were slippery with mud. Like Beth had reminded me, I was out of practice. Not only was I relearning all the techniques, my muscles hadn't yet regained the strength of student days. And of course, the consequences of falling would have been pretty sobering. So far so good, I thought, as I paused on a ledge a couple of feet above the water. Providing we had a safety line even Beth could get down without too much trouble.

'What do you think?' Rick shouted from the top. Even with his voice it was difficult to make out the words above the thunder of the water.

'Getting down's easy!' I shouted back. 'But I'm not sure about the water. It looks pretty deep and it's fast and furious. D'you want me to check it out?'

'Depends if you mind getting wet.'

'OK!' I shouted. 'I'll give it a go. Hold tight onto that rope!'

Somewhat reluctantly I lowered myself off the ledge and stepped knee deep into the river. It was icy. I breathed in through pursed lips. OK so far. If this was the extent of it we could wade through. Cautiously I took another step. This time I was bollock deep and I cried out with the shock.

'You all right down there?' Rick peered over. 'Oh, I see the problem!'

I looked up and saw him grinning. 'I'm coming back!' I called through chattering teeth. I stepped where I thought my foot had been before, on a boulder or a shallower bit of the riverbed. I must have missed it though because suddenly I was in up to my neck and a determined current was tugging me with it. I shouted in surprise then felt the rope tighten on my belt and the force of Rick's huge biceps battling with nature. Within seconds I'd scrambled out onto dry rocks and within minutes I was back at the top of the rift.

'Are you OK?' Beth rested a protective hand on my arm as Joe untied the rope from my belt.

'Well I wouldn't want to do it again in a hurry,' I panted and shivered. 'It wouldn't be so bad if you were wearing a wetsuit I suppose, but you'd need a line, the current's pretty strong.'

Rick shook his head. 'It's out of the question,' he said. 'We've no idea how much deeper it gets. No. If we want to explore the rest of this cave there's only one thing for it. We'll have to rig a high-level traverse.'

Chapter 15

Sling - loop of webbing, the most common dimensions being approx 3cm in width and 1m double length.

I pushed open the front door of the flat, giving it an extra shove to meet the resistance of the letters (mostly junk mail) and the freebie local paper wedged on the other side. It was half past eight, which meant I had time for a shower and a coffee and maybe even some breakfast before I had to leave for work.

There was no sign of Mike, for which I was thankful. It meant I didn't have to bother with small talk. His bedroom door was wide open revealing an empty, unmade bed. Not that that meant much, I think the only time he straightened it out was on the rare occasions when he changed the sheets. More significantly, there were no recently used coffee mugs; just old ones with dried on stains. This, coupled with the untouched post, suggested that he'd been out for the night and had not yet returned home. This wasn't unusual for Mike. Depending on what jobs he had on, his movements could be completely unpredictable. Sometimes his hours would follow a pattern for several days or even weeks. It wasn't uncommon for him to go out in the evening, dressed in jeans and leather jacket, looking as though he was just off to the pub, perhaps followed by a club or a party. Indeed, his work was such that this was very often exactly what he was doing. Then he'd arrive home the next day and sleep through the afternoon.

Because of the nature of Mike's work he'd warned me early on, ages before I moved in with him, not to acknowledge him if I bumped into him out on the town but to wait for him to approach me. This was mostly for my own safety, he explained, in case he was into something heavy. It was also that, because of my court appearances as an expert witness, there was a chance I might be recognised and risk blowing months of preparation work by his team, possibly even putting myself or someone else in physical danger. Personally, I thought he was trying to glamorise the whole set-up, but I agreed to go along with it on condition that he stayed away from me if I was with a woman. That last bit was just a joke at the time, seeing as I was happily married to Carole; but Mike seemed to take it seriously, winking and saying I was a sly old dog, the sort of bloke he could relate to.

I sifted through the post. There was nothing for me, hardly surprising as virtually everything still went to the house or to the office. I ambled into my room, turned on the radio, took off my clothes, throwing them onto the bed, then wandered naked into the bathroom and turned on the shower.

I'd spent the previous night with Carole. I'd learned, during the weeks of our separation, that ringing her wasn't a good idea. I think it was the stuff the counsellor had said about the time apart and keeping things business-like. If I phoned her, Carole either wouldn't answer (she knew it was me from the caller display on both our home phone and her mobile) or she'd curtly ask if I had something important to discuss. At first, I thought this was because she actually didn't want to speak to me; then I realised it was more likely because, if she took the call, she felt like she was disobeying rules. Carole had always been a very law-abiding person; always slowed down to thirty just before the speed limit sign, always turned the hi-fi off at eleven, even though our house was detached and no neighbour could possibly have heard it. I don't know whether she was born that way or whether it was the result of her working for a law firm for more than a decade.

Anyway, by chance I'd found that the best thing was to turn up unannounced. It started one evening some weeks previously when I'd gone round to collect my caving things. I'd tried to ring first, but of course she hadn't answered, so I'd driven round after work, rang the doorbell, still no answer. Well, I assumed she was out and, seeing as I needed the stuff as soon as possible and I still had a key, I let myself in. It turned out that Carole was in the bath and was terrified when she heard the sounds of someone rummaging round the house. 'Marty!

Thank God!' she exclaimed when she emerged, wrapped in a towel, hair dripping uncharacteristically on the carpet. She looked white and shaky, not like you usually do after a relaxing soak. I think she was genuinely scared and genuinely relieved. 'It's all right!' I laughed, and without thinking about it I went and put my arms round her. Perhaps that first time she was just glad that I wasn't a burglar, but I like to think she was pleased to see me. And I knew it was what she wanted as one thing led to another.

So, last night I'd just turned up. If I'd rung ahead and suggested going round then I know she'd have said no. But I figured that she was lonely and I was doing her a favour. It wasn't like I forced her into anything she didn't want. And we were still married for goodness' sake; it was what married couples were meant to do. She never said 'no' – well, not like she meant it anyway. In any case, in a few more weeks the trial separation period would be over and I'd be moving back in.

I squirted shower gel directly onto my head and rubbed my hair into a frothy lather. Then I repeated this procedure, aiming the gel at all those places modern hygiene standards demand that we wash on a daily basis. Water pelted in a chinking ripple onto the bath and with a lower pitched thud onto the plastic curtain, somewhere in the background the radio relayed a song by The Verve. As the water dripping from my hair ran clear I turned the shower off and pulled the curtain aside, peering through half-closed watery eyes for my towel and, realising I'd left it in the bedroom, I stepped out onto the lino floor and paused briefly to look at myself in the bathroom mirror, the only full length one in the flat. I wasn't exactly a pretty sight. This was nothing to do with last night of course. Carole had never been into anything kinky. I was wearing the battle scars of the previous weekend. I'd forgotten how much caving hurt. My mirror image was covered in bruises in different stages of healing and consequently of different colours and textures. I felt like a painting by numbers game in a child's colouring book. This had happened every week since I started caving again. I was sure it hadn't taken so long to get into the techniques and the moves first time around, but I supposed this time my body was older and therefore less forgiving. I just hoped I'd get re-accustomed to it soon.

I walked a watery trail into my bedroom and gave my head and shoulders a brief gentle rub, avoiding the more obvious of the bruises, before securing the towel round my waist. Selecting the cleaner of the two mugs on my bedside table, I headed into the kitchen.

The more secure I felt about Carole's feelings for me the more I was able to speculate about a possible renewal of my relationship with Beth. It was a kind of fantasy. Not the naughty kind, but more an intellectual game of 'what ifs'. What would I do if, when Carole asked me to move back in (because she definitely would, it was just a question of time), what if, at the same time, Beth said she wanted us to get back together? Although Beth had never actually stated this was on her mind, she had implied it in other ways. Every time we went caving I noticed how she fussed over me. Surely, if I could feel the chemistry between us then she must too. I'd never had the problem (problem?) of choosing between two women before, and suddenly I felt a thrill as the possibility – or even inevitability – of the scenario grew ever stronger.

For the first time in any of my relationships with women, I felt I could be objective. I could distance myself from my feelings and from the situation in hand. It was as though I was sitting on a hilltop, looking down on the different options and scenarios on offer to me. I could see the whole thing, what had happened in the past, what was going on now and what possibilities lay in store for the future. Looking at Carole and Beth from this viewpoint, I realised how different the two of them were. I wondered how I had become involved with women who were such opposites.

I suppose it all stemmed from their upbringing, from the attitudes of their parents. I remember the first time I stayed the weekend at Carole's parents' house. Now I know they were getting on a bit, and that things were different when they'd been young. But even so, it wasn't like Carole and I were teenagers. We were both pushing thirty and although we weren't actually engaged we'd been seeing each other for nearly two years and personally I counted spending more than a couple of hours with her folks as evidence of my commitment. Well, I thought under the circumstances that they'd put us in the same room, or at least adjoining ones (with a nod and a wink); but not a bit of it. Carole was assigned the spare room (with double bed) and I was relegated to the sofa bed in the lounge, the third and smallest bedroom having long since been converted into an upstairs bathroom. Well obviously if they wanted to play at keeping up appearances I'd go along with it. I enthused over the snug blankets that Carole's mother tucked over the sofa.

'I'll see you in a few minutes,' I whispered to Carole as she and her parents prepared for bed at the ridiculous hour of ten o'clock.

But she looked horrified. 'I'll see you at breakfast,' she said firmly. 'Please don't upset them, Marty. They've set their hearts on me having a white wedding.'

I was confused. 'Well you can have one,' I said, hoping that it didn't sound like a proposal.

The words tutted out as she glared at me. 'You have to play the game.'

Some game, I thought to myself, not exactly a lot of fun. The whole set up was so different from Beth's family. No chance of her growing up prim and proper. I thought about all this now though it wouldn't have occurred to me to make comparisons back then.

Anyway, all of that was history now. And I was left with the dilemma (albeit an academic one) of who to choose. Of course, I never actually resolved the fantasy, or even attempted to. I just reassured myself that when the time came I would know what to do. Whenever I played these mind games, the power that both women had over me diminished and I was back in control of the situation, back in control of my life. I never had to consider what I actually wanted, like what would make me happy. The thought of having the choice brought me a somewhat smug contentment.

I pulled the least crumpled shirt from the airing cupboard and prepared for work.

Chapter 16

Traverse - horizontal route, usually above ground level, sometimes aided by ropes.

As I stand above the streamway, at the start of the traverse, I'm feeling a bit woozy. I don't know if it's delayed concussion or just lack of sleep, but either way, I'm not in the best condition to tackle the most technical and potentially dangerous part of the cave.

For the first time I wonder if I've made a mistake trying to get to the camp. I've mostly dried out now thanks to the hike through Snake Passage and the boulder choke, and I stopped for a welcome drink of water out of the tankard in the Tap Room, as we came to call it, just ten minutes back. Now I consider whether I wouldn't be better to turn back and snuggle down as best I can in one of those warm, dry areas. I hunker down in the same spot where Beth and I waited for Rick and Joe ten months ago and weigh up the pros and cons. If I turn back now I won't have to do anything complicated, just walk and crawl and scramble a bit. I could do it in my sleep – and it may well come to that. Also I'd be near the entrance and ready to call for help in the morning.

On the down side, I'm low on supplies, half a pack of nuts and raisins low to be precise. And there'll be no comforts, no sleeping bag and no hot drink. I'm warm enough while I'm moving but what about when I settle down to sleep? I'll begin to chill down as soon as I stop, and if I lie or even sit down the ground will drain away my body heat. I try to calculate how quickly hypothermia could set in, wishing I'd concentrated harder on last year's pathology course. By contrast, the camp offers an almost cosy familiarity and the essentials of light, warmth and food. The only difficulty might be getting there. But I feel refreshed and more clear-headed after my brief rest. Surely my decision won't make that much difference in the long run. I stand up and clip my cows' tails onto the rope beside me.

I remember how we rigged it. Gradually, while the outside world moved from spring into summer, deep below the surface, in a place where there are no seasons, we tamed the streamway.

As with the digging, it was Rick who did most of the work. He inched his way, like Spiderman, high up along the rocky wall of the rift. Armed with fearsome equipment, tied with slings to his harness, he sunk bolts into the rock, each fitted with a metal loop through which a karabiner could be clipped. His insurance policy was a rope. This secured him to the previously installed bolt, beneath which he would swing (and indeed did, on a couple of occasions) if he missed his footing. The rift was longer than we'd expected and it took several trips till we reached a point where we could safely descend.

Today there is more water coming down than I've ever seen. As I watch it gushing beneath me I picture how heavily it must be raining in the outside world. Back in town, the torrential downpour will be bouncing off pavements, running in streams down the streets before tumbling through grids into storm drains. If it continues at this rate then, over near the border, there will likely be floods. The Severn will burst its banks, sweeping away cars and submerging the lower floors of buildings. Families will be rescued by dinghy or helicopter and cats will flee to the rooftops.

I could almost convince myself I'm better off underground.

In the past I've thought of this subterranean river as powerful and magnificent. Tonight it is angry, aggressive and malevolent, like it would happily sweep me away for the sheer hell of it. It's hard to believe that, once or twice, back in the summer, when the weather was much drier, there was no more than a placid stream meandering its way along the bottom. One time I'd climbed down at this point and waded through the gentle current, all the way down the rift, barely knee deep in water. This is not an option today, however, and instead I turn to the left, checking that the karabiners on my cows' tails are secure on the traverse rope before I launch myself out above the water. Then I set off, leaning out across the void with my feet braced against the rock.

When I reach the first of the bolts supporting the line, I pause for a moment to catch my breath and to rest my shoulder, which is aching quite badly. In a moment I will unclip the longer cow's tail from the rope and reattach it on the other side of the metal loop. Then, whilst holding firmly onto the line, I will do the same with the shorter one. Two ropes, two chances. Always make sure you have two chances. That's a good code to follow underground. Come to think it's a good rule for life in general.

I will have to repeat this at every bolt. They're like checkpoints, marking the sections of the traverse. The first one is the biggest leap, psychologically speaking, and I'm scared. After this, I tell myself, there'll be no turning back.

So I consider my options yet again for what I promise myself will be the last time.

I look down. Below me the river leaps and thrashes its way, rushing as though it is desperate to get through the cave as quickly as possible, anxious to surface once again in the frosty air of the Welsh mountainside, to breathe life-giving oxygen into its tired molecules and bask in the daytime sun. The river and me, both! Just one more push, I tell myself. Just a bit more effort along the traverse and after that it's little more than an easy walk to the camp.

I'm looking forward to reaching camp, no doubt about that, but then, I always am, even on a good day, a good trip. It's a milestone, two and a half hours' journey from the entrance. Whether it's a day trip or an overnighter it's good to stop there and brew a cup of tea. At one point we even took down a little portable CD player and some inflatable cushions, it was almost civilised, you could rest in comfort before going on to explore the further reaches of the cave. Today, just reaching the camp will be enough. When I get there I'll have some food and a drink – there'll be tea at least. In the very unlikely event that there is no gas, I can still heat up water in a tin mug held over a candle or night-light. I feel proud of myself thinking so creatively, and I was never even a boy scout. Then, after refuelling, I'll snuggle up in Fish's sleeping bag and get some kip. And tomorrow, warm, fed and rested, I'll retrace my steps to the entrance and one way or another I'll get out.

So confident am I, so certain of a predictable and positive outcome, that I've temporarily lost my fear. I take a deep breath and take hold of the cow's tail above me. It's time to be moving on.

Chapter 17

Bang - (slang) explosive substance, use of which requires a license in UK.

It was Wednesday again, and, as had become my habit, I was round at Rick and Joe's after work. It was a warm summer evening and I leant on the gatepost, watching Rick as he busied himself under the bonnet of the Astra.

'Fish seems OK to me,' I observed, 'a bit moody maybe, but then he always was. Artistic temperament or something.'

I remembered Fish at university. Although he was studying a technical subject, he was an artist too. He'd painted this kind of fresco on the wall of his room in Benson Street. It was full of strange shapes in different colours that leapt out at you alternately, first the red, then the blue, then the red again. It was like the shapes were living organisms, capricious entities invading your world. Especially when you'd dropped acid. And even when you hadn't. Rick once said there was a physical explanation for it, something to do with opposing colours and the way we perceive different wavelengths. The rest of us told him to shut up and have some more mushrooms.

Anyway, now as a mature, drug-clean adult, I'd been collecting Fish dutifully before each caving trip and sometimes to go to the pub in the evening as well. But I felt it was time to cool off a bit, to step back and let him manage on his own. It wasn't that I minded, he was a mate and I was happy to help out, but I was getting increasingly concerned that it was only a matter of time before Valerie blew my cover, realised that I wasn't exactly a model husband living with my wife and found out that I was taking Fish to spend time with 'that pair of queers' as she referred to Rick and Joe. Then the proverbial would really hit the fan, for all of us.

'He's certainly perked up a bit,' Rick agreed, 'but of course you didn't see him before. I think everything that's happened with the push on Quarry Cave has given him a new goal. The last trip was pretty exciting, he's rung me to talk about it a couple of times since.'

Rick was referring to the Saturday, a week and a half ago. I half closed my eyes and pictured it.

It was the first time we all went along the newly rigged streamway traverse and Rick was leading. We were close behind him as he arrived at the last bolt. Just yards ahead the rift ended and with it the streambed, the startled water tumbled noisily over a lip into the unknown.

Carefully we detached ourselves from the line and scrambled down to the level of the river. It was a mostly straightforward route with plenty of holds and strategic outcrops that would break your fall if you slipped. There was only one tricky bit where you had to step round a sharp corner, leaning directly out over the point where the water toppled downwards, this feature led to us naming the climb Lovers' Leap.

'Watch out for this move,' Rick warned, as he edged round to safety. 'Perhaps we should put a line on it next time.'

On this occasion, however, we had no extra ropes with us and, after completing the manoeuvre myself, I waited for Beth, who was immediately behind me, and took a precautionary hold of the sling looped round her belt as she leant outwards. The descent continued a further fifteen feet in comparative safety, dropping down into a small alcove beside the streamway. From that point there was apparently no way on.

We stood there in silence for a few moments, catching our breath and collecting our thoughts. Eventually, I stated the obvious. 'Looks like we'll have to rig a pitch over the waterfall.' I edged forward as far as I dared, trying to estimate the extent of the drop. But my courage only took me a couple of feet and all I could see was misty spray, glittering like gold dust in the darkness. I retreated and shook my head. 'It's a shame but I think this is as far as we can go today.'

Rick, who had wriggled out slightly further on his stomach, pulled back and nodded in agreement. 'Pity we can't see anything,' he said.

101

Fish, squatting silently on his haunches, spoke from the shadows. 'P-perhaps we could link our cows' tails and slings together and lower someone towards the edge to get a better look. Then we'd know w-what's ahead; w-what to bring next time.'

Fish's suggestion was the best option we had, so we secured Joe, being the smallest (well, strictly speaking the smallest was Beth, but none of us were going to let her take any risks), onto a makeshift line, looped the other end over a hefty stal that had formed conveniently close by and cautiously lowered him towards the edge. His legs were lost in the rush of water as he reached out into the void, arms outstretched like a sacrificial offering, his life, quite literally, in our hands. He paused there for a moment, a ghostly, ethereal figure, silhouetted in angelic pose in contrast to the hellish thundering of the water. He was saying something, shouting even, but his voice was lost in the cacophony. He turned and waved his arms, signalling to us to haul him back.

'What's it like?' Rick demanded, impatiently.

Joe was breathless with exhilaration, his face gleaming, radiantly wet. 'It's amazing! Like one of those trust games you play on team development courses, where you have to fall backwards and hope your colleagues will catch you.'

'No, idiot! What's the cave like?'

He laughed. 'That's amazing too.'

It turned out the river plummeted into a pool at least thirty feet below. Water was all Joe could see in any direction. A ladder from this point was out of the question because you'd never be able to stay on it – especially climbing back up – not with that weight of water crashing down on top of you. If that was the only way on then we would have to sink bolts for a traverse, starting in the safety of the small chamber we now occupied and extending out and round the corner, beyond the waterfall, then drop a ladder or an SRT rope from that point. To rig a pitch like that would be a complex and technical undertaking. It would take up huge resources of equipment, not to mention time. Our best hope was to dig around the chamber and look for an alternative route. But on that occasion there was no time to explore the possibility any further, not if we were going to make last food orders at the Quarryman's Rest and be home before the witching hour.

The sound of a spanner clattering noisily onto the tarmac, followed by Rick cursing, brought me back to the present.

'So when are we going to crack the next section of the cave?' We hadn't been down Quarry or any other cave for over a week and already I was missing it, getting twitchy with withdrawal. I toyed with a stem of bindweed that had twisted itself around both the gate and a nearby lavender bush. Back at the house I'd never paid much attention to the garden beyond occasionally mowing the lawn, which I'd always regarded as a nuisance and one of the drawbacks associated with married life. Carole had done all the complicated stuff like choosing plants and pruning them. By contrast, there was nothing green and living at Mike's flat, neither inside nor out (not unless you counted the mould growing on the outlet pipe of the toilet) and I was surprised at how much I was beginning to notice this lack, envying other people their suburban magnolias and herbaceous borders.

'Well not this weekend, Joe and I are off to Glastonbury.'

'Glastonbury? The festival? You mean you still go?'

Rick stood up straight, revealing a grubby T-shirt and arms smudged with engine oil and grease. 'Are you kidding? We never stopped; we haven't missed a year since the first time. Pass me that spanner will you.'

I carefully selected the appropriate tool and stepped across the pavement to put it in the outstretched hand as Rick disappeared again into the confusion of dismantled engine.

'Why don't you come with us?' His voice echoed round the car's components and arrived tinny and resonant at my ears. 'There's a good line up and I know someone with a couple of spare tickets.'

I thought about it. That first time that Rick referred to was at the end of our first year at university. I remembered it in a hazy kind of way – that's to say, it wasn't my memory that was at fault so much as the state of my brain while I was there.

Two things stood out from that first Glastonbury: Beth and drugs. Not necessarily in that order. There were five of us on that occasion; Taff didn't go, insisting that he was a miner not a hippy. Rick and Joe weren't yet a couple but they were seriously into the music, Joe especially, being a guitarist, was riveted to the lead solos. And I was with Beth of course. That weekend was the longest time I'd spent with her or any other girl, it felt like being married – or so I thought at the time. Meanwhile, Fish was this ethereal presence, like a ghost, haunting us. He was high on the atmosphere before he'd even had a sip of beer.

I remember lying on my back (come to think, I seemed to spend most of the weekend on my back one way or another) with the sun warm on my skin and bright on my eyelids. Like I was in some parallel universe that was closer to heaven. Beth lay next to me. I could feel her arm touching mine and smell the scent of patchouli on her skin. We were content just to be there. It didn't matter that we'd got soaked the night before or that the sound system had already broken down twice that day I was aware of Rick and Joe nearby, Rick playing air drums (if such a guitar equivalent exists) and Joe humming along with the guitar part.

'Hey!' Fish nudged me in the ribs as he spoke. 'Try some of this.'

I blinked at the shock of sunlight as I opened my eyes and took the joint that he held out. I sucked my breath in and the first drag seared straight through me. I struggled up into a sitting position, coughing.

'Really good stuff,' Fish informed me. 'Serious shit.'

Really good wasn't how I'd describe my initial reaction. It was like the smoke numbed my throat and my brain, even as I breathed it. I eyed the reefer dubiously as Beth calmly removed it from my hand, put it to her lips and inhaled like a pro. She nodded her approval to Fish as she passed the joint to Joe. I rubbed my eyes. We often shared a couple of spliffs back at the university but they never did more than make me a bit drowsy.

'This is the real thing,' Fish explained. 'What we get back home is like baby food compared to this.'

'Let's have another shot, I was half asleep last time.' I was determined not to appear like a child. This time I was more wary; I was ready for it. I just took a shallow breath and forced myself to hold it in my lungs for a few seconds. And as the wave of calm rippled through me I had to admit I could get to like it.

Fish stood up. I don't know if he was swaying or whether it was my eyes playing tricks. 'What say I score us some real stuff?' He addressed all of us. I had no idea what sort of 'stuff' he had in mind but like the others I nodded my agreement. So he disappeared, creeping barefoot over the sun-baked mud, weaving in and out of the colourful heaps of festival-goers who were stretched across the field, washed up like flotsam by the psychedelic tide.

My memory was vague after that. I remember Fish returning; goodness knows how he found us, he must have employed some sort of cosmic magnetism I suppose, some sort of transcendental global positioning system. He handed out some pills – which I must admit I was pretty scared of. I'd almost decided to put mine aside for a bit and wait and see what happened to the others (I persuaded myself this would be a noble thing to do, to watch out for them) but before I knew it I'd put the tab on my tongue, as Fish instructed me, and Beth had held a glass of beer to my lips.

After that I don't remember any individual details. It was as though the whole weekend condensed into one intense experience of colour and sound.

I fed on memories of the following few years' festivals as Rick continued to fiddle under the bonnet. I know I enjoyed them at the time but I was younger then, I was used to roughing it. Right now, in the cold light of day, all I could think of was a never-ending sea of mud. Then there were the terrifying toilets: little more than pits, filled with excrement and used tampons, surrounded by rusty iron screens. And the outdoor public washing facilities, which consisted of a cold tap and plastic bowls chained to tables, in which, for some inexplicable reason, beautiful people seemed determined to cleanse their private parts. Changing at the roadside to go caving is one thing but sorry, anywhere else I want my privacy.

'I think I'll give it a miss,' I said.

'Well suit yourself. I think you'd be surprised though. It's a lot better organised and ten times as many people.'

I shrugged. 'Is Beth going?' That was the one factor that might just change my mind.

'Probably not. I think she's scared of the mud, like you. Though how that can matter when you both go grovelling down caves, I can't begin to understand. No, this isn't gripping, pass the smaller one would you?'

'I might volunteer to work Saturday and Sunday,' I mused, almost to myself. 'Maybe take Monday or Tuesday off in lieu and save a day for flexi-time.' This building up of karma had become a habit. By volunteering to work on the weekends we weren't caving, I earned some bonus pay, and, more importantly, ensured that I wouldn't be required to do weekend work, apart from occasional emergency on-call stuff, for most of the summer.

Rick paused and looked up. 'If you're going to do that, why don't you take Sprat down the cave on your day off? He seemed really envious that he hadn't been able to join us for a trip yet when we were talking in the Red Dragon on Saturday night. He'd be able to advise us on rigging the pitch down the waterfall, or even using bang to break through to the lower level.'

A forecast of two days of heavy showers and the fact that Beth was planning to spend the weekend visiting her parents, decided me against going to the music festival, instead I made use of Saturday and Sunday by volunteering to work.

When I rang Sprat and suggested a trip down the Quarry on Monday or Tuesday he was very enthusiastic, especially when I described the chamber at the end of the streamway. He reckoned that it was almost certainly formed many years ago when the river ran at a higher level, and the only reason for it to have been etched out of the rock was because the water had found a way down through it; a way that would since have become blocked with rubble as the waterfall was formed. If the water had broken through before, then we could do the same now; that's what he reckoned, even if it meant using explosives.

So Tuesday morning found me in Sprat's shop, browsing through the caving guidebooks while I waited for to him to give last minute instructions to the student left in charge for the day. Mole Supplies was an Aladdin's Cave for cavers. Situated in a back street, the shop was very narrow. From the outside it looked little more than a kiosk, but inside, a string of tiny rooms stretched back, each crammed with a variety of caving paraphernalia. There were boots and batteries, wetsuits, boiler suits, fleecy undersuits and waterproof oversuits. Not to mention all the gadgetry that went with underground exploration. I'd known Simon Prat – Sprat, to his friends – since university days. I remember when I first started caving; Sprat had finished his degree a few years earlier. Whilst bumming around from one dead end job to another he'd noticed an untapped market. He rented a lock up garage and filled it with boots, helmets and oversuits which he bought in bulk from the manufacturers, then, at the beginning of each academic year, he kitted up all the new recruits to the university caving club. Twenty years on, Sprat's empire had grown to be one of the best-known caving supplies shops in the country.

Over by the till I saw the student nodding and Sprat giving him the thumbs up.

'OK,' Sprat called. 'Let's go and do it!'

A couple of hours later we were making our way across the hillside and then down through the cave.

'Bloody fantastic!' Sprat paused to take in the vista of the Snowy Mountains. He'd not been this far before. He was also suitably impressed with the streamway and admired Rick's neat rigging on the traverse.

We'd discussed what to take with us when we'd spoken on the phone the night before. There was digging equipment left over from the upper passages and stored just before the start of the streamway, which we could collect on the way. But Sprat said we might as well take some bang just in case we needed it, it would be a wasted trip if we got down there and found the stuff was too impacted to dig out by hand. I was secretly pleased about this, having never actually been on a trip where dynamite was used; but I'd heard stories about how you had to light the fuse and then run like hell because bang head (what you get from breathing in the fumes) is worse than any hangover.

Sprat carried the explosives in an old ammunition box – a watertight metal container like a small attaché case – and I carried the detonators in a sealed plastic drum. It was perfectly safe, Sprat told me, providing you kept the two components separate. I knew this was a rule that he frequently broke himself but he insisted I should learn to do it properly. Really I was glad I didn't have a bang license myself, I didn't want the responsibility.

As it turned out we didn't need it. Sprat leapt about frenetically when he saw the loose rubble around the edge of the chamber and immediately started scrabbling with his bare hands, intuitively seeking the way on like an unleashed sniffer dog. I refuelled with a Mars bar before I replaced my gloves and joined him, scraping at what had by now become a substantial hollow in the far corner.

Sprat was a weaselly sort of chap with piercing eyes and a slightly balding head compensated for by the hair on his chin. He was smaller and skinnier even than Joe and could wriggle into places where no man could follow – a job which he was called upon to do quite regularly in cave exploration. This time was no exception and he'd soon tunnelled down three feet into a hole that resembled a drain, just wide enough for him to slither into.

'It's going to go!' he yelped.

I grunted in agreement as I twisted the trowel, working loose a large stone near the top, gradually widening the opening. A thoroughfare big enough for the human ferret would be unlikely to accommodate me, let alone Rick.

'It's definitely going to go!' Sprat repeated the same words every few moments, it was like a mantra, a ritual chant that lulled us into an almost hypnotic state, driving us to work harder, however much our tired muscles complained. He was moving directly downwards now, as the passage extended, passing bucket-loads of rubble back up to me. The route he was uncovering twisted steeply in an anti-clockwise direction, wide enough for one person to slide down. As it emerged into the void beyond, Sprat squealed in glee and we named it the Spiral Staircase.

I don't know what we were expecting on the other side but what we found certainly took our breath away. A vast cavern as big as anything we'd explored underground – in this country at any rate – and within it an equally vast lake. It was awesome, one of those moments that make all the bruises and aching muscles, all the hours of hauling equipment, scraping and digging, all the pain and uncertainty worthwhile. Absolute perfection.

We must have stood there for ten minutes, Sprat and me, just staring. The surface of the water glowed golden in the beam of our cap lamps as it stretched away into infinity. Up near the waterfall the surface was choppy, leaping about, trying to move out of the way of the vertical wall of water pounding down into it. Further down the chamber, as the lake widened, the movement at the surface was almost imperceptible, if it weren't for boulders, rising here and there from the bed, it would have appeared quite still.

We scrambled down to the floor of the chamber and made our way between the lake and the rocky wall to our left. At times we had to clamber over boulders and edge our way around outcrops, at others we found ourselves walking on a flat beach, some twenty feet wide, as the water lapped beside us. We noted two passages off to the side but we didn't have time to explore them on this occasion. At the far end of the cavern we were clambering over boulders again. To our right, the previously benign expanse of water suddenly remembered its true purpose. It bottlenecked as the way ahead narrowed, gathering speed and momentum as it jostled its way towards a kind of giant plughole, where it swirled and spiralled before disappearing into the depths.

'You wouldn't want to take a dip in there on a rainy day,' Sprat observed, as we perched on a rock, watching the water disappear. He was right. Any more volume than this coming into the cave would make the feature treacherous.

As it was, there was no way to get safely past – not without getting seriously wet – so we retraced our steps. The waterfall was pretty spectacular now we approached it from down-river; it created a sharp, turbulent, wind chill and freshened the air with a dew-like scent. I paused to look over my shoulder as I stepped back into the Staircase. I was reluctant to leave yet eager to get back to the others and tell them what we'd found.

Chapter 18

Malachite - a copper carbonate mineral and semi-precious stone.

I'd been on a high for over a week. First there'd been the trip with Sprat, and the exhilaration of discovering the Lake Chamber. Two days later, Sprat had joined us at Benson Street and together the two of us had described it to the others. Then, on the Saturday, I'd been the one leading the group on our furthest trip into the cave yet.

But I guess not all of life can be perfect. Wednesday had come round again and I was back at Rick and Joe's. It had become a habit, going round there; a midweek mini-break where I got to spend some time with my mates; got fed, talked about caves then spent the night in their spare room. Just like old times, only more comfortable. That evening, Rick wasn't around. He was staying late at the university for a faculty dinner. Beth wasn't coming over either so we didn't have to eat vegetarian; instead, Joe had decided to cook steak and ale pie, which should have been a real treat for me, being a hardened carnivore. On this occasion, though, the sight of him chopping and pummelling those pieces of raw meat just made me feel sick.

The fact was it had been a particularly bad day at work. It had started off like any other, mostly routine stuff, going through the in tray, checking and signing reports and filling in analysis charts. I'd worked in the hospital lab since I finished my PhD so I was pretty much used to it by now. Like any job, you start off doing repetitive boring stuff. I think I spent the best part of two years analysing blood and urine samples. I was more familiar with bodily fluids than anyone ever wants to be. Then, when I'd proved I was reliable, I got promoted to a more senior position. I had more management and admin responsibilities but also more variety on the practical side, learning about histology generally and spending more time squinting down microscopes than shaking test tubes. It was only after I'd covered all the areas that the lab dealt with that I got the chance to specialise. And ironically, as Joe never tires of pointing out, the area that fell to me, and in which I showed most aptitude, was drug testing.

Now, it's a bigger field than you might think. You need a good general understanding of toxicology, never mind sound chemistry skills. It definitely isn't glamorous or exciting. Most days of the year you're not testing a heroin haul for purity (because I sometimes help out the police, testing stuff outside of the body as well as in). More often you find that someone didn't read their prescription properly and got side effects from taking too much of their medication or taking it with a glass of beer. And then there's all the athletes' stuff; routine testing for anyone involved in competitive sport to make sure they haven't chemically enhanced their performance. I found that my strength in all this was my intuition. Given a case history I could make a good guess at what someone had taken or been exposed to that might be giving them problems. I could go straight for bull's eye and save vital time.

That was ninety-nine percent of my drug-based work. It was rare that I had to deal with an intensive care case or, worse still, a fatality. Unfortunately, that Wednesday had been one of those one percent days.

The casualty was a twenty year-old male. He'd been brought in during the night but sadly had not responded to resuscitation attempts. That knowledge made me depressed from the start. But having come to terms with it, I decided my choice of action. Without the race against time I could do my best to explain what had happened. I wanted to be able to tell the grieving parents something more than the fact that their son had taken drugs (well, OK, a doctor would do the telling but I'd be responsible for what he or she said). Of course, I was only able to do this sort of work because I kept a distance. The victims were strangers to me.

On this occasion, I had a theory I wanted to pursue but I needed some more information first. I went through to my

112

office and took off my lab coat, hanging it on the peg on the back of the door. The computer was already switched on and I typed in the password to get at the report files.

I began to fill in my report. It was grim reading, I hated dealing with deaths, especially those of young people; and ones like this were so needless. I sighed to myself and put the kettle on to make a coffee. I was out of milk, fresh or powdered; it would have to be black. I'd got a sandwich from the local takeaway in the drawer. I took it out and slid it, on its paper plate with paper napkin, out of the bag. Then I poured the coffee and forced myself to turn back to the report. It was an unusual case for a drug-related death. More often they were overdoses and at least in those cases you felt the users knew what they were doing, knew the risks. Or often it was impurities – cheaper substances mixed with the drug to eke it out – that did the damage. But occasionally, like now, there was no obvious reason. It could have been a sad accident but equally it was possible the user already had a medical condition they didn't know about. I just had a hunch that the second option was the answer but I didn't have enough information to prove it on my own.

It was no good. I had to give this guy a fair hearing, so to speak. I didn't know who he was but I felt I owed it to him and to his family. I might turn out to be wrong in which case there was nothing lost but if he did turn out to have some medical condition that would have got him sooner or later then that would make more sense of his loss than just to say he took drugs and he died. I picked up the phone and dialled a number. There was no answer. I wasn't going to leave it. Of course, there'd be a full post-mortem and an inquest; but if there were more samples to be taken and tests to be done I wanted to do them myself, now, so that I could finish the report and then forget about it.

It was Dr Sherrin – Steve – on duty that day. We got on OK, went for a beer now and then. He wouldn't mind me dropping in. I closed the current file and stood up from the desk, tucking my shirt into my jeans. Then I set off down the corridor.

I could see that the office was empty as I walked through the main door. There was no sign of either Steve or his assistant. Although the computers were logged off and the cupboards and filing cabinets shut, in customary fashion, there was a jacket across the back of a chair and a steaming mug of tea on Steve's desk, so I reckoned he hadn't gone far. I turned to leave but then I realised it was four o'clock and I was hoping to get away early. And this wasn't something I wanted to put off until tomorrow. So I figured I'd just put my head round the door to the PM room and if one of them was there attending to whatever grisly duties (I really didn't like to think about that side of things) I could call them over, tell them about my concerns, ask for the fresh samples, then get the hell out of there.

The door was open just a crack. I stood close and called softly.

'Hello?'

I don't know why I called quietly. I mean, it wasn't like I was going to wake anyone up or cause Steve to inflict some mortal wound with his scalpel. I chuckled to myself nervously; I always seemed to act as though I was playing a part in some black comedy when I was in this neck of the woods.

There was no reply so I called again and, at the same time, pushed the door fully open.

I could see inside now. Without even having to step across the threshold I could see the whole of the interior. I could see, immediately, that there was no-one there - no-one alive at any rate. I could see the open swing doors in the far corner leading through to the fridges. I could see the scrubbed surfaces and the trays of instruments. I could see a couple of saws and what looked suspiciously like a cleaver; I tried not to let myself ponder on whether the room looked (or smelled) like a butcher's shop. And down the centre of the room I could see the dissection tables, one of which was occupied.

I could already see far more than I was comfortable with so I've no idea why I went in there, but some invisible force – or more likely some sick or morbid curiosity – drew me in.

He was lying on his back, arms neatly by his sides, completely naked. For some reason that shocked me. It somehow made him vulnerable, displayed for anyone to see. At least in life he would have had the choice. Perhaps it was those subtle changes that begin as soon as life ceases, the way the blood no longer feeds the tissues, the way the skin assumes a yellow plastic pallor, but as I approached his feet, I felt dissociated, as though he had never been a person. There was a long deep incision, starting from his throat and travelling down the centre of his chest, where his heart, lungs and liver had been pulled out, each in turn, slapped onto the scales like a new born baby or a joint of beef, and checked for signs of trauma or disease.

Suddenly, I knew that I shouldn't have gone in there; I didn't have the stomach for it. But before I turned to go I sneaked a look at his face. Now I knew this was playing with fire, that at the very least I'd feel shocked and saddened, but still I felt this compulsion, forcing me on. I froze, feeling that at any minute he would open his eyes and his mouth and start talking to me.

Then I realised that the face was familiar. I'd seen him in the Red Dragon several times with a pretty dark-haired girl, in fact I'd been talking to him, at the bar just a couple of nights ago. Perhaps I was wrong, that person had been full of energy, full of life, whereas this thing on the slab was white, the skin on his face drooping strangely. It was not so much a person as an impression made of wax. But I knew I was right. A strange tingling feeling began at my throat and spread to envelop the whole of my head. My ears burned hot. Jesus! I hoped he wasn't one of the caving fraternity. An invisible fist grabbed my insides and twisted them, causing me to bend double.

A figure appeared in the far doorway.

'Marty, I was about to call you – hey! Are you all right?' It was Steve's voice.

I felt hot, sick and dizzy all at the same time, my breath came in short, shallow gasps. I turned and ran out through the office. My stomach lurched and the room span sideways as though it was a sailing boat changing tack. I ran out into the corridor and pushed blindly down on the iron bar of the double doors of the fire escape. I was sick again and again, beside the tyres of a tired-looking metro, on the forlorn leaves of a shrub in a deathly dry tub and again on the dirty dusty tarmac. When my stomach was empty and I leant, almost upright, on the wing of the metro, Steve came out with a plastic cup of water.

'Sip it slowly,' he instructed. 'It happens to all of us.'

Too right, it does! That's what I was scared of.

'You OK?' Joe asked. 'You're looking a bit peaky.'

I shook my head. 'Bit of a headache after work. Mind if I get a few minutes' fresh air?'

'Of course. Go and sit in the garden. I'll get this in the oven then I'll show you what we've been doing with the bikes.'

I went outside and sat on a wrought-iron chair on the patio. I could have told Joe about what happened, he'd have been sympathetic, but I didn't want to talk about it. I was afraid that doing so would simply reaffirm the memories of a day I wanted to forget. I couldn't resolve it until I got the results of the tests the following day. There was nothing useful I could do until then. So I didn't want a post mortem (my stomach clenched at my unfortunate choice of words even though I didn't actually voice them) on it, instead I wanted to immerse myself in happier things.

Joe joined me a few minutes later and led me down to the outbuilding where their motorbikes were housed. 'We've spent all our spare time down here the past couple of days,' he said. 'What do you think?'

Both bikes had had a facelift. Even I could appreciate the work that had gone into them. The chrome gleamed and they looked like they were raring to go. Rick and Joe were going to a rally that coming weekend. We all knew about it because it meant we wouldn't be going caving.

'Where did you say you're going?' I ran my hand over the nearest bike, observing that it was far cleaner than the bathroom mirror back at Mike's flat.

'Matlock Bath; it's in Derbyshire. The rally isn't till Sunday but we're planning to ride up Friday night so we can do a bit of caving on the Saturday. A couple of the guys from a local club have offered to take us down a coffin level.'

'A what?' I shuddered, thinking back to earlier that day. Why is it that, whenever you try to avoid a subject, it seems to be waiting for you round every corner?

Joe laughed. 'It's a kind of mine they have up there.'

I laughed too but mine was the sort you do when you're nervous. 'You mean it's six feet under?'

'Well I think it is about that depth coincidentally! No, apparently the name refers to the shape of the passageway, the cross-section, the most economical way of excavating. Just high enough to walk when you're stooped, narrow at the top and bottom, and broader part way down for your shoulders.'

'Easy walking passage then,' I joked. 'What were they mining, copper?' I vaguely remembered seeing rock, green with malachite, when I'd been caving in the Peak District years ago.

'Lead, I think. Rick's got the details.' We went outside and Joe shut the door, securing it with a mortise lock and a padlock. 'Come on,' he said. 'Let's get a drink before dinner.'

Rope - two types of rope are commonly used underground. Static rope (ie with little stretch) is more suitable for abseiling or ascending, while rope with more stretch is used for lifelines and cows' tails as it absorbs the shock if a caver takes a fall.

I manage to hold my concentration for the length of the traverse, counting the bolt hangers as I transfer my cows' tails onto each new length of rope. Eventually I round the corner of Lovers' Leap, detach myself from the line and tumble down the Spiral Staircase.

Once I reach the top of Easter Climb I begin to relax. I know that, compared to what I've done so far, what lies ahead is a gentle stroll; that getting to the camp is inevitable.

Before I leave the Lake Chamber behind I pause and turn back to look at the waterfall. I've never seen it look that powerful before.

It was chance that I went out with Beth that weekend. With Rick and Joe out of town at their rally and Fish and Taff busy with family commitments, I'd hoped to build up some karma at work; but they were already fully covered. By Sunday afternoon I was getting bored. Mike was settled in front of the television watching a grand prix. I just had to get out.

Now, although theoretically I'd been hoping for an opportunity to get Beth on her own, experience told me that these relationship things usually played out much more easily and naturally in my head than they did in reality. There'd been several occasions in the past few weeks when I could have asked her out but it always seemed easier to leave it till another time. Just knowing that I could if I wanted was satisfying in a mental if not a physical sense. However, encouraged by my success with Carole, that afternoon I opted for calling round Beth's house on the off chance. Luck was clearly on my side because not only was she there but she was keen to get out. She wanted to collect a jacket she'd accidentally left up at The Quarryman's Rest after our trip to the end of the streamway the previous weekend, so it was an obvious suggestion to drive out there, go for a bit of a stroll, then stay for dinner.

The Quarryman's Rest was nestled high in the hills, tucked snugly between rocky outcrops. It had once served the men who extracted stone from the cliff-face beyond, but now the quarry was closed, the rows of tiny terraced cottages with their low ceilings and steep staircases had been pulled down, and what had once been a thriving community was reduced to a meagre hamlet, a couple of farms and mostly empty weekend cottages. I was amazed that the pub stayed open but I think it had become a retirement hobby for the owners, Huw and Gwen, rather than a profit-making business, though, to be fair, on fine summer weekends, they did quite a good trade serving food to day-trippers.

'Let's sit outside,' Beth suggested. 'We hardly ever get to see this place in daylight.'

I nodded agreement and took a long swig from my pint so it didn't spill as I ducked under the lintel of the side door.

The pub was a tiny place, little more than a cottage itself. It had a partially covered patio and a garden with a kind of miniature waterfall at the far end whose spray channelled into a rill that ran across the lawn. Here a mixture of walkers and smartly dressed escapees from the city sat on wooden benches beside wooden tables. It felt odd to be here when the place was busy. Usually we didn't arrive till mid-evening. When we were on trips, we'd made an arrangement with Huw and Gwen whereby we rang as soon as we came out of the cave and they had our food ready when we arrived. Sometimes, especially on a Sunday, we were the only customers. It also felt strange because we always came here with the others. It occurred to me that this was the first time I'd been on my own with Beth since we'd met up again. Or, to put it another way, the first time since we split up.

We settled ourselves opposite one another at the only free

119

table. I smiled at her, wondering whether she thought of our outing as a date. And also wondering whether I did.

I'd broached the subject with Joe on Wednesday, while we were eating dinner. I'd told him straight out that, the first time he and Rick invited me round when Beth was there, I'd suspected it was a set up, what with me newly separated from Carole and Beth newly arrived back from the States. But to my surprise he'd denied it. What's more, he'd suggested it would be a bad idea to even think of going there again unless we were very sure of our feelings. And I hadn't even told him the whole truth, the fact that I was confident I would soon be moving back in with Carole. We had an appointment booked to see the counsellor in a few weeks time at the end of our agreed trial separation. Of course there was a remote possibility that Carole would feel we still had some differences to work out, and if that was the case we might have to defer the moving in date a couple of weeks, but, either way, I felt confident that we'd soon be a happily married couple again.

If Joe had known all this I'm sure he'd have had more to say. I was quite surprised at how moralistic he'd become; but then, he'd been in a stable relationship for twenty years, he didn't appreciate what it was like to be on your own. I, on the other hand, had a different experience of life. Over the years, I'd learned that sometimes you should go for whatever you could get. I don't mean like being totally promiscuous (and that's just as well because these days I don't think I'd have the bottle or the energy for a string of one night stands) just that you should make the most of opportunities. Where Joe thought black and white, I saw infinite possibilities of grey. Right then, I saw no reason why one liaison should preclude another, especially as Carole and I were officially separated, and more especially because that break was her decision.

I hadn't always felt this way about relationships and sex and stuff. Beth and I had gone out for more than two years and I would never have considered being unfaithful to her, even though I had several offers and could easily have got away with it. But since then I'd developed a different outlook on life. And

120

what happened at work on Wednesday convinced me even more that you have to live life for the moment and enjoy it to the full.

Suddenly, it felt like my fantasy, the one where Beth and Carole both were competing for me, might soon become a reality. However, aside from the rights and wrongs and other people's opinions, I knew I wasn't cut out to lead a double life indefinitely. Goodness only knew how bigamists could carry it off. I just knew that I wouldn't be inventive enough to explain my absences or remember two sets of birthdays. The upshot of all this was I realised that if I wanted to get together with Beth it would be better to do so soon, while Carole and I were officially on a break. It would be easier to start it now, at any rate, to see if it was what I really wanted.

So I smiled at Beth across the table, wondering what to say. Maybe I should just come out with it and say it. Let's just get together; let's try again, give it our best shot. But it wasn't in my nature to say that sort of thing so I played safe.

'How are your parents?' I asked. I figured it was a good icebreaker and I'd always been genuinely fond of Beth's mum and dad.

I'd met quite a few of my friends' parents over the years and generally they followed a pattern. They were of the same generation and usually turned out to be much like my own mum and dad. A bit restricted, a bit moralistic, fairly predictable. Beth's though, were something different. Her mother was a yoga teacher. I remember she was often to be seen in their conservatory in leotard and tights, twisting herself into an array of knots and contortions that Houdini would have been proud to escape from. Every year she spent three weeks at an Ashram in India being spiritually reborn, then returned to float around the house in some higher state of consciousness.

Beth's father was a professor of philosophy at the university. He was also a member of the Communist party. I sometimes wondered if he was a spy. I could easily imagine him as a secret agent, travelling to London to keep clandestine appointments on a park bench with some mysterious gentleman in a trilby and trench coat, exchanging national secrets on carefully secreted microfilm and dodging poison-tipped umbrellas on the underground. As well as lecturing in ethics and Marxist studies, he frequently attended seminars and summits in various parts of the world, always taking with him his supply of cannabis leaves (home-grown in the aforementioned conservatory) stowed in the lining of his spectacles case.

I remember the first time I stayed over at Beth's place. I was all set to sleep in the guest room but Beth insisted I should share her room and her bed.

'I can't possibly,' I protested. 'What about your parents?'

'That's all right, they'll sleep in their own bed!' She giggled helplessly. 'No, seriously, they're cool about it.'

I wondered how many previous boyfriends had shared this privilege in her family home. Then I stopped thinking about it quickly, because, like so many things about Beth, I really didn't want to know the answer.

But what most surprised me on that first occasion was when, before we settled into her bed, she calmly started rolling a joint.

'Won't your parents mind?' I asked.

She grinned. 'They're cool about most things.'

I shook my head in wonder. The thought of my mother in her recently fashionable crimplene trouser-suit and with her neat shampoo and set or my father with his V-neck pullovers and pipe so much as uttering the word cannabis let alone being in possession of any was incomprehensible.

'Well.'

'Pardon?'

'They're well, thank you. My parents. Where are you, Marty? Out to lunch?'

'Sorry,' I laughed. 'I was miles away, thinking about when I first met them. I'm pleased they're OK. Say hi from me.'

'Will do. And yours?'

'Good,' I nodded.

I was becoming increasingly self-conscious. This wasn't how it was supposed to be. In the fantasy we fell into one another's arms and…well…nature took its course.

122

'Is something the matter?' Beth asked, after what seemed like an endless silence.

What was I supposed to say? Should I suggest a relationship, or a shag for old time's sake? 'I was thinking about work,' I said, as I fidgeted with my glass, 'it was a bad week, something really got to me.' I told her about the body in the mortuary.

She reached across the table and took my hand. 'That's dreadful,' she sympathised. 'You should have called me in the week, not bottled it up. Don't they have counsellors you can talk to at the hospital about that sort of thing?'

I know I looked horrified but I'd had enough of counsellors, thank you. I shrugged. 'It doesn't usually get to me. Most of the work's routine, there really aren't many tragedies like that one.'

Beth looked doubtful. 'So did he die because of the drugs?'

I shook my head. 'It was a heart condition that he was born with. It could have happened anytime, when he was playing football, running for a bus, even. I just hope he wasn't in the university caving club.'

'Fish or Rick would have heard by now if he was.'

I nodded.

Luckily our food arrived at that point and the conversation turned onto happier subjects. I leaned back in my chair, determined to enjoy the evening.

It was later on, when I dropped Beth home, she mentioned the subject again.

'Are you sure you're all right, Marty?' She twisted the key in the lock and pushed the front door open. 'You know, about finding that guy you recognised?'

I nodded. 'I'll be fine. It was a few days ago now; I've come to terms with it.'

She looked doubtful. 'Even so...talking about it, like we did, it brings it all out.' She hesitated. 'Maybe you shouldn't be alone. I mean...if you want, you could stay the night.'

I stopped, startled. All these weeks I'd been daydreaming about getting back together with Beth, imagining what I'd say, how I'd persuade her round to my way of thinking; and suddenly, here she was, propositioning me – or as good as – and I didn't know what to do.

I opened my mouth slowly, hoping the right words would form themselves. Maybe it was Joe's words, burning into my conscience; or the fact I hadn't had a proper drink because I was driving.

God, I want you. Yes, yes, yes! These were the words that buzzed inside my head.

'Thanks, but I've got an early start tomorrow, I'd best say good night,' were the words that came out of my mouth.

'Well, if you're sure?'

I wasn't sure at all. I wished she'd wrap her arms around me, kiss me, seduce me; make the decision for me. But she didn't. As I turned to get in the car, I told myself she probably meant that I could sleep on the sofa. And in any case, I thought, as I drove home, playing hard to get would work in my favour: there'd be another opportunity soon.

Unfortunately, I was wrong again.

Chapter 20

Aven - an area of cave with a high roof. From the French: meaning big cavern or cathedral.

The following weekend, on the Saturday, I arrived down the Red Dragon a bit later than usual. We were due to plan our next few trips underground and I hoped the others weren't deciding anything important without me. As it turned out, I needn't have worried; or maybe, in retrospect, I should have worried a lot.

I could see, as I made my way through the bar, that there was a newcomer in our midst. 'Who's been sitting in my chair?' I thought to myself, as I approached, and, 'Who's been eating my porridge?' as the stranger patted Beth on the hand and whispered something in her ear. She giggled and smiled at him in a way that made me want to puke. Everyone seemed to be having such a good time without me that, had I not been gasping for a beer, I'd probably just have turned round and quietly gone home. But hey, quit the self-pity! Anyway, at that point Rick saw me.

'Oh, Marty! I was hoping you'd make it. Come and meet Ashley.'

I made my way over to where Rick was standing as he interrupted the conversation going on beside him with a hand on the stranger's shoulder and a polite but insistent, 'Excuse me one moment but you must meet Marty.'

The stranger turned and shook my hand in a business-like way. He reminded me of one of those consultants who employers bring in from time to time. They're not your boss, not even an employee of your company, but their report on you could make the difference between your getting a promotion or your entire job being deemed unnecessary.

'Ashley Roberts,' the stranger announced, curtly.

'Marty,' I replied, surprised by the formality of his

125

introduction. 'Marty Wight,' I added, as an afterthought, feeling that his declaration of a surname bestowed a social advantage over me.

Ashley Roberts was tall and slim. He had impeccably-styled dark brown hair and a firm, smoothly-shaven chin. His steel blue eyes, startlingly pale beneath his perfectly sculpted, dark brows, twinkled, turning up slightly at the corners. He had no hint of a beer gut. In short, he was the sort of man women find attractive. Beth certainly did; that was obvious by the way she hung on his every word and positively drooled when he smiled at her.

'Good to meet you,' Ashley continued. 'We must talk properly, later maybe.' He was dismissing me already, eager to resume whatever he'd been discussing before I arrived, prioritising his conversations like a salesman.

'Excuse me but I'm going to get a drink.' I waved towards the bar in an attempt to resign before I got the sack.

A few minutes later, from the safety of the bar and a half-drunk pint of Pedigree, I watched Ashley Roberts in action.

Everyone seemed to be competing for his attention. It wasn't just our crowd either. There were plenty of people from the university caving club down the Red Dragon that evening, other clubs too. For each individual, it seemed, he had some quality, some achievement or experience for which they admired, envied or idolised him. And they weren't their usual rowdy selves either. Oh no! For Ashley Roberts, all these students, used-to-be students and hangers-on were on their best behaviour, politely waiting their turn to talk to this super hero.

I finished my pint, ordered another and, feeling a bit more fortified, returned into the throng to see what all the fuss was about.

I soon gleaned that it wasn't just Ashley's natural charm that was generating all the interest. Basically, there are three things that will guarantee your popularity in a caving club. The first is that you're fit and strong and game to take a few risks. The second is that you hold a bang license. And the third is that you've been on expeditions. Not just exploration close to home or caving holidays abroad but properly organised missions for weeks on end, discovering the previously unknown underworld of far-flung corners of the globe. None of our immediate crowd qualified on all of these counts. Sprat was the only member of the entire club who came close, and he was usually too busy with the shop to pursue the overseas bit very often. But Ashley Roberts had done it all and everyone wanted to hear about it.

It seemed like every conversation in the bar that night revolved around him. Ashley had been everywhere. He'd been in tropical caverns, warm and humid, where lofty avens sheltered flocks of sonar-squeaking bats; he'd plunged, semi-naked, into turquoise lagoons that stretched far beyond the beam of any lamp; and he'd travelled across subterranean torch-lit lakes by dinghy. He'd walked through ice tunnels that twisted, sharp and scalloped, through the very heart of glaciers and he'd sailed through caverns that sparkled with glow-worms. He'd even been in Lechuguila, with its sulphurous pools that bubble with deadly gases, where strange primeval creatures, bleached and blind, live in a world that breaks all the laws of nature. He'd explored the speleology in China and Vietnam, in Cuba and Japan. Ashley Roberts had been to those strange forgotten corners of the globe where even David Attenborough and Michael Palin feared to tread.

And he really knew how to play to an audience. He was like a film star, carefully sharing himself out so that even the minions got to exchange a few sentences, to receive a few moments of undivided attention from their demi-god. Often he paused and jotted down a few words on beer mats and scraps of paper. The information was varied, the names of caves, contacts abroad, occasionally his phone number or email. It looked as if he was signing autographs, a natural response to his fame.

He was certainly convincing; even Sprat seemed to be impressed. I joined in with the others, expressing envy at his adventures and congratulating his achievements, but privately I thought he was a bit of a pseud. I wasn't the only one to think so either.

'Upper class prat!' I heard Taff whisper to Fish. 'Thinks he's better than everyone else just because he's got money. I'd like to see the boy do a full shift of hard graft down a pit.'

It wasn't that though. You could tell, if you listened to Ashley – really listened and watched his movements too – that he was from a far humbler background and less privileged in education than Rick. Certainly he was well off, that was apparent straight away from the designer clothes (labels on the outside), which he wore with a casual elegance. I figured he'd probably bought his way onto some expeditions, just like the rich and famous pay to climb up Everest, or fly round the world in hot air balloons. But you still have to do the legwork, get fit, take risks. He'd found a way to make money and thereby achieve the lifestyle he craved. That's what really puts people's backs up. We can slag off the idle rich with hatred and envy, accepting that their privileges stem only from an accident of birth. But Ashley probably grew up in a similar family to Joe, Fish and myself. If we felt any jealousy it was only because we knew if we'd had the motivation to get off our backsides and organise our lives we could be in the same position that he was now.

I tried very hard to hate Ashley Roberts – and God knows I could find enough reasons – yet the fact was I couldn't bring myself even to dislike him. For all his irritating ways, he was fun and he was generous. Fair enough, there was plenty about him that I envied. But he never actually bragged about any of it.

And there was something more. Maybe it was his charm, his charisma, I don't know, but I got this strange feeling from the first moment I saw him. Something clicked when we shook hands (and we're not talking ageing joints here). It was that split second feeling of recognition you get very occasionally on meeting someone new. I didn't know him from Adam yet I felt some affinity, as though we'd been friends for a long time. Fish would doubtless say something esoteric, like we'd met in a past life. Later, when I thought about it logically (and soberly) I figured it was more likely that we'd bumped into one another

128

at a caving conference or some such event. The caving community, the hard core of it, is a comparatively small and close-knit circle of people.

But whatever the reason, I felt some sort of connection with Ashley Roberts that made me unable to hate him. Even when, at the end of the evening, he and Beth disappeared into the sunset together, still laughing and joking.

'Off goes Mr Smooth,' said Taff. 'Off to scent mark his territory.'

The others all laughed at the lewd comment. Normally I would have done the same, but on this occasion I just found it thoroughly distasteful.

Chapter 21

Sump - a section of cave passage completely submerged in water.

The day after meeting him, we had our first caving trip with Ashley; and naturally, we took him down Quarry Cave.

'Have you tried diving it yet?'

We were in the far end of the Lake Chamber, where, after broadening out into an almost serene pool, the water bottlenecked again before pouring down into a dark unwelcoming chasm between the rocks. This was where Sprat and I had stopped. It was as far into the cave as any of us had explored. We named it the Devil's Cauldron.

I looked at Ashley, in his sparkling state-of-the-art kit, with attempted hatred and sincere envy. I suppose I'd subconsciously been hoping that he wouldn't live up to his promises underground. How much happier I'd have felt if he'd been slow and clumsy or freaked at the sight of the traverse or the waterfall. But no such luck. Ashley Roberts sped down the entrance ladder like it was a flight of stairs, he slid effortlessly under the Big Slab and through the boulder choke, and, having stylishly negotiated the traverse above the streamway, he strode casually around the edge of the Lake like he was strolling along a beach on a summer's day, contemplating a paddle. By contrast I was painfully aware of how unfit I was – in caving terms at any rate; if anyone slowed down the pace it was me.

Now he lay on his stomach on a flat rock just above the water level on the brink of the Cauldron, peering down into the unknown, his helmet glistening wet with the spray. He was speaking but we couldn't make out what he said. His voice echoed before disappearing down the chasm.

'Pardon?' shouted Rick. 'Say that again. I think we lost a few words in the water!'

Ashley pulled back from the noise and the spray and sat in a crouch a few yards from the water. 'I said, have any of you dived through yet, to see if it opens up beyond the sump?'

Fish spoke quietly. 'I've been m-meaning to ask one of the guys from the d-d-diving group to come with me but I haven't got around to it yet. I don't want to do it on my own in case it's a long one and there're loose boulders or something.'

'Quite right,' Ashley nodded. 'What about the rest of you?'

'None of us dive.' Rick answered for all of us.

'Oh,' Ashley looked puzzled. 'I thought you did.' He looked at me, searchingly.

I was taken aback. 'I don't dive,' I replied hurriedly. I felt suddenly unnerved.

No-one else said anything, thank goodness, though Joe glanced at me sympathetically.

Ashley continued to look puzzled and stared at me intently. Inside I could feel myself beginning to shake, just a little. There was a pause, then he laughed and his face returned to normal. 'I just thought you said you did, but I must have been mistaken.' He turned to Fish. 'Well it looks like it's down to you and me then. We'll have to bring some bottles down here and see if there's a way through. Let's face it, the stream has to leave the cave somewhere, and where it does, we may be able to get out too!'

'Or discover a whole n-new section of cave,' Fish smiled happily.

And even though I couldn't quite relax for the rest of that trip, I was glad that Fish seemed happier than I'd seen him since we'd all got back together.

A week later, we were back again; taking the diving equipment in so Fish and Ashley could explore the Devil's Cauldron. We'd decided to leave the cars in a lay-by on the nearest stretch of road. It was a bit exposed but it would reduce the trek to the cave entrance to just over a mile, and that's far enough when you're carrying things like air cylinders.

Beth and Ashley had arrived together in his car. A confirmation, I feared, of their status as a couple. If I thought

131

about it – really thought – about the two of them together, then I'd have been gutted. So I didn't think. I saw it for what it was, a casual fling, the first step for Ashley as he slept his way round the female section of the university caving club (indeed he'd probably got a couple of others on the go already) then, when the super ram had serviced the whole flock he'd move on to pastures new. I'd met his sort before. I didn't blame him for it, I mean, what bloke wouldn't behave like that given half a chance? What bloke wouldn't go for Beth? It was my fault for hanging back, for not taking her when I had the chance. Now I'd have to wait until the two of them tired of one another; I gave it six weeks, tops. Meanwhile I consoled myself with imagining Ashley's shortcomings. I wondered what he was like in bed. If what people said about cars and their owners was true then Ashley, who drove a two-seater sporty job, with sleek red bodywork and a growling Cosworth engine, couldn't have much to offer in the bedroom department. Shortcomings! That was a good one! I smiled to myself and laughed out loud. Beth looked at me questioningly. That just proved the point really.

I'd called for Fish, as usual, and Taff had travelled up with Rick and Joe, so we had a full complement that day. We kitted up then squeezed the diving gear into our tackle sacks. Fish and Ashley were understandably excited; they were the ones who were going to be doing the exploring, breaking new ground, maybe even discovering a whole new section of cave. The rest of us weren't quite so enthusiastic. At best we were porters, carrying the heavy and cumbersome equipment so the stars of the show could save their strength for the interesting bit; we were like Sherpas, on an expedition up Everest. At worst we were risking life and limb. Because a tank of compressed air might be safe enough in the sea, but try dropping one onto a pile of rocks and the whole thing's likely to blow up in your face. The walk across the moor was a nuisance rather than dangerous but once inside the cave we'd have to be really careful.

We set off at a slower pace than usual, trudging up the well-worn path. I guess it was partly because we were thinking about all the unfamiliar kit we had to take that we overlooked it. It wasn't until we reached the cave entrance that we discovered we'd forgotten the key to the padlock. We'd made the entrance extra secure because of the deep shaft and there was no other way we could get in. Things weren't as bad as they might have been because we were pretty sure the key was in Joe's car rather than back in town, so after a short while of cursing and blaming one another, it was decided that Taff would run back while the rest of us waited near the entrance. We whiled away the time planning what we'd do once we got underground and how much we'd drink in the pub later.

It was more than half an hour before Taff appeared over the ridge, I was beginning to worry that the key wasn't there after all and we'd had a wasted journey. He looked concerned as he jogged up to us, bending over to catch his breath as he arrived.

'That's the last time we leave any vehicles there,' he panted.

'Why? What's happened?' Beth looked worried.

'Some prat was trying to break into Ashley's car.'

I smirked to myself. Really it served him right if he chose to bring something like that into the Welsh mountains. It was the obvious target for any thief, it just cried out, 'Try me! There're lots of expensive goodies inside! What about a joy ride?'

Ashley jumped to his feet in understandable anger. 'Is it all right? Has it been damaged? Did he get in?'

'Don't worry, boyo, he'd only got as far as fiddling with the door lock. Then I arrived so I saw him off.' He gave a satisfied smile and stroked his knuckles.

'You didn't hit him did you?' Beth sounded quite horrified.

Ashley wasn't so generous. 'Well it serves him right if you did.'

Taff laughed. 'Let's just say I don't think he'll be trying it again in a hurry.'

'Well done, mate,' said Ashley. 'That's the only language some people understand.'

I noted, with satisfaction, that Beth glared at him.

Three hours later, after the long-haul trip to get all the gear down, Fish and Ashley decided to do a quick recce. They weren't planning to do the whole dive that day. We hadn't taken a line for one thing, and you never dive underground without a line because there may be twists and turns, forks and branches, along the way, or the water might be foggy with silt. A line is your insurance policy to find your way out, like unravelling a jumper in a maze. But no-one wanted to leave without a quick glimpse of what was to come. So, in view of the current going down there, and in case they needed yanking back out, we tied them to the twenty metre length of rope we had with us, like we were fishing and they were the bait. Then they put on their weight belts and strapped an air cylinder each over their shoulders and disappeared into the dark gurgling hole. The rest of us waited. We expected to wait about ten minutes but it was much sooner than that when Fish's helmet broke the surface and Rick and Taff reached across to haul him out. Ashley was immediately behind and the two of them climbed onto the rocky ledge beside us and peeled off their cumbersome kit.

'Nothing doing,' Fish shook his head, 'a d-dead end.'

'It only went about thirty feet,' Ashley explained, 'then it just closed down. Obviously we'll go back another time and see if we can move some boulders, but I'm not hopeful. Plus, it was really hard work swimming back against the current. Any more water than today and you'd be stuck there for keeps.'

Neither of them was completely disheartened though, insisting that there was a good chance the streamway would reappear further into the cave.

Later, in the Quarryman's Rest, we sat waiting for our meals. The dive in the Devil's Cauldron had proved something of an anticlimax, but the main concern of the day was the attempted break-in of Ashley's car.

'It was probably a joy rider.' Taff puffed the words out of his mouth along with the smoke from his cigarette. 'Let's face it, boyo, it's hardly the most suitable vehicle to take on a caving trip.' He stared directly at Ashley. I could tell he was enjoying the opportunity to take the superior position. 'No, hear me out.' He raised his hand as Ashley opened his mouth to speak. 'This isn't jealousy talking. Of course I envy you that car – we all do – but there's a time and a place for it. You want to go cruising out on the open road, stop off somewhere where there're plenty of people about, that's fine. But you go driving that flashy number out into the sticks and then leave it in a lay-by for the day and you're asking for trouble. You've got enough spare cash. You'd be better to buy something a bit older and less conspicuous for your cave outings and leave the sporty car safely tucked up at home.'

I tried to catch Taff's eye. Well done, mate, I thought to myself.

'Actually it m-might not be as s-s-simple as that.' Fish took a long gulp of his orange juice. 'There's been a real problem with cavers' cars being broken into for some years now. People come out of their cave cold and w-wet and find the car windows broken and their dry clothes and towels gone.'

Beth looked surprised. 'Surely not. I mean, what's the point in that? Surely thieves know you wouldn't leave anything of value.'

I met her gaze, nodding agreement but Rick shook his head. 'I'm afraid Fish is right, Beth. You and Marty have been out of the caving scene for a while and things have changed, not all of them for the better. Some of the more popular caving areas have been hit really badly. It looks like the thieves know exactly whom they're targeting. If a group's gone caving the thieves know they've got several hours to play with. I know from meetings at the university club, there're some places you're advised to get changed at the caving hut and drive out in your kit, line the seats of the car with bin bags for the journey back. If you have got any valuables then generally you're better off hiding them in undergrowth near the cave entrance rather than leaving them in your car. Of course, if a cave is gated and padlocked then you can leave your stuff just inside the entrance. It's unlikely that cavers would steal from each other and if they did the local clubs will have details of who had

135

access at the time.'

Fish shook his head sadly. 'S-some clubs have even formed vigilante groups to hide beside the parked cars and s-scare off any thieves. It makes me s-sad that things have come to this.'

Rick looked serious. 'I really hope we're not going to have that sort of problem round here. I'd have thought the place was remote enough to discourage that sort of crime. Hopefully it was a one-off opportunist today, tempted by a smart sports car. I suggest that we play it carefully for the next few weeks, drive out here in old clothes and take wallets and things down the cave. And maybe not bring Ashley's car; there's no point in attracting attention. If it happens again we'll have to consider leaving our cars somewhere off the road. I suppose we could leave them here at the pub but it would be a really long walk.'

At that point Gwen arrived with our dinners and conversation stopped while we ate. It was only as we sat back sipping coffees, waking ourselves up for the drive home, that Beth asked the all-important question. 'What do we do now?' she wanted to know. 'We set our hopes on the Devil's Cauldron but even Fish and Ashley can't get through with their diving gear.'

'Oh, that's simple!' Rick's eyes were glinting and I think that he was secretly pleased that the Devil's Cauldron, which involved diving and therefore excluded him from participating, didn't provide a way on. 'There are two passages that we know of going off the Lake Chamber, we're going to explore them properly and discover the rest of the cave!'

Chapter 22

Column - formation that occurs when the stalactite above joins the
stalagmite below, linking floor to ceiling.

I had all sorts of plans for when I arrived at the camp: lighting a cosy candle, making a hot drink, sorting out some food – that sort of thing. But the reality is different. I've stumbled the last part of the journey with every joint and muscle in my body protesting, hating the sight of every glistening crystal and every shimmering stal along the way. They say that the body's urge to sleep is greater than its power to prevent it. I could so easily have just curled up in some sheltered corner and slept – and probably never woken up again. All I feel is relief as I emerge from the passage and see Fish's sleeping bag and camping mat rolled up in the corner. I'm on autopilot as I spread them out on the ground. My head is pounding. I pull off my chilly clothes and burrow, semi-conscious, into the musty-smelling bed. Fortunately I have just enough presence of mind to switch off my lamp before I fall asleep.

I can't remember if it was Ashley who first suggested we should set up a camp in the cave but certainly it was he who made it happen.

We'd been down the Quarry at least once a week for a while by then, not the whole group of us every time but at least two or three. Apart from the Devil's Cauldron, we'd explored both of the passages that led from the left hand side of the Lake Chamber. There was one, accessed by Easter Climb, just around the first rocky outcrop along from the waterfall; and another, with a more forbidding entrance, close to the Devil's Cauldron. But we'd only covered the first few hundred yards of each. We hadn't reckoned on the number of turnings, the climbs to higher levels and the pitches – some requiring ladders or ropes – to lower ones, that lay ahead. In short, we could never have imagined the enormity of the cave system we had discovered. On each trip we turned back after about four hours exploration in order to be out of the cave and home by midnight. So camping underground overnight was the next logical step.

'I've done it before often enough,' Ashley said, one night in the Red Dragon. 'I can make a list of everything we'll need. Obviously this won't be as complicated as an expedition camp, we'll only be intending to stay over one night at a time, two at the most, but just think of how much time we'll be able to spend exploring instead of wasting it trudging backwards and forwards across the hills. And it'll be fun, it'll bring the group together.'

He sounded like a management development consultant taking a team of desk-bound, cholesterol-packed executives out of the office for the first time in their working lives. I could have argued that the rest of us had known one another for twenty years or more, if we weren't 'together' by now we never would be. But he meant well. So we spent one weekend taking in the basics – a meths stove, night-lights and candles, mats to sleep on, dried and tinned food – all stuffed into tackle sacks and carried from the cars, lowered down the entrance shaft, passed from one to another through the boulder choke, pulled on ropes along the traverse and finally hauled to the dry and cosy (as far as any part of a cave can be called cosy) chamber where we planned to sleep. The other things – dry clothes, perishable food and anything we might have forgotten – we'd take with us the weekend of the camp itself.

Beth wasn't too happy about the toilet arrangements. Caves have a very fragile environment; each has its own microclimate, its own individual ecosystem. Some people reckon that even breathing disturbs the balance of gases and discolours calcite formations, but you have to draw the line somewhere. So the rule is that everything that goes into a cave must be brought out again. Food crumbs, the ash from carbide lamps, everything. Now it's OK to have a pee in fast flowing water, but that's the limit. So we took down a sealable plastic drum, together with a box of wipes and some plastic bags designed for used nappies, and positioned it a couple of minutes walk from the camp in a side passage; the Back Passage, Joe called it. There was a short section of streamway a few yards further down this same tunnel so you could kill two birds with one stone. In fact, after one of Joe's curries you could probably kill a whole flock of birds, but that's best not gone into. Beth still wasn't convinced and threatened not to come on the camp. Then she made her own arrangements. She decided that if she took a hefty dose of Imodium before the trip, she could avoid the dubious pleasure of using the facilities. And to be honest I think she had the best solution.

From my own point of view, I was quite glad of the camp because it helped keep my mind occupied. It was taking a bit longer than I'd foreseen to sort things out with Carole. A further three months' separation was what she'd requested, before she made any decisions. I was disappointed of course, but not unduly worried; I was sure she'd been talked into it by the counsellor. But on the positive side, it gave me the extra time I needed to get things together with Beth. It was obvious that her attachment to Ashley was just an infatuation. I told myself that the more she saw of him, the sooner she'd see that he was really just all talk. Their fling would come to a natural end and I'd be there for her, to tell her how he didn't deserve her, to take my rightful place in her life – and of course in her bed.

The camp took on a momentum of its own. We planned and we prepared and then the big weekend arrived. We each carried a tackle sack containing our sleeping bag, a dry change of clothes and the more perishable food. It took us longer to get there than usual, encumbered as we were, but it was worth it. It was just the hard core of us, Rick and Joe, Fish, Ashley and Beth, Taff and myself. I was glad there weren't any hangers-on from the club. It was three o'clock on a Saturday afternoon when we set out our beds and lit the stove for our first brew of tea underground.

And then we set off to explore. It was the first time we'd been able to concentrate our efforts beyond Camp David, as we'd named it, without having to worry about the time. We could enjoy ourselves without the constant worry of conserving energy and torchlight for the journey out. Rick, Joe, Fish and Ashley all had spare battery packs for their caving lamps; Taff, Beth and I had brought smaller compact head torches which would suffice for the less challenging walking and crawling sections of the cave. This was to be a one-nighter at the camp, a chance to test it out; but already we were thinking ahead, agreeing that, assuming everything went well, in a couple of weeks we'd come down on the Friday night and have almost two clear days in which to explore. We didn't do badly that afternoon though. Fish climbed up a calcited slope and found a way through into a series of upper chambers (the Mezzanine Level, he decided to call it). In one of them the stals had joined, forming an array of fine slender columns. We planned to return the next day and rig a hand line so that the less confident and agile of us (Beth and myself) could get up there too.

By eight in the evening we were all knackered, so we made our way back to the camp and set about cooking dinner. Beth arranged candles around the walls so that the chamber glowed as light as day - or so it seemed; after a whole day underground our eyes were finely tuned and accustomed to the gloom.

'Now's the time to party!' announced Rick. 'I hope you've all brought your contributions.'

It was Rick's idea that we should each bring something that you'd take to a party. We were all to keep our choice secret until tonight just to make it more fun. Beth's contribution, the only one we knew about, was to cook dinner, in this case 'one she'd made earlier' and transported to the camp in plastic containers to heat up on the stove at the appropriate time. This would be our party dinner just for tonight; on future trips we'd mostly use dried army-style meals for ease of carrying and planning. However, tonight we would dine in style and Beth had cooked a curry, although, in view of the primitive toilet facilities I wasn't so sure this was a good idea.

With only one stove and seven people to feed we heated the meal in three lots. As we had only taken a small plastic plate or bowl each this actually worked out quite well. And it felt almost civilised, as though we were eating several small courses. We were chilling down by then so we changed out of our damp muddy caving gear into dry thermals and track suits and huddled into our sleeping bags, which we had pulled close together.

'Where's the party then?' I asked.

Ashley had brought a bottle of whisky. He opened it, took a gulp and passed it to me. I took a few gulps, gasped as my throat smarted at the shock, then passed the bottle on to Fish who in turn passed it to Taff without taking even a sip. I noticed that Taff took a hefty swig though.

As the whisky began its second circuit, Rick took a packet of Rizlas from his bag, along with some tobacco and a small foil-wrapped package.

'It's a while since I've done this!' he laughed, as he joined two papers together and sprinkled a light covering of tobacco over them. Then he unwrapped the resin and held it so that a corner seared in the flame of his lighter. He sprinkled it over the tobacco and finished rolling the joint with well-practised ease.

'Not really my poison,' said Ashley, as the joint was passed to him. 'But this is a special occasion so what the hell.' He took a long drag and doubled up coughing and spluttering. 'Sorry for acting like a school kid; problem is I don't smoke.' He coughed again.

'Try this then.' Joe unwrapped his parcel and handed Ashley a slice of cake. 'I made a pudding for just this eventuality.'

'Wow, brownies!' exclaimed Beth. 'Why didn't I think of that?'

'Because if we'd all made them we'd end up stoned out of our brains,' Joe giggled.

Meanwhile the joint had come to me. I fingered it nervously, began to lift it to my lips then changed my mind and passed it towards Fish.

'God, what's happening to us all?' Rick laughed at me, despairingly. 'I know it's more than your job's worth and all

141

that but I hardly think we're going to get busted down here!'

'Force of habit,' I laughed. I changed my mind, took a couple of drags and passed it on.

The partying continued as we ate and drank our way through the various goodies: chocolates (Fish), more whisky (Taff, trust him!), and my own offering of chocolate biscuits. I didn't drink much because there were lots of people to share it but I was surprised at how the cannabis hit me; I suppose it was because I didn't get to do it very often these days. As for Ashley, who was eating it and therefore unable to gauge the effect until it was too late, he was totally out of his skull. I don't mean in a bad way but for someone who was usually Mr Control Freak he was giggling and joking like a kid.

'Marty!' Beth's voice filtered into my consciousness.

'Yeah?' I struggled to focus my brain. Beth was leaning across and shaking me by the shoulder.

'Are you on another planet or what? I said we ought to play a game or something, you didn't think to bring any cards did you?'

God she was just like she used to be twenty years ago. It was like we were in a time warp or something.

'Marty!'

'Let's do the time warp again!' I sang. 'No, sorry, I didn't think. We could sing some songs or something.'

'No.' She was emphatic, in a childish tantrummy sort of way. 'I want to play party games. Think of something, Ashley.'

Ashley, who by now was lying on his back in his sleeping bag, tried to sit up, blinked hard and lay back down again.

'You're all boring,' complained Beth.

'All right then,' said Rick, 'let's play truth or dare. I'm a brave man with nothing to hide, I challenge you all!'

Beth thought it was a brilliant idea. The first whisky bottle was empty by then so we set it down in the middle of the circle and Rick gave it first spin. We cheered as it slowed and eventually came to a stop pointing at Taff.

'Truth or dare?' Rick and Beth demanded.

'I'm too knackered to do any heroics,' he said. 'So it'll have to

142

be truth.'

Beth took charge. 'All right then. What do you regret?'

Taff thought for a while. 'Not studying for exams and going to university like you lot, I guess. And I really envied Marty when he went travelling. I'd have loved to have done that but sometimes I think I was born in a rut.'

Jesus! Someone envied me. The bottle was spinning again. This time it was Ashley's turn. He was getting a bit more together, though he was still pretty mellow and giggly. He also opted for a truth. 'Only,' he said, 'because a dare might involve standing up, and I don't think I can!'

'OK,' Taff said. 'Tell us something that changed your life.'

He didn't even stop to think, he just smiled. 'The death of my sister,' he announced.

We all went quiet. Beth looked sad. Ashley reached out and hugged her.

'Tell us about her,' suggested Rick, between gulps of whisky.

Beth glared at him. Then she took Ashley's hand. 'You don't have to,' she said.

'No, it's OK, really.' Ashley was still smiling. The rest of us, apart from Rick, were rather more subdued. We sat in silence as he continued.

'She was my twin; and you know what they say about twins – that one is more dominant, more bossy, one step ahead? Well it's true. And my sister was the dominant one; she made my life hell. Even when we were very little she was streets ahead and she was always telling me how useless I was. Sometimes I wished that she would just die and stop making my life a misery. I remember, when I was seven, I made an effigy of her out of Plasticine, and stuck pins in it. It didn't work of course. But the truth was that in those days I was a wimp; perhaps I was pathetic, like she said.'

Beth was leaning past Ashley and handing the current joint to me.

'Hey! Bring it back, I need more of that stuff!' He took a drag and started coughing again.

I rescued the joint before he dropped it. 'So how did she die?'

143

'In an accident. I was at college by then, we'd gone to opposite ends of the country; you'd think I'd have been free of her, but no. Anyway, the point is – and this is going to sound awful – in one sense I was almost glad she died, because that's when I started living. It was like I changed from this geeky nerd to a normal person overnight. So that's it really. I feel guilty for not feeling guilty…or something. But hey, the weirdest thing, and I need another drink before I can get my head round this…' Rick passed him the bottle and he took a couple of gulps. 'Yeah, the weirdest of all was that after she died it was like her spirit took me over. Suddenly I wanted to do all the wild, daring, risky things that she used to, I started getting a kick out of it. It was – and I know this sounds all New Agey – as if we were one personality and one spirit that divided in two when we were born, then, when she died, it – or they – became one again.'

He paused and took a gulp of whisky, then, in a more subdued voice, he continued. 'Although, in one way, I was glad she'd gone, in another, I'd lost the person who I was closest to, who I'd shared my life with since the moment we were conceived. And there isn't a day goes by that I don't think about her.'

We sat in silence for several minutes. Then, suddenly, Ashley sat up, cleared his throat and became Ashley again. 'We must make some decisions about what we're going to do tomorrow,' he said.

'Not till we've finished the game,' Beth insisted.

Then it was my turn and I chose a dare, because as far as I'm concerned, nothing is more frightening than the truth.

Chapter 23

Pretties - attractive cave formations.

When I awake I switch on my torch, wondering whether it's morning yet. I suppose, if I'd never spent a night underground, it would feel really freaky. But the fact that I've woken up in this very spot several times before, that I know what it feels like to open my eyes to total darkness, makes my predicament seem almost normal. It does spook me a bit that I'm on my own; but I've been caving solo on several occasions – not overnight, obviously, but on shorter trips – and I know that once I get on with the routine of eating, dressing and making my way through the cave, these activities will focus my attention.

Even when I think about the events of the past two days I'm able to rationalise it all. Now that I'm rested and thinking clearly, I can reassure myself that, although what happened yesterday was scary – OK, it was fucking awful – I'm dealing with it. I've done the hardest part; picked myself up, got to the camp and slept the night; and now I feel encouraged, having survived all that. I'm on a roll. Now all I have to do is get out.

My makeshift bed is in the supplies corner and I'm able to reach a box of candles without leaving the snugness of the sleeping bag. There are three left, together with some matches and half a dozen night-lights. Thank goodness we organised our camp well. I light one of the candles, holding it carefully at an angle while enough wax softens to secure it to the ground. Then I switch off the torch to conserve the precious battery.

Next to the candles there's half a bottle of meths for the stove, a container of water and an assortment of plastic and aluminium crockery and utensils. I rummage in the food box which is also conveniently within reach and find some tea bags and powdered milk, a couple of ready meals sealed in foil and a small pack of biscuits. Things are far better than I could have hoped and suddenly I feel more optimistic.

So. What to do first? I could do with a pee but that would mean a trip to one of the streamways. The sleeping bag is warm and cosy and I decide I can hold out for a bit. I'm remarkably hungry and realise I probably haven't had a decent meal for well over twenty-four hours. Sitting up in bed, I fill a small can with water from the plastic container and set it on the stove. When I've made my cup of tea I put one of the pre-packed meals on to boil. We removed all the wrappings to avoid carting unnecessary rubbish in and out of the cave so the contents remain a mystery until they're cooked.

Ten minutes later, my breakfast turns out to be chicken curry with rice. The smell, as I tear open the wrapper, is sensational. I feel I should pause and savour the aroma for a while. But I don't. I just grab a spoon and shovel it into my mouth with no thought of etiquette.

As I eat I wonder what the time is. I do a quick calculation. Four o'clock when I fell down the entrance shaft. An hour or two feeling sorry for myself, not to mention concussed; two and a half hours to the camp. That would put it at around nine when I fell asleep – early for me but then I'd been up most of the night before. I rarely sleep more than nine hours so I estimate it's probably around six now.

I wriggle my body around a bit, cautiously testing each part in turn and find that, now I've rested, apart from a bruise on my head that hurts if I touch it, I feel surprisingly good.

I think about Carole as I sit here eating. I think about how, if it weren't for splitting up with her, I wouldn't be stuck down here now. Our separation was the reason I got in touch with my university friends again. If I'm honest, I'd always felt a bit superior to Carole because I was a graduate and she wasn't. Not that it bothered me; in fact, I rather liked having the upper hand. Although she wasn't stupid, I'd never thought of her as the academic sort. So I remember how surprised I was when she told me she was going to give up work and go to university.

It was one night at the beginning of August and I'd gone round to the house. Beth and Ashley were all over one another

146

back then and I could feel my fantasy world slipping away. I needed reassurance that, whatever she or the counsellor said, Carole still wanted me. We were lying in bed, the sheets twisted in a post-coital jumble. I'd been worried things weren't going to get that far; it had taken longer than usual to persuade her that I was what she really wanted, but reminiscing about our wedding day and an extra bottle of wine had done the trick. Anyway, afterwards, rather than immediately getting up and making a cup of tea and tidying things up like she usually did, she started telling me about her plans for the future.

'University?' I was taken aback. 'You? Whatever for?'

She looked at me, hurt. 'You don't have a monopoly on higher education you know. I've got three 'A' Levels, I'm qualified to do the course and I've been offered a place.'

I expected her to be doing some pretend subject like sociology, but no, she was doing law with a minor in computer science. It was the obvious choice, she said, seeing as she'd been a legal secretary for years and knew the job nearly as well as the partners. And with all the new laws involving data protection and computer hacking, that side of things was a must.

'But won't it cost a lot?' I asked.

'I can get a loan. There shouldn't be any problem paying it back when I've qualified. And if by any chance there is, my parents have said they'll help out. Don't worry, I won't be asking you to contribute if that's what you're thinking.'

I'd sat there in silence, trying to picture Carole, first as a student and eventually as a solicitor or a barrister. Christ, I just couldn't get used to the idea.

Now, as I scrape the last of the curry out of the plastic bowl and lick the spoon clean, I think about what's happened to Carole since; and what's happened to me. And, just for a few minutes, I wonder, if I'd behaved better back then, whether it would all have turned out differently.

Chapter 24

Flowstone - blanket of calcite deposited on top of rock.

There was one trip into darkness that summer which didn't involve going underground.

At some unearthly hour of the morning, on Wednesday, the eleventh of August, we piled into Rick's Cavalier. It was the six of us, just like the old days; Rick, Joe, Beth, Taff, Fish and myself, and it felt almost like we were going to a festival. It was lucky it was the school holidays and Valerie had taken the girls to stay at her parents' for a couple of weeks; it meant Fish could get away without any problem. And it was especially lucky, I thought to myself rather selfishly, that Ashley was abroad on business and couldn't make it.

We knew that strictly speaking it was probably illegal for all six of us to travel in the one car, though, to be fair, everyone managed to get a seatbelt round them, even if it was shared. But we were satisfied that, even if it was illegal and uncomfortable, it was safe. And with the amount of traffic we knew would be out, it was the only way we could guarantee that we all stayed together. At six-thirty, when we arrived at Bigbury, on the south Devon coast, the car park was already filling up. When we'd stretched some life back into our limbs and queued at the beach kiosk to buy steaming tea in polystyrene cups, we shuffled down to the sand, shivering in the early morning chill and light-headed from lack of sleep.

Both Beth and Joe had brought food, enough for all of us, for breakfast and for lunch. We huddled together in the shelter of the rocks, eating bananas and honey sandwiches and wishing the clouds would go away and the sun show itself.

Eventually, we strolled across the sandy tidal causeway to Burgh Island and staked our temporary claim to a patch of land. All around us, people were gathering. All sorts of people: young, old, rich, poor. To our left, a young couple in brightly woven jumpers with beads plaited into their hair and rings through their ears, noses and eyebrows rolled what looked suspiciously like a joint. To our right sat a family group, the conservatively dressed parents sitting on matching stripy folding chairs while the children, impeccably behaved, tested out their protective cardboard-framed goggles.

At first we sat together on a blanket, the six of us, chatting and laughing. Then, as the sky began to darken and the temperature chilled, we drifted apart, pulling jumpers and fleeces over our T-shirts, taking our places, witnesses, arranging ourselves as though according to some pre-ordained plan.

Rick and Joe stood a few yards away. They were holding hands. It occurred to me that they rarely showed any public signs of affection. I suppose it just wasn't their way, they didn't need to prove anything to anyone, they may have been glad to be gay but they didn't feel the need to sing about it. They weren't shut away in any closet but neither did they publicise their relationship. The world of caving is one where men are men, why rock the boat? Today there was an air of innocence and intimacy about them, which I envied.

Taff leaned against a boulder where the rocks began to descend to the sea. He looked troubled, I thought, as he pulled on his cigarette with yellowed, work-worn fingers. None of us, with the possible exception of Fish, really knew what went on in his life or in his head. He didn't often talk about himself or his family. He'd grown up to expect days of hard graft, not to spend his time philosophising.

Perched on a rocky crag, like a figurehead on a boat, Fish was simply Fish, spiritual and solitary in some parallel universe at which the rest of us could only guess. At least he was looking a bit more cheerful than he had in the past few months.

We'd hoped for a dazzling lightshow, for the moon to drift across the brightness, but all we could see were clouds obscuring the sun. Eventually, at eleven o'clock, we stood poised in the unfamiliar half-light, waiting for it to happen.

Beth was standing directly in front of me now. Somehow,

imperceptibly, my arms had circled around her as we stared across the sea towards the western horizon.

A restlessness was growing, a feeling of foreboding in the chilly gloom, like the dark shadow of an impending storm. As the false twilight descended, seagulls screamed and circled in confusion. Then came the moment of truth. Totality. Darkness, broken only by the twinkling of camera flashes away on the mainland. Beth leaned back, her head resting on my shoulder. My arms tightened about her waist and my lips brushed briefly against her hair. Then a shining band of light appeared in the distance, at first just a thin line on the horizon, but in seconds it rushed towards us, growing in intensity as daylight returned.

Suddenly it was all over.

But it didn't have to be, not for Beth and me. I had as much right to her as Ashley did – more so, in fact, because I'd found her first. I'd bide my time until he was off guard, then I'd remind her that I was her first love and that I was the best.

Chapter 25

Scree - loose stones and rubble, often forming an unstable slope.

Eventually the need to pee persuades me out of the sleeping bag and into my caving kit. Having attended to the necessary in the nearest stretch of running water, I set off for the cave entrance, pausing only to stuff the packet of biscuits down my oversuit before I blow out the candle. I'm well fed now but I may have to wait an hour or two at the bottom of the entrance shaft for people to show up and I'll be glad of a snack. I set a leisurely pace. If my time estimate's right then it's still quite early and there's no point in hurrying just to sit around in the cold.

Now that I've thought about it more calmly, I've remembered the calls I made and the people I spoke to before I set off yesterday. And while I didn't actually state where I was going, providing the right people talk to the right other people, my whereabouts could be inferred. Now, I'm feeling so confident that I've convinced myself one of my friends will be waiting at the entrance with a ladder. They may already be walking across the mountainside. I might even catch up with them at the Snowy Mountains as they journey into the cave to meet me. I keep thinking these thoughts for the first fifteen minutes of my journey from the camp.

Then something causes my confidence to run out.

I can tell before I reach the Lake Chamber that something has changed, there is something different about the cave today. My optimism plummets and I fight the urge to panic. At first I dismiss my feeling as paranoia. Considering the less than relaxing nature of the circumstances and the fact that I slept fitfully through the night, it wouldn't be surprising if I were on edge, hearing things, seeing things that aren't really there. They say that if you're left in total darkness (which obviously I'm not, but the danger's there if my lamp gives out) anyway, they say it's only a matter of hours before you crack up completely. No wonder there were some weird scenes in those cave paintings from thousands of years ago. Hell, you wouldn't need drugs to hallucinate if you were stuck down a cave without a lamp.

But this isn't a hallucination. The cave sounds different. I'm walking along one of the dry, decorated passages that, in the past, was silent. This morning, however, there's a rushing noise. Puzzled, I walk faster and the sound gets louder.

I can taste it and smell it: moisture and cave. The noise is all around me now. No trick of the senses. I round the corner at the top of Easter Climb and the dreadful truth engulfs me. The whole chamber below is filled with noise and with water: water chasing down the fall, water rushing across the normally placid Lake and water filling the air with spray. Cautiously, I edge my way down the slope. I've never slipped on this section before but I'm taking no chances today. When I reach the bottom I try to shield my eyes with my hand but the spray reduces visibility to just a few feet and I feel like I'm staring into an impenetrable void. All around me is water, angry urgent water, thundering, crashing onto rocks; amplified a thousand times by a chorus of echoes. Sometimes the sound rises in pitch then mysteriously drops to a low boom. All the time, it's painful on my eardrums, drowning out my thoughts and shaking every cell of my body. My nerve cells go into overload. I can't see and I can't hear.

I have to back up a few steps in order to think straight. I pause for a moment and digest the scene before me, trying work out what must have happened. Perhaps there is more than that one stream on the top feeding into the cave. Perhaps others join it underground, all of them in flood, swollen with the torrential rain that must surely have fallen overnight. Above ground, with the added volume of water, rivers can burst their banks, aneurisms expanding and exploding onto the fields, like a safety valve. But down a cave, surrounded by rock, there's nowhere for the water to go.

I move cautiously forward again to the brink of the climb. Normally I would scramble a few feet down some boulders, then skirt around the edge of the Lake to the Staircase. Today that is impossible. There must have been one hell of a downpour outside because the water level has risen to within inches of the narrow ledge that clings to the wall at the start of Easter Climb. With the added turbulence it must be up at least four feet.

I edge my way out with my back pressed against the rock. If I can traverse around the wall of the chamber at this level then maybe I will be able to reach the Staircase without getting too wet. I don't know if it's possible because I've never had to do it. In the past there's always been an ample amount of dry rock pavement on a lower level. I move very slowly because I don't know what lies ahead, on the other hand I am very aware of what lies below. For a while I clamber round a sort of apse where the chamber bells out. Here there is some respite, it's like a harbour, protected from the spray. Although the level is still high, away from the full rush of the water and its associated clamour it has a comparative ambience of calm. I take the opportunity for a few moments rest before stepping back out into the confusion ahead.

When I step round the corner I will be just a few feet from the waterfall and also the Staircase. I brace myself and reach out for a secure handhold. Very carefully, I edge round. The draught generated by the waterfall makes me feel as though I am in a gale force wind, water pounds against my oversuit. Instinctively I hold tightly onto the rocky wall with both hands and prepare to make a lunge for the opening of the Staircase. But then I stop. Because there is nothing ahead except a huge bank of boulders and scree that must have been carried by the force of the streamway and come over the top, blocking the entrance to the Spiral Staircase. And in front of it falls the powerful force of a sheer wall of water. There is no way through.

'Fuckin' hell!'

In a cave no-one can hear you scream. Yeah, very funny! Shit! Things aren't looking good.

Then something changes, as I perch there, clinging on. The

153

sound changes. It's still crashing and rushing but there is something else as well, a terrible groaning and graunching, like that unseen giant is crying out in pain. I look up again to where the sound is coming from. Directly above me the top of the waterfall is moving, edging slowly but surely towards me. I gaze, perplexed, both my brain and my body failing to respond. There is a huge boulder about to fall on me and I can't seem to move. I remain paralysed – I don't know why – until the last moment, when a ton of murderous unrelenting rock is rushing towards me. Then suddenly I'm able to break free and I leap out blindly into the deadly torrent below.

Behind me, where I'd been standing a fraction of a second earlier, there is the most terrible splintering crash. But I'm already speeding away, carried by the impatient flow. Then I'm lifted, riding the crest of a tidal wave. There is so much energy in the water that I don't even feel the cold. Sometimes my head is under the water, then for a few moments I break the surface and take a gasping gulp of air. Then I'm away again. I try to lie horizontally as though I'm swimming, to save my legs from being pounded onto boulders.

Suddenly there are two high rocks ahead of me. I recognise them. They're normally clear of the water by several feet, like gateposts either side of the dark, sucking cauldron. I have to steer my way to the left now, because if I get carried down into the chasm ahead it'll be a one-way trip. I struggle to get upright and reach out with my arms; one moment I see the black hole approaching, the next I'm pulled back beneath the surface. I summon all my strength and push against unseen rocks in what I hope is the right direction. Then suddenly I can't move. I lift my head out of the water and find that I'm jammed in the crack behind the left-hand boulder. With a sigh of relief I haul myself, heavy with water, up out of the Lake to safety.

Chapter 26

Selenite - mineral which forms large transparent crystals.

Ten days after the eclipse we went on our second overnight camp down the cave. It was much easier this time because we'd left the bulk of our things – sleeping bags, stove, spare batteries for the smaller torches – down there from before.

I was glad of the distraction because things weren't working out as I'd hoped with Carole. I'd called on her three times since she told me about her plans to go to university. On the first occasion she'd been out and the house was in darkness – I'd sat outside in my car till after dark just to make sure. On the second she'd answered the door but not invited me in, saying she was getting ready to go out. And the third time I was sure she was in but was ignoring the door. I'd rung the bell several times and knocked loudly as well, and I could swear there was music playing inside. This made me really annoyed – I mean, it was my house too; I was still paying towards the mortgage. On the plus side, I figured Carole's behaviour gave me license to pursue my chances elsewhere.

As usual, the Quarryman's Rest on Sunday evening was the venue for dinner and debriefing. There was plenty to talk about after this second camp. The first time had been fun but other than sleeping the night underground we hadn't really achieved very much. To be honest, apart from Fish, we'd all been too hung over when we woke up the following morning to do anything other than stagger back to the outside world. But this time we'd been more restrained with the partying and as a result we'd explored much further than we expected, often turning back only because we didn't have the necessary equipment of ladders and ropes to go further.

'We need to make some decisions,' Ashley said.

'Him and his bloody decisions,' Taff whispered to me, as he took a gulp of beer. 'If he tells us to make any more I swear I'll

155

punch him.'

I nodded. Much as I liked Ashley, I was beginning to resent the way he'd just walked into our crowd and, more to the point, how he'd begun to take it over. Not to mention how he'd stolen Beth from right under my nose. But the fact was, regarding the cave he did have a point.

'The thing is,' Ashley continued, 'we've kept it secret so far, but what are we going to do from now on?' The way he said 'we', as if he'd been in on it from the start, grated on me; but I said nothing.

We pondered the dilemma for a bit. The only people we'd told about the camp were Damian and Sarah and Sprat. In fact we'd invited Sprat to join us this weekend but he was busy with the shop.

'No-one else apart from Damian and Sprat have been down the cave since Easter,' Rick said. 'Not many people want to hack all that way just to go to the Big Slab – and that's as far as anyone thinks it goes. The entrance is gated and padlocked; the university club holds the only keys. I suggest we keep it informal for a bit. If anyone wants to sign out a key, we tell them we think the boulder choke's unstable and warn them not to go any further. It's a white lie but justifiable, I think. And until we work out something more formal we don't talk about our explorations to anyone else.'

The rest of us nodded. Ashley looked dubious but at the end of the day he wasn't a full member of the university club like Rick and Fish were. This was a decision that wasn't his to make.

As the evening progressed, my concern regarding Ashley became less about the cave and more about his relationship with Beth. I winced as I saw her hand resting on his thigh. I thought about my resolve the day of the eclipse and decided I'd waited long enough. It was time to act.

A week and a half later, I got my opportunity. It was Thursday evening, warm and sunny, when I arrived at Beth's house.

'I thought you and Ashley might like to drive out to the country for a meal.' The words were rehearsed but I tried to make them sound casual.

Beth peered round the door, her hair dripping bubbles of shampoo onto the carpet. I could see from brief glimpses that she was wrapped in a rather scanty pink towel, revealing a long length of leg from her thigh to bare toes with varnished nails.

'Look, I'm sorry,' I continued. 'I've obviously caught you at a bad time. You can't stand here with the door open; you'll catch your death. I'll give you a ring later, or maybe tomorrow.' I turned as if to go.

'No, it's OK.' She pulled the door open. 'You'd better come in.'

I stepped into the hallway, glancing at my reflection in the full-length mirror, hoping I looked my best.

'I'll go and get dressed.' Beth set off up the stairs, taking care to pull her towel tighter around her body so that nothing showed.

'You're not that modest when you're taking off your wet suit,' I observed. It was a risky remark and I knew it. I seemed to get away with it, though.

'That's different. Go through to the kitchen and put the kettle on, would you?'

I topped up the kettle from the filter jug and took the coffee and tea bags out of the cupboard. I'd have preferred a beer or a glass of wine but I'd have to be careful if I was going to drive later. I went back out to the hall and called up the stairs.

'So what about it? Unless you and Ashley have other plans of course.'

Beth reappeared wearing tight jeans and a clingy purple T-shirt. 'I'm afraid he's been delayed. He's still in France.' She pushed past me into the kitchen and took two mugs off the hooks. 'He won't be back for another four days.'

'Oh, that's a shame,' I sympathised. I didn't let on that I already knew Ashley wouldn't be there. That I'd been round at Rick and Joe's the night before when he'd called from the Dordogne and told Rick he'd be away a few more days, having been persuaded to stay and do a trip down Berger, and could Rick please tell the Cave Research lot that he'd definitely be

157

back in time to do the China presentation at the conference.

'Well maybe next week then?' I suggested. I noticed how her hair smelled of apples. We sat down at the kitchen table and I smirked contentedly to myself. Ashley might be many things but he wasn't particularly observant, he underestimated the rest of us in many ways.

'Well I could still come out,' she said.

Inside I was cheering at how easy this was, outwardly I tried not to sound too eager. 'I suppose so, if you think Ashley wouldn't mind. There's plenty of stuff I should be doing this evening now I think about it, really another time would be better.'

'Ashley doesn't own me!' She was so abrupt she almost snapped. 'A meal in a country pub sounds lovely. What time do you want to leave?'

'Does an hour suit you? I could pick you up then if that's OK?'

'That's fine,' she said. 'But unless there's something you need to do at home you may as well stay here until we're ready to go. That reminds me, I got some photos developed of the last few trips. Now let's see, where did I put them?' She went through to the lounge and I heard her rummaging through the bookcase.

'Here they are.' She put the folder on my lap.

I browsed through the prints (which mainly starred Ashley) and managed not to make any sarcastic comments.

We had a pleasant evening out. I was on my best behaviour. I didn't produce the single malt till we got back.

'I'd thought Ashley and I might share a few drams...but seeing as he isn't here...' I waved the bottle dismissively.

'Well take it home with you.'

'I don't like drinking on my own,' I lied. 'We could save it till he's back from France.'

'Don't be silly,' Beth ushered me in, 'there's no reason why you and I should miss out. You can always get a taxi home or stay here the night.'

That was what I wanted to hear. Things were working out perfectly. We settled in the lounge to a background of Radiohead. As Thom Yorke wailed his inability to understand relationships, I felt a sense of solidarity. I filled the glasses Beth had produced and knocked the first couple back in one. I kept topping Beth's glass up before it was actually empty so she wouldn't count how many she was drinking. I told myself I wasn't trying to get her drunk or anything but I had noticed that she was becoming more controlled and careful since she'd started seeing Ashley, I simply saw it as my duty to help her loosen up and get a bit more carefree again.

Our conversation went from serious (our observations of Fish and his mental state), through silly (amusing anecdotes of our recent cave explorations), to very silly (nostalgia for our teenage years) until it finally dwindled to occasional words because we were so tired. At last Beth stood up. 'Time for bed,' she yawned.

I was sprawled out on the sofa. 'OK if I stay?'

'Of course.' She nodded and hiccupped. She was more than a little tipsy. So was I by then. 'You know where the spare room is. The bed's made up.' She stretched and sighed. 'Sorry but I'm beat. You stay up a bit longer if you want though. Just turn the lights off before you come upstairs.'

'Thanks,' I nodded, not moving.

'Well, I'll say good night then.'

'Night.'

As soon as Beth had left the room I punched the air triumphantly and mouthed a silent, 'Yes!' Everything was going better than I could have dreamed. This was my chance, not just an opportunity but practically an invitation. I'd missed one chance early in the summer and now I'd been given another. I certainly wouldn't let this one go. This was fate; it was meant to be. Any idea that I'd in any way engineered the situation was ridiculous; I fully believed that. I had a last drink, just for luck, then I stood and stretched. Wide-awake now, I took the stairs two at a time and headed into the spare bedroom, leaving the door open a couple of inches behind me. I undressed in the dark, dropping my clothes onto the floor before snuggling under the duvet. I could hear Beth in the bathroom, brushing her teeth, flushing the toilet, then padding barefoot across the landing. There was the sound of a drawer opening and shutting, her bedroom door was slightly ajar and a soft beam of light from her bedside lamp strayed across the landing. Then there was a click and the house was in darkness. This was it; it was now or never. I knew it was what we both wanted.

I waited a few moments, listening to the silence, then I crept silently out of bed, across the landing into Beth's room and slid under the duvet beside her. Last time I was in bed with her she was naked and smelled of patchouli. This time she smelled of cleansing lotion and the lingering remnants of Dune. She was lying on her side with her back to me, legs curled up like a child; she was breathing deeply and evenly. Already three-quarters asleep she hadn't even noticed I was there.

Cautiously, I put my hand on her shoulder and touched bare skin, I ran my hand down to her waist, I could feel her ribs moving as she breathed, she was wearing something that felt like silk – the way it slid through my fingers – it rippled slightly as she breathed in.

I nuzzled closer to her and began to kiss her neck, just lightly, little more than a friendly gesture really. She murmured, softly, in her sleep. I couldn't distinguish any words but I knew this was an encouragement; it couldn't have been anything else. I reached further and cupped her breast in my hand, kissed her neck, her back, her shoulder more hungrily. She began to stir. I intercepted her movement and rolled her onto her back, at the same time leaning against her, upon her, I kissed her fully and furiously on the lips. She wriggled and squirmed. God, she turned me on when she moved like that. I reached between her thighs. I was gone, lost, on a one-way trip.

'Bastard!'

My cheek stung hot and cold where she had hit me. Suddenly there was brightness; harsh, naked light illuminating

160

the room. I blinked and rubbed my eyes. Beth stood by the door, her hand on the light switch. In that second I was more scared of her than I've ever been scared of anyone in my life. More than the Valkyrie even – and that's saying something.

'Get out.' Her voice was slow and controlled, in some strange way it was more frightening than if she had shouted in anger. 'How dare you think you can take advantage.'

'Get out!' she repeated, a little louder this time. 'I don't know what you're playing at, Marty; maybe you just can't handle your drink. But to creep up on me like that, when you know I'm with Ashley, when I'm asleep for God's sake. Now just go.'

Slowly, self-consciously, I pulled back the duvet and stood there, naked and inadequate in front of her. I was shaking and numb, cold and afraid.

I've been in the water too long. Cold, ice-melt, Welsh mountain water. And I'm cold, too cold. Mind you, I'm not shivering any more. But they say that's a bad sign, it means you're getting hypothermia. What comes next? Confusion? Unconsciousness? Coma? I'm not giving in now, damn it! I've come too far for that. I'm going to take control, focus my mind and get myself back to safety. Once I'm back at the camp I'll be OK.

My hands are numb. I wedge them under my armpits to try and warm them and stumble along, arms crossed, as though I'm in a strait jacket. I might as well be. Shit, man, pull yourself together! You've got to keep the right mental attitude. Now watch where you're going, you can't afford to take a wrong turning and get lost again. I'm in a passage, dark and shadowy as velvet. Yet here and there it's encrusted with jewels shining in the night. I begin to sing in a weak and wavery voice. 'Star light, star bright.' My voice is crap. Beth always used to sing it really well – hang on though – star bright, Starbright Passage, that's where I am now. They're selenite crystals embedded in the limestone. I've seen them in another cave not far away. What's it called now? Aggy something. Agatha? No, stupid. Think. Focus your brain. Aggy, Aggy.

Agen Allwedd. The keyhole.

I went there years ago with Rick and Joe. Joe said the crystals shone like LEDs. Or was that Glastonbury? Hell, what's the difference? We were tripping on both occasions.

Glastonbury, that was something else. I remember lying on my back and looking at the stars.

'Lucy in the sky,' I suggested.

'LEDs,' Joe insisted.

We'd wandered earlier, around the stalls, where sunburnt traders wearing Moroccan scarves and Indian cheesecloth shirts sold beaded shoulder bags and prickly Alpaca jumpers. We bought pitta bread, salad and hummus – mainly because it didn't contain brown rice. God, I'd never seen so many drugs! There were a thousand different ways to inhale your dope, carved pipes of varying shapes and sizes, and glass bongs, blown in bright colours, that puffed clouds of pungent smoke. It was too late for the summer of love and most of the people were hardly beautiful – unless you'd really smoked a lot. Rick scored some acid. Joe and I stood and watched as he bartered with a dark, wrinkled man who looked at least fifty. He said he was only thirty-five. I looked at him suspiciously and hoped the stuff was clean. Notes changed hands and we went to find an empty patch of grass.

'Light emitting diodes.' Joe was emphatic.

Music washed over us in powerful waves. I thought we would drown. Oh Lord! Here comes the flood! Just another brick in the wall and we would build a new Jerusalem. All around, pot-headed pixies brewed evil-smelling mushrooms in their floating teapots. But we were in the modern age. We were Electrick Gypsies.

Hell, man! Get over it! You're going to make it! I'm shivering again, a good sign but still not pleasant, I pass all the passages we explored during the past year, The 'B' Arc, Millennium Doom. Doomed, that's what I am. I think the words in Fraser's Scottish accent. I'm back in 'Dad's Army' again.

Hey! I'm here. I'm back at the camp. It's the real thing, not just a dream, not just a can of coke. Coke? Jesus, don't let's go there. It's the only reason I'm in this mess. But here's the camp.

Thank you God. I promise to go to church when I get out of here.

Chapter 27

Resurgence - the place where a watercourse exits a cave into the open air.

With September came the weekend of the British Cave Research Association's annual conference. I'd been to a couple of these dos in the past, years ago, with Rick and Joe and Fish. In those days we couldn't afford to pay the rip-off conference rates charged by the university where it was held, so we'd slept outside in the car park, Rick and Joe in their car, and me and Fish in a tent, on the few square yards of grass between the tarmac and the side of the building. This year, being comparatively rich and grown-up, we'd booked rooms in the unnaturally pristine university accommodation and driven up on the Friday night.

I doubt I'd have bothered on my own but everyone else was going – apart from Taff, who didn't want to miss his weekend with the kids – so I said I'd go along too. And of course we were supposed to be supporting Ashley, who was giving a presentation.

At nine o'clock on the first evening, when Ashley was double-checking his notes ready for the following day, and Rick, Joe and Fish were in an impromptu surveying workshop, I found myself in the bar with Beth. It was the first time I'd been alone with her since our disastrous encounter.

'Look.' She stared into my eyes, like a schoolteacher about to administer six strokes of the cane. 'I'm going to write off what happened.'

I breathed a sigh of relief.

'I'm not saying I forgive you,' she went on hurriedly. 'You behaved despicably. But I'm putting it down to too much alcohol and the fact that you're still vulnerable and confused after splitting up with your wife.'

I mumbled an incoherent apology.

164

'I know what it feels like,' she went on, 'when you think your future's planned out, you think someone loves you, then you suddenly find…' She took a deep breath and pulled herself up straight to her full five feet and three inches. 'Well anyway, I understand, that's what I'm trying to say. I feel hurt and insulted, and right now I'm not sure I like you very much, but I do understand. Just don't dare tell anyone what happened,' she finished. With that she strode off in the direction of the ladies and left me standing, alone and suitably reprimanded, at the bar.

I ordered a beer, downed it in one, then bought a second, scowling into the glass as I drank. I hadn't been in the best of moods to start with. I'd received a letter, earlier in the week, from Carole's counsellor; I'd never thought of her as my counsellor, even though the two of us had often been to see her together. It was obvious that she took Carole's side right from the start. Well she would do wouldn't she? They were both women after all. And she clearly disliked men. Anyway, the letter said that I was going against our agreement by visiting Carole or even contacting her. It said that I must only get in touch if there was urgent business to discuss and that I must not call at the house without prior agreement, certainly I wasn't to turn up unannounced. If I did, then apparently a court order would be sought on grounds of harassment.

The nerve for God's sake! I knew that wasn't what Carole wanted. How dare this woman, this stranger, interfere! She was probably a lesbian feminist with a testosterone implant. She probably wanted Carole for herself.

I was angry but there was nothing I could do except stay out of the way for a while. On the bright side, absence was sure to make the heart grow fonder. If that was what Carole needed to realise how much she still wanted me then so be it.

I lit a cigarette and took a long satisfying first drag.

Back at the camp, back in the warmth of Fish's sleeping bag, as my mind gradually returns to a normal state of consciousness, I try to make sense of what has happened.

The journey back from the Cauldron had terrified me. I'd been aware enough to know that I wasn't thinking clearly; a combination of terror at being swept down the Lake, the onset of hypothermia from being so cold and wet, and sheer panic in the knowledge that either of these things could kill me. It would have been so easy to give up the struggle, to curl up in some corner along the way, basking in hallucinatory heat, and fall into an ice-cold terminal sleep.

But I hadn't. I'd forced myself to put one foot in front of the other until I reached Fish's sleeping bag, then to remove all my clothes and burrow into it. In the space of twenty-four hours, this item had been promoted from smelly health hazard to life-saving luxury.

Even now, the cold urges me to sleep. But I know I'm not safe yet. I still feel slightly spaced out, like I can't quite trust my senses or what they're telling me. Still in something of daze I light the stove and brew a mug of tea. Then I sip it, feeling the warmth radiate through me, and wait for my mind and body to recover.

It's amusing to think that back at university we used to pay money and risk prosecution to feel this way.

I guess it started with us sharing a couple of joints, but it was our first time at Glastonbury that really opened our eyes. After that, we wanted to explore further, just like we explored caves, stepping into the unknown. We sampled every mind-expanding, consciousness-altering, creativity-enhancing substance we could get our hands on. Cannabis, LSD and magic mushrooms were our idea of recreation. We drew the line at horse and coke, though, because we wanted to stay alive, and also we didn't have much money. Even speed we were a bit careful with. By our second year, Rick had already set his sights on a career as an academic and he reckoned there was only so much amphetamine sulphate he could take before his brain cells would fail to appreciate the concepts of quantum physics. So he saved it for late night parties and visits to his granny.

In the second year, when we'd tried everything the city clubs and the university black market had to offer, we started making our own. Or rather, I did, because I was the one studying chemistry.

I hadn't had any illegal intentions when I signed up for my course. I was at sixth-form college when I put in my university application and still living at home. Life there was so restrictive, what with my parents' old-fashioned conservative principles and their insistence that I set a good example for my younger sister, that to me, the prospect of being able to have a drink or a cigarette without having to sneak off in private, held enough excitement to keep me going for the next three years.

I don't remember who first suggested it. I think I was just messing around. It wasn't like I set out to synthesise an amazing new psychedelic substance – well certainly not with a view to using it. But we'd all read newspaper articles about people producing acid and stuff. I just thought I'd experiment to see how easily it could be done. In those days you had to work it out for yourself, it was a personal challenge, just like my DIY chemistry experiments in the garden shed when I was a kid. Today you can probably find step-by-step instructions on the internet. Back then it was guesswork. In the evenings, when the practicals had finished and the lab technicians had left for home, I'd work on my secret 'project'.

Generally it wouldn't have been that easy, not for under-grads anyway, but my course was project based, and from the second year on, having agreed a line of research with my tutor, there was nothing to stop me. Seriously hazardous or expensive chemicals I had to sign for and work under the supervision of a technician, but with anything else I was free to help myself and do my own thing, unhindered by watchful eyes.

Soon I'd set up a most unprofessional-looking array of flasks bubbling over Bunsen burners, and precipitates waiting innocuously in Petrie dishes. The result was somewhere between acid and speed, a sort of prototype of ecstasy, soaked in ground-up chalk, compacted and cut into tiny squares and coloured with food dye. 'Smartees', we called them – rather than 'Marty's', which could have landed me in trouble if word ever got out. They weren't to sell or anything, just a bit of recreation for Fish, Joe, Rick and myself to indulge in at home.

We wouldn't let Beth take any, though, even when she turned eighteen and regularly got legally drunk, because we didn't know if there were any side-effects, particularly long-term ones. The only effect that was noticeable at the time, besides the obligatory euphoria, was that they made you incredibly randy. This was bad news for me as I didn't think it fair to invite Beth round when I was out of my head and she wasn't. But it was very good news for Joe and Rick. In fact, I believe it was their first experience of Smartees which led to their first experience of each other, as it were. After being best mates for nearly two years, they finally realised – or at least admitted – that they were gay and madly in love.

Chapter 28

Fluorescein - dye tracing chemical used by cavers to determine the course of water.

It was a Sunday evening in October, and yet again we sat by the inglenook in the Quarryman's Rest, waiting hungrily for our plates of chicken curry and gammon and eggs. Only on this occasion we hadn't actually been underground; instead we'd spent the day dye testing the streamway, searching the surrounding hillside for the place – or places – where the water that ran through the cave re-emerged on the surface. We hoped that, where the water came out, we could go in, finding another entrance and hopefully a through trip. The operation had not been entirely productive.

We'd started the exercise in two groups. Rick, Joe and myself had parked in the usual place by the roadside and walked up the familiar track to the cave entrance. It was strange but far more comfortable to be walking that route in jeans and fleece jackets instead of the usual caving suits, and walking boots rather than Wellingtons or rubber lace-ups, certainly it was refreshing not to be encumbered with ladders and ropes and all the other clutter of caving. Not far from the padlocked grille that covered the shaft, a lively stream disappeared into the ground, the same watercourse that we swung above on the roped traverse down in the cave, though quieter out in the open with weeds and moss to soften its speed and no rocky enclosure to amplify its energy. There we poured fluorescein into the water, pausing to watch the glowing sunset-coloured liquid flow underground. Then, guided by Rick's compass and Ordnance survey map, we walked south, following the contour of the hillside. Soon we would strike off downhill and walk across the slopes to the south-east.

Fish, Ashley and Beth, meanwhile, had driven round to the west of the hills, some fifteen miles away along steep winding lanes, although only three or four as the crow flies. From there they would walk across the south-west reaches. The plan was for us to meet at a point due south of the cave entrance, having, hopefully, identified the river's resurgence. Of course, if it took some convoluted route underground and headed north then we were scuppered, but as the terrain to the south was mostly low whilst the land remained high to the north for some miles, this possibility was unlikely.

After half an hour's walking we were still on the upper level. There was no path and the going was slower than we'd anticipated, rugged underfoot with dips and hollows that we had to scramble round. At last we turned left and began to descend down a sheep track. As we dropped lower there were additional obstacles of brambles and gorse grasping at our legs as we trod briskly and purposefully across the moist ground.

We were on the lookout for the crystal clear streams that tumbled down towards the river, far below in the valley. If we came across one then we would attempt to trace it back, against the current, to its source bubbling up from the ground. We walked apart now, although still within shouting distance of one another, to cover more ground. I slowed my pace, focusing my attention on where I placed my feet, because a sprained or broken ankle would be a real nuisance for months to come. I was concentrating so hard that I felt like I was out there alone, just me and nature. As I walked, the smell of the withering bracken and the cold light of the autumn sun reminded me of a similar occasion at the beginning of our second year at university, though the search then was for something quite different.

I can remember it clearly. It was a misty day and the air hung with clingy autumnal dampness, hovering, chilling and giving the world a ghostly sheen. Every object, every person was surrounded by a hazy aura of lingering dew. Later it would shine in car headlights against the darkness of the night and envelop the world in fog. Fish looked wraith-like, skinny beneath his flimsy shirt, oblivious to the coldness of the air. The frayed bottoms of his jeans were already dark and wet from the grass. It was early November and we were collecting mushrooms (the magic variety) in readiness for Bonfire night. We thought their psychedelic effect might enhance the city firework display, scheduled to light up the sky over the seafront on November the fifth. The first time I'd tried mushrooms I was nearly sick. Steeped in boiling water, they made the most evil brew I had ever smelt in a teapot. But we did some experimenting and soon discovered that, when boiled in a cheap medium sweet sherry, they were really quite palatable.

So we scuffed our feet through the grass, shivering as a chilly breeze found its way through insufficient clothes.

Rick quickly grew impatient. 'This is a waste of time.' He wandered about haphazardly, kicking at the grass with his feet. 'Can't we just go caving instead and maybe score some acid down the union?'

Joe, meanwhile, was on his hands and knees, painstakingly searching the ground inch by inch.

Fish shook his head in dismay. 'You've g-got it all wr-wrong,' he protested. 'G-go with nature, you know? Free up your head and let the m-mushrooms find you. That's what Casteneda said the American Indians did when they were gathering peyote. Empty your m-mind, walk along and they'll be there in your path.'

Back on the seemingly futile hunt for the resurgence, I decided anything was worth a go. I tried emptying my mind and wishing for the elusive stream to gush across my path.

'Hey!' It was Joe, ahead and upslope of me, his voice dwindling in the breeze. I turned and climbed up the hillside and Rick backtracked, we both reached the place where Joe was waiting. At his feet, water sprung from between a mound of rocks, it was clear, noisy and moved with intent, hurrying away down the hill and disappearing back into the ground a few hundred yards on.

Rick studied the map. 'This doesn't seem to be marked. There's another one that is, though, a mile or so further on.'

171

'Well, marked or not, this is coming out of the mountain.' Joe stood his ground.

'Any sign of the dye?' I asked.

Joe shrugged. 'Nothing yet. But, you know, how long does it take? Do we sit here and wait for the next couple of hours or do we assume we've missed it?'

Neither Rick nor I knew the answer. Surprisingly, perhaps, this dye testing lark was something none of us, not even the supremely experienced Ashley, had tried before.

'We ought to get on and find this other stream on the map,' Rick insisted. 'Perhaps one of you should wait here for an hour or so then catch me up.'

There were three of us, but we had only one map and one compass between us. In the end we decided that Rick would go ahead on his own, on the basis that if Joe or I were going to get lost we'd be better off being lost together. So, while Rick disappeared into the distance, we sat up there by the spring, peering at the water every few moments, waiting hopefully for confirmation that the stream that surfaced there was the same one that travelled through the cave.

After an hour or more waiting on the exposed hillside, we were cold, tired and hungry. Eventually we had a call from Rick on his mobile. He hadn't found the stream he'd been looking for – it was almost certainly the one for which Joe had traced the source. We must have somehow lost our bearings. The others, meanwhile, had found a small watercourse with definite traces of the dye in it. Rick had met up with them and, having apparently fulfilled the purpose of the day, they were heading back to their car. Rick would retrace his steps and join us, then we'd decide on the most direct route back to the road.

By the time we arrived at Rick's car, we'd had enough. It had started raining soon after Rick had called and by the time he'd got back to us and we'd made our way back to the road (with several detours and wrong turnings along the way) our legs were soaked through. Suffering the discomfort of being cold and wet down a cave was one thing but above ground there was no exhilaration to offset it.

172

'What I can't understand,' mused Ashley. 'Is why so little trace came through. Are you sure you put it directly in the water, it didn't soak away into the soil?'

As we sat in the Quarryman's Rest, discussing the day, hindsight was proving to be, if not exact, then certainly a controversial science.

'We're not idiots,' I retaliated.

'Of course not, but anyone inexperienced can make a mistake.'

Ashley sat at the end of the table in a wooden armchair with an upholstered seat, while the rest of us occupied stools that were inferior by comparison. He seemed to have taken over as unofficial chairman, something he did too frequently these days and which was beginning to annoy me. Beth, meanwhile, sat at his side like some faithful servant, her hand resting on his knee.

'Let's face it,' I tried again, 'we cocked it up. Maybe we got there too early, or too late, I don't know, maybe some of the water goes another way, let's face it, it could travel miles underground.'

The others were silent – even Rick, unusually for him – I looked round at each of them in turn, failing to get any response.

'Well should we try it again?' I tried hard to control my exasperation.

Ashley was insistent. 'In my opinion it would be a waste of time. We've got our answer, albeit a faint one.'

'You don't think we should do a wider search of the hillside, check for any other watercourses? I mean...really we've done it the wrong way round. We should have checked out the stuff above ground first and had people waiting beside any major streams before we put the dye in. We should have a word with Sprat – I'm sure he knows more about it than all of us put together – and get his advice for next time.'

It was as though I was invisible or my voice had become silent or something.

'I think I'd have spotted anything there was to see by now.'

Ashley gave me a withering look. 'No. My vote is we spend a couple of days outside, have a dig round the area of the resurgence of the stream I found today. Then resume the exploration underground.'

'What do the rest of you think?' I grasped round for support.

Fish lifted up his hands and shrugged.

I turned to Rick and Joe who had been discussing something about motorbikes. 'Well?'

'Not really our area of expertise,' answered Rick. 'But personally I'm not really into all this messing about outside, I want to get underground again. Joe?'

'Well I think Marty's got a point.'

I looked at Beth. 'Looks like the casting vote's with you.' I stared at her, daring her.

She stared straight back at me. 'I think we should do whatever Ashley says.' Then she took his hand, which was resting on the table, squeezed it and smiled at him.

The food arrived then and the subject was closed.

Chapter 29

Phreatic tube - underground passage, often narrow and circular in cross section, hollowed out by water.

For what seems like hours, I huddle in this dank, smelly sleeping bag, dreading the moment when I will have to climb out of it and into my sodden caving things. These are rendered even less appealing because, in addition to being cold and wet, they're also coated with the gritty remains of the pack of biscuits (which failed to survive the ducking in the Lake). So I just lie here in the darkness. I'm at an all time low.

I go over the options, just like I did at the bottom of the entrance shaft yesterday afternoon. I figure I need to plan carefully what I'm going to do, while I'm relatively warm and dry. I need to conserve my energy, just like the light and the food, for when I need it most. Then, when I've decided on a course of action, I need to go for it.

This time there's even less in my favour. Rescue, in the short term, would be near impossible. I've seen for myself that the Spiral Staircase is impassable, and rigging a pitch down the waterfall would be dangerous to say the least – that's assuming the end of the streamway isn't blocked with boulders. Even when the water eases off, as it undoubtedly will sooner or later, there's no way I could get back to the entrance without someone else clearing the way from the upper level.

If I'd told someone for definite where I was going, if there was an official rescue call-out, then eventually, when the torrent subsides, they'd drop a line down to the Lake, or slowly and methodically clear the Staircase, just like Sprat and I had last summer. But there are too many 'ifs' in my reasoning and very little certainty, apart from the fact that I will shortly run out of light and food. So I sit in total darkness, conserving what resources I have.

Eventually I come up with a plan.

There's a possible way out of here besides the entrance shaft. We've been looking for it for ages, partly because the journey through the cave would become a through trip (there's something more satisfying about that rather than retracing your steps back the way you've come) and also because the current entrance is such a pain to get to. If there was one you could walk in, without a long pitch or a trek from the nearest road, then the cave would be much more popular. My current reason to find another entrance is rather more pressing.

OK, it's a long shot, especially so because I haven't been down here for a couple of weeks. I wasn't on the trips where people thought they were on the verge of breaking through. But here's the choice: either I have a go at finding the way through, or I sit it out at the camp in the hope of being rescued, growing colder and weaker all the while. There's no contest really. I reach for my fleece suit.

By the time I'm kitted up and ready to leave I've talked myself into a much more optimistic frame of mind. I have two chances. Word WILL get out that I'm missing. And people WILL come to rescue me. It's just going to take a bit longer than I envisaged. In the meantime I need to keep warm and the best way of doing that is to keep moving. If I find my way out in the process then so much the better. This is how I rationalise it to myself as I set off from the camp.

This time I take the opposite direction from before. I go the way that leads deeper into the cave. The first part of the journey is straightforward. I've done it many times. I take the well-trodden route, ignoring the passages that lead eventually to dead ends or pitches, and arrive in the comparatively new territory we've been exploring since Christmas. Here I wriggle down a long low corridor that Joe found not long ago. But at the end there are too many choices, I've not been this far before, I don't even know if I'm in the right place. I'm guessing. I take the passage that has what look to be scuff marks at the entrance. It starts off quite promising but soon it narrows and I'm bending double, then crawling. There's only one way on so I take it. I'm in a phreatic tube, a low rounded passage, sculpted

176

smooth by the passage of water. Water under pressure, below the water table, many years ago. Now it is left almost dry, since the stream has found another course. Flat on my stomach, arms outstretched before me, I pull myself laboriously along the tight and slippery tunnel. Is birth like this, I wonder?

It was five years ago that Carole got pregnant. Well, that's to say we didn't know she was, she hadn't done a test or anything, it wasn't as if we were trying. Carole had been on the pill since before we were married and Christ knows I certainly didn't want the responsibility of kids. Not then, anyway. The first thing we knew that something was wrong was when she got these stomach pains. It was late one evening and we'd been watching a thriller on television, it was almost eleven when it finished and we were pottering about, locking the doors, clearing empty glasses and crisp packets away, the sort of things you do before you go to bed.

Suddenly, as she was climbing the stairs, Carole doubled up, clutching her stomach. At first I thought she was playing a joke, acting one of the scenes from the film. I laughed and asked whether it was strychnine or arsenic this time. But she cried out in pain and sat down on the stair, her face flushed, her whole body shaking. I panicked; it all seemed to be happening so quickly. I called an ambulance, thinking that it might be appendicitis. There followed a frightening flurry of activity, sirens and flashing lights, stretchers and trolleys, oxygen masks and drips. The doctor in A and E said she'd have to go straight into theatre. He came out to speak to me when the operation was over.

'She's pregnant?' I gasped in disbelief.

'She was,' corrected the doctor. 'Not any more.'

'Well thank goodness that's all that was wrong.' I breathed a sigh of relief.

'I don't think you quite appreciate what I'm saying, Mr Wight. Your wife had an ectopic pregnancy, one growing in the fallopian tube. We had to remove the foetus along with the tube and the ovary as well I'm afraid. She could have died otherwise.'

An hour or two previously, I thought Carole had a bad dose of gut rot. Since then, she'd been pregnant, had surgery and was no longer expecting. It was hard to take it all in. I paused a moment and considered what really mattered. 'But she'll be all right now?' I demanded, anxiously.

The doctor nodded, happily. 'She'll make a full recovery.' Then he looked downwards, away from my gaze. There was something he didn't want to tell me. For a moment I was quite worried. Then he went on. 'This may affect her ability to conceive in the future. I think you should know that.'

I let out my breath, relieved. So what was the problem? She wouldn't have to bother to take the pill any more. It wasn't like either of us wanted children. Once she'd recovered from the surgery, everything would return to normal. They let me in to see her, just for a few minutes but she was drowsy from the anaesthetic and wasn't making much sense. It was well after midnight by then and they seemed to want to get rid of me. I was worried about Carole of course but they'd given her something to make her sleep and there wasn't anything I could actually do. So I got a taxi back home and watched the late film to take my mind off things.

As I squeeze my way further along the tube I hope to God the way ahead won't be blocked. There's no room to turn round. I continue to worm my way forward.

Then I hear it: the sound of footsteps. Someone else is here. Someone else is in the cave with me. And they're pretty close, judging by the sound. The alarm has been raised and a search party sent out. I don't know how it happened. I suppose the water level must have dropped and allowed them to descend down to the Lake. Any moment now I'll be rescued!

'Hey! Hello!' I shout with all my strength, then pause, lying quite still, straining my ears for the response.

'Hello!' My own voice echoes back to me. When it has hushed to a whisper I listen again. The footsteps are still there, rhythmically plodding their way, the hollow notes bouncing and resounding all about me. I try to gauge which direction they're coming from, but that isn't always easy in a cave. I shout first up the tunnel, the way I've been heading, then twist onto my side and turn my head uncomfortably in an effort to call back the way I've come.

Still there is no response. They can't hear me. What if they assume I've already got out? What if they return to the outside world and report that I'm not here? I should have written something in the logbook before I left the camp. I'm beginning to panic now. In one last desperate attempt to be heard I bang the roof above me, kicking it with my feet and thumping with my fists until my knuckles are bruised and sore. Then I flop flat onto my stomach, exhausted, my breath rasping with effort and frustration.

As my panting subsides I hear the footsteps once more, faster now, out of reach, tormenting me. Unceasingly they run, somewhere deep in the cave. Thank God! They must have heard me and even now they're trying to find a way through to where I'm lying. I close my eyes and feel the vibration of the boots as they run, all around, steadily thumping, pulsing up and down the passage. Just like my heart is steadily beating; just like my blood is pulsing through my body.

And then I realise the truth. There is no other person, no rescuer. The 'footsteps' that echo around me are nothing more than the desperate beating of my own heart.

In very low spirits, I crawl as far as I can down the tunnel, but it narrows, closing in gradually until eventually there is no way I can get through. Reluctantly I begin the slow and clumsy process of backing my way out.

Chapter 30

Straw - type of stalactite where the water feeds down the inside of a calcite tube, producing a long thin cylindrical formation.

I arranged to meet Carole in town on a Saturday afternoon. We'd decided that a coffee bar would be suitably neutral territory. I made the effort to be early. She always used to complain that I turned up late for everything. So I arrived ten minutes early, but even so Carole was already there.

I hadn't seen her for a couple of months. Not since that stupid letter from the counsellor, telling me to stay out of the way unless I'd agreed a visit. After the initial anger, I'd convinced myself it was my own decision to give Carole some space; I saw it as a bit of game playing to let her think she was in control, part of a long-term plan to get us back together.

That day I was confident that things were going my way. It was the first time Carole had suggested a meeting, a sure sign, I felt, that she was missing me. I was feeling very positive about the whole situation; it was as though I had now taken control of the game, that its outcome would be my choice, on my terms. I could give her a taste of her own medicine now, while I considered what I wanted, for a change. There was no need for me to move back into the house immediately, I could enjoy my freedom and consider my options. But I didn't need to worry about all that now. In the short term I had no doubt that the meeting that started in the coffee bar would soon adjourn back to the house, with or without a pub or classier restaurant on the way. By mid evening we'd be snuggled up together, perhaps in the cushioned comfort of the lounge, perhaps already in bed – it had been a while, after all, more than three months. Carole would ask me to move back in, she'd probably do that early on. But I wouldn't give her an answer straight away; I'd make her wait. In anticipation of the evening ahead I'd put a decent bottle of wine in the car.

At first I didn't notice Carole sitting in a window seat. I walked straight past her, looking for someone else. It was uncanny. I didn't realise a person could change so much in so short a time. Her mousy hair, now with shining highlights of burgundy, bounced in waves about her shoulders. I don't think I could ever remember seeing it in anything but the short and rather severe style in which she wore it when we first met. From her ears swung long brightly coloured pendants that reminded me of the stained glass in church windows; a denim jacket partly covered the vivid red jumper while, at the end of the tight fitting jeans, she wore flat plimsolls. Most of all, though, she looked so young. Her skin, previously drawn into fraught lines of worry, was now relaxed, giving her face a radiant softness, a kind of ethereal glow.

I don't know what I'd expected. It was the longest I'd gone without seeing her since we'd split up, or since we met, come to that. The old Carole, the one I'd married, didn't fit into this role, this picture. I'd liked her back then, but I realised in those first few seconds that I could grow to love this new person – really love her – in a way that I hadn't done before.

How well she'd fit in with Rick and Joe and the others, I thought to myself; it would be great introducing her to them when we were officially back together. It only occurred to me then, that Carole had never actually met any of my university friends. It wasn't that I'd purposely kept them apart. It had just worked out that way. When we first got together I hadn't been caving for more than a year and consequently I wasn't seeing so much of the lads. At a time when I needed a different direction in life, Carole offered a new, and therefore enticing, world. We weren't hermits, far from it, we socialised mainly with work colleagues, both hers and mine. Anyway, taking Carole, with her neatly pressed clothes and carefully applied make-up, into the spit and sawdust of the Red Dragon – much less down a cave – just wouldn't have crossed my mind. She had no brothers and sisters; she was the long-yearned-for, late-born child of what were then considered elderly parents. When we got married it was a quiet family affair in the village where her parents had retired to, there wouldn't have been room for an extended group of friends even if I'd wanted to invite them.

I kissed her on the cheek. I hadn't planned to; it was just spontaneous.

'You look really well, student life must be agreeing with you.'

'I'm certainly enjoying it. But don't you usually go out with your mates on Saturdays? I feel guilty dragging you away.'

She was so unselfish; it made me feel mean by comparison. The fact was, all the times I'd called round and shared her bed back in the summer, I'd never really told her anything about what I was doing other than the fact I was spending my spare time with old friends. I hadn't even mentioned that we went caving. Obviously I wouldn't have told her about Beth and my hopes in that direction, but mostly it was because keeping my life secret had made me feel I had some power over her. All that would change when I moved back in; I might even start telling her about it all when we were in bed later.

'I'm sure the break will do me good.' I pointed at her empty cup. 'I'll get you another tea, and something to eat.'

As I took off my jacket and settled myself for a nice cosy afternoon with Carole, I can honestly say there was nowhere else I'd rather be. The truth was, I was getting a bit pissed off with trips down Quarry Cave. Going underground these days generally involved measuring devices and compasses and long hours spent mapping the intricate network of pitches and passages onto a survey. And every time we came across so much as a puddle we had to go through the tedious and lengthy process of lugging diving gear down so that Ashley could stick his head in it and pronounce it a non-goer. What had started as exciting cave exploration was rapidly becoming more like a business venture. Anyway, as it turned out we were going somewhere different the following day so I wasn't missing out.

I looked at the menu. 'Let's have the most fattening, extravagant and expensive thing they've got,' I said.

It was so easy to talk. I don't know that we ever really did

182

before; we just went to work, came home and looked after the house and garden. Suddenly we had things in common. If only she'd gone to University ten, twenty years ago. We seemed only just to have begun our conversation when it was five o'clock and the cafe was closing.

'We could go and see a film,' I suggested.

Carole seemed reluctant. 'I have an assignment to do. Oh dear, we've spent the whole afternoon together and haven't discussed anything.'

'We've talked about all sorts of things, what else did you have in mind?'

She looked suddenly worried. For the first time that afternoon she seemed tense and uncomfortable.

'I want you to know,' she said, 'that what's happened wasn't planned. And I want you to try and be happy for me.'

I waited.

'I've just found out I'm pregnant.'

I stared, open-mouthed, in disbelief.

'I thought it couldn't happen,' she went on, 'after all, we'd been trying for five years.'

We'd been what? I wasn't aware we'd been trying anything, certainly not to have children. I mean – we didn't want them. Well I didn't, anyway. I wasn't ready. I'd always assumed Carole felt the same.

'Please don't be angry.' She sounded like she was about to burst into tears.

'I'm not angry. It's just taking a while to sink in.' I thought she couldn't have children, we both did, so it was kind of something that was never on the cards – a relief really, as far as I was concerned. I'd just never thought about it. Six months ago I wouldn't have been pleased by this news at all, but now, with this new Carole, I could see everything falling into place.

'I think it's marvellous news,' I said at last. 'It's just a shock, that's all, but I'll get used to it. I'll move back in straight away, if that's all right, and we'll try counselling again if you think it will help, I'll do anything you say. I'll clean up my act and I promise I'll make more effort this time. I'm really looking forward to being a father.'

'Marty!'

'What is it? I promise I won't let you down.'

She looked upset. 'Marty, you're not going to be a father.'

I was stunned again. 'What do you mean? If you want to stay on your own a bit longer, well I won't like it but I'll do whatever it takes and I'll pay you maintenance of course.'

'You're not listening to me. I feel awful now, but you said you didn't want children anyway. It isn't your baby, Marty. I've been seeing someone else, someone I met at the university.' She looked uncomfortable. 'I think that the quickest and easiest thing would be for you to divorce me.'

I was shocked into silence for several minutes. Then the words came out in an onslaught, like I just couldn't help myself.

'Pregnant! And it isn't mine! Well who the hell's is it then? We're married for Christ's sake!'

Carole was calm. 'We're separated Marty – and have been for almost a year. Just because we've had a couple of lapses…well they weren't my idea. Anyway, I've been trying to get you to talk for nearly two months now and you haven't even bothered to return my calls. It's always on your terms isn't it? Whenever you've wanted to see me you've pestered and harassed me until I gave in. But when I wanted to talk to you it was different.'

I knew she was right but I was reluctant to admit it, as though acknowledging my behaviour out loud made it real. 'Would it have made any difference?'

'These last few months? No. It was too late for us by then.'

I squirmed in my seat like a small child with parasitic worms. My day out was becoming a nightmare.

'So you're seeing someone?'

'Well, obviously. This isn't an immaculate conception and I don't do one night stands.'

I stared at her. Devastated. She was right; I hadn't bothered about her for ages. I'd been preoccupied with Beth, but naturally I wasn't going to mention that.

Suddenly she softened. She reached across the table and took my hand. 'You're trembling.'

Oh shit. I tried to pull myself together. I could fall in love with her all over again; properly, this time. Everything in my life was happening in the wrong order. Carole could see I was distressed, but her concern simply made matters worse, reminded me of what I'd lost, what I could have had, what, in truth, I'd never had.

She squeezed my fingers. 'Look, I'm sorry this has come as a shock to you. To tell you the truth I thought you were seeing someone yourself – not that that would have made any difference, not that that's why I've been seeing Cefn – but I thought you'd welcome the opportunity to get on with your own life.'

I swallowed and tried to concentrate on keeping my voice steady. 'So has this Cefn moved in with you?'

She looked defensive. 'Not yet. He has to sort some things out in his own life first.'

Ah! So he was married too.

'Don't look smug. It isn't like you think.' Her features hardened as she switched to efficient secretary mode, a safe neutral space. 'There are some practical issues we'll need to discuss. Obviously I don't expect you to pay towards the mortgage any more. And as soon as Cefn moves in I'll be able to buy you out – either that or we'll sell the place and split the proceeds. I want to be fair. I don't want to score points. Ten years of marriage shouldn't end in us hating one another.'

I tried to sound pleasant and understanding, more to save my dignity than anything else. 'So where did you meet?'

'I told you, at the university.'

'What? But term's only just started. You've hardly had time to exchange phone numbers let alone get pregnant!'

She sighed. 'Once again, it isn't like you think. We've been seeing each other for a while now – I've been going into the library since June, trying to brush up a bit before my course started. We wouldn't have planned a baby yet, obviously, but I thought I couldn't you see. After…well, after what happened;

185

so I wasn't taking any precautions. It's come as a real shock. But we're both very pleased about it and now we just want to get married as soon as possible. I'll still carry on with my degree.' She added this as an afterthought. I think it was meant to reassure me but instead it just highlighted the fact that the rest of her life would carry on as normal. I was the only bit that would have to go.

I shrugged. I was sulking, like a child whose favourite toy has been taken away. It was hardly surprising.

'Look, Marty, I know divorce isn't pleasant, but I just want it to be as quick and painless as possible.

Like the birth, I thought to myself bitterly. 'Right,' I agreed. I knew I should have said congratulations or something but I just couldn't bring myself to.

'Look, you've got enough to think about now. I hope that eventually you'll be able to wish me well and that we'll be friends. Let's leave talking about the business side of it all till another time.'

I nodded.

Carole stood up. I stared at her middle, trying to imagine what was inside, trying to see if you could tell yet. Or maybe trying not to.

'I'll get the bill,' she said.

'No, no. I'll sort that out.' I was really clutching at straws to save face now.

'Well, OK then. Goodbye Marty. And thanks for being so understanding.'

And she walked out.

Out of the cafe.

Out of our marriage.

Out of my life.

Chapter 31

Tourist trip - a sightseeing route in a cave that has already been mapped out. A trip that doesn't involve new exploration or digging.

A feeling of relief sweeps over me as I arrive back at the camp, although in retrospect it was probably foolhardy coming back here. When I finally extricated myself from that tight tunnel I should have rested, paused and taken stock, come to terms with the fact that firstly, no-one was likely to rescue me any time soon and, secondly, that I'd simply taken the wrong turning. I should have waited till I'd calmed down then set about finding the right way.

But instead, I found myself hurriedly retracing my steps to what has become my comfort zone, almost as welcoming and familiar as my bedroom back in the outside world. Now, by the light of a candle, I wince as I touch the bruises that are developing all over my body. They aren't just from the fall down the entrance shaft yesterday or even the impromptu dip in the Lake. These are also due to the fact that the more tired I get – and the more panicky – the clumsier my movements become. Even this past hour returning to my temporary home, too much time was spent banging my head on low bits of roof or tripping over boulders whose height I misjudged.

It's unlike me. I don't like danger and I'm usually very careful underground. There was only one occasion in the past year when I nearly came a cropper.

It happened back in November, in a different cave entirely.

The way Quarry Cave was going it could keep us busy every weekend for years to come, it could become an obsession; we could become a one-cave team. So, every few weeks, we made a point of going somewhere different; a nice predictable trip down a tried and tested cave. Not an easy ride necessarily, but a change from that same old hack across the mountain. And something we could chat about openly down the Red Dragon without giving away secrets of our latest discoveries.

Over the months we'd revisited some of our underground haunts from the old days. One time we went in Little Neath River Cave, with its entrance passage half way down the riverbank; a hands and knees crawl half submerged in water. And back in the summer we went in Dan Yr Ogof – a system that extends far beyond the electric lights and safety rails of the show cave – tumbling down the Abyss and floating down the icy route of the Green Canal, gasping at the cold, and clutching onto the old inner tyres that provided makeshift rafts. Then there was my all time favourite, Otter Hole, with its deadly tidal resurgence spilling in and out of the River Wye, and its Hall of Thirty, with stals bigger even than the Snowy Mountains, huge domes of red, black and white stretching as far as the eye can see.

On the day in question we'd agreed to go down Daren Cilau. Up by the old quarry workings, near Llangattock, its history of discovery was not unlike that of our own cave. For ages, all that was known of it was a long tedious entrance passage. Then these intrepid guys broke through and a year or two later it was one of the biggest known underground systems in Britain. I hadn't been in there for over ten years.

But unfortunately it fell on the morning after Carole's revelation about her pregnancy and needless to say I wasn't in the best of moods. After we'd parted the day before, I couldn't face going home. Neither could I face meeting the others in the Red Dragon. For one thing, I couldn't stand the thought of watching Ashley and Beth drooling over one another. And I certainly didn't want to 'talk about it'. I mean, who wants to go down the pub and tell their mates that some other bloke's got their wife up the duff? So I'd gone on this solitary pub-crawl, to places I was pretty sure there wouldn't be anyone I knew. Then I'd gone on to a club. I even thought about picking someone up for the night – a couple of girls half my age were giving me the eye, it wouldn't have been difficult – but for some reason I ended up going home alone.

That morning I'd woken with a headache, though less of a

hangover than I expected. I was tempted to cancel out of the trip but I knew I'd start brooding about everything. One advantage of going down a cave is that, when you're concentrating on staying alive, you don't have space to think about much else. So I'd thrown my kit in the car, grabbed a pork pie and a banana to eat on the way and set off for the hills.

Of course, I arrived late. When I pulled over at the side of the track, Joe's car was already there, as was Ashley's; but there was no sign of anyone about. I looked at my watch; half past eleven, even with the usual dithering about they'd have set off a while ago.

I looked at my watch again and at the cars in front of me. I could easily catch them up. It would take them half an hour to squeeze through the entrance crawls at least; much more, probably, because Rick and Taff were big blokes, it would take them longer than most to negotiate those tight passages, however fit they might be. In any case, a caving trip always takes longer the more people there are. Then I looked out of the window. Outside it was raining, dreary grey rain, quite heavy too. On the drive up it had been alternately overcast and drizzling, now it looked set in for the day. My kit was in the boot of the car, by the time I'd got it out and got changed I'd be soaked through.

I lit a cigarette. By the time I'd smoked it the squall might have passed over.

But when I wound down the window a couple of inches to throw the stub out, the rain was still hammering down, clattering on the car roof. I decided to wait a bit longer. It was then that I noticed the bottle on the floor. I reached across and picked it up. It was a red wine, a Cabernet that I'd bought yesterday; it must have rolled out from under the passenger seat. I'd put it in the car before I met Carole, in case we went back to the house. But of course, things hadn't worked out that way.

I read the label on the bottle, it was a good one; there was no point in wasting it. I opened the glove compartment and pulled out one of those Swiss army gadgets with which I succeeded in

189

extracting the cork. I'd just have a couple of swigs before I went down the cave.

The time passed more quickly after that. The wine was soothing and very warming. I smoked a couple more cigarettes too, just tobacco, nothing fancy.

Unfortunately, none of this really helped take my mind off things with Carole. I'd had time by now to take it in, and the more I thought about it the more fed up I became. It wasn't as if I'd been seeing anyone else, I mean, obviously things could have worked out differently with Beth; but she was an old friend, it was entirely different. Whereas Carole had clearly gone off with the first man she met and, what's more, she'd got pregnant. I wondered what he was like. Someone from the university, she'd said. Probably some spotty young kid half her age. I shook my head in disgust, wondering how I could ever have respected her so much.

By the time I'd finished the wine I really didn't care about getting wet any more, the rain was easing up in any case. I sighed and stretched my arms. I was too drunk to drive home so I put on my kit and went down the cave.

The entrance is one of the most unspectacular you're likely to see. Just a low arch, maybe a foot high and not much wider, hidden in a hollow at the bottom of a quarried rock face. If someone pointed at the insignificant hole and suggested going camping down it for the weekend you'd laugh at them. But this was exactly what many people had done, especially during the early stages of exploration. We weren't staying overnight, we were just going underground for the day, ten or twelve hours max, following a tried and tested route, the sort of thing that was known in caving circles as a tourist trip. I turned on my torch, flopped onto my belly and used my elbows and forearms as paddles to drag myself into the darkness.

The entrance series of Daren is a long low passage that zig-zags backwards and forwards for almost half a mile. Each section of twenty or thirty feet is joined to the next by a hairpin bend so that, after much effort of stooping and crawling, you have, in reality, progressed only a few yards into the hillside.

After the first couple of turns I'd left daylight behind and settled into the rhythm of the underworld, accompanied by the rattling echoes of stones dislodged beneath my stomach, or my boots and battery bashing against rock. Sometimes the roof was high enough for me to walk, albeit bent double, while at others I had to crawl flat out, my head turned to one side and my hands and belly bathed in icy water. Most caves have a tight squeeze and Daren's delight was known as the Vice, a nasty obstacle where the walls narrowed to a few inches at floor level, forcing all but the skinniest to crawl on their side, an arm and a leg constantly wedging between the unyielding rocks. I'd done this route several times before and even though it was years ago I knew the tricks, where to duck my head that little bit lower, where to place my hands and feet so they didn't become jammed.

After thirty minutes' methodical progress I finally emerged into a chamber high enough for me to stand upright. I knew I'd already be gaining on the others, although Rick was fitter than me it would take him considerably longer to squeeze his bulk through that first section. I stretched my limbs and continued across terrain that now typified the textbook description of 'easy walking passage'.

Now that I was upright I could feel the effects of the wine. I hadn't noticed it while I'd been crawling; the alcohol had simply acted as an anaesthetic, dulling the pain of the bruises which I'd doubtless been collecting. Now I was aware that the edge had gone from my concentration and I wasn't as sure-footed as usual. Not for the first time, I stumbled and landed on my hands and knees in a puddle. I considered, just for a moment, whether I should turn back. I could go now, before the caving became more serious, get back to the car and have a snooze. It wasn't like I'd be losing face; I'd been here before after all. But I suppose the wine had also numbed the part of my brain that controlled common sense. Bugger it, I thought. I stood up straight, took a deep breath and carried on.

When I arrived at Big Chamber there was still no sign of the others. I shouted then paused in silence, straining my ears for the sound of voices or of boots graunching on rock; but there was nothing. This was the point where the cave spread out into the mountain and for the first time there was a choice of ways on. Next to a watertight drum containing a first aid kit, there was a logbook, which each person signed, noting the date, time and proposed route. It was a safeguard for rescue call-outs. On this occasion it gave me the essential information of which way my friends had gone and how far they were ahead of me.

Rick, Joe, Fish, Taff, Ashley and Beth had passed this way twenty minutes ago, heading for the Time Machine.

The Time Machine. Was it the largest known underground cavern in Britain? Bigger than the Lake Chamber, even? I wasn't sure. There was another that came close in Agen Allwedd, just a mile along the track. And of course there was Gaping Ghyll in Yorkshire. I figured I'd catch up with the others at the seventy – a seventy-foot ladder pitch – along the away. It would take at least five minutes to get each person rigged to the lifeline and up the ladder even if they were really fit. Plus there were six of them. You never risked more than one person on a ladder or a rope at a time, not unless it was an emergency. Confident of catching up with them soon, I scrambled up the boulder slope and into Eglwys Passage.

I tried to remember the last time I'd been there. I couldn't remember any particularly difficult moves; indeed, it was easy straightforward passage with a bit of bending and wriggling here and there. Everything would have been fine if I'd caught up with the others before they reached the seventy; but of course, when I emerged into the chamber and gazed up the sheer wall of rock, there was no-one to be seen. I thought I could hear them, in the distance, high above, faraway echoes of the thudding of boots and the more tuneful sound of voices. I called out. But there was no reply.

The ladder was fixed, in a rather wiggly, moveable kind of way. Both the rungs and the sides were firm, unlike the twisty electron job we used to get down Quarry; it linked together in sections, like a caterpillar. It had to be like that to get it down the cave in the first place. By its side hung a rope, a lifeline, which you clipped to your belt, with someone you really trusted holding the other end. You wouldn't think of going up this pitch without. But I was alone and the wine seemed to take away the danger. I grasped the sides and put my foot on the first rung.

The ladder was in two sections; the first was precisely vertical, the second or upper half skewed slightly, following the curve of the rock. I was almost at the top and this time I could definitely hear them. There were clattering, clumping sounds, voices too, Beth's ringing laughter. The noises were muffled, distorted from bouncing off rocks and echoing their way round corners. I couldn't tell how far away they were. Immediately I thought of joining them and I shouted out so they'd know I was nearby. And that's when my foot slipped. I don't know whether I lost my concentration in my eagerness to join my friends or whether, woozy from the wine, I just didn't have enough co-ordination. Suddenly, as I stepped onto my left foot, there wasn't a rung where I expected one to be. I began to slide down the wall, screaming as I did so.

It seemed like an age that I hung there, my left hand gripping the rung, my feet thrashing about desperately searching for the ladder. I could hear the crashing and the voices getting louder. I shouted again.

Suddenly, something gripped my right wrist and hauled on it. Something or someone else grabbed various parts of my anatomy and my kit and pulled me, unceremoniously, to safety.

Moments later I lay on the ground a few feet from the top of the pitch, panting. Ashley was next to me. Seems he'd pulled me back from the brink single-handed, quite literally, he'd lifted my bodyweight with just one hand.

'Are you OK?' he asked.

I nodded. 'I thought only firemen could do that,' I puffed.

Beth looked startled, caught between admiration for Ashley and concern for me. Rick and Joe were standing over me shaking their heads.

Of course, there were exclamations about how lucky I was, and why on earth hadn't I self-lined with a hitch looped onto my belt? But I think everyone was too relieved at the outcome to question the real reason why the accident had happened in the first place.

Chapter 32

Helictite - formation that branches out from the wall of a cave.

For a while, I tried to dismiss what Carole had told me. I imagined her calling me and telling me that the pregnancy was a false alarm, that she and her toyboy had split up, that she wanted to give us another chance. But when I was honest with myself I knew things between us were over. And this in turn made it even more imperative that things with Beth should get back on. It was surely only a question of time until the perfect Ashley slipped up, and I had to ensure that, when he did, I would be there to help Beth pick up the pieces.

In the meantime, what I needed was to get things back on an even keel with her. Back to how things were before I pulled that stupid stunt trying to seduce her, better still, back to that time of promise and possibility before Ashley came on the scene.

Ashley Roberts.

It wasn't so much that I wanted him to go away, more that I wished he'd never arrived. My feelings towards him were confused. I quite reasonably resented the fact that he was going out with Beth, I resented the way he'd entered our close-knit circle, that he'd stepped in and virtually taken over just as we were discovering Quarry Cave. It was like we were in the middle of a reunion party, the six of us, having just met up again, when suddenly, someone who was never in our class to begin with, came and gate-crashed. It wasn't like he was unfriendly or anything; OK, he could be pompous and irritating sometimes, but we all have our faults; no, it was simply that he turned up in the wrong place at the wrong time. Any other time, any other place, and I'd have been pleased to think of him as a friend.

But instead I'd behaved stupidly and jeopardised my friendship with Beth, all because I was jealous of Ashley Roberts. And, because of his continued presence, it was difficult to find an opportunity to put things right.

Then, suddenly, I got my chance. It was one of those flat weekends when everyone had something else to do. Ashley was away on business, Rick and Joe had gone to a bike rally, Taff was spending quality time with his kids and Fish (very reluctantly I suspect, not least because it involved a visit to IKEA) was spending quality time with Valerie. That just left Beth and me, which was quite convenient really.

I didn't dare ask her out for a meal or anything, not after last time. I figured the only way I'd get her alone was if it was down a cave.

'We could set off early,' I suggested to her over the phone, 'and make it a day trip.' I wasn't going to push my luck by suggesting we camp overnight. She hummed and hahed for a while. I'd have to make it tempting. 'Perhaps we could explore the other side of the Lake Chamber – or anywhere else for that matter. You choose; we'll go wherever you like.' There was a brooding pause; I knew I'd almost won her over. 'And if we do find anything interesting it'll just be down to us,' I concluded.

'All right then. Pick me up tomorrow at seven.'

I thought that would do it. The fact was, I was looking forward to a private trip myself, not just for the chance to spend time with Beth but because we wouldn't have Ashley and Rick forging ahead, making all the decisions and generally telling us what to do.

And now we were underground, just the two of us. We went to the camp first and made a cup of tea.

During the past few months, Camp David had become more than an occasional overnight sleeping area, it was now our base within the cave. We kept a supply of drinks and snacks, along with cooking equipment and candles. We stored copies of maps we'd made, detailing different areas of the cave, and, in keeping with other major underground systems, we had a logbook which we signed when we explored beyond the camp, and wrote a brief report of each trip on the way back. On the front of this book were the words Cwar-yr-Ogof, the Quarry's official

Welsh name. Lots of caves with long or complicated names get abbreviated or simplified. There's Ogof Fynnon Ddu, here in Wales, which is known simply as OFD, and my particular favourite, Allt Nan Uamh Stream Cave, in the north of Scotland, which reduces to a wonderful, if unfortunate, acronym.

I unfolded the survey and spread the hand-drawn map on a rock. Already it showed a huge spider's web of passages. Later that day we would add any new ones we might find. And we'd write up our report in the logbook.

'So where shall we go?' I asked.

Beth leaned over the crumpled paper. Even in her caving overalls she was beautiful – more so in fact. Perhaps the contrast of the grubby suit emphasized her flawless skin. Incongruity. That was it. Wayward coils of hair had a cute way of escaping from under her helmet and the broad belay belt accentuated her tiny waist. I tried not to stare too obviously.

'What about the far side of the Lake.' She paused to sip her drink. 'Like you suggested yesterday.'

'Let's finish our tea and get on with it then.'

There were only two ways on from the Lake Chamber that we knew of so far. The first was accessed by Easter Climb, not far from the Spiral Staircase, a steep slope coated in shiny cream and yellow flowstone that looked like the sugary contents of a Cadbury's Creme egg. It looked as though it would be slippery and impossible to ascend, yet somehow our boots always gripped securely onto the surprisingly strong surface. Easter Climb was our usual route to Camp David and the way we'd come today. Then there was The Sewer, adjacent to the Devil's Cauldron. This started as a dark, forbidding route, lined with cruel, sharp edges of rock; then, further on, where sparkling crystals lit the walls and ceiling, its nature changed into something magical and it became Starbright Passage. These two routes formed an oxbow, joining together just before the camp. I don't know why no-one had bothered to explore the far side of the Lake before. Perhaps because it was not immediately accessible, the way was blocked at one end by the waterfall (forget trying to get past that) and at the other by the Devil's Cauldron. Also, the passages beyond the camp were going like crazy and it took all our time underground to explore those. Somehow, the fact that the far side of the chamber might hold even more exciting passages waiting to be discovered seemed to have been overlooked.

So we retraced our steps back to the Lake Chamber. It was great not to hurry, to just amble around at our own pace.

First we had to negotiate the Lake. The water was relatively calm in the middle section but there could be some deep areas. Beth, of course, had had the foresight to wear a wetsuit, whereas I was in my fleece.

'If we steer a path between the boulders we should be all right,' she suggested. 'I'll go first and find where the shallow bits are and you can wade across after.'

This seemed like a good idea and it also gave Beth an opportunity to take the lead. I took the precaution of roping the two of us together, just in case it was deeper than we expected or the placid surface hid strong underwater currents. In the end it wasn't too bad and I didn't get wet much above the knees. Once across, we wanted to search the wall of the chamber really thoroughly for likely passages. It had been done before, of course, by Fish and Taff but the trip had been somewhat hurried, and in any case, Beth and I hadn't actually been over here ourselves. We decided that I would start by the Cauldron and Beth would begin at the waterfall and we'd meet in the middle.

My section started off quite promising with lots of little corners and fissures in the rock to explore, but they all closed down after a few yards. I could hear Beth clattering away further round the chamber and hoped she was having better luck. However, all too soon we found ourselves standing next to one another.

'I suppose that's it then.' I couldn't hide my disappointment. 'We may as well go back to the camp and get lunch.'

'Yeah,' Beth agreed. 'Oh bother! I wonder when that happened.' Her hand reached frantically patting around her neck. 'It's gone! The chain must have broken or something.'

'Your charm necklace?' I knew immediately because she'd always worn it to go caving, ever since I first met her.

She nodded. 'The one Mum gave me.'

'Beats me why you wear it underground if it's so special.'

'That's the whole point!' She stared at me, exasperated. 'It's supposed to keep me safe.'

Of course, I remembered her explaining it years ago; it was some Zen symbol or something. 'Well check under your clothes; it's probably slipped down your wetsuit.'

She undid the first few inches of the zip and groped around underneath. God, I wished they were my hands down there. I mentally reprimanded myself for thinking lustful thoughts. I'd already learned I'd have to take it slowly with Beth and win her over gradually. She shook her head.

'Well maybe it's back in the car, it could have come off when you got changed.'

'No, I remember touching it when we had tea at the camp.' She looked suddenly dismayed. 'If I dropped it in the Lake then it's gone for good.'

I tried to be positive. 'The Lake's only a small section of the ground you've covered. Why don't we retrace your steps? We're not in any hurry after all. It's worth a try.'

Rather dejectedly Beth agreed and we started walking slowly back towards the waterfall. The rocks were overhanging and we were able to go right behind it so that there was a rock wall to our left and one of moving water to our right.

'What's that?' It was only chance that I saw something glinting on the ground.

Beth pounced. 'That's it! Oh Marty, well done! I'm so glad I haven't lost it.'

I offered to fasten it round her neck but she shook her head. 'Look, the clasp's broken.' She secured the necklace in a velcro pocket. 'You could fix my helmet for me though.' The cord on the back of her helmet, which secured the lamp cable, had come undone. She turned so that I could tie it and as she did so she looked up. 'Hey! Look at that!'

The cord was jerked out of my hand and I followed her gaze. Ten feet above was a recess in the rock. It could be nothing of course, or it could be the start of a passage. Beth reached to climb up but was too short to grasp the holds. I gave her a leg up and she scrambled up and disappeared head first into the opening.

'Anything there?' I called.

Her answer came back, hollow and echoey. 'Yeah. It's a passage.'

'Does it go?' That all important question.

'I think so.' Her voice was more distant. 'It turns a corner and…oh no! It's blocked, loose rubble though, we could easily shift it.'

I was about to climb after her but I held back. I didn't want to rush in and take over.

'What do you think?' I shouted. 'Shall we have a go at digging it?'

Her face appeared above me. 'Definitely!'

It took us over an hour to get to the camp and back. We were too excited to stop and make tea or anything, we just stuffed some Mars bars and packs of nuts and raisins into the cradles of our helmets, grabbed a bucket, rope, trowel and shovel and set off back. I got rather more wet on the Lake crossing this time, in my eagerness to get to work.

In the passage for the first time, I could see Beth was right. It was just rubble blocking the way ahead and it was soft and crumbly; no bang would be needed thank goodness. We took it in turns to scrape the debris out with the trowel, the other person using the shovel to deposit the spoil heap in the bucket. Every so often, when the bucket was full, we dragged it back to the entrance and tipped it out onto the chamber floor.

It was while I was doing the trowelling, I'd just pulled out a sizeable rock and suddenly I felt a draught. I signalled to Beth.

'Feel that?'

She nodded excitedly. We both knew that a draught meant one thing. There was clear passage ahead.

I scrabbled more frantically but it was difficult work in

200

cramped conditions. The tunnel we were clearing was low and by now I was lying on my stomach.

'Let me try,' said Beth. 'I'm smaller than you.'

We changed places and she worked steadily for half an hour. At last she stopped, moved the tools out of the way and wriggled over so that she was lying straight out facing the tunnel.

'I can see through!' she yelled.

She worked with her hands now, digging into the rubble like a mole. Then she started to squirm forward. Her head, shoulders, hips, knees and finally her feet disappeared.

At first there was the familiar graunching sound of a person crawling, pushing past loose rocks, then there were a few echoey footsteps, then nothing. I waited for what seemed like ages.

'Are you OK' I shouted at last.

There was a muffled voice, quiet, distant.

'I can't hear you!'

More footsteps and more graunching.

'Marty?'

This time I heard her clearly. I had already dropped onto my stomach and begun to wriggle through the dig. We met nose to nose in the tunnel.

'I take it it goes?'

'Come through and see,' she said quietly. She began to reverse the way she had come so I could get through. The tunnel was only wide enough for one and that was pushing it.

I didn't like it, squirming through all the compacted sandy stuff. That kind of debris always made me feel claustrophobic, like it could easily fall in and bury you. And very likely it could. I tried to push forward gracefully, to disturb the ground as little as possible. But grace and caving gear – with batteries and boots and goodness knows what sticking out everywhere – are two things that don't go together. At last I was able to raise my head and soon after to stand up. Turning my head, I played the beam of light around me.

It took my breath away. For several minutes, I stood there

speechless, unable to find the words to describe it.

'Fuckin' hell!' I said at last. 'Fuckin' cosmic light emitting diodes hell!'

'Isn't it amazing?' Beth's voice was faint and quivery. She was awestruck, just like I was.

I'd been in a lot of caves but I'd never seen anything quite like it. Long straws of pure crystal hung from the roof, glittering like chandeliers. The walls were draped with calcite flowstone, stained with manganese to majestic shades of purple. On the ground, in the waters of crystal-lined pools, nestled pearls: cave pearls, shimmering spheres, as perfect as anything you could find in an oyster. Stranger still, from the walls sprouted helictites: clusters of pure white tentacles reaching outwards like giant albino sea anemones.

Beth turned to me, tears in her eyes. 'It's perfect,' she said. 'It's perfect and we found it!'

She stretched her arms towards me and I hugged her. 'You found it,' I corrected.

'We stood there for a while just marvelling at the place. It was wonderful to be there, privileged, I suppose, drinking in all that splendour.

'To think,' said Beth as she shook her head yet again, 'that we're the first people ever to set foot here and to see all this.'

I smiled and took her hand. 'And it's our secret,' I said, 'until we decide to tell anyone else.'

Suddenly her mood became serious. 'Why can't you always be like this?' she asked me.

'Pardon?'

'Like you are now. Like you used to be. Fun. Normal.'

'Aren't I always?' I began to feel defensive.

'You know you're not.'

'Well things are different. You're with Ashley.'

'It isn't that. It's something more basic, inside you. Like something's happened, something that's changed the way you see the world.'

'Nothing you'd want to know,' I muttered.

'What?'

'We're not kids any more that's all.' I shrugged. 'Don't let's spoil today with some deep philosophical discussion, let's enjoy it.'

'Sorry,' she said. 'Let's get back to work. We need to find out how far this chamber extends and if there are any ways on.'

Duck - section of passage (usually low, requiring crawling) that is partially submerged.

The catastrophic rock fall in the Lake Chamber makes me wonder if anything else has changed further upriver, whether the streamway traverse is passable all the way to Lover's Leap, whether a new entrance has been carved out by the water rushing in. This wouldn't be the first cave to get rearranged during a flash flood. Long before I'd ever thought of caving, Swildon's Hole, on Mendip, used to have a vertical pitch known as the Forty Pot. Then in nineteen sixty-eight there was a flood and the force of the water simply washed it away. That part of the cave was changed forever.

I went down Swildon's several times back in my student days. In fact it was where I dived my first sump. To be honest, I wasn't too keen on the idea. None of us were. But it was only a short one, just a few feet underwater; Fish had assured us. We wouldn't need diving equipment or anything; all we had to do was hold our breath for a few seconds.

It was the end of the summer term and I'd been in the caving club nine months by then. We drove to the Mendips for the day, Rick, Joe, Fish and myself. Rick and Joe had done a short trip in this cave a few weeks before, with the university club; the time that I'd stayed behind and met Beth. And as for Fish, he'd been there dozens of times and knew the place better than he knew his way around town.

We parked the car at Priddy Green then climbed a rickety ladder into a disused hayloft where we were able to change into our wetsuits and overalls without offending the sensibilities of the locals. After that it was a short walk across farm fields to the cave. The entrance was a sink hole, a place where the water sinks into the ground. Fish explained these features were also known as swallow holes because the earth swallows the water;

and sometimes the caves associated with them were called swallets.

We were going to do what was commonly known as the 'short round trip'. Fish had already briefed us on it. It involved a twenty-foot ladder pitch, a cruise round the Trouble Series and back through the sump. Fish would lead in view of his knowledge and experience.

The first section was straightforward. It consisted of a series of short climbs down rocky walls and slopes. Carefully we lowered ourselves over water-smoothed shelves, dodging the icy spray that bounced and sang its way down cascades. When we reached the twenty there was already a ladder and lifeline rigged so we left our own tackle sack slung over a stal at the top. Fish assured us that if the other party came out first they'd rig our ladder before they left. In fact we met the group in question soon after, two men and a girl with a couple of teenagers, they were puzzling over a map and asked us the way to Tratman's Temple. Fish directed them and reminded them of cave etiquette regarding the ladder. 'They don't seem to have much of a clue,' he whispered to us when we were out of earshot. 'We'll probably end up rescuing them on our way back.'

The Trouble Series consisted of four uninviting ducks, icy cold and sinisterly still. I dread them to this day. Whilst not dangerous by caving standards, they have a doom-laden claustrophobic atmosphere, to be endured rather than enjoyed. I'd been through ducks before but the Troubles were something different. The first was completely sumped – water right up to the roof – and we had to bail it out for half an hour, scooping the water in our helmets. It was hot work, like a Roman bath, where you get sticky and sweaty before the cold plunge. Every so often we stopped and Fish bent over the pool, the side of his head breaking the surface of the water as he peered at what looked like a solid wall of rock. Then he'd straighten up, shake his head and the bailing would continue.

On the third occasion he came up smiling. 'There's two inches of air space,' he announced. 'Let's d-do it!'

205

For some reason it was decided that I should go first. I lay down on my back in the water, my nose lifted above the surface. I don't know whether it was due to my inadequate attire (at that time my kit consisted of a second-hand surfing wetsuit and a boiler suit) or whether that duck held the coldest water on Earth, but for two whole minutes my body convulsed and I gasped to catch my breath.

'You've g-got to lie still,' Fish instructed me, 'or the water will g-go up your nose.'

I'd already discovered that, thank you! I steadied myself and when my breathing had returned to normal I inched my way cautiously through the forbidding tunnel, trying very hard not to make any ripples.

After that first duck the other three seemed easy. When we'd all emerged, dripping and shivering, Fish took the lead again and we kept a brisk pace in an effort to warm up. We continued along sections of dry, easy walking passage – for once, a true and accurate description – then dropped down into the main drag. Fish pointed down the route which led deeper into the cave, explaining that there were a series of sumps, the first of which he'd free dived – just held his breath and hoped for the best – but it was a long way, he said, you needed to be a strong swimmer and even then you needed weights strapped to your belt to stop you floating up and crashing into the roof. We turned the other way, along which, Fish assured us, there was just one very short sump and after that we could be back above ground in an hour.

The chamber with the sump was small and unimpressive. Its only feature was a road sign (presumably nicked from somewhere in Wells), which indicated the way to 'Wookey Hole, avoiding city centre'. Rick saw me reading it and laughed. 'It's quite accurate,' he said. 'I was reading about it the other night. In theory, if you carried on through the sumps the way Fish pointed back there then eventually you'd surface in the show cave.' He paused and rubbed his chin. 'Unfortunately it can't be done – even with air bottles – you'd have to be microscopically small to fit through!'

'W-we can go this way though.' Fish had been waiting patiently. Now he indicated the way on. 'Here it is, Marty. Your first sump.'

I don't know what I'd expected. A deep pool of water, I suppose; in which I would stand, immersed to the neck, then bend from the waist for a brief second before standing straight once again, on the other side of a limestone barrier. So when I saw little more than a puddle on the ground I burst out laughing.

'I'll go f-first,' Fish told us, 'then you, Marty, then Rick, then Joe. The p-passage is very low so you'll need to lie on your stomach and pull on this.' He pointed at the rope which stretched out across the water. 'I'll be waiting on the other side so when I see your lamp I'll know you're on your way and if you're not through in a few seconds I'll p-pull on the rope. All you need to do is hold your breath.' He lay face down in what couldn't have been more than nine inches of water. 'See you in a m-minute or two.' And with that he slid away, first his head, then his body, and lastly kicking legs disappeared, all to the accompaniment of crashing, splashing and graunching noises. It was like he was being eaten by a monster, hidden in the rock. When the cave had swallowed its morsel, the noise reduced to an echoing memory and the turbulent water stilled to a gentle ripple, I knew it was my turn.

I lay flat out in water that was surprisingly warm compared to the Trouble ducks, took a deep breath, pulled on the rope, arm over arm, and slid into the sump. I kept my eyes closed because I didn't want to sting them in the, doubtless, silty water, but I could feel the rock roof above me as it clinked on the top of my helmet. Three pulls. Four. I should be clear of the sump by now, but no. If I raised my helmet even an inch I could still feel the rock clattering. Suddenly I started to get worried. Something must have gone wrong. Perhaps I'd turned down some unknown side passage. I'd have to try and back out, I wondered how much longer I could hold my breath. Then I lifted my head again and this time there was no resistance. I opened my eyes and pulled myself up onto my knees. Ten feet

207

behind me was the end of the sump. I'd been crawling along in six inches of water across a high, spacious, roomy passage.

Beside me, Fish rocked with laughter. In his hand he held a small stone and I realised what he'd done.

'You bastard!'

'Had you g-g-going though didn't I?'

'That was mean.'

'Didn't freak you though. S-s-seriously, Marty. You're OK with water. You're a strong swimmer. Why don't you have a go at diving? The club is running an introductory course in October. Then you could get your certificate. We could go exploring together. Once you can dive underground there's so much more to see, so many more places you can go.'

I shrugged, it sounded like a good idea. 'OK,' I agreed.

A beam of light was filtering out from the sump. Fish grabbed my arm.

'Time to catch the next one,' he grinned.

I smiled and picked up a pebble off the ground. 'This one's mine!' And as Rick's helmet emerged from under the rock I gently rapped the top of his head, tap, tap, tap, and laughed as he squirmed across the floor.

Chapter 34

Cascade - a series of small waterfalls, each one feeding the next.

I spent Christmas with Beth at her parents' house. It was by chance really, and the result of our spending time together exploring the Waterfall Chamber. I knew I wasn't her first choice but even so I enjoyed myself more than I expected.

I'd been dreading the festive season and it was all Carole's fault. In the past we'd always alternated. One year we'd spend Christmas Day with her parents and Boxing Day with mine, then the next we'd do it the other way round. It was a bit boring and predictable but it kept everyone happy. Carole diluted my parents and made spending the whole day with them more bearable, and in turn I rather liked her Dad. He and I used to disappear conspiratorially for a constitutional 'walk' while the dinner was being prepared; in reality this meant we sat in the local hostelry for a couple of hours. Then we'd stagger home, slightly pissed, to the intense disapproval of the women (apparently it was the only occasion each year he got even mildly drunk). Of course, Carole and her mother, being devout Methodists, thought I was leading him into sinful ways, but I reckoned I was doing the old chap a favour.

One thing was for sure, that scenario wasn't going to happen this year. I didn't know what Carole's plans were but I assumed they would include lover boy. I could imagine the visit to her parents, with them dismayed at the break-up of her marriage but at the same time thrilled at the prospect of grandparenthood. I decided to keep well away from my folks. Besides the visit being extremely dreary on my own (I knew my sister, together with husband and kids, would be visiting her in-laws) I just couldn't face all the questions that were bound to arise, nor all the tut-tutting, dear-dearing and 'isn't this all a sign of the times' comments.

So I wasn't really sure what I was going to do. Rick and Joe had invited me round to their house but I knew they were having Rick's mother (who was widowed and partially disabled) to stay. I didn't want to intrude, though I figured that if nothing else turned up I could just take them up on the invitation to dinner and skip the overnight bit. If I'd got my act together earlier I'd have booked a holiday abroad like Ashley had done; he was going on some serious caving thing in South America, something he'd planned before he got together with Beth. Not that I fancied the idea of dangerous exploration myself, but a week in the sun certainly appealed. It wasn't that I minded staying on my own, in fact in some ways it was what I'd prefer, but it wasn't a good enough excuse to let me off the parental visit or, worse still, the chance that they'd drop in on me.

Anyway, I hadn't planned ahead and before I knew it mid-December had arrived and I was beginning to dread the whole thing. So when Beth casually asked if I'd like to accompany her to visit her parents – it would be nice for old time's sake, she was quick to point out, they'd enjoy seeing me again – I graciously accepted.

Beth's parents had retired to a village near Hereford, to a modern detached bungalow within easy reach of all the necessary amenities. It wasn't a long drive, we could have just gone for the day, but neither of us wanted to forego drinking so we decided to stay Christmas night.

During the drive over we talked about the cave and our newly discovered Waterfall Chamber. We differed slightly on our opinions about keeping it secret. On that first trip, Beth had been all set to write it up in the logbook; but I'd stopped her, saying that we should wait a bit – at least until we'd been back with a camera and explored it properly to see if it extended further than that one chamber. We'd duly returned the week before Christmas and taken some photographs.

'So when are we going to tell the others about it?' Beth asked, as we sped down the slip road onto the motorway.

'Perhaps give it a bit longer,' I replied. 'Since we discovered it, that place is our responsibility. And as well as being outstandingly beautiful, it's possible that it might qualify as one of those sites of scientific interest, or whatever they are. I think we need to think about it a bit more before we announce it.'

Beth was doubtful. 'I can understand not wanting to tell the whole world, but we can trust our own friends. I feel mean keeping it from them.'

She was right, of course. In one way, I desperately wanted to share it with Rick and Joe and Fish. But if I'm honest, although I was concerned with the conservation issue, the most important thing was that it was a secret between Beth and me, like an invisible bond that held us together or a private club with only two members. And most importantly of all, it was a club from which Ashley was excluded.

But I didn't want to have an argument over it. 'We'll talk about it after Christmas,' I promised, hoping that other matters would crop up and that I could spin the situation out a bit longer, preferably till Ashley had left our group.

We arrived at her parents' place at midday, nicely timed to have a drink and relax before dinner. Beth disappeared into the kitchen with her mother while her father gave me a guided tour of the place.

'It's good to see you again,' he said as he ushered me along the hallway and opened doors showing me where cloakrooms, bathrooms and the like were located. 'Now, this is the master bedroom.'

I nodded appreciation.

'This is the spare room where Beth will be sleeping.'

I looked in another good-sized room with a double bed.

'We weren't sure if you'd be sharing so Mary made up the sofa bed in the library. Didn't like to ask Beth after what happened in the States, you know? Well if we've got it wrong you can always commute in the night.' He winked at me knowingly.

I wondered what had happened in the States. Beth had always changed the subject if I mentioned it. I wondered if she'd told Ashley. It was noticeable that Beth's father didn't mention Ashley at all. Whether that was out of courtesy to me or because he didn't know about him, I wasn't sure. Either way, the fact that I was there, being treated as a prospective suitor, gave me a smug satisfaction.

'Come and get a drink,' commanded Beth's father, 'and tell me what you're doing these days.' He poured two glasses of whisky and passed one to me. We'd moved into the lounge and I was standing by a large picture window, which looked out onto a bird table and ornamental pool. I took a gulp of my drink.

'Are you still making those drugs?'

I almost choked. Beth must have told her parents about it, all those years ago. I coughed and cleared my throat shaking my head.

'Sorry. Do you mean the Smartees?'

He nodded.

'No. That was a bit of fun when I was young. I'm a responsible citizen now.'

'Quite right,' he nodded. 'University's the place for all that. Try things out, experiment and get it out of your system, that's what I say. Unless you find something really good; in which case stick with it. Same goes for politics.'

I nodded politely; remembering the last time I messed with Smartees. We were in Benson Street; Rick, Joe, Fish and myself. It was our third year at university and we'd just finished our finals, last exam that very afternoon. By way of celebration, after we'd been for a curry and to the pub, we took some Smartees.

It was about two in the morning and things were kind of laid back. Fish had already been through his 'weirded out' phase and was sitting in an armchair, legs crossed looking completely compos mentis. Rick was spark out on the sofa, snoring quietly. I was wishing that I hadn't asked for my Vindaloo to be extra strong, but apart from that I was reasonably together. 'Sultans of Swing' was playing in the background, lulling us into a dream.

Then something really strange happened. Joe had been

sitting there quietly, cross-legged on the floor when suddenly he started shaking. At first I thought it was nothing.

'You OK, Spider? You cold? Shall I get you a cup of tea?' I asked.

He didn't reply; just shook even more. When he looked up, his eyes were wild with terror. I didn't know what to do. I was scared, scared of what was happening to him. I hoped we wouldn't have to call a doctor because they'd want to know what he'd taken. And basically the buck stopped with me. I'd get several years, I figured, if I admitted to making the stuff. Not to mention my future career and travel opportunities severely curtailed. If it came to it we could say we'd bought them in the pub, off someone we didn't know. But that wasn't the point. What was happening to Joe was the point.

Fish, meanwhile, was a bit more on the ball. 'Bad trip,' he said philosophically. He slid off the chair and sat next to Joe, putting his arm round him. 'Hey man, are you all weirded out then?'

Then Joe started to cry, sobbing uncontrollably. Fish held him tight and rocked him back and forth like a baby. He cooed, kissing him on the top of his head and on his cheek.

'C-cool it man. It's OK. I love you. I w-won't let anything bad happen.'

After a while Joe quietened down and Fish called across to me softly. 'You could g-get him that hot drink now, Marty.'

So I went out to the kitchen to make some tea. And when I got back Joe had fallen asleep. Fish too. They slept like babies in each other's arms.

But the episode had scared me senseless. This wasn't a game any more, not if people could get ill. I collected what Smartees we had left and flushed them down the toilet. And I never made any sort of drugs again.

'What about batting for the other side?'

'Huh?' I realised Beth's Dad was still talking to me.

'You know – swimming both sides of the river. That was something else I tried when I was at university. What about

213

you?'

Good grief! This was too much information – even from Beth's dad.

'Time for dinner!' Beth's mother called from the dining room. Thank goodness. Saved by the bell.

Beth and I went for a walk after dinner, while her parents were sleeping off the festivities. We'd had the obligatory overly large meal. Beth and her mother had had nut roast while her father and I had tucked into the more traditional poultry – 'So glad you're here,' he'd said to me, 'or I'd have been fed the veggie stuff too!' – all washed down with wine, red with the main course and a sweeter dessert wine with the pudding, not to mention brandy butter with hardly more than one ingredient. When at last we collapsed in the lounge it turned out there was more to come.

'What about a smoke?' Beth's father suggested. I honestly thought he meant cigars and nodded eagerly, but no; instead he rolled a serious joint. I was glad that some things hadn't changed.

Anyway, an hour or so later, while her parents were still well out of it, Beth and I went out. We'd had too many substances of various sorts to drive so we walked down to the river.

'You've never really told me what you got up to in the States,' I began. I remembered what her father had said and figured I'd feel my way carefully. If she changed the subject I'd back off. 'Did you enjoy your time there?'

She thought for a while before answering. 'At first I did. Though the culture's different. And the way they do business. I'm not sure I entirely fitted in.'

'Is that why you came back?'

She shook her head.

'Why then? From what Rick says you were doing really well.'

'Aren't I allowed to miss my family and friends?'

'Of course, but it sounds like you were earning enough to fly back for visits every few weeks, and – you know – whenever the subject's come up you've kind of hinted that something happened.'

There was a wooden bench close to the water. 'Let's sit down for a few minutes,' she said. 'If you don't mind.'

To be honest I was grateful. I'd had quite a bit to drink, not to mention the joint. We sat silently for a few moments, listening to the innocuous swish of the water as it bubbled round dormant stubs of flag iris, and wishing we'd brought bread for the optimistic ducks. I could feel that Beth was working out what she was going to say. I don't think she'd have told me about it under normal circumstances, but there's something about doing a potentially dangerous activity like caving, you feel a special kind of closeness to the people you share it with. It's different from any other sort of relationship. You've faced the same difficulties and overcome them; trusted your lives to one another; become brothers in arms. Anyway, I suspect it was largely because we'd recently been on a couple of caving trips together, trips that were a secret between us, that Beth chose to confide in me that afternoon – that and the wine and the cannabis.

'I suppose you've guessed it was about a man,' she began.

Had I? Did I really want to hear the sordid details of Beth's encounter with someone else? It was too late now. I'd just have to grin and bear it.

She continued. 'He was my boss. He was very rich, very successful, very attractive.'

Sounds just like Ashley, I thought to myself; luckily I had the presence of mind not to say this out loud. I nodded and tried to look concerned.

'I started seeing him three years ago. At first I thought he was just being friendly because I hadn't been over there very long and didn't know many people. He had a big place out of town, a kind of ranch, where he spent weekends, but most weeknights he used to stay in his apartment in Manhattan. He started asking me out to dinner, said he didn't like dining alone and he'd left it too late to arrange to meet up with friends, he made it sound like I was doing him a favour by joining him. At the same time, I didn't like to refuse because part of the time we'd talk about the business; the extra knowledge helped make up for my lack of experience; really I learned a lot from him.'

'I take it he was married?'

She nodded. 'I knew about that from the start, he never made any secret of it. But at that time we were simply business colleagues, discussing trade over dinner.'

'So when did things change?'

'I'm not sure there was a particular moment; it was all very gradual. Rob started mentioning his wife in passing, then she came into the conversation more and more. He told me they were married very young. It was practically an arranged thing, he said, not that they were forced into it, but their parents were great friends and it just seemed the natural thing to do, it made everyone happy. He said that, looking back, he didn't understand what love was, he didn't have enough experience to know that what they had wasn't it.' She looked up. 'These are the things he told me at the time and I had no reason not to believe him; now I suspect the whole thing was a pack of lies.'

Her eyes looked watery. I reached out to her and took her hand. 'You don't have to tell me any more if it's upsetting you.'

She shook her head. 'It's probably better to get it out of my system. Rob suggested that I should move into a bigger, more comfortable apartment. He said that he – the company – would cover most of the rent. Yes, Marty. I know what you're thinking, but it wasn't like that. Rob said it made more sense for tax purposes than giving me a rise in salary. After I'd moved he started telling me how his marriage was over. He and his wife led separate lives, he said; they'd slept in separate bedrooms for the past two years. That's when he started staying over. I've always said I'd never get involved with a married man but he told me that the marriage was simply a formality. I think I felt sorry for him. A girl friend once told me that half of all women have slept with a man because they felt sorry for him. Isn't that frightening?'

I thought that from my point of view it was rather encouraging, but I knew this opinion wouldn't go down very

216

well so I nodded in agreement.

'We only ever spent the night together at my place, never at his. I realise now that should have made me suspicious. And we were always on our own. I asked, sometimes, if we couldn't meet up with some of his friends for dinner or a drink; but he said he wanted me all to himself. By then I'd fallen in love with him so in a way I was flattered. He told me I was the first person he'd truly loved and what he wanted more than anything was for the two of us to get married and have a family.'

'So why didn't you?'

'His mother-in-law was ill with cancer – or so he said – he didn't want to upset everyone by asking for a divorce when the situation was so fragile.' She looked bitter. 'I had no reason not to believe him. He said it was breaking his heart having to wait, having to live a lie. We carried on seeing each other like that for two years. Meanwhile, my old firm back here had written to me asking if I wanted to come back at a higher grade. I turned them down of course because I thought it was all just a question of time. I got fed up asking Rob how his mother-in-law was; saying, oh how marvellous, when she was in remission; and, oh how awful, when it recurred. In the end I just wished she'd hurry up and die so the rest of us could get on with our lives. God, that sounds dreadful doesn't it?'

'Not as dreadful as manipulating someone by pretending someone else is terminally ill, if that's what he was doing. So what made you decide you'd had enough?'

Beth took a deep breath. 'I was at work one day and I had to go down to the foyer to meet a client. The receptionist was talking to a visitor, gave her a badge and waved her in the direction of the lifts. I asked who she was in case it was the person I was supposed to be meeting.'

'And I suppose it was your boss's wife.'

Beth nodded.

'So what was she like?'

'Very young. Very glamorous. Very pregnant. She was in town for a hospital appointment and to choose furnishings for

217

the baby's room.'

'Whew!'

'And that wasn't her first pregnancy, their elder child was born eighteen months previously, conceived just before I started seeing Rob seriously.'

'The wanker!'

'Pity he didn't stick to that.' She looked more angry than upset.

'I'm really sorry, Beth; it just shouldn't have happened to you.'

'Aren't you going to say it was my own stupid fault?'

'Of course not, you weren't the one who lied. I know it's awful. But thank God you found out when you did. You could still be there now, as his bit on the side while he carried on his double life. Did you confront him?'

She shook her head. 'I didn't dare; he was paying for my flat, don't forget. If I'd caused a fuss I could have ended up with no home, no job and no references. I got through the rest of the day – I don't know how – and when I went home I took all my personal things with me, except of course it didn't feel like home anymore. I started packing and in the middle of the night, and when it was nine in the morning here, I called my old firm and asked if the job offer was still open. They said yes and I was on a flight to Heathrow six hours later. When I arrived back in England I sent a formal letter of resignation. I'm afraid I was underhand and said I'd had to leave at short notice because my mother was ill – I had to do that, you see, or they'd have sued me for not working my notice; Americans sue everyone. And I knew when he read that, he'd realise I'd found out; and he wouldn't dare take any action against me then, in case I caused trouble for him.'

'I'm surprised you didn't want to cause trouble.'

'I'd have loved to but I wasn't prepared to sink to his level, and I didn't want to hurt his wife. Part of me hated her and resented her; but it wasn't her fault.'

We sat in silence for a while. The ducks had given up and swum away and wispy violet clouds marked the beginning of a wintry sunset. I contemplated telling Beth about Carole. About the pregnancy and everything. She'd told me her secret after all; it would be like a pact between us. But then I knew my own situation was different, it wasn't about the past so much as the future, people would find out soon enough, and in the meantime, so long as I didn't discuss it, I could almost pretend it wasn't happening.

'What do the others say about Rob?' I asked.

'Others?' Beth turned to me. 'No-one knows, apart from my parents and an old school friend. And they're not going to. What I've told you is strictly between you and me, it's no business of anyone else.'

'Not even Ashley?'

'Especially not Ashley.'

I smiled smugly. It was obvious the way things were going. I was the one Beth trusted with her innermost secrets. Ashley Roberts might take her out to expensive restaurants and send her flowers, but I knew things he didn't. I knew when I was well in there. Beth made it clear that Ashley simply wasn't important any more; not when it really mattered. All I had to do now was wait.

She shivered.

'Come on,' I said. 'It's chilling down and the light's fading. Let's get back and see if your parents are awake.'

Chapter 35

Pilot bulb - caving lamps generally have a halogen main beam and a much smaller dimmer pilot bulb which conserves the battery and is used when stationary or in easy terrain.

Back at the camp I'm starting to chill down again. There's the dilemma. Stay still for any length of time and you get cold, move about and you need food. I wish I knew what the time was. I'm trying to guess the number of hours I've been on the move and, consequently, the amount of light I have left in my lamp. It's OK here at the camp of course. If I rationed the night-lights for essential use only, I could stay here for a week. If I had more food, that is. I start to think creatively. I contemplate the possibility of fixing a candle on top of my helmet, like miners used to do before Davey invented his lamp. Then I could move about. Well I could if there was anywhere better to move to. If I could only free up my mind a bit more then maybe I could come up with some workable ideas.

I could do with some drugs, I think to myself. I've got some too. Stashed in the zip pocket of my fleece suit. I shake my head. Drugs used to be fun, happy pills to help you party, like a cherry on a cake or a whisky chaser. Would I really contemplate taking the stuff I have with me? Not for fun this time but more of an anaesthetic, a quick way out. I shudder and close my mind to the possibility. I've seen the good side of drugs, but also the bad.

It was midsummer, the end of our second year at university and we were back at Worthy Farm. The sun beat down relentlessly, baking a rich crust on top of last night's mud.

Rick and Joe lay entwined on the ground, Joe's head resting against Rick's chest. Usually they didn't go in for public displays of affection – a caving club being a place where men were men and all that – but here they were in a different world.

220

I stared at them as they embraced. Their movements were slow and slight, almost imperceptible as they gently stroked the bare skin of one another's arms. Occasionally Rick leaned forwards and they kissed on the lips, the merest brush. I was stunned at the tenderness of their touch; fascinated by the opposite qualities of their form. Rick dark, heavily built, his olive-skinned shoulders and back covered by a gorilla-like pelt of black hair. Joe appeared naked without his leather jacket, discarded in the extreme heat. I was shocked by his fragility and the redness of his bare skin in the sun. Yet they were drawn together like two halves of a whole, complementing one another precisely, yin and yang.

Fish sat cross-legged a few yards away. He moved his head and arms in time to the music and his hair, long and luxuriant, flowed about him in a dark undulating wave. He wore a loose white shirt that billowed in the breeze. It reflected the sun's rays in a dazzling crescendo of light, as though the brilliance radiated from within himself. He was an ethereal being, the chosen one, a saviour in a field full of sinners.

Beth, meanwhile, stood swaying, eyes closed dancing blind, her face and palms lifted skywards. The movement of her hips sent ripples swirling down the purple silk of her skirt, right down to the fringe that swept about her mud-spattered boots. She shook her head and the light played on her hair, shimmering on blonde ringlets. I got turned on just looking at her.

I shuffled my feet uncomfortably and readily accepted the joint that Taff passed me, balancing it between my thumb and forefinger in that way that, for some unwritten reason, was reserved for smoking cannabis. I took a long drag and held it deep inside, until my lungs felt like they were burning and bursting at the same time.

'There's a hell of a load of stuff here,' Taff observed.

'Yeah?' I was still thinking about Beth.

'Well, just look around you.'

I thought about handing the joint to Rick and Joe but couldn't bring myself to disturb the stillness and sanctity which

221

surrounded them so I passed it back to Taff and gazed about the field. He was right of course. I'd noticed it the first time I'd gone to a festival. Now I just kind of took it for granted and got on with my own thing, leaving other people to do theirs.

Taff blew out the scented smoke in a long steady stream. 'You know you could really shift a lot of Smartees somewhere like this.'

'I don't get you.'

'Come on. Here, Reading, Knebworth. A quid a throw, maybe even a fiver. One summer and you'd make a packet.'

I whistled. 'Hell man, I'm not a dealer. Smartees are just a bit of fun. For us.'

'Think about it though. What do you get on a student grant? Even less than me on a building site. All you'd have to do is make the stuff. I'd see to everything else. We could go halves.'

I shook my head. 'I don't want to get into trading. I mean – I don't want to be responsible if someone gets ill. And what if we got caught? Possession is one thing, I'd probably get a fine, but get done for dealing and I could be locked up for years. Sorry, mate, but it just isn't worth the risk. Anyway,' I stared at him, puzzled, 'I'd have thought you'd be against that kind of thing after what happened to your...ouch!'

Fish had rolled across and prodded me painfully in the ribs. I didn't even know he was listening.

'Sorry,' I muttered, embarrassed.

Fish stared at me intensely, shaking his head.

Back in our first year, soon after we all met, we were in my room listening to music, Rick and Joe, Fish and me. Rick was teaching us three innocents how to roll joints, how to glue the Rizlas together, how much resin to crumble in – because we hadn't started growing our own then – when, out of the blue, Fish started telling us about how Taff's older brother had died of a heroin overdose. 'It was only a few m-months ago,' he said, 'and I'm t-telling you so you don't put your foot in it, you know, d-don't mention heroin or ask about his family. He may seem OK but I've known him years, I know how hard he's taking it.'

And none of us had mentioned it until now.

'I'm really sorry,' I said again, 'I'm sorry about your brother and I'm sorry I reminded you of it. But I am surprised, though, that you're not more…well…anti the drug scene.'

Taff shrugged. 'No sweat,' he said, 'it was a couple of years ago now and I've come to terms with it.'

I nodded.

'Anyway,' he continued, 'it wasn't the heroin that killed him; it was the pit closing that did it. He'd been down there much longer than me, see? He couldn't imagine any other sort of life.' He took a long drag of the joint and sat looking at it as a piece of ash bent over and crumbled onto the grass. He shook his head. 'The drugs didn't kill him, they helped him, they were there for him when nothing and nobody else was. In a way they saved him.'

I struggled to understand his logic, and the idea of hard drugs in a sleepy mining community seemed incongruous to me. 'I'm surprised he managed to get hold of the stuff so easily.'

Taff laughed. 'Grow up, boyo! You from your nice clean middle-class home, thinking shit like that just happens in nasty run down inner city tower blocks. It's in your cosy little world as well, you know, not to mention half the villages in the valleys. Jesus, I've known where to get hold of gear like that since I was thirteen.'

I was shocked. I think Fish was too. 'But you haven't have you? I mean – you wouldn't?'

Taff blew a long column of smoke. 'I know it's there. If I need it then I guess it's only a question of time. And hey! If your little Smartees can help someone out and earn you a bob or two at the same time then where's the harm?'

'I'm not dealing. No way.'

'Mass murderers.' Fish had rolled onto his back and was sucking on a blade of grass.

'Huh?'

'That's what they are, dealers, they're mass murderers in slow motion.'

223

Bloody hell! This was all getting too heavy. I stood up, stretched and wrapped my arms around Beth. 'Fancy taking a stroll back to the tent with me?' I whispered in her ear.

And since I've been working in the lab, the horror story only seems to get worse. I remember back in the summer, a couple of days after I saw that poor guy on the slab. I mentioned it to Mike.

He shrugged. 'Yeah, what of it?' He didn't seem horrified like I was, or even surprised.

I wasn't exactly feeling tolerant that week. 'Well can't you do something about it?' I demanded. 'Make more effort to catch the people who are selling that stuff?'

'We know who the street dealers are,' he said, calmly, 'and we have a pretty good idea where they're stashing this latest batch.'

'What?' I just couldn't believe it. 'You know the stuff is out there but you do nothing? I've seen this poor dead chap get carved up and you could have stopped him getting those drugs in the first place?'

'Hey! Don't blame me! I'm just obeying orders. You know the game. You know what I do, you have a good idea how we operate and you know I can't answer questions. It's never simple. Sometimes you have to ignore the little fish, or nurture them and feed them, even; so that one day you can use them as bait to catch the big one.'

He was right. I didn't always approve of his methods, what I knew of them. But then, it wasn't a pretty business he was involved in.

'Have you noticed how they often have coloured lights in the toilets in clubs these days?' he continued.

'Vaguely,' I admitted.

'And do you know why that is?'

I shook my head.

'It's to stop people taking heroin, shooting up.'

'But how…?'

'Because they can't see their veins.'

224

Clearly I was lagging behind in my knowledge of modern street practices. 'But that's sick,' I answered. 'It will force people out onto the streets to find some dark alleyway. If something goes wrong there'll be little chance of them being found in time to get help.'

'But as far as the club's concerned it shifts the drugs off their premises. Not in my back yard and all that. This is the real world and it isn't always pretty.' His face hardened. 'I'm sorry if you don't like how I work but it really isn't any of your business. You get on with your job and leave me to get on with mine.'

He had a point, I supposed. I analysed what was in people's veins and Mike tried to catch the dealers who put it there. Neither occupation was most people's idea of fun.

'And anyway,' he continued, 'with your history, you're really not in a position to criticise others, are you?'

Back at the camp, I shudder. Fish is right; they're all murderers. I've been given the stuff in my pocket by a murderer. That's a good reason not to use it. I take the tiny packet out and rip it open, spilling the contents into the flame. Then I laugh out loud. And a thousand echoes laugh with me.

Chapter 36

Cave pearl - similar spherical formation to that found in an oyster.
Cave pearls are quite rare, typically found in shallow pools.

The festive season continued into New Year's Eve; traditionally one of the most celebrated nights of the year. What's more, it was the eve of the new millennium: an extra reason to party. But to us it was just another night down the pub, and the conversation, as always, was the cave.

We were in the Red Dragon. There were Beth and Ashley, Rick, Joe, Taff and myself. Fish was absent, building up karma by staying in with the Valkyrie so he could slip out and come caving with us tomorrow. We were discussing the following day's trip. Ashley wanted us to carry a load of diving gear down in readiness for him to have another push on the Devil's Cauldron.

'If we all lend a hand,' he was saying, 'we could get the stuff down there in three hours and still have time to look around a bit before we come back out.'

Rick wasn't convinced. 'Personally I'd rather spend the time making headway with the new passage. You've dived the Cauldron twice already and Fish is convinced it isn't going to go.'

While I was daydreaming, the conversation around me was getting heated.

Beth was defending Ashley. 'I think you're all being unfair. It's selfish not to help take Ashley's gear down. He's doing the dive for all of us after all.'

'Nobody's saying we won't help. I just think it would be better done one evening instead of a bank holiday. We don't get many opportunities these days with all of us together.' Rick's peace-making effort was failing.

I looked at Taff. He'd been fidgety and irritable for the last hour.

'What do you think?' Beth looked at me.

I shrugged.

Suddenly Taff slammed his fist on the table. 'Can't you bloody stop this fucking arguing? If we just got out there and got on with it we could have explored that cave ten times over by now! And some of us have other important things going on in our lives.' He stood up, picked up his jacket and stamped across the room.

He looked like he was heading for the door but turned at the last minute and went into the gents. Then I remembered a couple of weeks ago when something similar had happened. He'd been edgy just like tonight, although he hadn't actually lost it. Then, during the second part of the evening he'd changed. Suddenly he was sweet as pie, unnaturally calm. I hadn't thought about it at the time. If I had I'd have put it down to alcohol. But now I wasn't so sure and something about his behaviour didn't add up.

I stood up and made to follow him.

'And they say it's women who go to the loo in pairs,' laughed Beth. 'Must be something in the beer. So what do you say about tomorrow, Marty?'

'I agree with Rick,' I shouted over my shoulder as I hurried after Taff.

In the gents' toilets the room was empty. Grimy white tiles winked from the floor and the walls. The urinals gaped expectantly. There were two stalls, one of which was occupied, so I figured it had to be Taff in there. I went into the neighbouring one and, as quietly as you can do such things, climbed onto the already cracked seat. As I hoisted myself up I had this fear that Taff had slipped out of the pub unnoticed and I was about to view a total stranger having a crap. I put my hands on the dividing wall and pulled myself upright. Beneath my feet the toilet seat creaked ominously.

I peered over. It was Taff all right. He was sitting on the bowl, clothes intact, all except for his left sleeve, which was rolled up to just above his elbow. As I watched he withdrew the syringe. Oh shit, I was too late. He let out a sigh. Of what?

227

Resolution? Relief? Then he slumped, just let go physically and abandoned himself to the drug. He hadn't even noticed me – or so I thought.

Heroin. I should have realised before. He'd always said, hadn't he, that it was only a question of time? I just hoped that he hadn't taken too much, that it was clean. 'Hang on, Taff!' I called. 'I'm coming over. You're going to be all right!'

With that I hooked my right leg over the top of the partition, then scrabbled against the wall with my left foot in an attempt to get the rest of me over. It didn't quite work out how I intended and I overbalanced so that my feet stayed hooked over the top and my head and shoulders dangled precariously. I reached for the cistern, which mercifully was low level. 'Shit!'

'That's what usually goes down here. If I stood up now you'd go head first down the pan,' Taff laughed.

'You're OK!' I stated the obvious. 'Thank God.' The partition wobbled and I slipped another couple of inches. 'Er…I don't suppose you could give me a hand?'

He stood up, braced his shoulder under mine and unhooked my feet from where they were caught. I dropped down into the cubicle and we stood almost touching, face to face in the confined space.

'Hell, Taff. You shouldn't be doing this.'

He sat down again. 'I know, Marty, but…'

'No buts,' I said sternly. 'How many times have you done it?' I took his hands and turned them palm uppermost, studied his forearms. Apart from the fresh needle mark they were unscathed.

'A couple – but Marty it isn't what you think…'

'That's what they all say. People think they can control it, that it'll help.' I stared at him. 'But I've watched some of them get cut up on slabs.'

Taff sighed and shook his head.

'Look,' I continued, 'I can't talk about what goes down at work…' It was becoming bizarre, a serious subject in a ridiculous location. The stall was so cramped we were almost hugging one another. '…but trust me, Taff, there's some really

228

bad stuff around at the moment. Do you understand what I'm saying? I saw someone brought in only yesterday, they were half our age.' It was a lie, but a Persil white one under the circumstances.'

The syringe was lying on the floor. Best get rid of the evidence. I bent to pick it up. Then I saw something else, a small empty phial. I retrieved that too.

I read it three times just to be sure. 'Pethidine?'

I held it in front of his face. 'Is this what you've been taking?'

Taff started laughing. 'I tried to tell you.'

I was so relieved that I laughed too. 'But where did you get it? Why?'

He shrugged, 'You can get most things on the black market you know – I could probably order it on the internet if I owned a computer. And why? Because of everything that's going on. Because the kids are going to live on the other side of the world. Because for a few blissful hours it takes the pain away.'

'Yeah, if you're giving birth!' I giggled.

Taff shook his head. 'There I am holding a sensible conversation, rescuing you from diving head first down the pan, and you think I've just mainlined a load of horse. You've got no idea of the real world, boyo!' He laughed again. 'If you'd been concentrating in that film you'd know it's the junkie that goes swimming in the john!'

'Seriously though,' I tried to get back to what mattered, 'it isn't a good idea to take anything without supervision. This stuff is addictive too, you know? Very similar to morphine, in fact.' I scrabbled rashly for a bribe. 'I'll tell you what. I'll buy all your beer for the next month so long as you stay clean. Nothing but beer and baccy.'

That stopped him in his tracks. 'You serious?'

'Deadly – because that's what I don't want you to be.'

He scratched his chin, which wasn't easy pressed together as we were.

'Please, Taff. Give it a try. I'll help if it gets tough, you can call me anytime.'

'S'pose I could. It would save some money anyway.'

'Yeah. Think of that,' I encouraged. 'All the more to spend on beer.'

'I thought you were buying that.'

I stopped laughing for a moment, wondering if my offer had been a little rash and whether my overdraft could stretch that far.

Then we heard the squeaking of a swing door and froze, silent, trying not to laugh. There were no footsteps. It must have been someone going into the ladies next door.

Taff giggled. 'Better get out of here before we get arrested for cottaging.'

I turned and reached for the bolt.

Taff shrugged. 'It wasn't locked, it's broken, see?'

'Bastard!' I laughed.

We were still in there, both of us crammed in that tiny smelly cubicle, when suddenly there was a noise from the bar. People shouting something in unison, then a pause, then shouting again. This was followed by the sound of cheering, shouting and shrill blasts of what sounded like whistles and toy trumpets. Taff and I looked at one another then laughed.

'Happy New Millennium!' we both said.

Chapter 37

Rebelay - a fixed point in an SRT pitch where the caver transfers to a new rope or section of rope.

The candle's guttering, sending dramatic flashes of light and dark around the otherwise total blackness of Camp David. When this one's gone there's just one more left in the box. My last chance, I think to myself. A new beginning; or the beginning of the end. It sends my thoughts into places philosophical. In the past forty-eight hours I've had to reassess my life, big time. More than that, I've had to rethink stuff about people around me. I've been doing that in a smaller way for the past few months. And it all started with something I saw earlier in the year.

When you've known someone for a long time, you think you know all there is to know. You don't expect any surprises. They become reassuringly constant and predictable. And when you've known two people as a couple for twenty years, together they seem more rock solid than they do as individuals. They reinforce one another in a way that makes you feel safe and secure in their presence. Well that's how I've always felt, anyway. Maybe it's different for people whose parents have divorced. Even what had happened with Carole hadn't shaken my steadfast faith in human nature. However hurt I felt, however let down, the reappearance of Beth into my life helped me reconcile that Carole and I had never been right for each other in the first place. But a change in the relationships of my oldest, closest friends was something I couldn't begin to come to terms with. It shook the last bit of stability in my life.

The first time I suspected there was something going on between them was late January. It was a Saturday morning and we weren't caving because people had things to do. Taff was seeing his kids, Ashley was out of town, Joe had said something about being busy and Rick was fitting in some extra tutorials with a couple of students before their forthcoming exams. I needed a few things from town, like a birthday card for my sister. I'd forgotten last year's because I'd just moved out from home and, apart from the general disruption, remembering, buying and sending cards was one of the things Carole did. Anyway, this time my mother had phoned me a couple of days previously to remind me so I had no excuse. After that I thought I'd probably call in at Mole Supplies to pick up a couple of bits and pieces and have a chat with Sprat, then, later on, when he'd dropped the kids back with his ex, I wanted to go and see Taff, maybe go out for a beer with him and satisfy myself that he was doing OK, that he was clean.

After choosing the card and seeing to a few other errands I decided to stop off somewhere and have a coffee. Apart from anything else, I was desperate for a ciggy, I'd been smoking far too much since Carole's revelations but under the circumstances I thought it was quite justified. So I went into a cafe, a comfortably impersonal place with a self-service counter and wipe-clean tables. I chose a Danish pastry and a cappuccino and, after paying, picked up my tray from the counter where you collect sugar and teaspoons and looked around for somewhere to sit.

That's when I saw them, Fish and Joe. They were sitting at a table over by the far wall. I was about to shout hello and go and join them but something stopped me and instead I chose a table near to the counter. A pillar blocked me from their view and I lurked behind it, feeling somewhat furtive, trying to convince myself that I was just being polite and considerate, rather than barging in where I hadn't been invited. I peeped, surreptitiously, round the pillar. It was encircled by a garland of plastic ivy, pretty naff as far as taste goes but just the job for spying on people. It was more difficult than you'd think though. Suddenly I admired those private investigators – the ones you see on films – they made it look so easy. I pulled my chair over as far as I dared without risking being seen and leaned uncomfortably across the table. They were sitting opposite one another, side on to me. I could see more of Joe's face than of Fish's, they were deep in conversation and I could see that Joe was laughing; he seemed happy and more animated than usual. I leaned out a little so I could get a better look. Joe reached out and took Fish's hand. And Fish was positively beaming.

Suddenly I realised what was going on. They were having an affair. Jesus! I fumbled in my pocket, now I needed a cigarette more than ever. I lit up and peeked again. They were looking more serious now and Fish was doing most of the talking, Joe was nodding and adding the odd word now and again. I wished I could hear what they were saying.

'Excuse me, sir, but you're sitting in the No Smoking area.'

'What?' No, please don't disturb me now; worse still don't draw attention to me.

'You're sitting in the No Smoking area,' repeated the assistant, 'I'll have to ask you to put the cigarette out or move to another table.' She looked at me severely with the unbending authority of a teacher.

'Sorry,' I muttered, stubbing out the offending item in the ashtray offered.

As soon as she'd gone, I looked back round the pillar. I watched as they continued to laugh and chat as my neglected coffee grew cold and formed a skin across the surface. At last they stood up and made their way to the door. Outside the window, they paused and embraced. OK, not a full-on snog, but they gave each other quite a lingering hug.

Jesus! What was going on? Everyone was at it, it seemed: Fish and Joe, Carole and her toyboy. In a way I wasn't surprised at Fish – the homosexual thing, I mean. Back at university, when we were all in Benson Street together, if you'd asked me who was the one in four – if, statistically speaking, one in four of us were likely to be gay – then the prime candidate would have been Fish. And now, well, OK he was married but it hardly seemed a happy arrangement and anyone can swing both ways. Not me, obviously, I'm strictly a ladies' man, but I'm told most people have the potential.

Unwelcome thoughts started leaping into my head. All the

years Joe had been with Rick, I thought of them as a couple in a social sort of way. I never thought of the physical aspect of their relationship, of them having sex. But now he was having an affair with Fish, those were the images appearing before me. Shagging. What else is an affair about, after all? Suddenly, all I could see were pictures of Joe and Fish in bizarre contortions of homosexual acts.

I stood up, picked up my tray and moved to a table in the smoking section. It took three cigarettes to push it all to the back of my mind.

And then, a few days later, as if to confirm my suspicions, something else happened.

It was Tuesday evening and I was having a quiet night in, thinking about moving out. Now that it was clear I wasn't going to move back in with Carole, I was feeling the need to find somewhere that felt a bit more like home. Because it wasn't just the inside of this place that was unpleasant, the outside was just as bad. The building that housed Mike's flat was a monstrosity of brick and concrete and felt somewhat penitential. It had those awful iron handrails outside the doors, and dreary concrete lining the pedestrian entrance from the road. There was a mosaic of patched-up cement and broken paving slabs in the forecourt that made you wonder how many bodies were buried beneath. The structure itself was three floors high (we were at the top) and the halls and staircases had no doors, just covered archways. Although our entrance was round the back, necessitating fumbling round a grim shadowy path after dark, this somehow didn't deter tramps or passing drunks as evidenced by the smell of stale urine, multi-storey car park style, in the stairwell. In the alcove that housed the bins the word 'wanker' had been spray-painted across the dilapidated brick wall.

I guessed Mike had probably lived here for a couple of years. His work in the drug squad meant that he had to go undercover, to be a punter on the street, to request the services of dealers and to befriend them. Sometimes he might spend years on the same job, meeting contacts, gathering information. Depending on the outcome, he might stay on to work on something else, or he might, once his identity was known, move somewhere else in the country. He kept his gun in a locked cupboard in his room. I only saw it once, steely and sinister in its nest, like a newly hatched dinosaur. I wondered if he had ever used it to kill someone. I wondered if he knew what it felt like, to live, knowing that you are responsible for ending someone else's life. But I never asked. Because it really isn't the sort of subject that comes up as you crawl into the kitchen in the morning to get your first caffeine fix of the day or as you stagger in at night, out of your head on Old Peculiar. And, to be honest, if the answer was yes then I didn't want to know. I suppose I should have felt reassured, knowing there was a weapon there in the flat, but for some reason it only made me feel uneasy.

Apart from the fact that Mike was out a lot, the place had two things going for it. Firstly, it was near the centre of town, handy for my place of work and for staggering back from pubs and clubs. Secondly, it was cheap. I suppose I'd just grown accustomed to it, but the fact was it was a slum.

Anyway, that evening, the nine o'clock news had just started when there was a knock at the door. I looked through the spy-hole just in case it was someone dubious connected with Mike's investigations. He'd impressed on me always to do this and given me a special number to ring if I was in any doubt. I'd always followed his instructions religiously although so far I'd not encountered anyone out of the ordinary.

I figured that, if it were one of my friends, the most likely would be Taff. True to my word, I'd kept an eye on him since New Year. But this week was particularly bad for him because, the previous day, his ex-wife and kids had left for Brisbane, starting a new life of their own, and closing the chapter that Taff had shared with them in Wales. Not wanting him to be alone, I'd gone out for a drink with him. By nine o'clock he'd already drunk three pints to my one, but as long as it was only alcohol I wasn't too worried.

235

He'd tried to be philosophical about it all, saying that the kids would be better off. 'They'll have opportunities there,' he'd said, as he downed his fifth pint. 'I mean – what's left for them here, with the pits closed and everything? I'm sure the courts would have ordered them to stay if I'd opposed it, but it wouldn't have been fair would it?'

'But how will you get to see them?' I'd asked, as I passed him a cigarette and lit one for myself. The bar was almost empty, I wasn't used to it on a quiet night, forlorn chairs were slotted neatly beside tables, the flagstone floor was stark and cold, every noise, the chink of a beer glass, the scrape of a chair, even our voices, resounded loud and sharp without the myriad of bodies to absorb it. It was almost like being down a cave.

He'd shrugged. 'Megan will bring them back for a few weeks every summer. So they can all visit her parents, see? I'll get to see them then. And she's said I'd be welcome to visit them in Australia – but I can't see I'd be able to afford it.'

I'd seen him home and slept on the sofa in his flat, just to make sure he was OK.

So, that night, I half expected him to be looking for a drinking partner again. However, it wasn't Taff but Joe's slight form the other side of the lens and I opened the door in surprise. It was only then it dawned on me, this was the first time any of my friends had come round. Both Taff and Fish had sometimes collected me or dropped me off after caving trips but I'd always met them down in the street. No-one I knew had actually stepped across the threshold.

'Come in...er...sorry about all this.' The hallway was cluttered with Mike's bicycle, two pairs of scruffy trainers and a rubbish bag destined for the aforementioned self-abusing bins; then there was several weeks' worth of junk mail which was forming a heap in imminent danger of suffering a landslide.

Joe looked around, clearly embarrassed. 'I hope I haven't caught you at a bad time, only I uploaded the first set of photos from my new camera at lunchtime and seeing as you're on the way home...'

I was equally embarrassed as I led the way into the lounge.

'Hang on, I'll find you somewhere to sit.' I scooped the last week's newspapers and an ashtray off the sofa, tripping over the TV controller as I did so and consequently spilling fag ends over the upholstery and amplifying the newscaster's voice to a frightening number of decibels.

'We're not used to visitors,' I explained. 'Let me get you a beer.'

'No, really, I'm driving.'

'Well a coffee then.'

I persuaded Joe to sit on the freshly brushed sofa rather than follow me into the kitchen – he really would have been horrified to see the entire contents of the crockery cupboard immersed in greasy water in the sink. I picked out a couple of mugs and washed them under the tap.

'You're working late!' I shouted across the hall.

'Yeah. I thought the extra hours would dry up after Christmas – once all the millennium bug fixes were done. Now, there seems to be just as much panic over the new European currency. Goodness knows if it will ever happen, but it has to be coded into every billing program for every company that's going to take the damn things.'

I searched through the cupboards looking for the ground coffee, hoping to redeem myself and prove I hadn't become a complete slob. I was feeling a bit uncomfortable; not just about the mess the flat was in but the fact Joe had turned up now, a few days after I'd seen him with Fish. Maybe one of them had noticed me that day and Joe was going to ask me to keep quiet about it. I'd been thinking about it since. And the more I thought, the more their affair seemed obvious. It explained why Fish had seemed so much happier these past few months. I'd remembered times at university – especially that time when Joe had a bad trip on Smartees – when Fish had practically declared his undying love for him. For all I knew it might have been going on for years.

'But do you really need to work this many hours? I mean, it isn't like you need the money or anything?'

'Well they're making it worth my while. And I may have

237

some extra expenses coming up soon.'

Extra expenses? Jeez, what if he meant he was going to buy Rick out of the house? I finished making the coffee and joined him in the lounge.

'Do you want to call Rick and let him know you're here?'

'No thanks; he'll be out. He was planning on seeing Ashley to talk caves.'

'Those two are getting thick as thieves aren't they?' Shit! I shouldn't have said that. What if that was part of it? What if Ashley swung both ways too? Stranger things have happened.

Joe took one look at my face and laughed. 'I'm glad he's found someone equally eccentric to make plans with, it means I don't have to hear about it every night.'

I nodded. If Rick was out with Ashley a lot then that gave Joe more opportunity to see Fish. I knew I should be ashamed of the way I was thinking; it really wasn't any of my business. 'So let's see these pictures then,' I said.

Joe was the nearest we had to an official photographer. He'd learned the tricks of how to take pictures underground. How to run an extension lead from the hot-shoe on his camera to power a hand held flash unit. How to position specialist slave units behind rocks and round corners so that they picked up signals from the camera and triggered concealed flashguns, backlighting formations and waterfalls. How to set up the camera on a tripod with the shutter locked open so that one person could become many, illuminating the length of a passage, rope or ladder in a series of pre-planned exposures.

Now he'd bought a digital camera – more for surface use really – and this was his first shot at testing it in a cave environment. We browsed through the stuff he'd read into the computer. It was great for places full of shiny white calcite but in the dark or dull areas of a cave the light wasn't really enough.

'At least it's small and lightweight. It'll be useful to have with us to keep a record of what we're doing.'

'Fish seems happier these days,' I said, as we paged through the pictures on Joe's laptop. 'Maybe it's his turn for some good luck.' It was an innocent comment but I watched carefully for a reaction.

Joe nodded. 'Yes, Rick and I have noticed. We're not half so worried about him now. And I'm sure a lot of that's down to you, being there, supporting him when he needed someone.' He was completely calm and controlled, no hint of embarrassment or guilt. But after what I'd seen it didn't convince me. If anything it made me even more suspicious. Perhaps the affair had been going on so long that they were good at lying about it.

And then, right on cue, his mobile beeped the arrival of a text message. Sitting next to him, in order to look at the photos, I could see the screen display indicating it was from Fish. He picked the phone up and clicked into the message. I couldn't see the details, of course, but he seemed really pleased as he read it and afterwards he tapped in a quick reply.

'Nothing important,' he said as he set the phone down on the table. 'Now, have a look at the traditional ones.'

We looked at the other photographs, the ones he'd taken on the SLR. They were really good – though nothing like the ones Beth and I had secretly stashed away – but really I couldn't concentrate. All I could think of was what was going on between Joe and Fish. Eventually we'd looked at all the photos and he stood up. 'I'd best be going soon,' he said. 'If I could just pop to the bathroom first…'

'It's down the corridor, on the left.'

And then, after he'd left the room, I did something I'm really not proud of. His mobile was still on the coffee table, next to the SLR photos and the laptop. It wasn't that I was being nosy – I just needed to know for sure. So I picked it up and clicked to refresh the screen. <1 message. Sender – Fish> it announced. I clicked on 'read'.

<Everything's arranged. Suggest we don't tell anyone yet. Valerie won't be pleased. Love 'n' peace. Fish.>

Arranged? Oh my gosh…were they planning to run away together? I was so horrified, I paged into the 'sent' messages to read Joe's reply.

<You're brilliant! Can't wait. Love, Joe.>

I just couldn't believe it. I sat there for a few moments, staring at the words. Then the sound of the toilet flushing brought me to my senses and I hurriedly clicked back to the home page and replaced the phone on the table.

'Are you sure you're OK?' I asked as Joe put his jacket on. 'And Rick?'

'Course we are. You know us. Why do you ask?'

I shrugged. 'I guess you always seem to be watching out for other people. I just hope you're looking after yourselves.'

He laughed. Was it a little forced, maybe? What would I know? I couldn't make sense of my own life let alone anyone else's. He put a hand on my shoulder. 'I just want my mates to be happy,' he said. 'Talking of which, I don't like thinking of you in this dump. If Rick and I had realised what sort of place you were staying in we'd have insisted on you moving in with us from the start. Please will you reconsider now?'

He was right. This was a God-forsaken hole and there was nothing I'd have liked better than to go back with him to Benson Street there and then. But I was worried about him and Rick. This thing with Fish; I didn't know for sure how far it had gone or how serious it was. Maybe it had started innocently – with Joe trying to pull Fish out of a depression – and then got out of hand. Whatever was happening, I felt if there was any chance of Rick and Joe working through it, they needed their space. So I said no.

'OK then, here's what we'll do. Rick will be home by now so I don't need my key.' He took a bunch of keys out of his pocket and worked the front door one off the ring. He handed it to me. 'Here, take this. As soon as you change your mind we'll be expecting you.'

I took it. 'Cheers.'

'And don't leave it too long.' And before he left he kissed me on the cheek in what I guessed was a homosexually platonic way.

Chapter 38

Alpine bunk - a communal mattress on which a number of people sleep side by side.

It's only when I light the new candle, and in its comparatively clear and steady light I see the logbook, that I realise its contents might hold the key to my way out. It hadn't occurred to me to look at it until now. I'd been more concerned with cooking food and trying to stay sane.

But now it seems obvious. Instead of trying to remember the snatches of conversation I've heard over the past few days, all I have to do is read the accounts recorded here.

So I turn to the last few entries and read the summaries of the two most recent trips, one written by Rick and the last one in Sprat's scrawling hand. And in retrospect, the descriptions make it obvious where I went wrong a couple of hours earlier.

It's clear now where I should have turned off the main drag, and I read the details of the most likely route to the outside. The descriptions of the tight water-filled passages I'll need to negotiate fill me with dread. The fact is. I'm not good with water underground. It isn't so bad if it's in a big open area such as the Lake, or if there are other people around. But what I'm reading about the way on is starting to give me the shakes.

I try and tell myself it'll be OK. After all, I didn't always feel this way. In my second year at university I got my diving certificate and did a couple of specialist courses on cave diving. Then I went on trips with Fish. I remember how we went in Wookey Hole, past the show cave all the way to the first sump. Then the fun really started; a whole series of submerged passages interspersed with glistening chambers, places where hardly anyone else had been, a whole different lost world.

But I guess things can't always be fun. And when they got too heavy I locked everything away in the back of my mind and moved on.

After almost a year of caving again, I thought the bad stuff was safely in the past. Then, in February, we went on a trip to Yorkshire, and the old ghosts resurfaced.

The plan was to go in Gaping Ghyll, a famous cavern up near Ingleton. We drove up on the Friday night in readiness for the cave on Saturday. It was the first time the group of us had gone anywhere other than Quarry Cave since the trip in Daren before Christmas.

Admittedly there were all sorts of things going on which meant I wasn't in the best state of mind to start with. By the time we arrived at the caving club where we were staying, and spread our sleeping bags in a row along the alpine bunk, it was almost eleven; too late to go out to a pub. While the others were in the common room, attempting to light a log fire in an ancient stove, I slipped upstairs and raided my bag for my emergency beer supply. I pulled out a can of Pedigree, sat on the bunk and snapped the ring pull; then I downed the first half in one go.

It had been a tiring journey and I really needed a drink. We'd travelled up in two cars: Ashley, Beth and Taff in one and me, Rick, Joe and Fish in the other. I'd driven the second half with Rick beside me, directing me the last few long miles, along steep twisting lanes that wriggled across misty moors, eventually arriving at the caving club. And all the while I'd been aware of Fish and Joe in the back. I could see them in the rear view mirror, making those knowing signs new lovers do when they think no-one's watching; a smile, a nudge; they were almost imperceptible. But after what I'd seen in town and read in the texts it was like they were screaming their declarations of passion for me alone to hear.

I took another gulp of beer. If I'd driven with Beth and Ashley I'd have felt equally uncomfortable for different reasons. It was like I couldn't win these days. I really wanted a cigarette but that would have to wait as there was a no smoking sign in the bunk room and I didn't want to take my beer downstairs, I only had a couple of cans – hardly enough to restore my own sanity let alone to share round.

That was when Joe appeared. He was light on his feet and I

242

hadn't heard him climbing the steep stairs. Suddenly he was standing there in the doorway and I looked guiltily at my drink, like I was sixteen again and been caught out by my Dad.

'Want a swig?' I offered the can to him as he sat down beside me on the bunk.

He shook his head. 'You deserve it, you've been driving,' he said.

I nodded. 'It's just to help me unwind after concentrating on the road,' I agreed. 'It'll help me sleep.'

'Better to drink it now than before caving tomorrow,' Joe laughed. Then suddenly he was serious. 'What happened to you that time before Christmas?' He didn't have to specify more than that. My drunken caving adventure in Daren stood out as the only stupid thing any of us had done underground since we'd met up again.

I shrugged. I'd escaped a cross-examination at the time, what with the preparations for Christmas and the explorations in Quarry Cave. Only now did it occur to me that I'd never told anyone about what had happened with Carole. Maybe it was time I did.

I looked at Joe. 'That was a bad day,' I said. 'I'd just discovered my wife of ten years was pregnant with someone else's baby.' And I told Joe the whole story. About how I'd been seeing Carole on and off since I moved out; how I'd clung on to the hope that we'd patch things up.

When I finished we sat in silence for a few moments, then Joe spoke. 'That's heavy,' he said. 'That's one hell of a revelation for any man to take in.'

I nodded, gloomily.

'Have you met him – this new chap?'

I shook my head. 'Good grief, no! And I don't want to. At least living in a big city there's no reason our paths need cross. Presumably he's a law student too. When they've finished their degrees they'll probably move to London and be barristers together.' Please go far away, I thought to myself.

'Well I'm really sorry things didn't work out for you,' Joe said. 'Any time you want to talk you know where I am.'

243

'Thanks,' I murmured, as I downed the last of the beer.

'See you downstairs in a bit,' Joe said. 'Hopefully the others have got that fire going.' And he disappeared down the twisting staircase as silently as he'd arrived.

I was relieved. There were other subjects he might have wanted to talk to me about – like him and Fish, for one – that I just didn't want to think about right now.

The next day dawned and Gaping Ghyll beckoned. At that stage I was looking forward to it. My head was so tangled up with Carole and Joe and Fish, I didn't have space to worry about anything else. I thought I'd be glad of the distraction.

The main entrance to the cave was a three hundred and sixty foot abseil pitch alongside a thundering waterfall. You didn't have to be a caver to go down it. On the August and Whitsun bank holiday weekends a couple of local clubs set up a chair attached to a winch and lowered sightseers in and out of the main chamber.

We weren't taking that route though. For one thing we didn't have enough rope with us. Instead, we hiked across the moor to a lower entrance. This was known as Bar Pot and technically it was a separate cave, though it was part of the same system. After a series of short climbs and ladders we came to the longest pitch. It was a hundred feet; straight down a sheer exposed wall. Rick did the rigging, making sure there were ropes to clip our cows' tails onto before we hung, poised, over the vertical drop. Taff went down first, winding the rope round his descender then testing it with his full weight before unclipping the longer length of rope from the karabiner above him. Then he was off, sliding down into the blackness, the rope buzzing behind him. The rest of us followed in turn.

From the bottom of the pitch it was an easy enough stroll through to Gaping Ghyll. Beth was the only one who hadn't been there before. She marvelled at the vastness of it all. To be honest, it's the kind of place that's impressive even if it's your hundredth time. They say it's so big that you could fit York Minster inside it.

Not surprisingly, Ashley was the only one of us who'd ever abseiled down the main pitch.

'You wouldn't want to do that today,' he told us, authoritatively, as we gazed up towards the dot of daylight, our view distorted by the mist from the waterfall. 'After last night's rain there'd be too much weight of water on you.' He was probably right. The spray seemed to fill the entire cavern.

We sat on boulders far enough from the water not to get soaked, and ate the chocolate bars we'd brought as snacks. Then, after another stroll round, Fish, Joe and Rick set off to begin the ascent up the pitch. With seven of us to get up the rope, one at a time, it would likely take an hour for everyone to return to the upper level. If we all stood waiting our turn at the bottom of the pitch we'd get cold. So we agreed that Beth and Ashley would follow in ten minutes and Taff and I would bring up the rear. Ashley was impressing Beth with an account of how he ascended the main pitch beside the waterfall. Not straight up through the water but a complicated route involving bolts and rebelays. Neither Taff nor I could be bothered with listening to him so, with time to fill, we wandered off further into the cave system.

After a few minutes we found ourselves in a passage that followed the course of a stream. At first the route was narrow and we had to straddle the water, then it opened out into a series of chambers. Taff said it was a likely area for fossils and he hung back, examining the rock. I carried on, walking alongside the water, until the way ahead was blocked abruptly by a sheer wall of rock. At my feet the water pooled at the same level, presumably it disappeared into a sump. I paused and sat on a boulder and that's when it came back to me. As I looked into the pool, memories that had previously been safely confined to the distorted depths began to bubble to the surface.

I began to think about the last occasion I'd been on a caving trip to Yorkshire. It was fifteen years ago that Rick, Joe, Fish, Taff and myself had travelled up here. But it was a different trip entirely; different accommodation; different cave.

The place we'd booked to stay turned out to be Spartan as

caving clubs often are. I remember a wooden dining table and some chairs plus a couple of winged armchairs that might have been deemed too tatty for the local homeless shelter. The decoration wasn't up to much either; in fact it made our student house seem palatial. The place was damp – hardly surprising as it was left unoccupied half the time. That and the fact it was out on its own on a bleak Pennine hillside at the mercy of the weather made it little wonder that a mouldy smell emanated from the plaster and rain certainly found its way through the roof from time to time.

Across the hallway, the kitchen was even worse. In the middle of the room stood a kind of platform with shelving beneath and an area on top for the preparation of food. To call it a work surface would have been misleading, conjuring as that does, an image of polished pine or freshly scrubbed Formica, emanating an aura of cleanliness and hygiene. Instead, a wooden structure, adorned with peeling paint, supported a grimy slab; across which, gas rings strode like huge mechanical spiders.

A metal jungle of pans defied anyone to touch them, balanced in precarious towers, only occasionally glued together with the remnants of bygone meals. The cold stone of the floor challenged and beckoned, daring the defenceless skin of bare feet to cross its bleak expanse.

But worst of all, where sullen, grease-streaked wall met ceiling, a gap stretched between the sections of plasterboard. It was just wide enough for a wiry pink tail to swing down defiantly. And on the floor below, an invitation teased and tempted. 'Roland, this is for you,' read the card beside the bowl of rat poison.

As undergraduates, we wouldn't have batted an eyelid at that place, more likely we'd have relished the squalor. But we were much more fussy and grown up by then. Rick and I were in the third year of our PhDs, Taff was labouring on a building site which was one better than Fish, I suppose, who was unemployed again, while Joe was the only one gainfully employed, working as a computer programmer; compared to the rest of us he was well rich.

Rick, Joe and I had been first to arrive and deposited our sleeping bags and overnight packs in the bunkroom. By the time Taff and Fish pulled up outside an hour later, it was already mid-evening. Taff took one look at the kitchen facilities and suggested that, rather than mess about trying to cook, we go straight to the pub. We all voted this was the best option and set off for the nearest village, taking both cars.

At eleven o'clock, suitably fed and relaxed, Rick, Joe and I prepared to go back to the hut. That's when Fish announced he wouldn't be joining us. 'There d-doesn't seem m-much point in going back to sleep in that mess,' he said. 'Taff and I have got all our stuff with us and the landlord s-says there's an outbuilding we can stay in – or we could s-sleep in the car.'

'Jeez, sounds like the nativity,' joked Rick.

'Well don't stay up too late,' I suggested. 'Don't forget we've got a dive to do tomorrow.'

I'd noticed that the bar showed no signs of closing and suspected this was the main reason Fish was eager to sleep at the pub. I was also keenly aware that, this being a diving trip, it would be Fish and I who had the serious business to do the following day.

But Fish was unperturbed. He gave that innocent stare through dark lashes. 'S-stay cool, Marty,' he said. 'I could swim in my sleep. Have I ever let you down?'

I had to admit, he seemed to have this ability to float through hangovers while the rest of us were moaning and cursing. In any case, there was nothing I could do. So, rather reluctantly, we parted company and Rick, Joe and I headed back to the delights of the caving hut, hoping that the rat – or rats – hadn't nibbled their way into our sleeping bags.

Suddenly the memory stopped. Like the film had broken on a spool or the bulb had blown on a projector. I looked up from the pool to the wall in front of me. It was particularly dark, harsh, forbidding rock. It felt like the walls of the cavern were closing in on me. I could feel my breaths coming fast and shallow as I tried to control my thoughts.

247

'Marty! You OK?' Taff was standing behind me. 'You're shivering,' he said.

I was certainly shaking but not because I was cold.

'Come on,' he said, 'let's get back to the pitch and get out of here.'

'Good idea,' I said, standing up. 'You lead the way.' Sometimes it's great not to have to take responsibility, to let someone else take charge.

Chapter 39

Bedding plane - horizontal strata of rock, often partially eroded and forming a low flat space in a cave.

A couple of weeks after the Gaping Ghyll trip, I went round to Beth's to show her the latest photos of Quarry Cave and to separate out the ones of the Waterfall Chamber before the rest got passed around the crowd. I sat in silence while she looked through the pictures.

There were plenty of shots of the group of us. Beyond the Lake Chamber the cave continued to surprise us. There were passages and chambers connected by short climbs; some of them were tricky enough to require hand lines – or even ladders, if they presented a sheer pitch. Sometimes the streamway reappeared – water that had gone through the Devil's Cauldron, presumably – and formed cascades over smooth, shiny flowstone before disappearing again into rocky tunnels too tight for us to follow.

Some places were quite spectacular. There was Starbright Passage, with its dark velvety walls and ceiling encrusted with sparkling selenite crystals. There was the Breakfast Bar, where golden embryonic stalagmites shimmered in puddles, like poached eggs in a pan. There was Discworld, a flat circular chamber, part of a bedding plane, with three gnarled and twisted stals, stained black with manganese, which we named The Wyrd Sisters, rising from the floor.

Then there was a huge maze – the Monkey Puzzle Tree – where tight, twisting tunnels looped and threaded, branching and doubling back on themselves making us completely lose our sense of direction.

'This one's quite good.'

'Hmm?'

'This one – with the straws backlit. It's atmospheric.'

I wasn't listening to her, instead I was focusing on a small box folder tucked amongst a collection of paperback novels on the bookcase. I spotted a familiar word printed on the spine.

'Yeah. Beth?'

'Yeah?' She carried on browsing, holding the next picture at arm's length, half closing one eye and squinting at the print.

'Do you still read the tarot?'

She paused and looked up.

I wondered for a moment if I shouldn't have mentioned it. She used to read them a lot back in our student days. I remembered the last time.

It was a Friday night and we'd not long arrived back from the pub. We'd run back to Benson Street through the January chill. We were in downtime, returned to Earth in the aftermath of Christmas but not yet begun to get twitchy about finals. Beth had her mock 'A' levels coming up but that didn't stop her spending time with us - or more specifically me - on the weekends. We'd lit the gas fire in the front room and already shared a couple of joints, as much to warm us up physically as to chill us out mentally. I'd been in the kitchen preparing the contents of the fridge - a packet of sausages which I'd grilled and half a sliced white loaf which I'd toasted, successfully disguising the occasional green patches around the crust - to satisfy the communal munchies.

I loaded up the plate and pushed open the door.

'I'm a fool! I'm a fool! I always knew it.' Rick was dancing around the room. He laughed and grabbed the shade that rested precariously on the table lamp, balancing it on his head.

'Mind the cards!' Beth sat cross-legged on the floor. She reached out and scooped up the tarot deck that was spread in front of her, gathering the cards into the folds of her skirt. She was dressed in velvet that night, a dark patchwork of green, purple, burgundy and orange; jewel colours; round her neck hung a single amethyst on a leather thong. I looked at her and thought lustful thoughts.

'Pass the tucker, Weed.' Rick reached out his hand. I took a slice of toast to go with the sausage that was already clenched between my teeth before handing him the plate. 'I'm the fool,' he announced again, triumphantly, between mouthfuls. 'Who's next? Fish?'

Fish lay on the floor on his back, giggling quietly. 'N-not me. I'm t-too weirded out.' He rolled over onto his side, still giggling.

'You then, Weed.'

'Uh.' I was unable to speak without dropping the sausage but I shook my head vigorously. Beth had read my cards before, loads of times. I didn't take it seriously of course, but I generally went along with it to humour her and often it was a bit of a laugh, like now with Rick. Only sometimes it gave me the creeps, I couldn't say why, probably when I'd had dope or was tired. Tonight was one of those times.

'Looks like it has to be you then, Joe.'

'I'm tired, I can't be bothered.' He was spread out on the sofa, eyes half closed.

'Come on, Spider, don't disappoint the lovely lady.' Rick wasn't giving up easily, he never did.

'Look I don't need to…' Beth looked up at me. I was pointing upwards trying to hint at an early night.

'Nonsense! If I'm a fool I need to know if anyone round here has any sense or if we're all just one big circus of clowns. Now shuffle those cards and tell Joe how clever he is.'

I wasn't paying much attention to what was going on. I was aware of Joe reluctantly pulling himself upright and rubbing his eyes as I crossed the room to the stereo unit to turn over the record. It was Pink Floyd's 'Atom Heart Mother', fairly seriously weird – even when you were stone cold sober and hadn't taken any drugs. Really I just wanted to get my hands on Beth, but I'd have to wait another ten or fifteen minutes before I could start persuading her about what I had in mind.

Rick was rolling a cigarette, a straight one this time, no dope. I went and sat next to him ready to bum a few drags while Beth shuffled, cut and dealt the pack. I thought about making some coffee – we'd run out of beer – but I couldn't be bothered, anyway there was probably no milk.

'Come on!' Rick called, each time another card was turned

over. 'These are all boring ones. I just want to know if he's a fool too,' he slurred. His attention span rapidly waning, he sighed heavily, put the cigarette to his lips and lit it.

Beth turned over the last card, the most important one in the reading she always said.

Rick leaned forward to look. 'Whoa! Careful with that axe, Eugene, or what?'

To be more precise it was a sickle, brandished menacingly in the arms of the grim reaper.

'Hey? You telling me I'm about to die?' Joe was wide-awake suddenly. He spoke with more than a hint of panic, it was the cannabis talking.

'Of course not!' Beth sounded cross. 'I keep trying to tell you lot this isn't a parlour game. You have to read it in terms of your situation and the question you had in mind when I shuffled the pack. You did have a question didn't you?'

Joe shrugged. 'I told you I didn't want to do it.'

'Well it's about possibilities, not certainties or anything literal. It's probably reminding you that if you don't work you'll fail your exams.' She looked up at me. 'Make some coffee, Marty – I don't care if it's black – then I think I might go home.'

While Beth carefully wrapped her cards in the psychically protective silk scarf she always kept them in, I went through to the kitchen and filled the kettle. My mood had plummeted from an optimistic high to a mournful sulk. Not because of Joe's cards – that was all just a load of hocus-pocus – but because of Beth's decision to go home. I searched around the sink for a clean mug, wondering how I could get her to change her mind. The scalding hot drink would take a while to cool, that would buy me some time.

When I returned to the lounge and set the mug on the hearth near to where Beth sat, the atmosphere had returned to a sleepy, dreamy equilibrium. Conversation, such as it was, covered mundane topics such as who was going to go to the shop in the morning and whether Rick should grow a beard.

We all jumped when the telephone rang. It was almost midnight. We just sat there at first, letting it ring, each thinking it would be for someone else. At last, Beth lifted the receiver.

'Hello? Yes? No, that's all right, no-one's gone to bed yet.' She passed it to Joe. 'Your Aunt Helen.'

'Hello?' That was all Joe said, after that he just sat and listened, not even making the usual polite hmm and aha noises that you utter to show that you haven't gone to sleep.

The rest of us sat in silence looking questioningly at one another. I was on the point of suggesting we should leave the room so that Joe could talk in private, when he simply said 'Thank you,' and 'goodbye,' then quietly put the phone down. He sat motionless, staring straight ahead and we all sat there with him for what seemed like ages. At last he spoke, his voice was a whisper, barely audible.

'That was Aunt Helen, Mum's sister. Mum had a stroke earlier this evening. She died on the way to hospital.'

'Shit! Oh God man, I'm sorry.' The words were inadequate but I had to say something.

Fish pulled himself into some semblance of consciousness and crawled across the room to drape an arm round Joe's shoulders. Beth reached out and took his hand. Only Rick stayed seated on the sofa, staring silently, his brow wrinkling, his lips pouting, gradually contorting his face. Suddenly he leapt up, eyes ablaze, he pointed at Beth.

'This is all your fault, you and your bloody cards! Do us all a favour and get out before you cause any more trouble!' He pushed the startled Beth roughly aside and knelt down in front of Joe, taking both his hands and kissing him lightly on the forehead before pulling him into a protective hug.

I put my arm round Beth as she stood up. She was shaking.

'Come on,' I said. 'Let's get some air while things calm down.' I led her out to the kitchen and opened the back door. She had started to sob and I pulled her closer, hugging her to my chest.

'I didn't even want to do it,' she mumbled between tears. 'Rick insisted. I didn't make anything happen. Joe's mother must have died hours before we read the cards.'

'Hush! It was just bad timing, a horrible coincidence.'

'Rick thinks I'm some sort of witch!'

'No he doesn't. He's lashing out because he's upset. He's probably worked out that it all happened while he was showing off down at the pub and he feels guilty about it. Anyway it's Joe who matters, his feelings.'

Beth sniffed and rubbed her eyes with a purple velvet sleeve. She bent down and dropped the tarot cards onto the cold cracked concrete of the doorstep. 'Can I borrow your lighter?' She held out her hand.

'This isn't your fault. And you're good you know? Your readings have made me question things I do and helped me make decisions.' It wasn't strictly true but I wanted to be supportive.

'Whatever. I don't want to read them any more. Lighter please.'

The two of us stood there shivering, watching as the flames enveloped the cards, the plastic coating making them shrink into miniatures before finally dissolving into a black crackly heap.

'The tarot?' Beth looked at me suspiciously. 'I thought we left all that behind years ago. We burnt the cards, remember?'

How could I forget? 'But you bought another set?'

She looked at me doubtfully. 'Well yes, but I haven't used them for ages.'

'So you could do a reading for me now?'

Beth sighed. 'I'm not sure I can tell you what you want to hear. It wouldn't be about predicting the future, Marty. I'm not going to try and tell your fortune or anything stupid like that so please don't ask.'

'No of course not.' What was I doing? Clutching at straws or what? 'I just need some ideas and encouragement you know? Like I'm feeling in a rut.'

'So talk to a friend, or a counsellor, or a careers adviser.'

'Please.'

I don't know what I was hoping for. It wasn't like I believed in the cards or anything. Not really. But Beth did. Maybe if she did a reading for me it would be another bond between us, a secret. The Waterfall Chamber had worked its magic for a while but it hadn't got us together; and anyway, it would probably be common knowledge soon. Maybe if the right card came up – like the lovers or a knight in shining armour – Beth would see herself in it; maybe it would help convince her that the two of us should be together.

She shrugged and collected the photos, sliding them carefully back into the folder. 'All right then, but I've told you the conditions.' She pulled the file off the shelf and took out the cards. 'This deck had only just been printed when I bought it; the cards are very positive and optimistic. I want you to have a look through them before we start and familiarise yourself with them.'

Beth spread the cards on the carpet where we were sitting.

'What? No silk scarf?'

'That stuff's just to set the mood. It's your attitude that's important.'

'I have the best intentions.'

'Don't joke, Marty, or I'm not doing it. This is about freeing your mind of everyday clutter so you can make decisions based on your intuition. I'm not going to tell you how long you're going to live and how many children you're going to have. That isn't what it's about.'

'I couldn't agree more,' I lied. I studied the images in front of me. They were very different from the stark, frightening pictures Beth had dealt when we were at university. Instead, these were based on the legends of King Arthur and the Knights of the Round Table, the Major Arcana featuring characters such as Guinevere, Gawain and the Lady of the Lake. The pictures were detailed illustrations, delicately and sensitively painted.

So we began the reading. The routine was much the same as before. Beth gathered the cards and shuffled them, then, asked me to cut the pack whilst concentrating on the question I was asking.

My mind was full of questions; that was the problem. Where

255

does my life go from here? Will I get together with Beth, shag her senseless and have lots of kids? Or will I just sit about like a sad loser while my wife gives birth to someone else's child?

Luckily Beth didn't ask what I was thinking. She, at least, was taking this seriously. Her brow furrowed in concentration as she dealt the cards face down onto the floor in front of us.

I didn't pay that much heed to most of the reading. There were pictures of swords and swamps and the Holy Grail. Beth talked about failures and opportunities and the need for care and concentration but she was right, none of it told me anything I wanted to hear. I yawned as she turned over the last card.

'This represents your life from now on – oh!'

The image was of a skeletal figure holding a bundle of bloodstained rags. Positive pack or not there was no getting away from it, this card was Death. The hairs on the back of my neck began to prickle.

Beth was waffling on about how, despite the image, it was a very positive message about new beginnings. I didn't pay much attention. How stupid did she think I was? Death was staring me in the face and she was trying to make out it was a good thing.

I stood up. 'I'd better go, I've got an early start.' I needed to get away from there and have a stiff drink, preferably several. I hurried out to the car, without thanking her, without a proper goodbye and forgetting the photos, only wishing I'd never suggested it in the first place.

There's a cave down on the Gower; Paviland, it's called. They found some old bones there, really old. It must have been one of the first Homo Sapiens Sapiens, the first modern humans, to live in Britain. And his friends had laid this guy out, respectfully like, and painted his body with red ochre. They left his staff too, broken into pieces, so no-one else could go casting spells. He must have been a really powerful person.

A cave makes a really good tomb.

I'll try not to think about that.

Chapter 40

Carbide lamp - most lamps used down caves are electric, powered by rechargeable batteries. An alternative type burn calcium carbide, which, although it gives a bright light, leaves a residue which is messy and potentially a pollutant. Consequently, carbide lamps are often banned in finely decorated or ecologically sensitive caves.

'We ought to have a meeting,' Ashley said.

It was a Saturday evening at the beginning of March and we were in the Quarryman's Rest. For the first time in weeks we were all there, Rick, Joe, Beth, Fish, Taff and of course Ashley; we'd all been down the cave. There hadn't been many trips recently. Joe, worried that work would dry up after the millennium, had found himself just as much in demand adapting finance programs for the new European currency, Rick had been grading exams for the first semester, Ashley had been out of the country a lot, installing computer security all over the world. And Fish seemed to be busy on matters of his own. It wasn't to do with Valerie, she seemed happy for him to spend time with us these days. In fact I'd rung him a couple of times to get Valerie's surprised response of, 'Oh, but I thought he was with you!' I'd fumbled for excuses, telling her I'd forgotten he was working late before meeting me. Fish was so much happier, I should have been pleased – and I would have been if it weren't for the fact that I knew about his liaison with Joe. I found myself noting each time Fish's absence coincided with Joe's overtime.

'So what about it?' Ashley continued. 'We need to make some decisions about the cave.'

What Ashley really meant was that he would make the decisions and the rest of us would (hopefully) agree with him. I suppose he was right though. There were still some areas left to survey but we reckoned that even now it was easily the biggest natural cave system known in Britain. It had pretties as well –

and not just the ones Beth and I had found. Despite our attempts to keep our discoveries quiet, the Quarry was being talked about in caving clubs up and down the country – one or two had even come on tourist trips as far as the Lake Chamber; even now, Rick was preparing an article to go in one of the specialist magazines. Very soon there would be a deluge of clubs wanting to explore it, to look at the pretties, to dive the Devil's Cauldron, maybe even to stay overnight at the camp. With Rick and Fish on the committee, we could probably call the shots at our club. But that meant there was a lot for us to do. We had to think about whether we were going to take guided groups, we had to get the survey finished, professionally printed and decide what we were going to charge for it, we really had quite a busy time ahead of us.

Rick suggested we have the meeting in Benson Street. We could use the map room, where we could all sit round the table and, unlike holding it on club premises, where we would doubtless be disturbed by other club members wanting to muscle in on the action, it would just be invited guests. He also suggested that we could stay on for a drink afterwards.

I wasn't concentrating. I was watching Joe and Fish who were sitting opposite one another, making secret gestures when they thought no-one was looking. Nothing too obvious: a raised eyebrow here, a knowing grin there; I tried to look away but my eyes were constantly drawn back. Every word that passed between them, every glance, screamed out at me, it was so obvious. No-one else seemed to notice but I suppose that was because they didn't know what I did, they hadn't seen what I had. I felt very uncomfortable about it and also really sad. Joe and Rick had always been the happiest, most stable couple I knew, they'd been together so long it was impossible to think of them as anything other than a permanent fixture. And aside from their personal happiness, if they split up, the whole dynamic of our crowd would change, nothing would be the same again.

'What do you think, Marty?'

'Huh?'

'Wake up, sleepy,' Beth laughed. 'Are you on for a meeting and general get together in a couple of weeks time? The rest of us can make that.'

I nodded quickly.

'That's decided then.' Ashley beamed at us all.

So that's how we all came to be assembled in one hundred and one, Benson Street.

I couldn't help but chuckle at the map room. Ten chairs had been placed around the table. We'd invited Sprat as well, and Damian and Sarah, because Damian was chairman of the university caving club that year and Sarah the secretary. In each place there was a notepad, a pencil and an upturned tumbler; in the centre was a decanter of water. Joe saw me laughing and came over to me, grinning.

'I thought, if Ashley wants a meeting he can have one,' he whispered. 'I've just got to hand out copies of the agenda then we can decide who's going to be chairman. Do you think I should have sent out formal invitations asking everyone to wear suits and ties?'

'Definitely not!' I laughed. 'Ashley would beat us all hands down at power dressing.'

I nominated Rick as chairman of the meeting and Fish seconded it. Joe nominated Beth to take the minutes but she said that just because she was a woman she wasn't going to pretend to be a secretary. In the end Fish offered to do it and throughout the meeting he noted everything down in his neat, flowing artistic writing.

We dealt with all the issues on the agenda. Beth and I had decided to keep quiet about the Waterfall Chamber for a bit longer. We'd discussed the question of access to the cave several times in the past few weeks and Sprat said we had grounds to restrict anywhere beyond the area at the beginning of the Lake Chamber because of possible damage to formations and danger with features such as the Devil's Cauldron. We also voted to ban carbide lamps because of all the pretties.

Consequently, we'd taped off that area a couple of weeks

previously, before the first party from another club made their trip; and the base of the Spiral Staircase now looked like the entrance to a police crime scene, with stripy tape and 'do not cross' signs arranged strategically. Anywhere beyond that, we voted to have guided trips, supervised by at least one of our group. This had the added bonus that we could safely leave things at the camp, knowing they wouldn't be disturbed, and ruled out the soul-destroying possibility that, after all our hard work, it might be a group from another club who finally made it a through trip by breaking through to the outside world. For Beth and me, with outsiders stopping at the Lake and our own crowd concentrating on pushing the area beyond the camp, it meant we wouldn't have to worry about the Waterfall Chamber being discovered for a while yet.

By nine-thirty we were through.

'That it then?' asked Taff. He looked like he was dying for a drink and a smoke.

'Just one more thing,' said Rick. 'Any other business?'

'Well there isn't any is there?' asked Ashley. 'I mean we've covered everything.'

'There is one more thing actually,' said Joe. 'Though strictly speaking it isn't to do with the cave.'

We looked at him expectantly.

'I'd like to say happy fortieth birthday to Rick, from me, from everyone – and if you'd all like to come downstairs it's time to party!'

Joe had got a real spread laid on in the dining room, with expensive champagne, the whole works.

'How did you manage to organise all this without Rick knowing?' Beth was impressed. 'In his own house as well.'

'Ah, that's where Fish came in. He kept Rick out of the way for the day while I sorted out the food.'

'Well done, Fish,' Beth congratulated him.

'And there's another secret Fish kept,' Joe continued. 'In fact he's been keeping it in his garage for a couple of months now. Is it ready?' He looked up at Fish who nodded. 'In that case,' Joe continued, 'I'd like everyone to step outside where Rick will open his birthday present!'

Joe led the way out into the back garden where a large lumpy shape loomed in the darkness of the lawn. 'As I said, today is Rick's fortieth birthday. And for twenty of those years he's been my best friend and my housemate. So I wanted to mark the occasion with something really special. Go on,' he told Rick, 'do the unveiling.'

The shape was covered by a tarpaulin, which Rick carefully peeled back. There, gleaming in the moonlight, stood a Harley Davidson.

'Wow!' Rick stood and stared. 'Wow, wow, wow!' Then he hugged Joe while the rest of us cheered.

'We'd already planned to take some time off,' explained Joe. 'Take the bikes round Europe. Now we'll do it on the Harley.'

'I'm really impressed,' I told Joe. 'It must have cost an arm and a leg.'

He smiled. 'Well you knew I'd been working overtime. There've been a lot of well-paid opportunities for programmers recently. Anyway, it's worth it, it's what we've always wanted.'

'So when are you going abroad?'

'In a couple of days. We're getting the crossing to Roscoff on Tuesday – which reminds me, you've already got a house key so if you need any of the stuff about the cave while we're away you can get in.'

'I'll water your plants too if you like,' I offered, completely forgetting that I would be away myself for the next few days.

I felt so stupid. To think I'd assumed something romantic was going on between Fish and Joe. And all the time they'd been planning this. Thank goodness I hadn't said anything to anyone.

Down the cave I think about the meeting and Rick's party afterwards. I laugh when I remember it's my own birthday in a couple of weeks. For the past year I've been dreading the day when I turn forty but right now my only concern is that I might not make it that far!

Chapter 41

Regulator - also known as an octopus (colloquial), device which dispenses compressed air from a cylinder at ambient atmospheric pressure.

Now that I've read the accounts in the logbook I'm pretty sure I can find the route they describe. But the battery on my lamp is low; I can't afford to get it wrong again. So I'm psyching myself up for this final push. I figure it's been a while – and a lot of activity – since breakfast, what I need is a meal to set me up before I set off. I take the last foil pack (trying not to think of it as the last supper) and set it in a pan of water to boil.

The following Friday evening I rang the bell and waited. I was at Beth's, at her invitation. I'd been away all week, on a course in Bristol; DNA as a diagnostic tool; not entirely my specialty but it was becoming such a big thing these days; everyone had to learn about it. So I hadn't had any contact with anyone – except for Rick and Joe who'd called me on my mobile on Wednesday night. They were heading for Nice then hoping to make the Spanish border by the weekend.

'Ask Fish about the cave.' Rick had sounded excited.

'What? I can't hear you. The signal isn't very good.'

'I think we've found the way through! Hasn't Fish told you?'

I remembered that Rick and Joe had planned a trip down the Quarry before they went to Europe. It had been arranged for the Monday after their party but not many people had been free to go. I was away on my course. Beth and Taff were both working. Ashley was in London. So that had only left Fish and possibly Sprat able to go with them.

'I've been out of town, I haven't seen him.'

'Well make sure you do.'

'OK! Enjoy the rest of your holiday then.'

'Yeah. Bye.'

Trust Rick, to call me from abroad just to tell me about a cave! Still, if they were right it would certainly be exciting. Indeed, I'd meant to call Fish as soon as I got back, earlier that afternoon. But then there'd been this phone message from Beth, asking me to go round in the evening. So everything else had gone out of the window, including a message from Fish as it turned out, but Rick had already told me what it was about so I figured the details could wait till tomorrow. There was no sign of Mike – in fact the flat didn't look like it had been lived in for several days, but then it often looked that way. I was glad of the couple of hours to myself before it was time to go out. I had a shower and ironed a T-shirt and some fresh jeans. I had a glass of wine while I was getting ready, just to relax me a bit.

The door opened.

'Come in,' said Beth. 'Pour yourself a drink, dinner won't be long.'

She hovered about in the kitchen while I had a couple of drinks. She hadn't mentioned what it was about but I guessed probably the Waterfall Chamber. Of course, it could be her way of showing she was getting interested in me again. The dining table was set for two, it was meticulously neat with perfectly placed knives and forks, mats and napkins, but there were no flowers or candles, the sort of thing someone like Beth would have for a romantic evening.

Beth had cooked a vegetarian chilli, with a fruit sorbet for dessert. While we ate, she broached the subject of the Waterfall Chamber.

'We've kept the secret long enough,' she said. 'It isn't fair on the others not to share it with them.'

I nodded, knowing she was right.

She continued. 'And it will be for all of us to decide how we control access for other clubs now the cave's going public. Maybe we'll put a gate across it like they have with the columns in Ogof Ffynnon Ddu. But it isn't just our decision to make, Marty.'

We talked about how we'd wait till Rick and Joe were back then we'd take everyone down and show them together. Sprat too. In a way I was glad Beth had made the decision for me.

Eventually we sat in the lounge, sipping coffee. I was disappointed that the evening hadn't turned out to be the romantic proposition I'd been secretly, if unrealistically, yearning for. But there was still hope for that another time. We were silent for a while then Beth spoke.

'There's something else I want to speak to you about,' she said.

I began to feel almost hopeful.

'I want to talk to you about Ashley.'

So far so good.

She continued. 'I know you've always had your doubts about him. And I want you to know that I've considered the things you've said very seriously.'

Thank goodness. She was coming to her senses at last; she'd obviously realised he was all talk.

'I'm glad,' I said. 'I didn't like to say anything but it was obvious he wasn't right for you. I mean, he's a nice enough bloke to go for a drink with and all that, but...'

'Marty!' She looked furious. 'What the hell are you talking about? He's kind, generous, successful, caring, I have no intention of splitting up with him. In fact I was so moved by Rick and Joe last week – it was their twentieth anniversary for goodness' sake, as well as Rick's birthday, they've been together for longer than most married couples – anyway it got me thinking about what I really want in life. I want to settle down, get married, have children. I'm going to suggest to Ashley that we get married.'

I was stunned into silence. Carole pregnant, Beth marrying Ashley, I couldn't cope with all this.

'But you can't!' I said at last.

'Marty, I'm doing you the courtesy of telling you this because we were close once and because I thought we were friends now. What's the matter?'

I just kind of exploded. 'You're an idiot,' I said. 'He isn't clever or brave; he's just a prat who likes taking risks. You'll be making a real fool of yourself.'

'There's no need to be abusive! You're just jealous because Ashley's everything you're not.'

'Yeah, a lunatic,' I muttered.

'All right then,' she fumed, 'if you want some home truths you can have them. You've changed. You're impossible these days and it makes me really sad, knowing that once I really liked you – loved you, even.'

She paused for breath.

'Of course I've changed,' I said. 'So have you. We've grown up.'

'Grown up? That's one thing you definitely haven't done, you act like a spoilt child most of the time. For God's sake look at yourself! You're consumed with jealousy, you smoke too much, you've got a drink problem and as for your attitude to women – it's disgusting. I'm not surprised Carole went off with someone else. I bet you didn't even manage to stay faithful to her while you were married.'

I scowled and shrugged. Beth had no right to turn the inquisition on me like this.

'Well did you? Go on, tell me you never had affairs.'

I squirmed. There was no point in trying to lie to Beth. She knew me too well. 'One or two I suppose, but only with people from work. It was just sex, nothing serious, I'd never have let her find out, I had too much respect for her.'

'Respect? You don't know the meaning of the word. Respect is about how you treat people, not about cheating on them then gloating because you think you've got away with it. You don't respect anyone, you're just a liar.'

I stared in front of me. Everything Beth said was ridiculous, of course, but I wouldn't lose my temper with her. Then she stared at me, her eyes were aflame. Jesus! She was scary.

'Did you ever...' she enunciated the words slowly and clearly, in a cold emotionless tone of voice, '...did you ever cheat on me when we were going out together?'

I was genuinely shocked, horrified at the thought. 'No! How could you think that?'

'Well you seem to have found it easy enough with your wife.

265

I'm beginning to wonder if I ever knew you at all, maybe it was just a sham.'

'Not with you. Never. I idolised you, for God's sake. Now I can see you were out of my league. Looking back I wonder why you bothered with me.'

Gradually she calmed down. She spoke to me more softly. 'Perhaps that's your trouble, Marty. You don't even respect yourself. I don't understand you these days; you were never like this when we were younger. It's as if I don't know you any more. What's happened to you?'

I stood up and shrugged. 'I'd better go.'

'Yes I think you'd better. Do yourself a favour and sort yourself out. I'd really like us to be friends, but the way you behave these days…' she shook her head.

I grabbed my coat from the peg in the hall. 'Thanks for the psychiatric dissection,' I growled. 'I'll go back to my padded cell and make way for Mr Wonderful.'

One last meal then I'm off. I'll feel more positive when I've eaten. I've done enough caving to know that you can only run on adrenalin for so long, then you need food. Low blood sugar makes you edgy and depressed; it makes you more likely to make mistakes. And I can't afford to do that now. In any case, I'm hungry.

It's only when I tear open the foil pack I realise something is wrong. Instead of a tasty meal, the scent that wafts in the steam reminds me of the sickly smell of a chemistry lab. It isn't food that I tip into the bowl but the sticky melted contents of the first aid kit.

Chapter 42

Pot - alternative name for cave, usually one (or part of same) comprising deep vertical pitches.

I stamped into the flat and slammed the door behind me. Jesus, I needed a drink. I looked in the fridge and in my cupboard. Nothing. I looked in Mike's cupboard. There was a bottle of white wine. I'd have preferred red but it would do. I grabbed the corkscrew and a glass and took these and the bottle into the lounge. I certainly wasn't going to wait while it chilled.

The cork came out without resistance and I downed the first glass in one. I poured another.

I hated Beth, for being so wrong about everything, and also for being right.

I searched through my CDs (I'd collected them from Carole's because they weren't her taste anyway), chose a Led Zeppelin and turned the volume up loud. 'Immigrant Song' just didn't work on quiet anyway. I turned the phone off and the answering machine right down. I wanted to wallow in my anger and self-pity without interruptions. Beth would want to apologise of course, she was probably trying to call me right now. Well, she would just have to stew!

I poured another glass and sang along to 'Gallows Pole'. As I was drinking the fourth I was unaware that a phone message was coming through. Or another as I downed the fifth. It was by chance that I turned my mobile on. I only wanted to see if Beth had sent me a text message, and to have the satisfaction of knowing that if she had I was choosing not to reply.

There was a message. I paged into it eagerly. <Marty, please call the hospital urgently. Graham>

'Shit!'

I dialled the number. 'Hello? Dr Hall, please. Graham? Hell, I'm sorry, I forgot I was on call.'

'No you're not, don't worry. But could you possibly get

down here? We've got someone, just been brought in, he's had quite a cocktail by the looks of it, alcohol and probably several street drugs besides. I know it's not your night but it's your area of expertise and I'd really value your opinion.'

'Er…yeah…of course. I've had a couple of drinks though,' I added tentatively.

'Don't worry; you won't be making life or death decisions, but an unofficial opinion would really help.'

OK, I'll be there as soon as I can.'

'If you could. This one's still alive and I'd like to keep him that way.'

I put the phone down and picked up the car keys. Then I looked at the empty bottle and thought better of it, picked the phone up again and called for a taxi. Then I grabbed my jacket and headed out of the door. I didn't stop to turn the CD off and I certainly didn't stop to check the answering machine.

Nothing could have prepared me for what I found at the hospital, or whom.

Fish's face was pale and lifeless. Plastic tubes invaded his nose, throat and veins. He looked insignificant, lying there surrounded by machines straight out of a science fiction film. Flashing displays described the action of his heart and lungs. I felt sick. Déjà vu. Just like fifteen years ago, two weeks after the dive he never made it to. I stared at him, wondering what, if anything, was going on inside his head.

Valerie sat beside the bed clutching the limp hand in hers. Her face looked strained, the muscles stretched taut. Behind her the ventilator hissed intrusively.

'He could breathe on his own,' she claimed, defensively. 'But the doctor says if they keep him sedated and do whatever they can artificially then it'll give him more chance to recover.'

I thought she was coping OK but suddenly she burst into tears. She turned to me, grabbed my arms and attached herself like a limpet, sobbing noisily into my chest. It was the closest, mentally or physically, that we had ever been.

'Oh Marty!' she wailed. 'It's all my fault.'

'Don't be silly.' I rested my hand awkwardly on her shoulder wondering whether I should stroke or hair or something. It occurred to me that I didn't know much about comfort or affection unless it was a sex thing. I fumbled for the right words. 'Of course it isn't your fault. How could it be?' For the first time ever, I actually felt some sort of sympathy, some compassion for Valerie. Did she know that he was full of alcohol plus a cocktail of drugs? I didn't know what the police had said at this point; didn't know how much it was my professional duty to keep under wraps. They'd have mentioned the alcohol, anyway; there was no law against drinking. 'It isn't your fault,' I stated definitively, 'not unless you poured a bottle of whisky down his throat. Even then, that alone wouldn't have done this.'

She shook her head, pulling back from me slightly. 'It's what I said to him earlier on, when he got in from work. I told him I've been seeing someone else, that I want a divorce.' She sniffed. 'And now he's gone and done this to himself. I should have broken it to him more gently.'

Taff stood in the corner, as he had since I arrived, shuffling his feet like a naughty schoolchild. I looked at him questioningly. At first he looked puzzled then he realised what I meant.

'No way!' he said. 'Yeah, he called me and we met up. Yeah, he told me what had happened. But he didn't drink, I swear. He's never touched a drop; not since…'

I extricated myself from Valerie, who by now was quietly sobbing, and reattached her to Fish.

'All he drank was lemonade,' said Taff, 'and anyway,' he leaned over to me and spoke in a whisper, 'for some reason he seemed surprisingly happy that she was planning to leave him.'

'So did you leave him in the pub?'

'Oh no. We left together. He said he had someone to meet later and before that he wanted to drop by on Ashley – see if he was back from London. He needed up to date copies of the Quarry survey for the printers, he said he'd tried to contact you to get the key to Rick's and when there was no reply he decided to see if Ashley had a key or a copy of the survey or…I don't know. That's where he was going anyway, I walked part of the way with him.'

I looked suspiciously at Taff. Although I'd got closer to him and was beginning to lose my prejudice, I still didn't know quite how far I could trust him. Especially where drink and drugs were concerned, especially after the episode at New Year.

'What time was that?'

'For Christ's sake, Marty! You're worse than the cops. I've already told all this to them.'

'Sorry,' I said. 'I'm just trying to build up a picture of exactly what happened and when. In case it can help Fish. The more details the doctors have the more chance they have of giving him the best treatment.'

I looked at Fish and wondered what conclusions the hospital staff were drawing. They'd have got hold of his medical notes by now surely. They'd have the details of what happened before. The overdose, a cocktail of downers washed down with alcohol. It was this very hospital he was rushed into. A suicide attempt they'd said, by someone very depressed; a cry for help at the very least, certainly not an accident. They'd say the same now.

Graham nodded to me that he wanted a word and we stepped outside into the corridor where we could still observe the bedside through the glass panels but our conversation could not be overheard. Although he'd been at the hospital less than a year, I knew Graham quite well by now. He was the first choice on call in overdose cases so quite frequently we came together to discuss clinical whys and wherefores. Sometimes, if our shifts coincided, we went for a beer and a game of darts afterwards.

'I'm sorry,' he was saying. 'I had no idea you were a friend of the patient. If you'd rather we called someone else in…'

I shook my head. Then, for the first time in all the confusion, I noticed someone else I knew well sitting in the waiting area.

'What's that woman doing here?'

'Oh,' Graham looked across. 'She brought the patient in.

She'd given him CPR – made a professional job of it too, had his heart and lungs working again by the time the ambulance arrived. If it weren't for her he'd certainly be dead. I'm sure she'd talk to you if you want more details for your report.'

'Thanks. I'll see to that now.'

I hurried over to her. 'Carole? What the hell are you doing here? How did you come to find Fish?'

'Marty! Thank God!' She looked up and I saw that she'd been crying. She looked dishevelled, like she didn't care about herself. She was holding a half empty plastic cup of liquid from the drinks machine. I gently took it from her, set it on the table and lifted her up into my arms. Our embrace seemed to last an unnaturally long time, it felt strange hugging her like that, the baby, half way to being a person, pressing against my stomach. When at last I pulled away I repeated the question.

'Fish?' She looked puzzled. 'What are you talking about, Marty? I just want someone to tell me what's happening to Cefn.'

I looked at her. Then I turned round and looked through the glass partition at Fish. She'd told me she was seeing someone from the university and I'd just assumed it was another student. And as for Carole, she'd no reason to know Fish was one of my friends. I'd never mentioned any of them to her by name, nor even told her about the caving. No wonder I'd never put two and two together. And neither had she. And to think I'd paired Fish off with Joe, if it wasn't such a tragic situation I'd have laughed.

Carole gazed up at me. 'You know him don't you?'

I nodded.

'He never really talked much about his friends. We agreed I'd wait and meet them when we could be together properly. I knew he was married of course, but he was planning to leave her – I mean he is planning to – when he's better. He will get better won't he? I want to go in there and hold his hand, but I can't while she's there.'

'Look,' I said, 'there's no point in us sitting here. Come over to my office and I'll make you a proper cup of coffee. You can

271

tell me what happened.'

So I settled Carole into the comfiest swivel chair I could find and set a mug of decent coffee on my desk in front of her, quickly sweeping out of sight any paperwork that referred to Fish. Then, a little calmer, she told me her version of events.

'He was supposed to come over earlier this evening. When he didn't turn up I was annoyed but there wasn't much I could do, I could hardly ring him at home. But then by ten I was getting really angry and I called him on his mobile. The first couple of times I tried it was on voicemail. I decided to give it one more go and this time he answered – but he was strange, incoherent, I thought at first that he was drunk. His voice was slurred; it was difficult to make out the words. But he kept repeating the same thing, that and something about being 'weirded out'. I couldn't get any more sense out of him than that.'

I shivered. I remembered trying to communicate with Fish myself when he was in a state like that.

'It was lucky he was able to tell you where he was.'

'Oh, he didn't exactly. But he kept saying 'Ashley'. Then I remembered seeing this business card with Ashley Roberts written on it. Ever since September, since we knew we were going to be together, Cefn's kept a few odds and ends at the house. He has a notebook with numbers and addresses by the phone. I'd never looked in it before, I wouldn't pry, but this was an emergency. Sure enough, right near the beginning was an address and phone number for Ashley Roberts.'

'Quite the sleuth,' I commented.

'Don't joke Marty, I was worried about him.'

'Sorry,' I held her hand. 'So you drove round to his flat?'

She nodded. 'Yes. I tried to ring first but there was no answer. So I looked up the address in the A to Z and drove round. There was no answer when I rang the bell but the door was unlocked. He was inside, unconscious. I called an ambulance straight away then I tried to resuscitate him. After a few minutes he spluttered and started breathing again.'

'Thank God you did all that first aid training.'

'He will be all right won't he? I can't understand it, he never drinks alcohol.'

I took a deep breath. 'Have you spoken to the police?'

'Briefly. They were round here earlier. I think I'm supposed to make a proper statement tomorrow. I was so scared about Cefn I didn't really pay much attention to anything else. Why, Marty? If he went out and got drunk why do the police need to know about it?'

I wondered how much I should tell her.

'Did you tell them about your relationship? About the baby?'

She seemed flustered, close to tears again. 'I told the police, yes. But not the doctors or nurses, I haven't had chance.'

I wondered whether I should tell her that Valerie had asked Fish for a divorce then everything would be out in the open. But what if Valerie changed her mind? People often do in traumatic situations. Or what if she lashed out at Carole and it made her go into premature labour? I decided it was safest just to keep quiet. 'Look,' I said at last. 'I'll have a word with the doctor and see if he can take Valerie away for a chat and give you chance to sit with Fish – I mean Cefn – for a few minutes. And I'm sure if I explain the situation the doctor will tell you all the details even though you're not strictly family.'

'Or you could tell me,' Carole suggested.

I hesitated. I really didn't want to be the one to tell Carole about the drugs. 'It would be better for you to talk to a doctor,' I said. 'They'll be able to tell you about what treatment they're planning. Then I'll see you home. There's nothing else either of us can do here tonight. One thing's for sure, you saved his life; you did everything you could. Whatever happens now, I want you to remember that.'

Half an hour later Valerie was persuaded to get some fresh air and a coffee and to try once more to contact Fish's parents. I stood guard in the corridor to make sure she didn't return unexpectedly while Carole snatched a few moments with Fish. I was subdued. My tests confirmed that his blood contained heroin, cocaine and alcohol. The combination was known as a 'Brompton cocktail' and it had once been advocated,

273

controversially, within palliative care, for inducing the perfect death. For a moment I wondered if Fish knew that? I shuddered. In my book there was no way the words perfect and death could ever fit together. An hour earlier I might have believed that Fish had attempted to take his own life. But knowing what I did now, about Carole and the baby, it seemed he had everything to live for. And from what Taff said he was looking forward to it. Something just didn't add up.

They would take a lot of coming to terms with, the events and revelations of those last few hours. Not only what had happened to Fish (and goodness knows, I had sinister feelings about that) but the fact that he turned out to be the mysterious Cefn, the hated toyboy (as I had previously viewed that unknown stranger) who had stolen my wife and got her pregnant. Of course, I knew really that it wasn't like that. My marriage had ended a long time ago. Still it was an uncanny coincidence. It would certainly take some getting used to. It was hardly Fish's fault, how was he to know that Carole was my wife? That was the biggest irony of all, it occurred to me at four in the morning, when I finally got to bed, the fact that Carole had never mentioned me. All the time that she had been seeing Fish she'd never talked to him about me, apart from a brief mention that she was waiting for a divorce, I suppose. And Fish too for that matter. Here were two of the people I thought I was closest to and they'd never even spoken my name.

Chapter 43

*Gour pools - natural water features found underground where a pool -
or often a string of pools - have been hollowed out of the rock by the
action of water. The liquid is further retained by the formation of gour
dams (deposits of calcite etc) on the lower side.*

I woke up late the next day, and instantly the horror of the
night before came back to haunt me. There was no sign of Mike
as I poured boiling water over the teabag in a rather grimy mug
and picked the post up off the doormat. I glanced in his room
on my way to the shower but his bed looked like it hadn't been
slept in and a mug containing the dregs of at least two-day-old
coffee stood on the bedside cabinet. I noticed that the door to
the gun cupboard was swinging open and the interior was
empty. I just hoped to God he was out catching whoever had
done this to Fish. I shivered, went into the bathroom and
turned on the water.

When I was dressed I called the hospital and asked about
Fish. He was stable, comfortable (hah, hah!), but still hadn't
regained consciousness. I spoke to Graham too. It turned out
they'd taken a closer look at him. In addition to bruises around
his wrists and shoulders they'd found a small puncture wound
going into a vein on his left arm. Fish was left-handed; if he
wanted to stick a needle into himself it would be into his right
arm. The most likely scenario was that he'd been physically
restrained and injected with heroin and cocaine, and that while
he was out of it, alcohol had been poured forcibly down his
throat. I felt numb. I couldn't imagine what sort of person
would do something like that, or why.

I thought about calling Beth to tell her what had happened,
then I remembered she would be getting ready for her big night
with Ashley. I decided against contacting her, telling myself it
was to spare her the anxiety but knowing really that, since it
wouldn't benefit Fish, I just couldn't be arsed. Not after

everything she'd said. She could find out for herself. Better still, perhaps her precious Ashley could break the news to her. Luckily I wasn't expected to go into work. I'd been scheduled on call for that weekend but Graham said he'd spoken to my department and they positively insisted that, under the circumstances, I take the time off.

I didn't want to be with Carole. I know that sounds mean but I'd done the caring supporting bit the night before, there was a limit to how much I could take of her declaring her love for someone else – even when it was Fish. And there was no point in my going to the hospital since there was nothing more I could usefully do. So I decided to do the one thing I knew how. Go caving.

It was while I was getting my kit together that Rick called. It was on my mobile and his name showed up on the display. At first I wasn't going to answer, if this was just a social call I didn't want to have to tell him about Fish, then I thought maybe someone already had and he was after an update. I clicked the call button.

'Weed! How goes it?'

Shit! He clearly hadn't heard about Fish. 'I've got the day off; I'm just off down the cave. What are you and Joe up to?'

'We're in a bar in Barcelona. It's raining at the moment so we're not on the bikes yet, that's why I'm calling now.'

'Have you called anyone else?' I decided to hedge round the subject.

'When we're on holiday? You must be joking! No. We just wanted to ask you a favour seeing as you have the keys to the house and seeing as we're planning to stay on an extra week.' He proceeded to give me instructions about watering plants and cancelling newspapers. I agreed to everything without really thinking about it and without much chance of remembering it later.

Suddenly Rick sounded excited. 'Hey, did you say you're going down the cave? You've been talking to Sprat then?'

'What are you talking about?'

'What I was trying to tell you when we lost the signal a

couple of days ago. We think we've found the way through! Hasn't Sprat told you about it? Or Fish?'

I decided to phrase any references to Fish carefully. There was no sense in worrying Rick and Joe about him when there was nothing they could do, especially since they were on holiday, they really needed the space and the time. I knew if I told them what had happened they'd leave the bikes behind and be on the next flight back and that wouldn't do anyone any good.

'I haven't spoken to either of them. I've been away on a course all week. I only got back last night. What's this about breaking through?'

'It was the day before we set off, Monday. Remember we said we'd go caving with Sprat?'

I vaguely remembered the trip being planned.

'And we think we've found a goer! Down past the gour pools.' He went on to describe the passage. It started with a tight crawl, then there was a duck, almost submerged but with just an inch or two of air space and a couple of dips in the roof where you had to hold your breath. At the end of it, apparently, was a passage blocked with loose boulders and a serious draught.

Normally I'd have been really excited about the discovery but under the circumstances it was painfully insignificant. I had to feign interest.

'I can't believe Fish hasn't told you yet,' Rick continued, 'I'll give him a call.'

'Don't do that!'

'What? Is something wrong? Don't tell me. There are problems with Valerie, right?'

'Something like that.' There was some truth in my answer, making it easier to sound convincing.

'OK. I'll lie low as far as Fish is concerned. I don't want to make matters worse. Strange he didn't even tell Ashley though, or Taff.'

'I expect he had other things on his mind. And Ashley's been away a couple of days too.'

277

'Yeah, well Sprat said he'd try and get down again later in the week.'

'Perhaps I'll ring him then, see if he wants to come with me, even though it's Saturday…'

'Do that. If he can't get away then at least he can give you more precise directions. Just be sure and give me a call if you find a way through.'

'I promise. Look, the signal's breaking up, give my love to Joe.'

Phew! I needed a strong coffee before I thought about anything else, really I could have done with a whisky but I knew that wasn't a good idea. I made the drink and sat down in the lounge. I dialled Sprat's home number, it would be far more sensible to go caving with someone else, and he was good fun to be with, he'd help take my mind off things. What's more, maybe we'd find the way through that Rick had been so excited about. There was no reply. I dialled the shop. It was one of the student helpers who answered; he told me that Sprat had gone caving, left about half an hour ago, he hadn't said where.

It was unusual for Sprat to take a Saturday off. I figured, in view of what Rick had just told me, he was headed for the Quarry too. He'd probably tried to call Fish already, and most likely tried to ring me while I was talking to Rick.

Hell, I just had to get out. If I met up with Sprat, that would be great. If not I'd go on my own, like I would have done anyway. Really I should have called Taff, told him where I was going and warned him not to say anything to Rick and Joe. But my head was spinning. I grabbed the bag that contained my caving kit and headed out of the front door and down the steps.

In less than an hour I was parking the car. I'd turned off the road before the lay-by and driven down one of the old quarry tracks. Strictly speaking it was off limits but it was that bit closer to the cave and quite frankly I just didn't care. I pulled on my oversuit and boots (I was already wearing my fleece) and strapped the battery and helmet to my belt. Then I slung a coil of rope and my kit bag over my shoulder and strode out across the grass and heather. I didn't have any real plans about what I

278

was going to do underground, get down to the camp for starters I supposed, then explore one of the further passages, there were a couple yet we hadn't written off entirely.

Obviously I'd keep a look out for the place Rick had described, but I have to admit it wasn't my main concern today. And it was difficult to picture what he was saying from a few crackly words. Exploring, however exciting, could wait till another time. Today I just needed the cave to keep me occupied for a few hours, to take my mind off everything that had happened. There was a chill wind picking up and dark indigo clouds were ganging up on the horizon. I vaguely remembered hearing a weather warning on the car radio, but with any luck I should be back in the car if not the pub before the rain started.

It was sheltered where I'd parked. It was only when I stepped out from the hoof-trodden dung-strewn sheep track, up onto the top that the weather hit me. It was already blowing a hooley. The wind was screaming, tearing through the grass. If there had been any trees up there it would doubtless have torn through them too, or more likely uprooted them. Sometimes it whined, high in pitch, sometimes it rumbled, deep and resonant like thunder, and sometimes it stopped altogether, pausing to take a breath then suddenly blow again and take me unawares. I was tempted to turn back there and then. If it had been a normal day, if all the stuff with Fish hadn't happened, then I'd probably have called it quits and gone straight to the pub. But that day I needed to battle with the elements. Afterwards, I knew I'd feel better. The thing about suffering is that it's great when it stops.

I'd been going about ten minutes when the rain started. Just drizzle really but the wind lashed it painfully into my face, stinging my cheeks and my eyes. I pulled the oversuit hood up over my helmet and tightened the toggles and bent my head towards the grass. I was looking forward to getting underground.

A few yards before I reached the entrance, I felt for the padlock key in my pocket. It wasn't until I was sitting on the ground, tying a habitual knot in the end of the rope that I noticed the ladder hanging from the iron bolt just inside the grille. I tugged at the padlock. It was firmly shut with the entrance grill closed tight. Either someone was down the cave or they had left the ladder behind – by mistake or on purpose so that it would be ready for the next trip. I decided the latter was more likely. Then I remembered, of course, it would most likely be Sprat. I hadn't seen his van but it was probably parked further along the road. I cheered slightly at the thought of meeting him down the cave. As the ladder was in place it made sense to use it, so, in the customary fashion I left my rope attached to the grille, and after a few moments thought, and having removed my cows' tails for the traverse, I decided to leave the kit bag there as well. If, by some chance, Sprat left first, without having crossed paths with me, he'd lower the bag that contained my harness and ascenders down to the cave floor and rig the rope ready for me to get out – or more likely he'd just leave the ladder.

With these extra things to think about, I completely forgot my key, leaving it behind in the lock as I climbed down into the cave.

Having reached the bottom I started my journey through the entrance series. I moved quickly, converting fear and frustration into speed, twisting my body this way and that in well-practised turns and ducks as I negotiated the meanders and dogleg turns of the passage. On a solo trip you travel at your optimum speed, not quite getting out of breath yet keeping your momentum. Your body works efficiently and you can cover a lot of ground with surprising ease. I very soon reached the boulder choke where the obstacle course forced me to slow down as I climbed under and over the haphazard terrain. I stopped running on adrenalin and reality took its chance to creep up on me. What I hadn't considered about caving on my own was that, on the easy bits where I didn't have to concentrate too hard, I would have a lot of time to think. I thought alternately, of Fish (which made me anxious) and of Beth and Ashley (which made me angry). Occasionally I also thought of Carole but this just made me confused.

280

When I reached the top of the streamway I clipped the two karabiners on my cows' tails onto the traverse rope. Then I made my way along, leaning out from the rocky wall, stopping to transfer first one then the other krab to the next section of rope each time I came to a metal loop. Below me the river crashed over boulders. It seemed louder than usual – probably just because I was on my own. When I came to the shelf where the river cascaded down to the lake below, I unclipped from the line, scrambled down to the opening on the left and went down the staircase in a controlled slide, collecting a few bruises as I encountered rocks along the way. I skirted round the edge of the lake, leaving the waterfall splashing down behind me on the right. I'd soon be at the camp where, with any luck, Sprat would have detailed his way on in the logbook. He might even be taking a break over a mug of tea. This thought cheered me.

I don't know what made me take a detour round to the Devil's Cauldron at the far end, the satisfaction of seeing the water disappear into the unknown, perhaps. Either way, I stood there for a few moments, listening to the water gurgle down between the rocks, like someone had pulled the plug on a giant bath. I enjoyed the feeling that it was just me there. Me and nature. I was turning to go when something caught my eye, something shiny and red. It was on a rocky ledge on a lower level so I hadn't seen it from where I'd been standing. I turned back and clambered down to where the object was lying. It was a tackle sack. Immediately I wondered whether it belonged to Sprat or to someone else, maybe a group from another club who had borrowed a key – though, if that was the case they, they shouldn't have come this far without one of us accompanying them. I picked it up to see if there was any indication of the owner, initials inked just inside maybe, like I usually did with mine.

But I didn't get that far. The sack was heavier than I expected and as I tried to lift it some of the contents spilled out onto the rock. It was a cellophane pack containing a white substance. The cellophane must have caught on a sharp edge of rock causing it to puncture and the crystalline contents to spill out

281

onto the ledge. I stooped down and dipped my fingertip in the sugary pile, sniffed it and tasted a fraction on the tip of my tongue. I didn't need my professional training to tell me what it was.

Chapter 44

Ascender - metal device which can be pushed along a rope in one direction only, used to travel up a rope in SRT.

The flame of the candle stands almost upright in a straight stem with hardly a movement of air to make it waver. After so long in near darkness, it seems to glow like a burning sun.

This is it. I've got no food left, nothing to lose. I'm going to have one more push at getting out. But before I do I'm going to leave a record. Just in case something goes wrong (I tell myself this would take the form of getting trapped and waiting to be successfully rescued rather than anything more final). I take the logbook and pen which we had used to record our explorations and under the last entry, the one in which Sprat described this newly discovered passage, I write in a few sentences. Briefly, I describe what has happened, who is responsible for my being here and why. Then, like all the other trips done before, I describe as best I can where I am now heading. If by any chance a rescue party – or anyone else for that matter – should find a way through during the next few hours, they will know where to find me. What I have scribbled is impersonal, addressed to anyone who may read it. I toy with the idea of writing short individual messages to my friends. Just in case. Yet as I try to form the sentences in my head I see that tarot card again, and feel a kind of premonition, as if I would be signing my own death warrant. I decide against it.

I switch on my lamp, blow out the candle then I'm on my way. I've memorised the route before I set off. I can picture every inch of it in my head, even the part at the end where I've never been before. And all the time I'm treading the familiar path, I'm thinking about that trip to Yorkshire, the one fifteen years ago.

In the morning, after cooking and eating a hearty breakfast

(we'd left our food in the car overnight, safely out of reach of the rat) we set off to the cave. We were up here to go diving – well, Fish and I were. Rick, Joe and Taff were going to be our entourage and carry all the gear in. We were meeting up with someone who'd contacted Fish through the cave diving group and persuaded him to organise it. Apparently she was one of those wild adventurous types. I didn't know. I didn't really care. I was just going along as an extra because Fish had asked me to, because I'd dived that system with him once before.

We met up with her at a lay-by as near as we could park to the cave entrance. Her name was Gina and she did a lot of deep sea diving, treasure hunting on ancient wrecks; navigating her way around barnacled hulls and treacherous rigging. She was young and pushy, a striking girl with spiky hair and a fearsome temper. I didn't want anything to do with her; women like that frightened me in those days – still do in fact. I decided I'd have to do the dive because I'd promised Fish. But I'd just be a passenger; I'd leave all the talking and decision making to him.

Fish and Taff weren't there when we arrived. They still hadn't turned up fifteen minutes later when we'd changed into our kit.

Gina wasn't impressed. She paced up and down in her blue wetsuit. 'He said ten o'clock,' she said, looking at her watch. From the scowl on her face it was clear patience wasn't one of her virtues. 'So where is he then?' She directed the question at me. I mean, hell, how should I know? I wasn't his keeper.

'Weed killer,' sniggered Joe.

'I'm wilting,' I whispered back.

She stared at Joe this time; a piercing look with steel blue eyes, freshly sharpened steel at that. 'Well don't just stand there giggling,' she commanded. 'Start carrying the gear through, it'll save time later.'

Eventually Rick made an executive decision. 'I'll go and look for them,' he said. 'Maybe they've overslept or their car won't start.' We took the rest of the kit out of the car before he left, so we could start taking it up to the cave like Gina suggested.

Half an hour later, just as Joe, Gina and I arrived back at the road, Rick returned. He was alone.

'Well?' I asked, in a low voice.

'Fish is ill,' he said. 'Puking his guts up with no sign of recovery.'

'Shit!'

'Yeah; that too, probably. According to Taff, the two of them decided to have a nightcap. That was when we left last night. And it seems that after a few whiskies they discovered the pub had a lock in. So they had a few more. Taff's OK but Fish is wrecked. He's sick as a dog, Marty. There's no way he can dive today. I doubt he'll be able to stand upright before evening.'

'Shit!'

'What's going on? When's he arriving?' Gina stood in front of us. Hell, was she frightening.

'I'm afraid he's been taken ill,' said Rick. 'We'll have to reschedule.'

'Impossible. I've come here to dive this cave and I'm damn well going to do it!'

'We can't,' I protested. 'I've only done it the once and I'm not as experienced as Fish. It wouldn't be safe.'

She glared at me. 'Well in that case,' she said, 'I'll just have to do it on my own!' And with that she took her kit bag out of her car, slung it over her shoulder and headed off towards the entrance.

I called after her and she turned briefly.

'Well?' she asked. 'Are you coming or not?'

I'm certain I've found the right place. It all fits Rick and Sprat's descriptions, the slope of the approach, the way the stream joins from the right, flooding the passage into a duck. I crouch down to peer through the rocky archway, my head tilted horizontally just above the surface of the water. There's only a couple of inches of air space, it should be more than that according to the description in the logbook, a foot at least for the first part, but the others came down here before it rained.

I shiver at the thought of it. The water is icy and I feel like I've only just begun to dry out after my adventure in the Lake, although surely that was hours ago now. I face the facts. Even if this passage is the one detailed in the logbook, I'm not sure I'll be able to get past the deep section, and even if I do there's no guarantee that there will be a way through to the outside. But there's only one way to find out and I have to go for it. I take a deep breath and lie down on my back in the unwelcoming water.

The chill leaves me breathless and it's a full minute before I can breathe normally. With my head tilted slightly back so that my nose is in the air, I shuffle forward, arms pressed against my sides, propelling myself onwards with my heels and trying very hard not to make additional ripples. I can't see the way ahead, my view is limited to the rocky roof a few inches above me, there is no alternative but to keep going, trusting that the passage will soon widen out. I'm in luck. It does. It opens up into a small pear-shaped chamber with room to sit up, my head and shoulders clear of the torrent below.

From there on, however, things don't look so good. Ahead, the passage is completely sumped; water meeting roof. My heart sinks. I wonder how long it goes on like that – indeed whether it opens up at all. The way on looks to be roomier than the squeeze I've just come through, but even so it won't be as easy as swimming underwater at the leisure centre pool. I sit for a precious few moments to prepare myself, knowing that the longer I wait, the colder I will become.

At last I kneel in the water, I take two deep breaths in and out, on the third I breathe in as deeply as I can, tuck my chin down towards my neck and plunge into the inky tunnel. I open my eyes, blinking at the coldness, squinting slightly for protection. With my hands I feel the sides of the tunnel and propel myself forward. I try to kick my feet but my knees bang and scrape painfully against boulders.

The passage widens a little – I can tell by my outstretched arms – but there's no sign of the surface breaking into an air pocket. I've been counting the seconds and I know that I have to turn back now, while I can, before I run out of air.

* * *

'OK!' I shouted after her. 'Hang on!'

It was against my better judgment, but what could I do?

We made our way into the cave, Rick and Joe carrying the heavier items of gear to the water's edge. Then Gina and I kitted up, strapping the cumbersome cylinders onto our backs. Joe looked at me sympathetically as I waded out into the pool. It was black and dingy, like oil, and just about as inviting.

After that, Gina and I were on our own. The water was slightly silty, with dark particles of iron-stained clay suspended in its chilly depths that reduced the visibility to just a few yards. I carried the line, unravelling it behind us like an old jumper in a maze. The walls were black with manganese, swallowing the torch beams and spreading gloomy shadows. Beneath us, hostile rocks scraped at our knees. It was a challenging swim, but hardly enjoyable. We surfaced in several chambers, enjoying the brief respite of bright calcited walls and the opportunity to breathe normal, if stagnant, air.

At last we came to a bell-shaped cavern, completely flooded but with room to stretch upright and tread water. This was as far as I'd come in the past and the end of the line as far as the survey was concerned. I signalled that we would rest a few moments before turning back.

Gina explored around the walls of the chamber; with unnatural energy she scrabbled and scraped at rubble slopes, like a rabbit going to ground. Suddenly she pulled back a huge boulder, sending a swirl of debris about us. She appeared before me out of the thickening mist and waved her arms excitedly, pointing at the low passage she had uncovered. I shared her enthusiasm, but in a more restrained manner. When she signalled that we should carry on I looked at my watch and, calculating that we had used one third of our air supply, shook my head vehemently. She ignored me and pulled away more of the clutter, widening the entrance.

I'll never forget her face as she turned to wave to me, mocking and teasing, her slightly upturned eyes, framed by the facemask, sparkling with the carefree disobedience of a mischievous child.

287

I grabbed at her arm, swung her round and pointed at my watch. Violently, she shook herself free and her eyes flashed with emotion. I tried to read her thoughts; single-mindedness, bloody-mindedness, anger? Way beyond my understanding, that was for sure. Then she turned her back on me and wriggled through the opening. I remember her flippered feet waving as she disappeared.

I was angry and frightened at the same time. I stuck my head into the entrance of the tunnel but my shoulders wedged fast against solid rock. Perhaps I was relieved that I couldn't follow. If I had done, things might have turned out differently, one way or another.

The waiting was unbearable. The walls of the chamber seemed to close in on me, squeezing my body so I felt I could hardly breathe. Every few minutes I looked at my watch. At last, knowing I was cutting it fine, I made the decision to return alone. Before I left, I tied the line off onto a rock. Just in case.

I surfaced, cold, breathless and miserable, dragged myself out of the water and collapsed onto the muddy floor. With Joe's arms around me I hung my head and cried.

I'd almost run out of air.

Just like now.

Chapter 45

Iron pyrites - a sparkling mineral found in caves, also known as fool's gold because of its tendency to be mistaken for something more precious.

Suddenly a figure loomed out of the water.

The eyes, clear blue and slightly upturned, gazed at me through the frame of the diving mask.

'G-Gina?' I stuttered. I stood rigid, frozen in shock. I was looking at a ghost.

The figure pulled the mask away from his face. 'I guess we did look pretty alike,' Ashley said. His voice was calm and without emotion.

I was open-mouthed, haunted, forgetting for a moment the comparatively unimportant detail of what I held in my hand.

Ashley lifted his hand and wiped his face. Water dripped from his chin and from his nose. He stared at me.

I remained motionless, still clutching the pack of coke. My legs were shaking. I sat down on a boulder and set the cellophane parcel on the ground. I was vaguely aware of Ashley pulling himself out of the water, tugging a second tackle sack behind him. After removing the weights and diving gear he checked both his new cargo and the one I had opened, pushing the package I'd removed back into the first tackle sack. Then he stacked the diving gear on the rock beside me.

'Why don't you keep this,' he suggested. 'I'm getting some new kit soon anyway. I'll need Trimix for the deep caverns in South America.' He was too calm. I'd just blown his cover. Why didn't he threaten to kill me or at least leave me bound and gagged? Instead he was offering me all this expensive equipment. Perhaps that was it. A bribe.

'I don't dive any more.'

'Maybe you should.'

I couldn't hack this. Here was someone I thought I knew. A

mate. And in the space of a few seconds I had to deal with not one but two disturbing revelations about him.

'The diving accident – you knew all the time that it was me?'

He smiled. 'It's a small world, the caving fraternity.'

'But you never said anything.'

'I realised early on that it was something you hadn't come to terms with. I like you, Marty, I like your friends, I didn't want to upset you.'

Tears were flooding my eyes. 'I was leading the dive, I was responsible for her, I killed her. Or as good as.'

'No, Marty, you didn't kill anyone.' He looked up at me then, in that deep piercing way he had that cut through all my secrets. 'I don't blame you for what happened and you shouldn't blame yourself. I knew Gina all her life. I know what she was like. I can picture what happened, you telling her to turn back, spelling out the danger; and her telling you to go to hell and striking out on her own. She was never a team player, Marty. She lived for risk and she died because of it. It made her special. There's no point in regrets or recriminations. Damn! I wish I'd talked to you before. I didn't realise just how badly you felt.'

I sniffed. 'I should have waited for her. Or gone after her, made her turn back.'

'You'd have waited forever. You'd have died yourself. What good would that have done? You have to put it behind you now and move on. I have, and so must you.'

I had relived her death over and over so many times. Imagining what it would be like to be lost; to be trapped maybe, or for your gear to fail. Then to gasp for air and find there was none. And to die there. Alone. It was three years before they found her body. Jelly in a rubber mould.

'What about you?' I nodded at the packages. 'Is that what you call moving on?'

Ashley laughed. 'Get real. You're hardly in a position to judge – the man who manufactured his own mind expanding cocktail!'

How did he know about the Smartees? Beth, I suppose, or

even Rick, must have told him, probably just a passing comment, no big deal, because they didn't know what I knew now.

'That was years ago,' I sighed. 'It was just a bit of fun. I was a kid mixing chemicals in a test-tube, it was only for myself and a couple of friends, I never made money out of it, it's hardly the same thing as smuggling cocaine.' I hoped I didn't sound too defensive.

Ashley stared at me, intensely. 'But what if it was now? What if you had a student loan to pay off? What if none of you had suffered any bad effects from the stuff and people were asking you, begging you, to sell it to them? Can you really be sure you wouldn't do it?'

'There's no comparison,' I retaliated. 'You had us all believe you worked with computers when really…I mean, Christ knows what the street value of this is. And coke is almost as serious as it gets.'

'OK, let's clear up a couple of points,' Ashley began. He was calm and methodical. 'Firstly, I install computer security systems; that's what I do, that's my job, you know that yourself, you've seen me do it. Secondly, I don't deal in crack. All right, I know it's easy enough to make – what's the formula, washing soda or something? You're the chemist, you probably know more about that than I do. But what people do with it is up to them. I know it sounds stupid but this is a hobby, I don't do it for the money. OK, it's a lucrative business, I'm not denying that, but that isn't why I do it. I'm providing a service, giving people a choice. No-one has to buy it, no-one has to use it, but if they want to then the stuff I import is good, it's clean, there are minimal impurities. If someone wants to do coke then this is as safe as it gets. Yeah, it's illegal, but it's not the big deal it used to be. If the law changes it'll be just another energy shot, like a double espresso. Until then there's a trade. I work for myself, no middlemen, no crooks. OK there's an element of danger for me. Getting caught, mainly. But I enjoy that, just like I enjoy the danger in caving. That's the buzz for me, that's really living.'

I felt perplexed. He wouldn't be saying these things if he'd seen people laid out on a mortuary slab, or if he'd seen Fish yesterday. It was all too much to take in. 'But why coke? I've never seen you take it yourself.'

'You're right; I don't touch the stuff. I suppose it's in memory of Gina; it was her favourite high. God knows, she was probably out of her head on it when she did the dive.' He paused for a moment, looking kind of introspective, sad, even. Then he snapped back into his business-like, efficient self. 'Come on,' he said as he jumped to his feet and held out his free hand to help me up. 'Let's get out of here.'

The scenario that I found myself in was entirely surreal. I felt like an actor, playing out a part, reading a previously unseen script. I wished I knew what was going on in Ashley's mind. Did he still think of me as a friend – if indeed he ever had? And if so would that friendship count for anything now? Or was I just an expendable pawn in his game, an obstacle that had inadvertently got in his way and must be removed?

Ashley tied the cords on the tackle sacks while I looked on, open-mouthed. I thought about trying to reason with him, do a deal, offer to cover his tracks until he'd left the country. I felt myself wondering if he'd ever killed anyone. If he'd pointed a gun at someone's head and cold-bloodedly pulled the trigger, whether he'd spiked the goods he supplied and so sent someone just as certainly to their death. I know he made out he had nothing to do with the seedy side of the business and I wanted to believe him. But how would I know? I was just a chemist, not a tough police officer like Mike. I only knew how to set up reactions in a test tube; I wasn't trained to deal with people or situations like this.

During this time, Ashley never turned his back on me. A precaution, I suppose, in case I took a swing at him while he was off guard. He hung the shiny red sacks, one across each shoulder and, without a word, set off in the direction of the entrance. I felt some small relief that he paid little attention to me. I followed a short distance behind. As we approached the climb and the river traverse, I thought of the evidence I had provided in the past, the cases I had come to know almost as well as the police with whom I liaised. I thought of appearing in court, of hearing about these hideous people and how they worked, their psychological make-up, their greed, their complete disregard for human life. I tried to force myself to accept that Ashley was one of these. Not a friend. Not an ordinary person, but a callous, hardened criminal.

We came to the climb up the spiral staircase – a bit more tricky going up than down. He was so calm I just had no idea what he was going to do. He was a professional that was for sure; he wouldn't take any risks or leave any loose ends. Perhaps he was planning to pay me off. But he couldn't be sure I'd accept.

Then, suddenly, I remembered Fish, lying in a coma in the hospital bed. What was it Taff had said? He'd tried to persuade him to stay for another drink but he'd refused because he'd already arranged to meet someone (fair enough, that was Carole), but before that he was going to drop by Ashley's. Where had Carole found him? Ashley's flat!

I hadn't really thought about the implications of it when I was at the hospital. I'd been more concerned with what was happening to Fish and the shock revelation about him and Carole. Now I put two and two together and felt sick at the result. Fish must have turned up unannounced at Ashley's flat, walked in on some deal, seen something he shouldn't have. And that was the price he paid. Ashley must have done that to him; Ashley who we'd thought was our friend but who turned out to be a dangerous drug-dealer. Now I'd just walked in on a similar scene. And I was in a desperate dilemma. Kill or be killed. That's what it might come down to, if I was going to get out of here alive. I'd have to think fast.

We reached the top of the Staircase and Ashley was just in front of me, cool, confident, just about to scramble up to the traverse, looking directly ahead. I stood behind. To my left the streamway plunged over the rocky ledge and down into the Lake below. I waited till Ashley's feet were level with my shoulder, then I took my chance. I grabbed his left ankle and tugged, pulling him off balance, tugged again so that he fell down into the rushing water, then I lost my own footing so that I started to slide down with him. The tackle sack had broken his fall or I think he'd have come off worse. Meanwhile, I found myself lying across his chest, leaning out over the waterfall.

I don't really know what happened next, Ashley had hold of me, he was pulling, or pushing, I couldn't tell, it all happened so quickly. I kicked and struggled and then I saw a fist coming towards me. This was it. Nemesis.

'Are you OK?'

'Dunno. I think so.' I felt dazed and my chin hurt. I rubbed it and saw a smudge of blood on my glove. I was wet too, soaked, but, in the short term, at least, that wasn't important.

'I'm sorry about that but I had to do something or you'd have killed us both.'

I laughed that sort of nervous chuckle that slips out at the least appropriate moments. 'Instead of just you killing me, you mean?'

Ashley sat down beside me. I noticed, then, that he'd pulled me up to the rope and clipped on my cows' tails. 'Marty, I have no intention of hurting you. For God's sake, if I wanted to kill you I could have just let you fall down the seventy in Daren that time, remember? When you were drunk.'

I took a deep breath. 'That was before I knew about all that.' I pointed at the tackle sack. I paused, wondering if laying the cards on the table could land me in any worse trouble. Hell, I was in up to my neck already. I went for it. 'And I know what you did to Fish.'

'Fish? I haven't done anything to him. I don't know what you're talking about.'

'Don't play games,' I said. 'Last night, when you pumped him full of alcohol and coke and heroin, then left him to die.'

To give him his due Ashley looked genuinely surprised. Horrified, even.

'Why did you try to kill him?' I asked. 'Was it because he found out about your little drug operation or for his part in what happened to Gina? I'm guessing that seeing as you seem

294

to know all about my part in it, you also know that Fish was supposed to be leading the dive if he hadn't got pissed out of his mind.'

'Yes…yes, of course I know all that. Fish was no more to blame than you were. OK, he got drunk, but he could just as easily have been ill with food poisoning, the outcome would have been the same. But what's all this about last night? What do you mean? Is he all right? Tell me what happened.'

I told him about how I'd been called out and how Fish was lying there on a ventilator. I told him what Taff had said. And Carole. How Fish had been found at Ashley's flat. And how they'd found the puncture mark from a syringe.

The colour drained from Ashley's face. He sat there with furrowed brow for what seemed like ages, then he spoke very slowly and seriously. 'Look, Marty, I can't tell you everything, there isn't time, and anyway there's lots of stuff it's best you don't know. But I can promise you I had nothing to do with anything that's happened to Fish. As I said, I like you all, I have no reason, no wish, to harm anyone – and I certainly don't deal in heroin!' He paused for a moment, like he was making one of his decisions. Slowly and calmly he continued. 'As it happens, I was out of town last night. I was still up in London, sorting out some arrangements for the trip to Cuba. I left my flat on Monday morning and haven't been back since. I drove directly here this morning. I know I can't prove that to you now but when you get out of here there are people who will vouch for me. You can ask them. I'd like you to do that just so that you – all of you – know that I wasn't involved.'

I touched my chin again and winced. 'So what do you think happened to him? Could someone else have been in your flat?'

Ashley looked uncomfortable. He mused for a moment. 'Maybe,' he said at last. 'Maybe someone thought they'd find this haul stashed away there,' he patted one of the tackle sacks, 'and decided to help themselves. Not that I'd be stupid enough to keep it at home.' He stared directly at me. 'Marty, I'm going to give you some advice.'

'I'm all ears.'

'This isn't a joke believe me. When you get out of here, just remember that you can't trust anyone. Even the people who you think are close to you.'

'Do you have to talk in riddles?'

'I'm trying to protect you. Can't you see? The less you know the less danger you'll be in.'

I breathed out slowly, the warm air whistling over my teeth. Who did he mean? Not Rick, surely. Or Joe? He and Rick had been very chummy after all, but any thought of involvement in Ashley's game was unthinkable, and in any case they were away, out of the country. Taff was the only one who might be into dealing, but Fish was his childhood friend, no way would he harm him.

'Please believe me,' he continued. 'Look. I can tell you some of it. Like I've brought forward the trip, for instance, I'm flying to South America tonight.'

'Why are you telling me this?'

'Because it doesn't matter any more.'

'You mean you're going away for good?'

He hesitated. 'Well, after what you've told me, let's just say I don't think I'll be able to come back for a while. That partly depends on you and what you tell the police about the stuff you've seen down here. Though you wouldn't have any evidence of course.'

'What about Beth?'

'She'll meet someone else. We were just having a bit of fun and she knew it. I'm not stupid, Marty; I know that Beth, like any other women I've been involved with, was basically impressed by the size of my bank balance. Beth likes me because she thinks I'm some fantasy figure. If she's in love...well...then she's in love with the person she wants me to be, not the person I am.'

I thought about telling him what Beth had said but it was a bit late now and there didn't seem much point.

He continued. 'I'm going to make a suggestion and I need you to trust me on this.'

I nodded.

'There's a possibility that someone will be waiting to meet me by the car. Yes, I know I said I work alone, but what you've just told me changes things. There are clearly dangerous people who've been checking up on me. It's possible I've been followed. I don't want you to get into any danger so I want you to stay down here, just for a few hours. As soon as I'm at the airport I'll call someone and make sure you get out OK.'

It sounded a bit convenient to me and I had no guarantee he'd actually do as he said. 'Why not leave the ladder?'

'Because if someone's watching I need it to look convincing and I want to make sure you stay out of the way until it's safe. Believe me, it's important that you aren't seen with me; that you don't get mixed up in this. I've been taken for a ride myself by the looks of it. Please Marty.' He looked at me directly, piercingly. 'What you've told me about Fish...this is serious stuff. This time I'm in far more danger than before. That's my lookout; I chose to take the risk. You didn't and now I feel responsible for you. Please do as I ask. All you have to do is sit tight for an hour or two, then, as soon as I'm on my way, I'll call someone you know and tell them to come and get you out.'

'I don't like the idea. Anyway, my car's parked on the quarry track, it's nowhere near yours, so even if you have your meeting I'd be well out of the way.'

'Well if you're determined then there isn't much I can do about it, but seriously, Marty, I really am only thinking of your safety.'

So was I. All right, so maybe I could trust Ashley (and deep down I believed he was genuine) but what if this 'someone' decided they wanted him out of the way too? Permanently. He couldn't tell anyone where I was with a bullet in his head. It horrified me to face the reality of the game I was caught up in. 'Look,' I suggested, 'I've left my rope and ascenders at the top. You could rig them for me and take the ladder. I'll wait half an hour then climb out.'

Ashley shrugged. 'OK,' he agreed at last. 'But make it an hour. I don't want you walking into any danger.'

And there was nothing I could do but take his word for it.

'Well,' he said. 'It's getting late and I have a plane to catch. Let's get on.'

It was a strange journey out. Normally we'd have been laughing and joking, but instead we walked in silence. Because there was nothing left to say. Along the traverse, it wasn't so bad; you always had to concentrate anyway. And the Snowy Mountains demanded your attention. But then there were the endless long winding passages, and the boulder choke – that was the worst – it took ages, mainly because Ashley was carrying those two bulky sacks. Normally I'd have offered to take one, but knowing what they contained I just couldn't.

I got to thinking again, about unsavoury subjects. Like if Ashley hadn't tried to kill Fish (and I truly wanted to believe – no, I truly believed – that he hadn't) then who was responsible? Taff could have been lying about getting him drunk. God, I really didn't want to be thinking in that way.

At last we reached the entrance shaft. Ashley was still in front; he stopped to clip the tackle sacks onto his belt.

'Well I hope things work out for you,' he smiled. 'Let go of the past, Marty, and start living again. To be honest I'd always thought that you and Beth...well, never mind. Good luck anyway.' He held out his hand. I shook it but I couldn't bring myself to wish him well.

He started up the ladder then. First, one rung, then the next, one foot in front, the other behind, like a dance, his arms weaving through the rungs, hooking over them, palms towards his face, holding himself upright. The rustling and scraping echoed down beneath him, like an invisible trail. Ripples of movement rolled down the wires. Then they stopped and I knew he'd reached the top. There would be a few moments while he opened the grille and hauled himself out. I waited. I watched the ladder. And when a faint quiver told me it was free I began to climb. I'd made my decision much earlier. I'd rather take my chances on the surface than wait down here.

Then I heard voices, up above me. There were two of them, and although the words were unclear it was obvious from the tone that they were arguing. I paused for a moment, straining my ears; it wasn't difficult, they were hardly whispering. One of the voices was Ashley's, obviously. The other I recognised instantly.

After that, things happened fast. Someone was swinging the ladder, deliberately trying to dislodge me. I held on as long as I could but I swung into the side of the shaft and banged my head on a rock. I hurt. I lost my hold on the ladder. I fell to the ground. I hurt even more. Something fluttered down after me, something white, dancing like a feather. It landed on the ground by my side, a tiny cellophane pack containing a white powder. Enough coke to blast me off this mortal coil and into an eternal orbit. And Mike's words fell down around me.

'Die happy!'

Chapter 46

Descender - an abseil device for travelling down a rope. Caving descenders do not twist the rope. They sometimes include a braking device which activates if the caver lets go.

As soon as I'm out of the water, I collapse in a heap, panting. I'm very sure now that I've found the place Rick told me about over the phone, the same tunnel Sprat described in the logbook. But I'm equally sure that, with the cave in flood, where previously the water stopped inches short of the roof, it now fills the passage completely, forming one or more sumps, too long to safely free dive.

It's only when my slow, defeated journey has brought me almost back to the camp, that I remember Ashley's diving kit, left beside the Devil's Cauldron. I hesitate momentarily before taking that route.

As I reach the end of Starbright Passage and continue into The Sewer, the hum of rushing water fills the air. I can't remember seeing the air cylinder and regulator when I climbed out of the Lake earlier, but I was hardly in a state to notice. I remind myself there's every chance they'll have been swept into the Cauldron.

By the time I emerge into the Lake Chamber the water is deafening. I'm pretty sure, from the thunderous noise and the spray that fills the air, there's more of it than before. It's only just peaking. If my exit from the cave depends on its subsiding I could be in for a long wait.

So when I see the diving gear safely stacked on the ledge behind the Cauldron and know that it has been spared a one-way trip into the sump, the decision of what to do is made.

It's a long laborious trip to carry the gear back to the camp (where I pause for a rest) and then to the small chamber at the start of the flooded passage. There I kit up, strapping a compressed air cylinder onto my back for the first time in fifteen years, clenching my teeth in trepidation as I bite onto the mouthpiece. The gauge indicates that the tank's low. Neither Ashley nor I had envisaged my using it this soon.

I practise breathing, slowly and evenly, before I reach the sump. Then I know I have to go for it. The way ahead lies under a low shelf of rock. I lie flat on my stomach and drag myself cautiously into the tunnel. After a few yards the flooded passage opens out a little and I'm almost swimming. Like a plough, my outstretched arms push aside rocky rubble and I lift my head a little so that my helmet bounces tap, tap, tap against the roof. I think of the way ahead and how there is no space to turn round even if I want to. Fuelled by panic, my breath hisses and rasps, deep and fast. I'm using up too much air.

I steady myself, tell myself to breathe slowly, shallowly, to move forward steadily, deliberately. My legs paddle freely now. The roof gets higher and I wish I'd worn the weight belt. If it weren't for yesterday's rain I could probably almost walk it. I'm going to get out of here. It's going to be all right.

I surface, pulling the mask away from my face, and gasp in deep breaths of longed-for air. I have confronted my demons and won, I am still alive whereas they will never have so much power over me again. Strengthened by this knowledge I now have belief, rather than simply hope, that I will get out of here alive. I take a few moments to reassess the situation; later, when this crisis is over, I will reassess my life.

But I'm not out yet. I'm optimistic though. Not just because the passage beyond the sump is like Rick described, but because the nature of the cave has changed. I can't say exactly what is different, whether it's the colour of the rock, the texture, the smell or the humidity of the air. All I know for certain is that it feels different, different like the cave entrance, several twists and turns before the bottom of the shaft, different in a way that could be physical, or might be the knowledge that the outside world isn't far away.

Since the sump I've been paddling through knee-deep water. Now, a few yards ahead, the passage forks. To the left, the streamway splashes noisily under a low boulder; to the right, a narrow tunnel continues. I wait a few more moments to compose myself, unstrapping the cylinder from my back and piling it with the regulator and mask near the water's edge. Then I squeeze down the passage to the right.

After ten yards I stop. A pile of rocks blocks the way. They are quite small and loose; I can pick most of them up with one hand. I begin methodically to move them aside. I have no idea what lies beyond other than the hopeful indication of a slight but constant draught. But the activity gives me something to think about, to focus my mind, and it helps me to warm up a little.

The work is therapeutic, meditative almost. Occasionally I switch off my lamp for a while, conserving those last flickering vestiges of light, and work in total darkness using the sense of touch alone. I have lost all track of time, I have no idea whether it is mid-day or midnight nor even what day it is. More than anything now I want to sleep. I could so easily just curl up and drift into slumber but know that I must not. Humming tunes to myself I force myself to carry on.

I fall into a rhythm. Beginning each time at the roof of the tunnel, in the top left hand corner, I clear the stones, progressing to the right; then I do the same with those below. Although impatient, I work carefully. The last thing I need now is a roof fall, or indeed any uncontrolled movement of rock. Sometimes the rubble is resistant, glued together with a finer mix of silt or soil, then I have to prise at the lumpy surface with my fingers and pull it, crumbling, towards me. I've done this plenty of times before, plenty of times during the last year, with Rick and Joe, with Taff and Fish, and Beth, digging out the debris that so often clogs up tunnels. I don't have any bang this time though, or even a shovel, or, more importantly, anyone with whom to laugh about it. All those times before were really no more than a game; only this one is for real. Occasionally I think of Mike, and each time I shudder in disbelief. I feel light-headed as I accumulate piles of spoil by my left side and push it decisively behind me. Each time, when I have moved the debris at floor level, I flash my torch on briefly, surveying the new barrier before me, then move forward a few inches to begin the exercise again.

It's during one of these breaks, when I've completed a section and flashed on the torch to look at the next wall of stones. In darkness once more, I edge forward. And that's when I first notice. The gentle draught of earlier has increased to a strong and steady breeze. I switch the light back on and look more closely at the rocks before me. They are interspersed with soil, lovely fresh crumbly soil. In a state of frenzied excitement, I scrabble haphazardly at the material in my way, all the careful method of earlier has disappeared and I have only one thing in mind.

Escape. I sit back on the grass, dizzy with exhaustion and relief. In the dark hours that had seemed so interminably long, I had dreamed of this moment; its image had carried me onward when my body had wanted to give up. I had dreamed of an ethereal freshness, of breathing deep breaths of sweet-scented air, of colours so vivid that I could be tripping, and sunlight so bright that it burned my eyes. Yet as I sit here, alone on the dark mountainside, all I'm aware of is the overwhelming and pungent odour of sheep droppings.

It's dark. It must be evening, or even the middle of the night. I can hear that rustling munching sound that sheep make as they graze, eerie in the darkness. Then I think, what the hell, I'm out now, I can use the last of the light in my back-up torch. I switch it on and look about me. The range isn't very far, but I can see the sheep's eyes glowing. They're strange animals by torchlight. Their form is misty and insubstantial but their eyes shine like lights. Several times in the past I've surfaced from a cave in the dark and set off across the fields thinking I was heading towards the welcoming lights of a caving hut or a farm, only to find that I'd been following a flock of sheep.

But this time it's the other way round. As I stand upright I realise that the scrub by the entrance is in fact a hedge and, whilst the ones nearby are real enough, the 'sheep' further away turn out to be the lights of a building. Filled with relief I climb over a nearby gate and down a flagstone path past dustbins and some crates and knock on what I assume is the kitchen door.

Chapter 47

'Do they fit all right?' asked Huw.

I'd never been in the kitchen of the Quarryman's Rest before. I sat at the table, peculiarly dressed in a brown and cream check shirt, V-neck sleeveless pullover with diamond pattern and a pair of trousers cut very generously around the waist and held up by a belt. In front of me stood the remains of a large glass of brandy and a mug of cocoa.

I smiled and nodded affirmatively as I tucked into a double helping of bacon and eggs.

'You get that down you then lad. Sounds like quite an adventure you've had, going down a cave on your own and getting trapped by a rock fall. We'd better call that friend of yours and tell him you're all right.'

'Who's that?' I asked, immediately suspicious. Oh God, what if Mike was checking to make sure I hadn't escaped? What if I was still in danger?

'That local boy, the one you call Taff.' Huw paused to top up my brandy. I thought it was amusing the way he spoke of us as though we were little more than children; amusing but also affectionate. 'That Taff, he was round asking about you this morning. Seems that smart good-looking one had told him you might have had an accident or something. He rang him earlier apparently, from goodness knows where. Anyway, Taff went off up to the cave then came back here a few hours later and said it was flooded and he couldn't get through, said he'd try again tomorrow and hope the water had gone down. He had a friend with him, a skinny boy with a beard.' That would be Sprat, I thought to myself. Huw called to his wife. 'Get the phone, Gwen; we'd better ring him before he goes to bed or calls out the cave rescue.' He turned to me. 'He gave us a number, see. Just in case. Then we'll see about a bed for you for the night.'

'Thanks.' I said, wondering how that one word could mean

305

enough.

Taff came over to collect me the next morning. We'd spoken on the phone briefly the night before, just enough to let him know that I was all right and to warn him that Mike was dangerous – though Ashley had already told him that, apparently. I'd asked if he could bring me some clean, dry clothes and was surprised when the jeans and sweatshirt he handed me turned out to be my own.

'How did you get these?' I asked.

'I went over to the flat late last night. After we spoke. There wasn't anyone there. I collected all your stuff actually...well...what I figured was yours. I hope I did the right thing.'

'Hell, I'm just glad I don't have to go near the place again. You didn't have a key. How did you get in?'

'I've got a hairclip and a screwdriver,' he grinned.

'But weren't you taking a hell of a chance?'

'I took my cousins.'

'Ah.' I'd met Taff's cousins a couple of times: hefty lads from solid mining stock. You didn't argue with them.

'Still, it's a good thing Mike wasn't about.'

Taff snorted. 'More like a pity, if you ask me, boyo. We could have shown him exactly what we thought of him.'

After I'd thanked Huw and Gwen yet again, we drove up to the quarry road where my car was parked.

'Where are you heading now?' asked Taff. 'Your stuff's at my place. I expect you could stay a few days if you don't mind the sofa.'

'Thanks. But I've got the key to Rick and Joe's. I can stay there – till they get back, anyway.'

Taff looked dubious. 'We'll see,' he said, severely. 'Come back to my place first and check I've collected everything.'

As it turned out, Taff insisted on staying with me in Benson Street until Rick and Joe returned a week later. We had a discussion then, the four of us. We didn't include Beth. Her feelings were understandably mixed. She went off to stay with

306

an old school friend, which was probably the best thing.

We sat in the lounge, Rick, Joe, Taff and me. It was just like that night after the pub a year ago, when the whole thing started. Like everything had come full circle. Except this time Taff was stone cold sober. We wanted answers; we wanted to know exactly what had happened to our friend, and why. Fish had come round from the coma by then but he was still in hospital, heavily sedated. Even assuming he made a complete recovery, mentally speaking, Graham had warned me he probably wouldn't remember the hour or two before he passed out. Meanwhile, the police had closed ranks. They simply referred to it as a drug-related incident. So we tried to fill in the gaps: to figure out what happened and why.

We reckoned it went something like this.

Fish met Taff for a quick drink. Then he set off to meet Carole, calling on Ashley on the way. He knocked on the door of the flat and there was no answer, but seeing as the door was ajar and he could hear noises inside he went in anyway. Except it wasn't Ashley in there. It was Mike, ransacking the place. Why was Mike there? Not on official police business, that was for sure. Who knows what goes on in the dirty world of drug dealing? Most likely he'd worked out Ashley was shipping coke in and was hoping to find where he'd stashed it, either to force him into a deal or just to help himself. I was inclined to believe what Ashley told me down the cave, and I doubt he realised Mike was onto him.

So Fish went in. Perhaps Mike assumed it was Ashley, until he'd overpowered him. Perhaps Mike wasn't alone. There could have been more of them. When Mike saw it wasn't Ashley, he couldn't risk him talking; not right then, it could blow the whole thing. Especially if he assumed Fish was one of Ashley's dealers. So he poured a load of alcohol down his throat and injected a nasty cocktail into his vein.

We sat for a while, trying to digest it all. The story lay like a lump of dough in our stomachs.

Joe scratched at his chin. 'So Mike made it look like Fish had gone to the flat, helped himself to gear of various sorts, had

307

himself a fix and overdone it. All self-inflicted.'

I nodded. 'Except he didn't know Fish was left-handed.'

Rick picked up the story. 'That could have made it more complicated. But then Ashley fled the country – very convenient for Mike, very convenient for the police generally. Fish is found unconscious in Ashley's flat. Mike says Ashley's been bringing in coke – if he says anything at all. Ashley takes off. Ashley must have done the deed. It's an open and shut case.'

'What about DNA?' Joe looked at me. 'Isn't that what you were studying just before this happened? Surely Mike's DNA will be all over Ashley's place, not to mention fingerprints.'

I shrugged. 'Mike would have thought of that. He'd have worn gloves, latex probably, no fibres, no residue. And he'd say he'd been in the place as part of his investigations.'

We sat in silence for a while, indeed, Taff had been quiet the whole time. Then he suddenly burst out. 'I've got it! Something that was niggling me.' He looked at me. 'When I went round to get your things, I didn't know which was your room and the first one I went in, on the desk there was an ID card or some such with a photo on – I checked to see if it was yours – it wasn't but the person looked familiar.'

We all looked at him expectantly.

'I've been trying to think where I met him before and now I've remembered. It was the bloke I thumped back in the summer, the one who was fiddling with Ashley's car. So that was the person who nearly killed Fish. God, now I wish I'd given the bugger a proper kicking!'

We all nodded. Not that we condoned violence but these were exceptional circumstances. And Taff saw it as a personal thing, avenging what happened to his friend.

'So Mike was onto Ashley from the start,' Rick pondered.

'Looks like it,' Taff agreed.

'Do you think Mike had done this sort of thing before?' Joe asked. Because if he had then surely he'd be pretty well off. Why would he stay living in such squalor?'

'Well it doesn't do to flaunt your ill-gotten gains,' Rick

308

observed, 'And whether or not he was officially undercover, he needed to fit in with the people he was mixing with; a suburban semi wouldn't cut it. I suspect this was his first shot. Ashley – whatever illegal stuff he's done – is hardly a hardened criminal, he isn't your typical dealer who'd shoot you soon as look at you. He was an easy target.'

They talked on about how Mike would have played it. Not keeping official records of Ashley but instead following him and studying him. Waiting for the crucial moment when he could cash in on the deal.

But I wasn't really concentrating. I was thinking about how Mike must have known I was connected with Ashley from the start. That time he tried to break into his car, he must surely have recognised my vehicle parked nearby. When he shook the ladder and I fell down the shaft...for the past week I'd been telling myself that Mike wouldn't have known it was me down the cave; that whatever sort of shit he was, leaving someone to die, he wouldn't do it to his friend, his flatmate. But now I realised he must have suspected it was me – or at the very least, one of my mates. I felt sick.

'Are you OK?' Joe was looking at me, suddenly. 'Sorry. I can't imagine how you must feel talking about this.'

'Not exactly good,' I agreed. 'But it needs to be sorted out.' Then I told them what I'd just been thinking.

'This is serious,' Rick said. 'Perhaps Mike thought Fish was some dangerous drug dealer – not that it excuses what he did to him, but let's be generous and allow that maybe he told himself he was just putting a nasty criminal out of action for a few hours. He wouldn't have known Fish was teetotal making the alcohol hit him so badly. But if he had any idea it was you down the cave, that makes him sinister on a whole new level. What have you said to the police?'

'Nothing,' I said. 'There was no official cave rescue call out, no-one notified the police I was missing, so technically I don't need to make a statement.'

I thought back to my escape from the cave. Basically I hadn't wanted any fuss. Once I'd got to Rick and Joe's I'd rung work and told them I'd been trapped down a cave and had a bit of a fall as well and didn't feel up to coming in for a few days. Graham had called round to Benson Street, assured me that Fish was stable and insisted on checking me over. I'd been vague about what happened. As far as anyone outside our group was concerned, I'd gone caving to take my mind off what had happened to Fish and got trapped by the rock fall and floodwater. There'd been no need to mention Ashley or what happened at the entrance. After that I'd pretty much slept for forty-eight hours. To be honest, it wasn't until Rick and Joe got back that I was beginning to think clearly. And only when we had that conversation that the full horror of it all really hit me.

'You have to tell the police about Mike,' Rick said. We can't let him get away with it.'

I was hesitant. 'I'm not sure it will do any good. And it will mean incriminating Ashley.'

'I agree with Rick,' Joe said. 'Mike will have worked out by now that it was you he pushed off the ladder – even if he didn't know at the time. So you won't be any safer staying anonymous. In fact, if you make a statement against him, there's no way he'd dare touch you. Plus, you owe it to Fish. OK, he's woken up now but he hasn't spoken coherently to anyone yet; there's no guarantee he'll make a full recovery.'

'And you don't need to incriminate Ashley,' Rick continued. 'You can say you met up with him when he was already on his way out of the cave. There's no reason you should know what was in those tackle sacks; you'd assume it was his diving gear. You tell the police Ashley was in London Friday night. They'll be able to check his alibis. In any case, if it comes to it it's far better he gets a record for shipping coke than attempted murder.'

I still wasn't happy about it. I could see how easy it would be for Mike to wriggle out of any responsibility. But the others were insistent. So I made a statement and was assured the matter would be thoroughly investigated but that I should understand that Mike was a senior officer who had been working undercover. It was most likely that I had misunderstood his words or actions. In the meantime I was reassured that he was currently on leave and that on his return he would be transferring to another force.

It was months later that I received a letter saying no charge had been made seeing as there was no evidence, no witness reports and therefore no case to answer. Quite simply it was Mike's word against mine. It was much later in the year when I heard through the grapevine that Mike was living in Liverpool where he'd received a promotion.

After my adventure down the cave I took a week off work. By the time I went back I'd recovered physically and Fish was out of intensive care so I thought I'd be all right. But I wasn't. Just the thought of the lab made me feel sick, and any mention of a PM report left me a quivering wreck. I decided I just couldn't do it any more and two weeks later I handed in my notice. My boss wouldn't accept it though. He said how much the department valued me, and whatever my experiences in the past (I'd told him all about the Smartees) they all contributed to my expertise now. Eventually he persuaded me to take six months paid leave and reconsider my job on my return.

Meanwhile, Beth was fretting over Ashley and Carole was fretting over Fish. Taff was fretting over his kids, but at least he was happy for me to provide therapy in the form of a drinking partner, he didn't demand a shoulder to cry on or deep and meaningful conversations late into the night.

Hell, I needed a break!

So I thought, why not have one? Without rent and bills to pay I figured I could afford not only my own expenses for a trip to Australia but enough to treat Taff as well. I'd have a travelling companion and he'd get to see his kids.

And that's how we come to be here, Taff and me, the proverbial odd couple, enjoying the Australian sun, sand and surf. I suppose it sounds like I'm running away again, like I did all those years ago. But it feels different this time.

311

Back home things are gradually sorting themselves out. In a film, things would be black and white, so to speak. Fish would either make a full and miraculous recovery, to live happily with Carole and their child for ever after. Or else he'd die, regaining consciousness just long enough for me to promise that I'd stand by Carole and raise their child as though it were my own. Its dark and beautiful looks would ensure that Fish would never be forgotten.

But of course, real life is rarely that simple. There's this middle route that's long, painful and dreary. People with brain damage, undergoing months of physiotherapy, rarely make good cinema. After coming out of the coma, Fish spent two weeks in hospital followed by a month in a rehabilitation centre. Not for any sort of addiction or dependency but because his motor functions were seriously impaired as a result of the chemical onslaught on his system and the precious seconds his brain had been deprived of oxygen. He probably should have stayed in longer but Carole was determined that he should be home with her in time for the birth of the baby.

I'm a bit worried about how I'll feel, seeing the three of them living happily together in my house. I feel envious sometimes, of course I do, that's only natural. Because I was falling in love with the new Carole and, as her husband, I felt that I should have first refusal. It's taken me a while (and several conversations with Joe) to realise that so much about her now is to do with her being with Fish. If she were with me then all those changes, all those different aspects of her personality that I admire, would disappear. When she had the baby – a little girl – she changed again. Even from a few home movie clips, sent by Joe, I can tell she's suddenly discovered this new purpose in her life.

Joe tells me that Beth's been spending a lot of time with him and Rick, going round there straight from work so she doesn't have to be home alone. It sounds like she's pretty much as confused as I am. I still hold out this hope that maybe, when I get back and the dust has settled, the two of us might get together; but I'm trying not to think about it too much because before that could happen I have to sort out my feelings for Carole, and Beth has to sort out hers for Ashley.

Ashley Roberts.

Things started getting complicated when he arrived and they're still unravelling now he's gone. Rick's had a couple of postcards from him from Cuba, with an open invitation for all of us to go on awesome caving expeditions. I think Rick would like to take him up on it but Joe's not so keen. He still blames him, indirectly, for what happened to Fish, and what nearly happened to me. But I daresay that, as usual, Rick will get his way and he and Joe will take a holiday out there. I won't be hurrying though. And Beth certainly won't.

But on a lighter note, I suppose the thing that's changed most in all this is the cave. The Spiral Staircase is completely blocked, both from the top – you can't even get into the chamber by Lovers' Leap any more – and from the bottom where a huge scree slope in the Lake Chamber extends across the Staircase and the waterfall itself. That same pile of boulders also blocks the entrance to the Waterfall Chamber. Only Beth and I know what's behind there and for the moment that's how it's going to stay.

Whilst you can put a line down from the streamway traverse and pick your way down the boulders to the Lake (Rick, Joe, Taff and Sprat have done it a couple of times) it's not a good idea. The whole thing's so unstable that one wrong step and you could have several tons of rock crashing on top of you. I've no doubt that, in time, people will clear the Spiral Staircase and get to do the through trip. But for the moment The Quarry has become two separate caves, the Upper Quarry, accessed from the hilltop, and the Lower Quarry, accessed from behind the pub. I don't have to tell you which is more popular!

My knowledge of the cave, as it is now, comes from my friends. I haven't been back (though I had plenty of opportunity before I set off on my travels). Nor do I intend to in the foreseeable future. I haven't been down any cave in fact. Joe says I should get back on that horse but personally I'm happy to put it out to grass for a while.

I may not have been down a cave for a long time but there's one hobby I have resurrected. It was when we took a trip up to Cairns and went out on the reef. Taff, always a strong swimmer, suggested we go snorkelling. But he didn't stop at that. He was so impressed with that glimpse of the underwater world that he wanted to go scuba diving too. He'd never fancied it down a cave, he said, but this was different. There were properly organised trips, he insisted, they even took beginners like himself, so with my experience I'd be perfectly safe. He was right of course. It was brilliant.

That was the start of it. After a week diving in these idyllic warm seas full of amazing creatures, I began to feel differently about it. It was so different from the claustrophobic water-filled tunnels of a cave. Now I'm doing a diving instructor's course. And when I'm qualified, if I can instil enough regard for safety into my students such that just one accident is avoided then it'll be worthwhile.

Taff, meanwhile, has been working as a lifeguard. Turns out he got his lifesaving certificates years ago. He got chatting to the guys at the nearest beach to where we've been staying in Brisbane and after a quick refresher course they took him on. For the first time in his life he's found something he can do that he enjoys. He fits in; he's respected. And of course he gets to see his kids regularly. If he can get a full visa I think he'll stay here.

He stands up and shakes the sand off himself. 'There's a smashing Sheila up there by the surf club,' he grins. 'I'll see if I can charm her with a tube of the old amber nectar!'

www.ingramcontent.com/pod-product-compliance
Lightning Source LLC
Chambersburg PA
CBHW030022180626
46810CB00001B/168